Praise for *A Journey to St. Thomas*

"Rather than a pilgrimage to the shrine of Saint Thomas in Canterbury, these voyagers take a cruise to the island of St. Thomas in the Caribbean. Their personal stories, told in rhyme, combine to form a witty and penetrating commentary on life in our time."

—**Benedict H. Gross**,
Professor of Mathematics Emeritus,
Harvard University

"Regret the loss of verse with rhythm, rhyme and some ribald storytelling? Then join the Survivors' Club on the good ship *Froth*, as its cast of frolicsome characters tell their modern *Canterbury Tales*. Narrative verse in Josiah Hatch's skilled hands turns out to open the doors to commentary on contemporary life and foibles, social satire, and good old-fashioned comedy. Chaucer would chuckle. So will you."

—**Robert Connor**, Director and President, Emeritus,
The National Humanities Center

"The book is truly intriguing and unique. The linguistic flow, the telling observations, and the apt illustrations—a panorama of the whole modern scene coming from that small collection of characters on a vessel."

—**David Boyd**, past Dean and Professor Emeritus,
Northeastern University; D.Phil, Oxford

"Josiah Hatch's *A Journey to St. Thomas* is playful, clever, and compassionate. To me, his poetic writing reflects a keen respect for the value of the individual in human social life."

—**Ian McCallum**,
South African author of two anthologies of poetry,
Wild Gifts (1999) and *Untamed* (2012),
and the award-winning book, *Ecological Intelligence*

"The book is an explosion of intellect, imagination, and erudition controlled unerringly by a stunning empathy for the dangerously diverse narratives that occupy the minds of contemporary Americans. In poetry, this master craftsman has found the right medium. . . . Hatch's rhyme captures more vividly than prose possibly could the author's wit and the poignance of his characters' tales. He is our Whitman and has produced a work of genius."

—**Tom Farer**, University Professor,
University of Denver

"Josiah Hatch's *A Journey to St. Thomas* could not be more fun. Hip, instructive without being didactic, the tales tickle an old funny bone grown outworn by desuetude. All this and heroic verse."

—**Bruce Ducker**, author of
Dizzying Heights: The Aspen Novel

"A tour de force. Read, recite, and enjoy."

—**Bob Baron**, author and publisher;
past Chair, Wild Foundation

"Tales for our time, indeed: a stimulating mix of occupations representing much of the range of US society. Modern cruise passengers in the age of COVID as pilgrims à la Chaucer: it's a clever conceit. Writing in iambic pentameter over nearly four hundred pages is no small feat, and Hatch has devised myriad entertaining rhymes to keep it going."

—**Scott E. Casper**, President
of the American Antiquarian Society

"*A Journey to St. Thomas: Tales for Our Time* is a twenty-first-century reimagining of *The Canterbury Tales*. Like the original, it is . . . written in verse and consists of twenty-four tales, but not by pilgrims, rather by cruise passengers on a voyage to St. Thomas in the Virgin Islands. Ranging from an evangelical preacher to a social worker, they tell enthralling stories of mystery, suspense, magic, murder, horror, and comedy. Intended to be read aloud, their tales are ingenious and satirical, exposing at times the corruption, inequity, and hypocrisy of small-town America. Other stories are simply entertaining and fun."

—**Andrew J. O'Shaughnessy,**
Professor of History, University of Virginia

A Journey to St. Thomas

Tales for Our Time

Josiah Oakes Hatch III

Illustrated by
Cathy Morrison

Fulcrum Publishing
Wheat Ridge, Colorado

Library of Congress Cataloging-in-Publication Data

Names: Hatch, Josiah O., III, author. | Morrison, Cathy, 1954- illustrator. | Chaucer, Geoffrey, -1400. Canterbury tales.
Title: A journey to St. Thomas : tales for our time / Josiah Oakes Hatch III ; illustrated by Cathy Morrison.
Description: Wheat Ridge, Colorado : Fulcrum Publishing, [2023] | Includes bibliographical references.
Identifiers: LCCN 2023012587 (print) | LCCN 2023012588 (ebook) | ISBN 9781682753347 (hardback) | ISBN 9781682754597 (ebook)
Subjects: BISAC: FICTION / Adaptations & Pastiche | FICTION / Literary | LCGFT: Narrative poetry.
Classification: LCC PS3608.A86163 J68 2023 (print) | LCC PS3608.A86163 (ebook) | DDC 811/.6--dc23/eng/20230410
LC record available at https://lccn.loc.gov/2023012587
LC ebook record available at https://lccn.loc.gov/2023012588

Printed in the United States
0 9 8 7 6 5 4 3 2 1

Illustrations by Cathy Morrison
Cover art and design by Cathy Morrison
Interior design by Patty Maher

Fulcrum Publishing
3970 Youngfield Street
Wheat Ridge, Colorado 80033
(800) 992-2908 • (303) 277-1623
www.fulcrumbooks.com

To my best friend and wife of nearly fifty years,
Caroline Borden Hatch,
This book is lovingly dedicated.

Contents

Foreword

Geoffrey Chaucer and *The Canterbury Tales*

By Robert C. Baron

Diseases have been around as long as humankind. The Greeks, Romans, Egyptians, Jews, Muslims, and others have documented major outbreaks of diseases, often spread by trade from one region to another, or from one people to another. Dr. Charles Clark in his book on AIDS has an excellent description on the history of plagues that were sent by God as punishment for our misdeeds or to blame other people. In the introduction to this book, he wrote: "1348 was a terrifying year for the people of Europe. Strange and agonizing death struck many thousands of people. There was no obvious explanation for who would become ill and for those who would die."[1] Perhaps one-third of the people in Europe died from an epidemic of bubonic plague that came to be called the Black Death. In some places, it was more than half. The disease was extremely contagious, and death was sudden. A person could be very healthy, and within a few days, dead.

The Black Death had a profound effect on English society. For example, it created a labor shortage: wages went up as peasants left the land and moved to where the jobs were. And because of the high mortality rates and the feeling that God was punishing people, religious beliefs were undermined, and the authority of the Church was questioned. A century later, Martin Luther wrote a Bible in German, and William Tyndale wrote one in English, both of which further challenged the behavior and competency of Church leaders.[2]

People in England who survived the plague soon forgot it. There is a paucity of mentions of the illness in the English literature of the time—unlike in the Italian writings of Dante Alighieri and Giovanni Boccaccio.

Among those who lived during this time was a young boy, perhaps eight years old, named Geoffrey Chaucer. Some of his neighbors and friends died, but he and his father survived. Born in the early 1340s, he was educated at St. Paul's Cathedral School, learned Latin, and received a rudimentary classical education. He then attended law school at the Inner Temple in London. London was a small place with a population of 40,000 people. A century later, in 1500, there were about 75,000 people.

Chaucer's father, John Chaucer, owned a family pub and was a vintner who sold wine to King Edward III. He obtained a position for his son as a page in the retinue of the Countess of Ulster, the wife of the Duke of Clarence and the daughter-in-law of the king. Chaucer advanced in position and was a squire during Edward III's invasion of France, when he was captured by the French but then ransomed by the king. The Hundred Years' War, which had begun in 1337, lasted throughout his life and beyond.

During his twenties, Chaucer was employed in military and diplomatic missions to France, Flanders, and Spain. In his thirties, he was on trade and diplomatic missions to Genoa, Florence, and Lombardy. He was named clerk of public works. When he was forty-five, Chaucer was appointed justice of the peace in Kent and later knight of the shire and member of parliament from Kent; he received a pension from the king in 1367. In 1374, he was appointed controller of customs. During his lifetime, he served three kings: King Edward III, Richard II, and Henry IV. Geoffrey Chaucer died on October 25, 1400, and was buried in Westminster Abbey.

It is not for his diplomatic service that Geoffrey Chaucer is remembered, however; it is as a poet. The first major English poet, Chaucer read and admired Ovid, Virgil, Dante, Petrarch, and Boccaccio.[3]

Chaucer was an honored poet during his lifetime.[4] He translated *The Romance of the Rose,* a thirteenth-century French poem, and wrote *The Book of the Duchesse, The House of Fame, Anelida and Arcite, The Parliament of Foules,* and *Troilus and Criseyde*. But, he is best remembered for *The Canterbury Tales*.

As he got older, Chaucer had more time for his poetry, starting *The Canterbury Tales* in 1387 and continuing it until his death in 1400. It tells the story of a group of pilgrims who traveled together to Canterbury, a sacred place where Archbishop Thomas à Beckett was killed in 1170 after King Henry II said: "Won't someone rid me of this turbulent priest?" whereupon four knights went to Canterbury and murdered Beckett in his own cathedral. Afterward, miracles were said to have taken place, and Thomas à Beckett was canonized. (Alfred Lord Tennyson, T. S. Eliot, Christopher Fry, Jean Anouilh, and others all wrote of the murder.) Canterbury then became one of Europe's most important pilgrimage centers.

Chaucer planned that each of the two dozen pilgrims would tell four stories—two going to Canterbury and two coming home—but he finished only one story for each. He wrote *The Canterbury Tales* on vellum, as this was long before printed books were available. Scribes copied his writings and in some cases finished a story. Then, in 1450, Johann Gutenberg developed movable type and adjustable molds. Soon printers all over Europe were involved in the production of printed works. The first edition of *The Canterbury Tales* was published in print by William Caxton in 1476, a lifetime after Chaucer's death.

There are many editions of *The Canterbury Tales*, some in the original language, some translated to modern English in poetry or prose; some are of the entire book, some are of individual tales. *The Canterbury Tales* continues to be taught in high schools and colleges.

Why has this poem lasted seven centuries? Perhaps most of all because Chaucer is a supreme storyteller. His narrative skills are outstanding, and in each tale, he develops individual characters and dialogue. The stories introduce the reader to a variety of people—of different occupations, places in society, ages and temperaments, and include both clergy and laity. Through Chaucer, we get a view of fourteenth-century society.

Chaucer wrote in Middle English at a time when most writings were in Latin, French, Italian, or Anglo-Norman. If you listen to someone read aloud the original text you hear the rhythm, the sweep of language, the beat. In a prose translation you miss the poetry of the language but still get the strength of the stories.

Poetry is meant to be read aloud. At the end of this book is a bibliography featuring some classic poetry you may wish to enjoy.

Geoffrey Chaucer told the stories of people from two dozen professions. He probably knew people in most of their occupations and had empathy for many. In *A Journey to St. Thomas*, Josiah Hatch also tells stories from two dozen professions. Some professions—for example, lawyer and physician—share similarities with Chaucer's characters, while others are unique to their time, such as pardoner or private lender.

Infectious diseases are phenomena of groups rather than individuals; they are more easily spread between large groups living close to each other. A plague affects many people—rich or poor, pious or sinner, young or old. Anyone can die. It is the great leveler. But not all die, and those who live will often develop resistance to a given disease. And plagues can come back frequently. Humans have some twenty years between generations and the disease may periodically return, affecting the next generation.

Records of the past are not complete. Estimates of the number of deaths where the Black Death occurred range between 25 percent and 40 percent. When Europeans conquered North and South America, they brought measles, mumps, smallpox, yellow fever, cholera, and typhoid fever. Since the Native Americans had no immunity to these diseases, infection rates were high—sometime 30 percent, sometimes more than 90 percent. New World Native Peoples were not conquered by weapons but by European diseases.

The 1918–1919 Spanish flu came in three waves. It is estimated that 675,000 Americans died, or about 6.5 percent of the population. The records for the COVID-19 are incomplete since the virus is still affecting people, but current mortality is below 0.3 percent.

A short biography of the author of this book is on page 391. Let me add a few comments. Josiah Hatch studied the classics, Anglo-Saxon literature, and music theory at Princeton, Oxford, and in Italy. His work at the Smithsonian, his law degree, and his work as a practicing attorney and professor at the Josef

Korbel School of International Studies at the University of Denver all contribute greatly to this work.

Hatch has written text and music for two musicals for the Denver Cactus Club and numerous musical pieces for the University Club's 12th Night programs. He wrote *Forbidden Carols of Christmas*, which was published in 2018, as well as a law book for West Publishing in 1990.

I have known Josiah for a quarter century. His ability to quote long literary passages in English, Latin, Greek, and other languages makes him unforgettable. In an article, Josiah wrote: "In doubt, after a time, of the relevance of most of what I learned, I committed a great deal of it to memory, with the thought of sorting it out later, leaving my head overburdened with poetry, history and literature. My studies tend to burble out from time to time, causing general consternation."[5]

His voice is strong and melodious, and he was chosen to narrate the film *Wilderness in America*. These and other qualities make Josiah Hatch's work the culmination of a life of scholarship, literature, and entertainment.

Let's move on and let the author tell why he wrote *A Journey to St. Thomas* and talk about the characters, the two dozen stories, his choice of meter and rhyme, and what he hopes you may get from the reading of his poetry.

Notes

1. Charles F. Clark, MD, *AIDS and the Arrows of Pestilence* (Golden, CO: Fulcrum Publishing, 1994.)
2. Brian Monahan, *God's Best Seller: William Tyndale and the Writing of the English Bible* (New York: St. Martin's Press, 2002.)
3. Richard West, *Chaucer: The Life and Times of the First English Poet* (London: Constable & CO, Ltd, 2000).
4. John Gardner, *The Life and Times of Chaucer* (New York: Vintage, 1977. Reprinted by Barnes and Noble, 2009.)
5. *The Literary Club at 600* (Denver: Privately Published, 2021.)

The Origins of This Book

In its format and approach, *A Journey to St. Thomas* seeks to pay tribute to the fourteenth-century master poet, Geoffrey Chaucer. Chaucer, like Dante, showed his contemporaries the power of the vernacular for creating accessible poetry. His approach of letting characters tell their own stories, even while they inhabit a different overall narrative, enables Chaucer to present his complex society as an amalgam of individual perspectives.

The Canterbury Tales is a collection of the tales and vignettes of a broad collection of characters thrown together in a common venture: a pilgrimage to the shrine of St. Thomas à Becket in Canterbury. The purpose of their pilgrimage is to give thanks to St. Thomas for helping them through prior illness: "*That holy blissful martyr for to seke / That hem hath holpen whan that they were seeke.*" In the majority of cases, the "*sekeness*" was one or another of two forms of *Yersinia pestis*, the pathogen that caused the infamous Black Death. This bacterial pandemic, spread by rat fleas and by even deadlier aerosol emissions from sick patients, killed a very large percentage of European society—25 to 40 percent by various measures. Chaucer was a small boy when the plague first arrived in England in 1348. The next five years were devastating to the island's population. Thereafter, waxing and waning surges of infection persisted for fifty years and sporadically beyond. During the time of plague, Chaucer saw members of his family and the families of his patrons succumb to the disease and watched his society's turmoil worsened by the pandemic.

Our time echoes Chaucer's in engaging ways, but, when the writing of this book began in 2018, the common experience of plague was not one of them. Instead, the author was struggling, as everyone in this age seems to be, to make sense of political discord, propaganda and prevarication by leaders, economic hardship for those without advantages, cries of elitism and resentment, and the perceived inability of the ordinary citizen to make any difference. These are echoes, in fact, of the age in which Chaucer wrote, when two centuries of rule by French-speaking Norman kings and their favored elites had created class war, factional infighting, and extremes of wealth and poverty. At the same time that the two synthetic languages, French and Anglo-Saxon, were morphing into an English vernacular now called Middle English, promoting common access to literary texts, society experienced further destabilization caused by pandemic and social unrest.

The fourteenth century in England was socially fraught, even without the Black Death, just as our time has had myriad troubles made worse, but not created, by a pathogen. This was the century of Wat Tyler and the Peasants' Revolt, when resentment of the high-living king, his oligarchical retainers, and their indifference to the suffering of the poor erupted in class protests. Before long, there were attacks by bands of vigilantes, creation of *villeyn* armies, alienation of the commons, large-scale destruction of property, and persistent and fatal retaliation by the state. It was the age of Richard II and the wars between oligarchs that eventually resulted in Richard's abdication and murder. A foreign "forever war"—the "Hundred Years'" conflict between England and France—brought passionate nationalism and military preferment into the mix. In short, with its geopolitical unrest, polarized political factions, uneven wealth distribution, climate disasters that brought famine from unexpected periods of intense cold, and demagoguery and social ignorance on all sides, the time is, to a certain extent, reminiscent of our own. Finally, as if to complete the parallels between the ages after two years had gone into the writing of this book, our own plague, COVID-19, suddenly arrived in our world.

As economic, political, and social chaos increase in our own society, the technique of *The Canterbury Tales* is useful in showing a broad cross-section of our complex age through the stories told by individual travelers of our age. There have been two large impediments to bringing about this book. The first is the danger of trying to emulate one of the great icons of English literature. A cat can look at a king, as the saying goes, and the author acknowledges at the outset his lack of intent and capacity to reach the mastery of the original model. Second, in Anglo-American culture, it is not a common experience to go on pilgrimages, or seek the intervention of particular saints. Therefore, instead of going on a religious journey to ask help from St. Thomas à Becket, our collection of characters are embarking on a package tour from New York City to the island of St. Thomas in the Virgin Islands. They are a group of unmarried lonely hearts, thrown together by circumstance, traveling in hopes of lightening their lives.

The great Roman poet, Juvenal, thought that there could only be two ways to deal with chaotic societies. You could grieve or you could laugh. He chose laughter. Chaucer, with his mild, but still pungent, satire, balanced good humor and despair. Neither his pilgrimage nor the stories told by the participants seem polemical in intention but rather allowed readers some space in which to view themselves and their society without feeling personally attacked. All this he accomplished through placing stories within a story. His characters tell their own tales in their own way, leaving the reader to view the range of different narrators as a broad composite of the age.

Chaucer was an advantaged young man, whose family was well known at court and whose skills were employed over the course of his life by the royal establishment. His point of view may be criticized by contemporary champions of equity, diversity, and inclusion as limited. Like *The Canterbury Tales*, our modern emulation is selective: it reflects the perspective of an author who, while aiming to be invisible, works with a cast of travelers drawn from his experience as an overeducated, securely middle-class relic of an earlier age.

Finally, there is a deliberate choice of form in this book, which relies on a dated medium—narrative poetry in heroic couplets, presenting the overall adventure in meter and rhyme. Modern directness and accessible meaning are meant to render access much more comfortable. The choice to write a modern work in verse is the product of the author's belief that much of the magic of *The Canterbury Tales* lies in an oral presentation of the text. Since the advent of the electric light, families and friends have ceased reading aloud to each other, as each person can now easily take the book to a bedroom, library, or read on the internet. Similarly, public declamation, a form of presentation carefully nurtured over past centuries, has largely succumbed to video and teleprompters. Poetry, however, arose out of communal experience and depends on oral expression for its full meaning. We encourage readers to test the author's assertions by reading passages of this book aloud to each other.

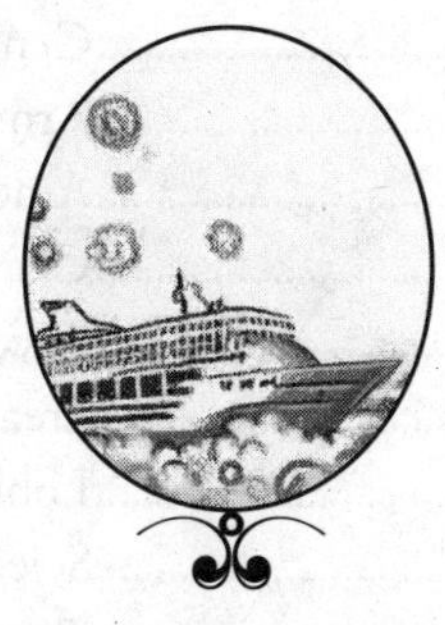

The List of Characters

For those who are fans of *The Canterbury Tales* and want to refer to tales that are, to some extent, modern counterpoints, we offer this list.

Canterbury Tales	A Journey to St. Thomas
Knight	General
Squire	Army Captain
Yeoman	Aide-de-Camp
Prioress	Charity Queen
Nun's Companion	Accountant
Monk	Preacher
Friar	Lobbyist
Nun's Priest	Scientist
Clerk of Oxford	Teacher
Sergeant of the Law	Business Lawyer
Franklin	Builder
Guildsmen	Five Jolly Businessmen
Cook	Bartender
Shipman	Pilot
Doctor of Physic	Physician
Wife of Bath	Widow of Los Altos Hills
Parson	Social Worker
Plowman	Welder
Miller	Shop Steward
Manciple	Private Lender
Reeve	Farmer
Summoner	Sports Recruiter
Pardoner	Insurance Salesman
Host of Tabard	Cruise Director

When Fall has flung the dead leaves to the lawn,
And Night has pulped them in cold rain till dawn,
While every plant that pleased the world is dead,
Each casually murdered in its bed;
When cold winds rake the rubbish heaps and send
Wet notices no one you know has penned—
Soiled scraps, blurred ink, the kind of thing
That some sepulchral summoner might bring;
When blackbirds struggle with the grieving sky,
To croak their witness that the world's awry,
"Our life is pathless, we can only stray."
Small wonder people try to get away.
Some couples may take out a second trust
To satisfy their edgy wanderlust,
Then folk of many different types and styles
Develop fervent longing for the Virgin Isles
And use whatever means they can secure
To see St. Thomas on a package tour.

These pilgrims of the modern sort would trek
Downtown themselves to book a penthouse deck
Where they alone would toast the isle's allure
Splashed in full color through the cruise brochure,
Gloating, as if they owned it privately,
Along with nearby portions of the sea.
Divorced, and short on funds, nevertheless
I thought a modest trip might ease distress.
Perhaps I might meet someone dressed in silk
Under the moonlight. Something of that ilk.

I passed by cruises billed as "European"
And cheap-cheap tours on ships flagged Eritrean
(Having had dreams in which I walked the plank
For cutthroats, who all sniggered as I sank).
The travel agent whom I found by phone
Cut short my long, apologetic drone
And launched into his own, well-practiced spiel:
"I've got the perfect package—what a deal!
"We've come up with bereavement fares this Spring.
For those whose other halves have taken wing.

"You qualify if you have lost your spouse!"
(Well, so I had, and with her half my house.)
I found that I'd agreed to sail with twenty-nine
Whose marital status was not far from mine.

We were a "Survivors' Club," a mere device
To give us access to a discount price.
(I ask if "survivor" required Her to be dead:
The agent laughed. "At least to you!" he said).
But then he said, should someone snoop,
I'd blend in well among the mourning group—
We'd all share staterooms. I could don a mien
Consistent with my loss. If I came clean,
He said, I would not have to "disembark"
Mid-ocean to be hors d'oeuvres for some shark.
It seemed that there was not another way
To get a discount, so I said, "OK."

Our ship, the *Ocean Froth*, oppressed the quay,
And dazzled like an iceberg on the sea,
A floating torte of countless frosted decks.
Scanning them from below wreaked hell with necks;
You needed binoculars to find the top
And maybe an astrolabe or turboprop.
Within her labyrinthine layers she'd hold
Up to five thousand passengers, all told,
So closely packed that one precocious sneeze
Could gain the status of widespread disease
In just a day, and with an extra night,
An international disaster site.
Our berths were up on Deck H-115,
The steward told me. I had never seen
A ship so vast that every fire drill
Required some wilderness survival skill,

Knowledge of maps and compasses at least
And how at night to tell the west from east.
Each deck was subdivided into planes
With quadrants, sections, subsections, and lanes,
And elevator banks and corridors
Both fore and aft, unfolding by the scores.
At length by hide-and-seek I found
The berth where I felt destined to be drowned.

I kicked the shoes from my beleaguered feet,
Which airport concourses and lines had beat,
And started to undress and wash my face,
Hunched in the tiny lavatory space,
When, in my roommate came, and not just him,
But many others, squeezing limb by limb
Into the cabin, which had been assigned
In error by the computer mastermind
To the entire group "Survivors' Club."
Converging like the spokes around a hub,
And buzzing like a hive of angry bees,
We waited for the purser and the keys,
For thirty minutes. Trying not to stare
At my new polka-dotted underwear,
We stood around and giggled until we
Decided we might be good company.

We made for St. Thomas late that afternoon,
Under a red and inauspicious moon.
At seven, when the evening meal was served,
We found a lengthy table was reserved
Down in a room outfitted with a bar
And filled with chattering guests from near and far.
Our table sign had lilies etched in black:
Betokening our loss. No turning back.

There was no menu, though, for every meal
Served all alike, part of the package deal.
Drinks were not included, but the ship
Supplied some table wine to start the trip
In penance for the mix-up in our rooms.
It was a bit like grog, with fire and fumes;
Those who needed more to aid their slumbers
Found that the bar would bill by cabin numbers.
Beside a window looking over seas
Grown gray with dusk, as with some grave disease
We sat at last assembled as a group,
Awaiting the first course, chilled melon soup.

To pass the time I'll share my own reviews
Of these, my new companions on the cruise—
Both who they were, and whom they meant to be,
Foibles and fancies as revealed to me,

And why they thought this venture would be fun;
Let's start with one whose working life was done.

There was a General, a forthright man.
His greatest pleasure was to map and plan.
For thirty years he'd served in foreign wars
And fought in mortal battles by the scores.
Shipped out of "Rot-C," wet behind the ears,
Into the Tet Offensive with his peers,
He climbed their bodies strewn about at Hue
But never wept and never ran away.
When he was wounded fighting near Khe Sanh,
Leading his squad with every bullet gone
He called in air support, the prospects dire,
And lost six months to wounds from friendly fire.
From infantry battalions in Kuwait
He led reconnaissance to calibrate
Iraqi strength and safeguard the Brigade.
And in Afghanistan his daring raid
Against the Taliban's secluded caves,
Sent numerous assassins to their graves.
For this, our grateful state, though slow to thank,
At last retired him with a step in rank
From colonel all the way to brigadier
With medals at which neophytes might peer
If he should wear them, which he never did.
He kept them in a locker where he hid
Old deeds, diplomas, tokens of esteem
He never looked at, for he did not dream
Of personal accomplishments or fame.
He'd seen his peers shirk combat just to claim
Prestigious posts in Washington, D.C.,
The lifelines of a desk-man's pedigree.

But he disdained such bureaucratic strife
For all he had to offer was his life.
He knew about a battle's deadly cost;
His face was marked with every man he'd lost.

And yet, despite his known ferocity,
He showed not a bit of animosity
When those at dinner would hold forth on war
And strategies that they lacked talent for.
He thought the greatest tragedy was death,
The foremost that of his life partner, Beth,
For whom he had arranged this trip at sea
To celebrate their pending liberty.
He'd stood down Fate, only to bury her—
No battle plan existed to deter
The march of aching illness through her bones.
She was a song now, rife with overtones,
That made him reach for her each night, but clutch
Cold pillows, so devoid of needed touch.
Without her, it was clear that his attire
Would never win a battle with the dryer;
You could not guess his value from his dress:
His navy blazer had been worn to shininess,
Its middle button hung from a frayed thread—
The top and bottom did the work instead.

His daughter, Julia, sat just next to him,
A Captain, sharp of mind and strong of limb,
Her hair bobbed dark beneath a duckbilled cap.
Near forty, she was energy on tap,
And quite a lovely woman: tight of frame,
With eyes that put a sunny lake to shame.
And yet, as is the case with such a lake,
Below a certain depth she went opaque;
For she commanded cyber-operations,
Sniffing the coded trails of foreign nations.
And she was as accomplished in the field:
There were no weapons that she could not wield,
Or tests of stamina she would not try.
She shot as well as any macho guy

But when off duty, as I've heard the tale,
No one would ever take her for a male.
She did not see herself as someone's wife:
There was too much she wanted from her life,

So if some hero thought he'd bring her down,
And did not heed the warning in her frown,
He soon would find his body on the floor,
For she was skilled in all the arts of war.
Yet, Julia, not Amazon nor Artemis,
Would give a worthy man the kind of kiss
That left him weak-kneed, craving just one more.
So sometimes, if he was not from the corps,
And was as courteous as fit and fair,
He might stand awed as she let down her hair
And sweetly made his fondest hopes fulfilled.
Rumors that trickled back to base were killed.
Her private life she kept strictly unknown,
Both for her father's sake and for her own,
And laughed off disappointed gibes that she
Belonged in Sappho's own sorority.
The General stood apart and let her run,
As proud as he would be of any son;
And yet he grieved that chiefs of staff unseen,
Would one day find a chance to intervene
And elevate some less accomplished man
In keeping with their buddy-system's plan.
For now, he smiled; she gave his cheek a peck
And went to run ten laps around the deck.

He brought his aide-de-camp, who'd followed him
Into retirement judging that the glim
Was off the service once his boss was gone.
He shaved his head, which left his features drawn,

Making it seem he was a single scowl,
One unified expression, pate to jowl.
His ways, plain-spoken, kept him in the field
For he was quick to challenge, slow to yield
If orders from on high made little sense.
Or, for some reason, seniors took offense
And sent him into combat, sure that he
Would first exasperate the enemy
Before he killed them, or himself was killed
And either happenstance would leave them thrilled.
The General found him stalwart and astute:
He liked the fact the man would not salute
And jump to orders that he knew were wrong.
Their bond was loyal, and it was lifelong.
No one knew better how to get supplied
Outside of channels when those channels died.

No one had better sense when he was faced
With quandaries that might leave them all disgraced;
For, such decisions were quite foreign to
That medal-decked, but acquiescent crew
Who hold the Pentagon's dark canyons from
Rank interlopers who one day might come
To dominate those corridors and toss
The aging bureaucrats into a fosse.
Now, knowing that his dear friend had no chance
Without him to stay safe or to advance,
The General had brought him on this cruise,
To find the time and place to disabuse
His pal of thoughts civilian life would bless
Him with high wages and a choice of dress!
He knew the wind blows cold down alleys where
Some broken veterans slump in despair.

A queen of charity was next in line
And glistened like bright pyrite in a mine.
And she had brought an entourage along—
They sat before her, half a dozen strong!
For she was empress of her charity,
And would wield censure and hyperbole
Against despoilers of the sea and land
(And these were many, you must understand).
Although she had to fight against her name
(Fiona Flake), she still put foes to shame
With ready wit, and unrelenting zeal.
Her press releases carried barbs of steel.
And if she bid offending folk to cease
Their depredations or forgo their peace,
Industrialists and presidents alike
Would trundle wearily up to a mic
And humbly seek the pardon of the press.
Fiona was quite tall, six feet, no less,
Direct of gaze and rather slow to smile,
She could pick out a donor from a mile
And almost wiggle with affected glee.

She had a secret meeting in a cay,
Clandestine and conveniently, remote
She had to rent an ocean-going boat
To sail from Nassau with her retinue
To this location out of common view.
She was concerned about the ship's slow pace
And wished they'd burn more oil and start to race!
Her staff of five was all around her set
To do small tasks and check out those she met:
Sandy, her loved administrative aide;
A scientist; two publicists; a maid;
And one boy intern, trained to bring more drinks
While keeping the expression of the Sphinx.

Her scientist lent gravitas to all.
He was a modest man, as round as tall,
But smart as a whip in all those terms of art
Ms. Flake would throw around to play her part.
He had as many publications and degrees
As there are leaves on consequential trees,
And in his field he had celebrity;
But it was Phytopharmacology.
More central still to Ms. Flake's entourage
Were her twin bulldogs, Gwyneth and Defarge.
Down at her feet they sat for every meal
And did not beg, but neither came to heel.
Once in her lap, they'd lick her on the lips,
Nibble her ears and kiss her fingertips—
A lover would think twice about their place
In line if he gained access to that face.
Even the loaf she tore and passed around
Was something most sent onward with a frown.
She'd lost her partner of some twenty years,
But never afterward was seen in tears.
She seemed a human who lacked human cares,
But liked the company of polar bears.

A telegenic preacher formed a part
Of our small Order of the Lonely Heart.
Whether his wife was dead and gone awhile
Or having her along would cramp his style
We never knew. He was a handsome man
And groomed to flutter pulses. Fit and tan
In tailored suits and snow-white collar, he
Could reconcile net worth and piety.
His cufflinks, intricately wrought of gold,
Portrayed an angel bearing a billfold.
He was the pastor of a megachurch,
A shrine of soaring glass and polished birch

Concealing more circuit boards for sound and light
Than Broadway venues use on opening night.
For, stagecraft was this reverend's stock-in-trade.
His Sunday "gate" left rivals in the shade.

His church, First Chapel of Christ's Covenant
Was built with an urban-renovation grant,
Where low rents once had sheltered many poor,
All soon relocated or were shown the door.
The reverend, though, insisted the depraved
Evictees were far fewer than he saved
Each week in person or on pay TV,
When they tuned in to form his laity
And pledge their cash. By God, donations soared
After he preached the gospel of Our Lord.
So many came to donate bonds and stocks,
His parking lot comprised two city blocks.

His glaring eyes and unwiped, sweating brow,
His penetrating words, enhanced somehow
From his position in his pulpit high,
Condemned the pusillanimous to die
To this world and the next, unless they showed
Their zeal to plumb their wallets and unload
A pledge to Christ from all that they would earn.
Did not St. Paul aver that God would spurn
A wealthy man who might refuse to see
That greater than hope and faith is charity?
Lethal injections had his grim assent;
He loathed the evils of big government
And panned them in each sermon to his flock
Using examples guaranteed to shock,
Like criminals who while out on parole
Murdered or raped, or at the least they stole.

Abortionists he'd put in dungeons where
They'd nevermore enjoy the outside air.
His terrified parishioners would vote,
As if the Lord had written them a note.
But as to why God brought him to this ship,
This preacher kept a tightly buttoned lip,
Until he realized how much we were struck
To silence by his energy and pluck.

Then he revealed he was researching how
A ship was managed, from the stern to bow,
Because, in a vision, he'd been called to make
A sacred floating church, for Jesus's sake.
God sent the vision of a yacht, The Dove,
Conceived in faith, constructed out of love,
With crosses both astern and on the prow
And rows of chairs between, should space allow.
So, since his board had given him the rope,
He'd come to give that sacred project scope.
In dreams he felt God's salt wind in his hair,
And saw his congregation kneel in prayer.
The broad horizon was his reredos
Thunder his music, lightning at the cross!
He heard his sermon broadcast on TV.
Didn't Christ still the winds on Galilee?
Did He not walk barefooted on the waves
To demonstrate the faith that always saves
As He would prod men to release their souls
From the encumbrance of their large bankrolls?
The boldness of this vision startled me.
It seemed ecclesiastic piracy,
But, listening, I soon came to understand
The conduct mirrored what he did on land.

Next to the preacher sat a lobbyist
Who viewed him as a partner for a tryst,
As evident to everyone who sat
Around them and observed their whispered chat.
This former senator, so I was told,
Stepped down after one term to pan for gold.
She now earned money from an oil concern
And made gains vanish from their tax return;
Though you may think it dull, she made a mint
Covertly and without a fingerprint.
She'd had the strength to trade her aging face
For polymers of architectural grace.
In alcove lighting, when the cocktails flowed
She was an houri, but when features showed
In harsher light, the young men hit the brakes:
Her cheeks were smooth, but drawn as are a snake's,
With angles and taut lines that scuttlebutt
Attributed to nip and tuck and cut—
Lip augmentation, chin reduction, and
Abrasion of some skin that was too tanned.

She'd found, alas, in her benighted trade,
A woman had to fight to stay a maid.
She had, in fact, been chased around the desk
By men both high-and-mighty and grotesque,
But if they ventured further to extort
Erotic conquest, out of love or sport,
They found themselves down in the parking lot
Shivering by their limousines, for naught.
She would not be some trophy of the hour,
But lived and died through pull and naked power.
And if one wronged her, he would find, in season,
He'd been denatured for no rhyme or reason!

She saw scant need to see a moral told,
But was content to eat her dishes cold.

Nor was she ever reticent to stoop
To earning stolen dollars from a group!
For neither principle nor worthy cause
Gives equal-access rights under our laws.
Money it is that gets you in the door,
And deeper access costs you even more!
She saw the rivers of expenditure
That flowed around the Hill like rich manure
And thought, why shouldn't I take some of that?
I'd never earn it as a technocrat!
Raw influence is the way to rise above
Those common folk who cannot push and shove.
Indeed, as soon as she had witnessed how
The Congress splurged to feed a sacred cow,
She lost her love for prudent government
And fought to get a piece of what was spent.
She'd bought a little sailing yacht she docked
In the Potomac, and it was well stocked
With after-dinner drinks and rare champagnes
That could be-jumble a John Maynard Keynes.
The Carryforward was the vessel's name,
And those who sailed were never quite the same
When they stepped off as when they came aboard.
For passengers were tied tight with the cord
Of indiscretions they racked up offshore.
Her mics picked up their every belch and snore.

We were agog at all her savoir faire
But did not know why she was sitting there;
As marriage was not in her history,
Her joining us was still a mystery,

Till she, in conversations after drinks,
Confessed, amid veiled hints and solemn winks,
That she would travel on this cruise each year,
To carry cash and make it disappear
Into a bank beyond all moral bounds
That would convert it into British pounds
Without a trace as to its origin
And send it out by wire for storage in
An institution whose deep privacy
Would strip the money's genealogy.
She then admitted that she'd never wed,
Much less confined attentions to one bed,
But joined because her client company
Both owned the ship and let her sail for free.

The face beside hers all but disappeared
Into the brambles of a bushy beard.
Some rimless glasses gleamed above the blur
Of this great symphony of facial fur.
I thought at first, he had the modest goal
Of trying to conceal some scar or mole.
But then, his second-most distinctive trait
Was that he focused only on his plate.
When he looked up at others, his cold eyes
Would stare right past you toward some distant prize.
His ways and means were furtive, as it were:
The beard obscured his lack of character.
You would perceive, had he been less hirsute,
A dearth of principle most absolute.
For such a fuzzy man, he was a troll
Who only would converse if paid a toll.

He was a private lender. Through finance
He offered businesses a second chance.

With capital he'd earned from real estate,
Renting apartments to the desperate.
He brought the skills he'd used on needy folk
To lend to businesses whose budgets broke.
In truth, he was a salesman who could make
A baby-rattle from a rattlesnake.
He cultivated young developers
Who had inventions, but were amateurs:
Beginners, still quite vulnerable to guile.
He'd listen to their prattle for a while
Then lend them funds on terms to drag them down
Until, at last, he'd run them out of town
And seize their assets. He was quite a pro
At sensing opportunities for buying low.
After his fees and interest bled firms dry,
He'd dress up the remains and sell them high.
As owner of their stock, he'd come out well,
And do-gooders could simply go to Hell.

A secret rule that was his party line
Was "Mine is mine, but also yours is mine."
After the chumps defaulted on their loans,
He'd suck the marrow from their fiscal bones
Through new agreements at a higher rate
And punish them for daring to pay late,
For, as he told his pals after a drink,
All squids taste best when cooked in their own ink.
This bear-like man was genial to his prey,
Quite friendly and available all day
To run the numbers till their needs were met;
But his solutions always took more debt.
Though warm as sunlight was his first hello,
He would turn colder as the loans would grow,
And when they reached the threshold of default
He bound the wounds with iodine and salt.

He was a far from sympathetic man
But knew the way to execute a plan.

He never gave a thought to what might be
If all the country's lenders did as he.
The welfare of the nation mattered naught.
He found economists quite overwrought.
If prices fell, then businesses must fail.
He'd sell them short and still he would prevail.
As for the reason he was on this trip
He'd come along, he said, to get a grip
After his wife's demise, although, in truth
As usual he was not saying sooth.
Foreclosures brought him tickets that could not
Be transferred or cashed in; so on the spot
He thought he'd come and thereby skip
The funeral baloney with a trip.
A week ago, her terminal ennui
Propelled his third wife off the balcony.
He wondered, when she stepped off of the brink,
If forty stories gave her time to think
Of all the inconvenience she would cause
By forcing his business to be put on "Pause"?

A woman in a faded gingham blouse
Sat to his right, and tried in vain to rouse
The lender to conversation, but gave up
At last and stared into her coffee cup.
Her hair was faded red, shot through with gray,
Her face quite round and open as the day.
She was her grade school's "Teacher of the Year!"
A status that made notices appear
In the School News and on the cork-lined board
Outside the Teachers' Lounge, but no reward

Beyond that was expected or received.
In truth, she was quite shy and, so, relieved
That further hubbub was not de rigeur.
Doing some good was quite enough for her.

Her fellow teachers, shocked that thirty years
Of energy, self-doubt, and sweat and tears
Could be so disregarded by the school,
Made secret contributions to a pool.
And thus amassed, in time, a little fund
That, when it was presented, left her stunned.
They'd bought her tickets, sent her on her way,
And given her a stipend for each day.
(Of course, to get a discount, her dear friends
Vouchsafed she'd lost her spouse. It all depends
How you define that word to judge it true:
Her teaching was the only love she knew.)
She'd given life to children, drop by drop.
Nothing but death would ever make her stop.
She swapped their cynicism for a goal,
Some purpose that would grip them, heart and soul.
She brought them school supplies when budgets failed
And intervened when they were hurt or jailed.

Despite all this, of course, the state
Encumbered by the rich, the good-and-great,
Required accreditations most severe,
Yet cut her basic living, year to year.
She made her home in a large trailer park,
Where no one wished to wander after dark,
And skipped her dinner so that sometimes she
Could help a student dodge insolvency.
She was a cheerful person, with a smile
That would illuminate a cubic mile,

And listened earnestly if you would share
Letters you'd like to write but did not dare.

The sleek man to her right wore casual clothes
That cost a fortune. Everybody knows
Those ads suggesting that you have not scored
Until you buy things you cannot afford.
He was a lawyer, smug with certainty,
Who plied his trade in Washington, D.C.
Though he maintained some children and a wife
They did not play a large part in his life.
Most people thought him single, for he chose
To play the widower if that would dispose
Of obstacles to success in any case
Or baggage during a romantic chase.
Family were problems one and all, he thought,
Demanding cash or gifts that might be sought
In lieu of love: for such he had no time.
Weren't they grateful for his rapid climb
Up to the very pinnacles of power?
Did they not know, when he came home to shower
And throw things, he was merely stressed and worn
From winning wealth for them! He could but scorn
Such insolence, entitlement, and greed.
How dare they say that they could be in need!
How dare they try to make him share their guilt!

He lived in a reality he'd built
And into which he never brought a soul.
There were some others' secrets that he stole
To make sure that his fortune was assured
And built to last as long as he endured.
His family knew nothing of the tail
He hunted, nor that some of it was male.

His worldliness made him the confidant
Of criminals whose infamy he'd flaunt.
He said he'd deem a rat an honest man,
As long as he coughed up as the meter ran.
No one would say he had the common touch
But then, he found he did not need it much.
Fear was his currency and métier
He'd scorch the earth for clients who would pay.
An ordinary person could not brook
His giant fees unless he was a crook.

His premium rates were in the stratosphere,
Though corporate clients did not shed a tear
About the cost. They wanted something more
Than lawyering: a safety net, rapport
With those who were their business overlords—
The mandarins who serve on corporate boards.
So, when the monthly invoice came around,
High charges reinforced how skilled and sound
The judgment of the board had been to hire
A person of such quality and fire.
His suite of offices eclipsed Versailles,
But officers were thrilled; for, those on high
Could tell they'd hired the cream of all the cream
To be the leader of their legal team.
He worked associates hard, but paid them well,
Then tossed them out when stress began to tell.
Hope springs eternal, and this lawyer knew,
He'd quickly find two dozen more to screw.

But, overall, the ploy that made him rich
Was legislation passed at fever pitch
Whenever some new party came to power.
His chosen team was primed for such an hour.

Persuasive people that he would engage
Would stir the pot of democratic rage
That actually concealed a selfish cause,
Then lobbyists could make that into laws.
The portraits in the Capitol might weep,
But congressmen cast votes as if asleep.
Content with a vacuity of knowledge,
Adorned with bits their staff picked up in college.
He stood by, solemn-faced, as they
Came to his clients to learn what to say.
Some decades later when our Highest Court
Would puzzle through a purchased law's import
To see what legislators might have meant
In volumes of congressional intent,
They'd find the legal cupboard all but bare:
It made Supreme Court clerks pull out their hair.
For years to come the statute would entangle
Squadrons of scholars searching for an angle
Into the larger meaning of the law—
A contest that would end up in a draw.
Its author never would express a view
Until someone would hire him to construe
The statute as an expert for a court.
He charged a lot for matters of that sort!

Meanwhile clients marveled at the vim
With which he'd climbed the legal jungle gym.
They'd double his bonus and contracted rate
And send him delicacies by the crate.
So why was he consorting with us folk
Aboard a cruise that he must think a joke?
We gathered that some client was aboard
And wished simply to hide among the horde
Of commoners until in good time, they
Could finally reveal their powerplay.

Next up there was a builder, one of those
Who grabs exurban acreage and throws
The whole caboodle into Master Plans,
Prepackaged right down to the garbage cans
That sit beside the driveway of each home.
The houses, like the teeth of some great comb,
Are so identical in plan and tone,
You'd need a bloodhound to pick out your own.
Each has a lawn, but not too much to mow,
With clear views of front doors up and down the row":
Knowing the neighbors well was thus assured,
But very often not to be endured,
Seeing that only several feet could stand
Between you and their son's electric band,
Tossed plates and glasses, weeping, shouting spells,
And such alarms as haunt suburban Hells.

You might as well be in their living room
Absorbing their life story from the womb
Though it might leave you little chance to pique
The envy of your neighbors with a sleek
Addition to your look-alike estate,
New front-door decorations will look great.
Some orange pumpkins lit on Hallowe'en
Will cause a next-door neighbor to turn green.
And just before Thanksgiving, you could string
More Christmas lights than God's imagining,
Such as would cause the city grid to brown
And leave in utter darkness half the town.
These things the builder knew, but rose above;
Evasions were things that he had plenty of.
His own estate was in the country, by
A verdant park, far from the hue and cry
And there he'd entertain such folk as might
Give all his further projects a green light.

Five jolly businessmen, rotund and able,
Sat in the empty spaces at our table.
They'd won the grand prize at a sales convention,
But viewed this cruise, the prize, with apprehension.
They'd never left their safe United States
And thought they'd wandered upon risky straits.
The first sold ceiling fans and lighting mounts:
The next bought air conditioning accounts;
A third insured the businesses of all;
The fourth sold brackets for a workshop wall
The last dealt second-hand appliances.
They'd joined in desperate alliances
To slow the underselling of their stock,
By chain stores that made millions moving schlock..
They all were pillars of their modest towns
And wore civic equivalents of crowns.
They were coordinated in their dress:
Blazers and gray trousers always pressed,
Lapels sporting awards from social clubs
Or their community's small business hubs.

At dinner, they would always wear striped ties,
But collars were all open otherwise.
With well-scrubbed faces, short hair, aftershave,
They advertised the reason to behave.
And make their living in a modest way;
Yet vote against interest on election day.
The politicians whom they voted for
Knew well their yearning for the days of yore,
And harped the timeworn customs that folks feared
Would be supplanted by the new and weird.
They were all vestrymen, commissioners, and such
And did not like new customs very much.

They loved their carports and their bungalows:
Their values fit them like a suit of clothes.
No wives could come along, unhappily,
Their prize did not include a coterie.
They thought their wives might want to sit and crow
In their distinguished husbands' afterglow,
More than complacent to be left behind:
To this, they found their spouses disinclined.
And when the husbands pushed ahead to leave
They joined us fully qualified to grieve.

A bartender was with us! Bless my stars!
So needed on a ship with twenty bars!
In fact, as we continued on our trip
The cruise line hired him, acting on a tip.
But he was here to pick up new ideas,
And spend the tips he'd garnered over years.
Strange drinks were his passion, he could make
An egg nog from raw egg, a Bellyache,
A Monkey Gland, a Mule, or Sazarac
Or pour a bourbon with a brown ale back.
He sported tattoos and studs in his ears,
Embodying the tradesmen's darkest fears
But gained on them by serving them himself
His own concoctions, far from off-the-shelf.
So sad that drugs had made his nose run free,
For strange martinis were his specialty.

An airline pilot was aboard our boat—
How curious to find such a one afloat!
He was quite affable, though reticent
About his past and home. He seemed content
To sit and listen to the rest of us.
I never saw him fret or make a fuss.

He wore a pilot's shirt, short-sleeved and white,
Not apt to wrinkle if you spent the night
Slouched in an airport, hangar, or hotel.
This ocean-going suited him quite well.
Around his neck he wore a good luck charm
Which would have caused air passengers alarm—
The patron saint of travelers, St. Christopher,
Holding a four-leaf clover, so to spur
Both God and pagan Luck to lend him aid.
And yet he did not seem to be afraid,
For he had spent his whole life in the air,
Riding the gusty winds from here to there.

From when the stork first brought him to his mom.
He handled every journey with aplomb.
Mere nervousness was not a barrier
To flying fares for a large carrier
From continent to distant continent,
As long as you were seen as confident.
In times when normal airline work was slack,
He'd pilot charter flights both there and back
To places like Tashkent and Samarkand.
I wondered if he carried contraband.
He seemed to favor countries that were wild
Where flight plans and the like were never filed.
And he feared nothing—nothing—so said he,
But also glanced behind him constantly.

A general practitioner was there—
A doctor, affable and debonaire.
Weary of doing rounds on clinic wards,
Retired from a dozen major boards,
He'd signed on with the cruise line as a lark
To deal with heath conditions on our bark!

Should some poor passenger fall sick aboard,
Or stagger as if run through by a sword
Or sit down, turning white with sudden pains,
He'd save their lives or pack up their remains.
Efficiency gave medicine its clout,
Dosing and closing, cases in and out
Within the twenty minutes carriers required.
He'd not be there, if, later, folks expired.
Meanwhile a perfect paragon was he!
Respected for his wit and bonhomie.
His colleagues would refer him patients and
He always paid the favor back again.

His close relations with drug companies
Had given him in life a certain ease.
They courted him and took him off on trips
About which not a word came from their lips.
They'd sell the latest pills they had turned out—
Outrageous cost would give the drug more clout
For those of means, who could afford to pay.
For others, he would find another way:
Perhaps free samples of old medicine
And something to be rubbed into the skin.
He'd also throw in terminology
From Chinese medicine, about the chi,
And urge a lower carb, high-fiber diet,
Prescribing enough drugs to keep them quiet,
With a referral to another doc
Who'd never take them, on or off the clock.
But even that advice was not for free:
He made sure that he always got his fee.

There was a widow from Los Altos Hills,
Who wore a dress that would have brought on chills

Had she been less than seventy years old.
Designed the dress herself, so I was told:
Clinging and flowing, cut along the bias,
It drew frank stares from men, even the pious,
And from the other ladies of her town
Long probing looks that ended in a frown.
Her jewelry was such as seldom seen
Outside the gravesite of some pagan queen;
Her purse and heels made out of softest leather,
Had cost five thousand dollars altogether.
Her skin was soft and flawless, and her cheeks
Enhanced by deftest surgical techniques,
Would blush and dimple every time she smiled.
She had the fresh face of a sinless child.

But suitors found her passions quite alive,
For over time, she'd caught and married five,
Beguiling them on their initial dates,
And all of them had left her large estates.
She spent it all on trips around the world
And not a sight escaped her as she swirled
From place to place—the holidays in Rome,
Summers in England, where she kept a home
In Mayfair, winters on tropic cruises or
Ensconced in her château along Côte D'or.
Despite her poise and regal countenance
She was a person full of common sense
Who loved a bawdy joke and repartee
As gourmandizers love a fricassee.
Quite hard to shock, she craved the give and take
The way a wolfhound loves a sirloin steak.
She'd bed a lover, if she liked his looks,
And teach him things they never put in books.

A good man of a moral cast of mind
Sat quietly and ate, as if inclined
To think that every meal might be his last.
His calling often furnished no repast.
He was a social worker and a priest
Sent by a congregation in the East
To keep him safe from physical collapse,
Or spiritual exhaustion perhaps.
No doctors worked as hard or long as he.
For, licensed though he was to take a fee,
He would not do so when he thought that meant
He might be taking from the indigent.
His own needs were, to him, of little weight,
Compared to those of some poor reprobate.
He was quite learned in theology,
In medicine, and sociology.

And yet, he'd travel miles by car or bus
To bring a patient crutches or a truss,
Knowing he would not otherwise find aid,
Though for such help, he never would be paid.
He thought of how his Lord would heal the sick
And comfort every raving lunatic
Who stopped Him on his way through Galilee,
Whether he was a serf or Sadducee.
Also, it was his duty, being well,
To try, by illustration, to impel
The fortunate in life to take their cue
From his example and embrace his view.
He thought that, if the wealthy did not care
To feed a homeless beggar in the square,
Why would less favored people take that on?
Press photographs of black ties on a lawn

At country houses where champagne and brie
And evening dresses posed for charity—
Those made him scowl and heavenward raise his eyes.

He knew that if a beggar dared surprise
These sponsors in their own beneficence
By showing up at one of their events
He'd stumble with security details
Past the mixed salads, aubergines, and quails
And fly unceremoniously out the gate
Into the inconsiderate hands of Fate.
Such grand occasions gave rich folk a way
To streamline pity and drink Beaujolais.
He found no mission in such nice pretense;
His storefront clinic was his recompense.
Though small, it doubled as a parish church
And those who found it made no further search,
Not even if their lives were a disaster.
They saw in him a true and gentle pastor.
He would not mince words if he thought you wrong,
But strove to coax your inner thoughts along
Until you understood the consequence
Of errors and devised some recompense.
Nor did he leave his conscience on the shelf,
But every day kept true to it himself.

He brought with him a welder, his own brother,
Different from him as one cat from another.
This sibling stayed down in the family home
And ate there every night and did not roam.
He watched the changing neighborhood for signs
Of urban blight, or dealers with designs.
He was the guardian of the neighborhood.
Their parents died, but he was there for good.

His welding was a good construction job
With high-scale wages, seeing that the Mob
Took fees from every dollar that he earned.
But he paid up; no sense in getting burned.
He liked them better than the government,
Which did the same; for every dollar spent
They threatened to expend another five,
Whether or not taxpayers would survive.

His palms were rougher than a pilgrim's feet,
His face burnt brown, his limbs tough as mesquite.
And weathered also was his soul down deep:
The Bible says that, as you sow, you reap,
Which meant, he thought, hard work could conquer all,
And he must work until the Lord would call;
But meanwhile, foreign imports, lulls, and taxes
Cut down construction projects as if axes
Alternated blows. He'd have to fold
His hand and ask assistance to grow old.
Already he could hardly pay his bills,
And age was creeping up, and with it pills,
Arthritis pain and braces for his knees.
He lived in terror of some new disease
That would destroy his self-sufficiency.
He kept a pistol, if that had to be.
His brother, hearing his profound distress,
Had asked in Bible Study to address
The state of mind he found his sibling in,
And if such desperation was a sin
Beyond God's grace if you died all alone.
Cruise tickets showed up promptly on their own,
Non-refundable—that was no surprise!—
He'd use the cash for good works otherwise.

The shop steward was next: a piece of work.
Mere hints of injustice made him go beserk.
His strength was on display, for he could win
Any armwrestle others might begin.
He was a compact man, though muscle-bound,
He'd knock the doors off hinges with a pound
Of one huge fist or break them into bits.
His beard was red and bristly as a spitz
And broad as if he used it as a spade.
These attributes threw rivals into shade.
For he was steward of a factory
That turned out airplane engines sea-to-sea,
The statutes of collective bargaining
Were scripture he applied to everything, .
He'd protest actions by the management
That cut his members' pay by just a cent
And call them arbitrary and unfair!
For health and safety issues he would dare
To call a strike and follow through, despite
The kickback from all interest-groups in sight
And studies backed by management that found
The right to strike both sketchy and unsound.

He won more than he lost, and his reviews
By union officials awarded him this cruise.
He was as rough in looks as in his life:
He never won a partner or a wife.
The right of his nose displayed a wart
That many reddish bristles did disport!
His nostrils, which widened as he groaned and tried
To pin a person's arm to Naugahyde,
Were vast and black and flecked with ambergris—
No person had a mouth as wide as his.
And yet, he was a player and sang songs,
Of unrepentant women and their wrongs.

He was quite free with cash, I came to see;
And, whether this was impropriety
Or open-handed thanks, or just largesse,
It's not my duty to find out or guess.
He played a guitar, too, and would regale
The travelers with songs of cuffs and jail.

The rawboned man who'd taken the next chair
Looked so ferocious, with his weathered stare
And rural manner, his red-knuckled hand
That fiddled with a napkin and the band
Of ancient sweat that stained his Stetson (which
He flung onto his chairback with one pitch)
That city types around him turned away
And grimaced, as he gave a friendly: "Hey!"
(As if to say that they'd rather sink the ship
Than share a cabin with him on this trip.)
He overlooked their rudeness, for he knew
That though he lived on barley and beef stew,
Behind his looks he owned a mind so keen
That, had they stopped to look behind the screen,
They would have grown quite silent with respect.
He managed an industrial farm, unchecked
By normal limits on prosperity,
(Or so investors joked delightedly).
It dwarfed the lender's puny balance sheet.
The lawyer's enterprise could not compete
With sales of exports measured by the ton.
Each deal in soybeans, wheat, or corn, when done.
Brought in receipts of millions for his firm.
His salary alone would make them squirm.

He knew world markets for commodities
And hedged his losses easy as you please.
So, though he was a rustic and plain-faced,
He caught the wealth his rivals only chased.

Flowcharts and forecasts were his daily bread:
He stood financial downturns on their head.
Accounts for investors were so competent
That not a one would question what he sent.
That reputation let him source supplies
At home or globally, through lows and highs.
Boxcars of compost and insecticides
Came trundling in, dependably as tides.
He also knew a lot about the law
But used it only to induce the shock and awe
He needed to conclude a troubled sale
And add a rich new chapter to his tale.

And yet, he also knew to play the host
When lobbyists would fly in from the coast
Or congressmen would junket at the farm.
He'd take them pheasant hunting and disarm
Their staff of questions as he gave them guns.
Instead of price supports and overruns,
They spoke of how a pheasant would reveal
His presence, with a rush of cochineal
And sunlit gold that so entranced some men
They never thought of shooting birds again.
In small talk, at the farm, after the drinks
A careless man might say just what he thinks,
But this man knew to drink only enough
To help him listen to the vapid stuff
That passed for policy, and action plans
They thought would wow them in the hinterlands.

At length when tongues would slur and lids would droop,
He'd rise and send them bedward in a group,
And never mention how he had to find
Illegal workers every year, to mind

The harvesting and baling of his crops:
For US workers thought the wages slops,
Unworthy of a patriot's family line.
He chose to take on men who'd work, not whine.
Too bad if they chattered in a different tongue—
The soybeans would not fail to grow among
Workers whose speech they could not understand
Or shrivel when harvested by a foreign hand.

He'd grown up on this land and knew it well,
For that alone they'd hired him. He could quell
A dust-up among neighbors, win their thanks
Although he was no longer from their ranks:
He too had watched the local banks foreclose
On his small family farm, when credit froze
Back in the eighties. He was still a boy
And, decades later, nothing could alloy.
The grief he felt as townsfolk leveled blame,
As if some negligence had wrought this shame.
He could not wait to grow and move away,
To find some training that would lead to pay.
Chicago beckoned, and he learned finance,
And how to trade commodities, enhance
His profits with derivatives, and try
Never again to be left high and dry.
At length, as he made peace with moneymen,
He came full circle back to where he'd been,
But now quite safe, with income and renown.

And yet his family's blood called from the ground:
So he would drive out in the depths of night
Beyond the glimmer of the furthest light,
Where silence struggled with the homeless wind,
And thoughts were lost and resolution thinned.

He'd gaze up at the purple pulse of stars
Fronting a void oblivious of memoirs
Until his plans were lost in their array.
In hours that loomed until the sky turned gray.
He thought of what the wind says when it sighs:
The prairies gone, farms taken as a prize
By men with pools of capital who knew
As little about farming as voodoo.
The tracts they would assemble, swap, and trade
Or borrow on, scrape clean, proceed to grade
Were legacies of homesteading and grit
From those who vowed they never would submit.
That work, erased now, fallow, dry, and brown
Awaited some executive countdown
To turn into deep furrows, well supplied
With water and the latest pesticide.
Yet he could see, in springtime every year,
Small memories of homesteading appear
As clumps of orphaned iris rose to sing
And wonder where their farms had gone this spring.
At last, when he felt all that he could feel,
He'd climb back in the truck and turn the wheel
Till he could cut the engine and steal in,
Pull off his boots and throw them in the bin,
Hang up his coat and think of how his spouse,
Would tell him he let night into the house.
After some forty years, she'd hit the wall
And moved to California. All in all
She'd rather help her mother, who was ill,
Than hang around and share his inner chill.
The papers came much later, telling how
He'd starved her of affection so that now
They would not live together anymore.
He went out on the porch and shut the door

And sat there thinking of the dispossessed,
Feeling that he had failed a moral test.
Those people that his moneyed folk had skinned,
How would they fare out homeless in the wind?

The CPA beside him had the looks
Of one inseparable from corporate books.
She kept accounts for some great firm back East
And knew more secrets than a parish priest.
She also did the taxes of the queen
of charity and kept her business clean.
Saw that every bill was paid on time
Without complaint, before a clock could chime.
Even the most unpunctual demand
She met with calmness and a steady hand.
Such was her skill with numbers on account
That she was able always to surmount
Inquiries aimed at some numeric truth.
She'd ample methods to outfox a sleuth—
Although her clients might not pay her well
She drew sufficient income to dispel
Misgivings that she was dispensable.
Such a result would be incomprehensible.
For, if her customers were hard to please,
Her deft accounting put them quite at ease,
And if she was a bubble off of plumb
She'd smile at how she made them all look dumb.

A sports recruiter was the next in line—
He wore a jersey with the number nine
In white, across a faded purple field.
The name below his nape had checked and peeled
Off of the shirt but stayed fresh in his mind.
A life of beer and chicken wings had lined
His belly with an unathletic bulge
And even now, he'd happily indulge

In any round of drinks and merriment.
Although his days of coaching were long spent,
He had some value as a memory,
That raised funds for his university,
Recruiting hopeful prospects for the team,
Telling them all they had to dream the dream,
And hinting at great riches sure to come.
He certainly knew how to beat that drum.

At high school games he'd always have a spotter
Wooing best players for the alma mater,
Their parents, too! If steaks and ale
Alone were not enough to close the sale,
Then scholarships and stipends did the trick.
He'd let those carrots dangle from the stick,
And, in hard cases, maybe bring a date
With a degree in how to titillate.
His face was pocked with adolescent scars
And creased from long years puffing foul cigars,
Which he would chain smoke on the topmost deck.
He wore a whistle chain around his neck,
As if he might be called to referee
A pick-up game—though that was hard to see—
But still, somebody's mental bells might ding
If people saw the chain and champions' ring
That flashed and sparkled when he raised his glass
And threw an imaginary forward pass.
Though out of shape, he seemed to be in rut:
He constantly was sucking in his gut
And giving passing water nymphs the eye.
But never managed a successful try.

He and his buddy, an insurance man,
Would, after dinner, lead a caravan

Of thirsty folk down to a nearby bar,
And there they'd stay until the morning star
Shone in the east and we were long abed.
But if you had insomnia instead
You'd find them in a sports bar on our deck
Each with an arm around the other's neck,
Recalling college cheers and gridiron plays
And trying to recapture younger days.

His pal, the insurance sales baboo,
Sold policies for risks you never knew
Existed. Though, you'd audibly observe
That this was your vacation; he'd the nerve
To try to sell you coverage right now:
"If not now, then when?" he would allow.
Alone, the boutonniere on his lapel
Should make it clear that he was here to sell!
He looked peculiar, thin with lank blond hair
That grew in places, but not everywhere.
My thought was: radiation accident;
But I am told there was no such event.
He and the sports recruiter were a pair,
At least, there seemed to be a bonding there.

They'd sing old songs of love and suffering,
The coach on bass, the salesman buffering.
But once he spoke, his figure took on weight:
He was a most persuasive reprobate.
His briefcase was stuffed full of policies
That, he averred, would set your mind at ease.
He also brought exhibits, which he used
To show you what befell folk who refused
To buy the coverage they'd entertained:
A vial of poison pills that he explained

Killed off a man who failed to get "Whole Life"
Before he married his much younger wife;
A fire-charred splinter from a property
Not yet protected by a policy;
A bit of an exploded tire that led
To crashes which left everybody dead.
With these, he might persuade a fervent nun
To buy insurance for a future son.
In conferences, when he was panelist,
He'd mesmerize the audience and twist
Their fear of the unknown to his own use.
And though you might consider it abuse,
He would persuade the audience to buy
Annuities they could not justify.

I have described, as briefly as I could,
What I learned, or thought I understood
About my companions who put to sea for this long trip
From Brooklyn Pier 13 on such a ship,
How we had met each other that first night
And stowed our gear and went to get a bite.
But now, dear reader, your indulgence, pray:
If I speak plainly what I heard folk say.
Do not ascribe their choice of words to me!
I just recount, not joint and severally,
A true reporting of their every word.
And tell you everything I saw and heard,
For, I have always had the tendency,
To find real life far stranger than TV.
And so it proved on this odd escapade.
Don't blame me for mistakes the others made,
Their follies or the attitudes they had.
Consider how Christ Jesus would, when mad
At sinners, repeat their words that gave offense.
And Plato, too, said sound must follow sense.

If I upset some moral applecart,
That is most likely due to lack of art.

Because the Froth held thousands in its hull,
Each having been assured, "This won't be dull!"
A cruise director was assigned to every group
To make sure travelers would form a troupe.

He doled out aspirin and Dramamine
If any choppy waves were on the scene,
Hosted and entertained to smooth out bumps,
And cheered up anyone down in the dumps.
Our host was a playful and resourceful man,
Insightful, too, and quick to make a plan.
He found we were a disaffected bunch—
Some grieving, some upset, some out to lunch,
Few likely to watch movies or a show.
In all, we made a miserable tableau,
Too senior on the whole to sing or dance,
Too unalike to find on-board romance.

"Dear People," said he, "We are all a team
"In merriment, to make this cruise a dream
"Conveying you toward joy and novelty.
"I know you folks have paid a lot to be
"Our passengers to Charlotte Amalie.
"You'll love St. Thomas; that I promise you
"And there you'll find so many things to do
"That you will be ecstatic that you came—
"But till we get there, I propose a game!

"*Now you are all delightful folks*, I find,
"Who've had the instinct to leave cares behind.
"I'll wager you have stories to recount.
"Yes, privacy, I know, is paramount.
"But if you play our game the time will pass,
"We'll give you license to refresh your glass
"Courtesy of the *Ocean Froth*, as often
"As you come to take a part. We'll soften
"Every heart, you'll meet amazing friends.
"It's magic for each person who attends.
"This exercise will occupy you all,
"From now until we reach our port of call.
"If you agree to trust me, raise your hand!"
His challenge loured above our little band.

Then, as in grade-school class, intrigued but tense,
About a question that makes little sense,
Reluctant to be first, hands straggled up.
"Unanimous," he said, and raised his cup,
Toasting our willingness; though only he
Could swear that there was unanimity.
"So, let me tell you what you have agreed.
"Each one of you, as these next days proceed,

"Will search your store of memory and thence
"Tell us a story of a true experience,
"(Perhaps not yours), to teach us or amuse
"The group, and at our journey's end, we'll choose
"From all the stories told, which one was best.
"And if we've chosen yours, then all the rest
"Of us will buy you a delicious dinner,
"With fine champagne, to toast you as the winner.

"*Now, just to make the contest* a bit snappier,
"And possibly happy, or a little happier,
"I'll volunteer that, absent your dissent,
"I'll serve as Referee of Merriment.
"Come see me if you feel a little shy
"And I can give you something sure to fortify
"Your spirits. As to that, I guarantee
"If you will let those spirits wander free,
"Your presentation will be far from stale
"(To the extent you recollect your tale)."
There was some muttering from all around
The tables, but, as most of us had downed
Some cocktails to alleviate the grip
Of weariness from the connecting trip,
We readily agreed that he could be
The arbiter of our frivolity.
That being said, we stood up from our feast
To raise a final glass—I did, at least—
And go to bed, or to inspect new bars,
In my own case, I said my au revoirs.

The next day, soon as dawn began to spring,
Our cabin telephones began to ring.
It was our host, who said that we should rise
Because we would be jet-lagged otherwise.

We'd meet for breakfast and then plan the day
And free time till we had to make our way
Back to the dining room, to consummate
Our soggy promise to participate
In storytelling. All of those who could
Renege on their commitment surely would,
Whether they might claim hangovers or lack
Of talent, or plain diffidence, their track
To safety ran straight to the bright-eyed host.
He stood among the tables like a post,
And in his hand, he held a sheaf of straws
From which he said we all must make our draws,
So he could set the order of our tales.
We moved to do this at the pace of snails,
But such was this host's talent to disarm
Even the lender yielded to his charm.

So, everyone among us drew a straw.
And most then gave a secretive hurrah,
For, whether by chance or fate or hostly fraud
The General lost the draw and won the nod.

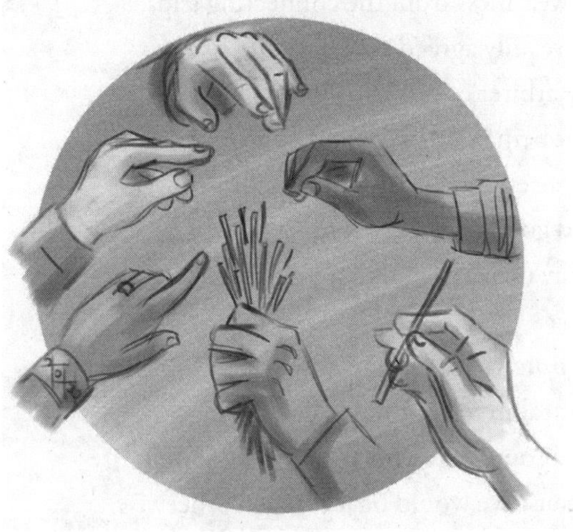

His daughter, Julia, who was there with him,
Patted his hand and said she'd go and swim.
The rest of us applauded the result.
For he, of all of us, was most adult—
Composed by training and by temperament,
As I have told you. He did not resent
The honor, but collected himself, and then
To our surprise, declared he would begin
Right there at breakfast; said he might as well:
"Now, sit down all of you, and I will tell
"A wartime story I've not told a soul."
We smiled and sat and listened to the whole
Of his account of honor, love, and crime,
Nor noticed we had lost all sense of time.

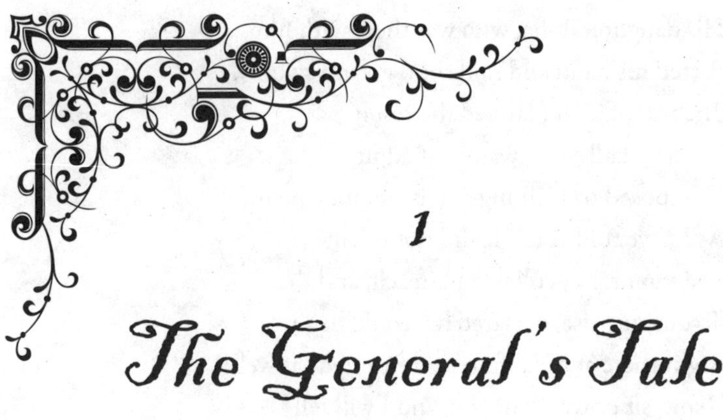

1

The General's Tale

Betrayal, I will tell of, and romance,
Both dressed in camouflage by circumstance,
And of obsession's horrifying price:
Murder, repentance, doubt, and sacrifice.
To come along with me, you must forsake
The comfortable pablum of the fake,
The patriotic stories told to you,
And settle for a narrative that's true.
Statistics do not teach: they count the dead—
But not the ones destroyed in heart and head.
It seems that under every casualty,
Lie twenty injuries we cannot see,
And are discovered only when the men
Come home with dreams they can't turn off again.

We, who are safe and snug and look at things
Like war with the dispassion safety brings,
May think that some nobility or creed
Is what makes troops commit themselves to bleed.
But if you view why folks enlist for war
You'll seldom find that it's esprit de corps.

Escape from poverty; the hope of fame;
A father's stern command; a sense of shame;
A quest for honors; some too-fertile date;
A gangland contract sure to seal one's fate:
All these are the compulsions that will drive
Young folks to fight and maybe not survive.
Nor on the whole do we care why they do
This work, as long as they're not me or you.
Each person's reasons, they say, are their own:
If some crazed tyro signs up to atone
For wild misdeeds—escape the tracking hounds
Before the county sheriff can find grounds
To lock him up—why should the public care?
His life and ending are his own affair.

Far different if the well-to-do were drafted.
Then you would see all orders tightly crafted,
Instituting rules of safe deployment,
Reasonable breaks for self-enjoyment,
And countless limitations on abuse
To let their own child live to see the truce.
And so, our force consists of volunteers.
They get small thanks from their civilian peers
For choosing risks a sane man would refuse,
Just to become statistics in the news.
Somewhat like ancient gladiators, they
Do gruesome work for insufficient pay,
Nor look for some assurance of our thanks.
Yet comradeship grows thick among the ranks.
In young folks, common danger can instill
A fervor that can subjugate the will.
Reliance is a stronger bond than love
Or fear or inspiration from above.

An NCO served out of Pakistan
In the mid-eighties. None knew where he'd gone

When he departed for Islamabad
Or what he had to do, not even God.
He never was acknowledged to be there,
And none could find his papers anywhere.
However, through his sacrifice, he rose to be
A sergeant major in the infantry:
Indeed, he was assigned to Special Forces.
Whose deeds are only known to unnamed sources.
Let's call him Kane. The officers that knew
His orders were in southwest Asia, too,
And unacknowledged. At that time, of course
The Soviets held Afghanistan by force
And every nation-state that bordered it
Was worried that the country might submit
And start a trend of domination so
That none knew if they'd be the next to go.
Regardless of their policies they turned
To the US, but made sure that no one learned
They had. And, thus, a secret scheme was hatched
To give insurgents ordinance that matched
The power and lethality of all
The Russians used to keep the land in thrall.

Training and advisors were supplied
To countries that for decades had denied
The US any role in their affairs:
And even now took reasonable cares
To keep their partnership out of the news
And publicly express opposing views.
Thus, men like Kane were told to carry on,
Though based in China and in Pakistan.
There these US personnel were tasked
With training Afghan refugees, as asked,
In tactics, ordinance, and how to kill
The enemy in silence and with skill.

Kane was a soldier's soldier, one who knew
Men follow only if led by someone who
Will suffer hardships equal to their own,
And never whimper, snivel, carp, or moan.
He led the kinds of missions that would end
Only with no more bullets to expend.
His reputation as an NCO
Attracted youth impatient to go
Find enemies to fight—if no attack,
Were imminent—or if camp life seemed slack.

There was about Kane some wild gallantry
That worked like catnip on young infantry.
Indeed, Kane was a model of a man
So angular, wasp-waisted, with élan
That made him seem invincible to those
He led to danger, sometimes by the nose.
It was inevitable that he became involved
In forays not acknowledged or resolved.
They based him in Peshawar, where he found
A number of Americans were bound
For training exercises and directing arms
Toward hidden depots on Afghani farms.

A colonel, a person we will christen Zeke,
Began to call on Kane when facts were bleak—
A murdered Pashtun squad, a renegade
Who'd some pro-Russian sentiment betrayed
Over and over, Kane gave him sound advice:
Dispassionate, straightforward, and precise.
Moreover, he would take steps on his own,
To fix things, though just how remained unknown.
In time, the colonel so relied on Kane,
When any desperate threat came down the lane,

He'd quickly choose him over higher ranks
To lead reconnaissance and guard their flanks
From sneak attacks and sudden sniper fire.
Kane was as cool as snow and tough as wire.

Zeke and his NCO were unique men,
But wrote the same text with a different pen.
The younger man had death-defrauding nerve.
The colonel added prudence and reserve:
Though he was brave, he liked to think things through,
Knowing that lives would hang on a miscue.
But once decided, he'd be out front.
And ready fully to assume the brunt
Of loss, if generals up the chain might carp.
But he was deemed both competent and sharp
By those in charge—a seasoned middleman
Between the armies, US and Afghan.
Beyond all that, the men were closely linked
By qualities as strong as indistinct
To those who did not share their bond.
They both were willing to advance beyond
The limits that a situation might impose.
They both were careless of themselves and chose
The dangerous assignments. Both disdained
To yield an inch of dominance they gained.

It's not surprising they became fast friends,
Each by duress propelled to common ends.
So it was not surprising that this Kane
Became almost a son to Zeke. So plain
Was it to others that they thought of them
As Gemini, or fruit grown on a common stem.
His wife also was taken with Kane's looks
His savoir faire, a face from storybooks,

And he was frequently their welcome guest
When all had opportunity to rest.
But more on that in time: for men so rough,
To be trusting was remarkable enough.

For all his skills, Ezekiel's greatest worth
Was as the best liaison man on earth.
He had spent decades in the Middle East,
As US interests in the place increased.
He soaked up languages, he learned to quote
The Koran without hitting a wrong note,
While those in Washington had backed the Shah,
And found themselves at odds with Al-Fatah,
Zeke burrowed deep into his bailiwick.
He courted leaders, never played a trick,
Until his stature among Afghan chiefs
Was of a man respecting their beliefs,
So long as they did not endanger troops.
Like them, he thought ideologues nincompoops,
Whether they belonged to them or us,
Why waste the time on such abstracted fuss!
He smiled, that once the Soviets were gone,
The Afghan earth, we thought, would cease to yawn,
And swallow foreign troops by regiment,
Leaving behind a tale of lives ill spent.
So we'd make fiefdoms democratic blocks
With laws, due process, markets, bonds, and stocks?

Ezekiel knew full well that was a dream,
A "shining-city-on-a-hill" type scheme.
For ages, tribes had fought over these lands:
Medes and Persians, Greco-Bactrians,
Hindu Shahi, Kushans, Hephthalites,
Saffarids, and Samanids and Kidarites,

Ghurids, Ghaznavids, and Timurids,
Mughals and Hotakis, and Durranids,
Then Turks and Brits, the Russians, Pakistan.
And not a one was able to hang on
To see things through. Of all the conquering hosts
Nothing remained but unrequited ghosts.
Ezekiel still had hope that, if he did his best,
The US might fare better than the rest.

In South Afghanistan the Soviets held power,
But in the north sat chieftains, grim and dour,
Ruling their feudal states. They saw no need
To recognize a "state" or intercede,
For their world antedated all the lines
The British drew for national confines.
They culled from centuries of self-governance
A Pashtunwali code for sustenance.
So foreign nation-building left them cold:
They'd seen it come and go, for they were old.
However, at this time, the Soviets
Were dropping bombs from overflying jets
And blowing people up, both as support
To their regime in Kabul and for sport.
The Russians' partisans were city folk
To whom the Pashtuns were a rustic joke.
Burning their food and killing their elite,
Which they attempted from five thousand feet,
Were thought to be passable expedients,
Saving of manpower, time, and armaments.

Zeke was a major then, expendable
If things went wrong, but otherwise dependable,
He had been sent covertly to recruit
Reluctant tribal chiefs, to constitute

An opposition force that could attack
The Soviet pillagers and beat them back.
He'd offer guns, artillery, and aid,
But the gift that really did persuade
Was shoulder-fired missiles that could turn
A warplane into fiery crash and burn.
In every village he was entertained
As Pashtun hospitality ordained,
And he, in Pashto, made his arguments:
He told them that it made a lot more sense
To take to war back to the enemy
And so preserve their independency.

He made one enemy—Abdullah Kahn,
A tribal chieftain known in Pakistan.
He ruled with power that would have shamed a tsar.
From mountainsides northeast of Charikar.
The warlord's stronghold in the Hindu Kush
Was stone and ice. There was grass or brush
Or shrub or thorny tree that one could find;
The air was thin, the gusts cold and unkind.
The major was kept waiting for an hour,
A demonstration of the warlord's power,
But then was shown to an inner space,
The *mehmankhana*, or men's meeting place.
He came alone and wearing Pashtun dress,
With no appearance of uneasiness.
An old *bukhari* belched both heat and smoke
And clothed the ceiling in a sooty cloak.

His bearded host was wind-cured, cracked, and dark,
With raisin eyes, deep-seated, and a spark
Behind them that bespoke a wily mind
Quick to respond to injuries in kind.

After the cushions and the tea and talk,
About his health, his family, the walk
He had to take to reach the citadel,
Abdullah let the major know that he
Looked to the US for security.
Against betrayal by a rival chief
Who might be bribed to enter as a thief
And take his chattels, wives, and property,
Blaming it on a stray insurgency.
The major said he could not promise, but
The gratitude of the United States was what
Would best protect Abdullah from his peers—
That, and the ordinance shipped through Tangiers,
To be delivered to these very peaks
By roundabout delivery in weeks.

The major left, with an uneasy heart,
Unsettled by the way he'd played his part.
He could not promise that the USA
Would intervene in some homegrown melee,
Nor had he promised! That was beyond his cure.
And yet his host had pressed him to ensure
Just that. His Pashto might have been unsound
And led him to linguistic marshy ground,
But he was sure that no such coin was spent.
His fears in this regard were prescient:
Within a month, he got a short report
Saying that men had sacked Abdullah's fort
Using the selfsame cataclysmic arms
The US gave to ward off other harms.
The major was distraught, because he felt
He'd been a cat's-paw in the damage dealt.
And yet requests for details lacked response:
The high command was busy for the nonce.

Then some weeks later he received by mail
An eight-track tape that pierced him like a nail.
There sat Abdullah Khan, addressing him
In Pashto, both his voice and aspect grim.
He sat in the same audience room, while fumes
Wisped up like ghosts of slaughter from their tombs.
On tape Khan unwound bandages that cloaked
His right eye socket. The raw pit evoked
The savagery, misprision, and deceit
That now he laid down at the major's feet.
His compound had been set on fire, his wives
Were lucky to outrun it with their lives,
All but the youngest daughter had escaped,
But two of those escapees had been raped.
And Khan's commander, a dear childhood mate,
Was crucified over the compound gate.

The major watched the tape a hundred times
And mused on justice for inhuman crimes.
Each time the old man's mumbling, never loud,
Reached out and fell upon him like a shroud:
"All Edens hide some serpent underneath,"
The warlord murmured, "But you gave ours teeth.
"You'll say you were not here, of course. These men
"Misused your weapons; this is not your sin.
"Yet well you knew their nature when you gave
"Them power to send my family to the grave.
"And to what end? So you could say you won
"A skirmish in a war that's never done?
"And the worst insult is you came among
"Our people speaking to us in our tongue
"To indicate to us you were a friend,
"While your intent, I find, was only to upend
"Our way of life, involve us in your war,
"And use us to perform a thankless chore.

"Surely as I no longer see the sky
"On my right hand, I now will prophesy
"That you will lose someone to you as dear
"As those I've buried with a futile tear.
"*Nyaw aw Badal!* You must share my grief!
"'Revenge is justice!' That is our belief,
"And, like unbroken sunlight, I will be
"Around and on you, beating ceaselessly
"And patiently as now upon these stones,
"That crush so many of my rivals' bones."
Attendants helped the old man from the floor
And carefully two-stepped him to the door.

The major sent the tape straight to the top:
But no one tried to make the menace stop.
The Pakistani General in charge
Was unimpressed by it, both by and large.

He said he thought this Kahn had struggled for
A feudal lifestyle doomed from days of yore.
Then he, because of wealth and family,
Had been entitled to the fealty
Of all within the precinct he controlled.
Now, modern knowledge purposed to remold
The governance of all the Afghan lands,
Through diplomatic layings-on of hands,
As soon as we could tame its wilderness.
The General thought the major should not stress.

So months went by, and soon the proxy fight,
Became intense. The Soviets felt the bite
Of the insurgent warriors in the North
And foreign fighters traveling back and forth
Across state boundaries, where those did exist.
They sensed the chance for conquest had been missed.
Ezekiel, now Lieutenant Colonel Wendt,
Wished he could be sentenced to time spent.
He was a hostage to protracted war
And sometimes wondered what he stayed there for.
But then Abdullah Kahn reminded him
That memories were long and futures grim.
One cold, high-desert morning, when he went
With specialists to tour some far event,
His jeep exploded, killing the poor man
Who turned it on to make sure that it ran.
And only one month later, to compound
The tension, he opened his front door and found
His ID fixed by a knife blade to the deck,
Its point run through his photo at the neck.

Of course, MPs in bright-red armbands came,
But never found a person fit to blame.

No Afghan refugees were brought to book.
And so the colonel took the time to look
Under his vehicle before he left
On any trip and guarded against theft.
Kane, as his confidant throughout this time,
Reported each new incident as crime,
And by investigation learned that Khan
Had taken credit for attempts upon
The *kaffir* colonel, whom he swore he'd kill
Before he lived to climb another hill.
The threats continued, and there were close calls,
Enough to make Kane fortify the walls
Of Zeke's camp quarters and Humvees and jeeps:
For now he knew Abdullah played for keeps.

That summer, Zeke made Madison his wife,
Although he knew he wed too late in life.
They met over a punchbowl at some fete
That military units pitch to celebrate
The idea of corps loyalty in their troops.
Too soon it would descend to pukes and whoops.
Zeke was as nervous as a new recruit
Out on a date in an ill-fitting suit.
And then he sloshed his drink all down her front
And dabbed it with a napkin. To be blunt
She put her arms around him as he did,
To steady him; and as his fingers slid
Across soft cleavage, he was truly blest
To feel the concupiscence of her breast.
Men run from love, or feel some higher call,
Which oftentimes leads onward to a fall:
Yet when it comes, love carries all before
And leaves the seaman on a foreign shore.

She was a beauty, younger by ten years.
One loving look from her could end his fears,
All setbacks, grievous losses, formal blame
Were disregarded, and his wife became
The only thing in life that he desired.
Simply to look at her was to be fired
With ardor, tenderness, and reticence:
He gave up every grip on common sense.
And so they married, with his army chums
Making a canopy of swords, with horns and drums
Conducting them to hopes of greatest bliss.
They solemnly affirmed that with a kiss
Which lasted so, so long that invitees
Who watched began to feel unease.
And yet, their marriage was not trouble free.
She pined whenever phones rang, for then he
Would pack his duffel and set out to sea.
Eventually, married bliss grew somewhat tired.
And after seven years, he had not sired
A child. Was there some tinge of shame in this?
Their bond had been a paradigm of bliss,
The more intense because they had to weigh
New orders that could come on any day.

They'd won a six-month leave in Germany
To live at some huge base incessantly,
And so, at best, theirs was contingent joy
That circumstance could easily destroy.
And then, he had some spells, unnerved
By feelings that his joy was undeserved.
The colonel's prior military days
Involved close combat, man-on-man displays
Of sheer brutality, the kind of acts
Left off official records of the facts.

The army thought him surgical, but he
Remembered the dank and blood-soaked filigree
Of every operation, and he knew
That, one day, retribution would come due.
That did not make him the best company
For spouses wanting peace and constancy.
And yet, at night she washed away all fears
With understanding laughs and fervent tears.

The colonel gladly shouldered all the weight
Of their discomfort, sure to complicate
The course of his career. But what of that?
He'd give up the career in nothing flat
If she demanded that he change his life.
It was the very least he owed his wife.
But she determined that he should persist
Because she knew the man that she had kissed.
He was as dear as any God devised,
And, of all friends, the finest and most prized.
With love, the colonel wore his wedding ring
Not on his hand, but on a leather string.
Next to his heart. He was convinced the amulet
Would either keep him safe from any threat
Or, after death, serve as an epitaph,
If his remains were somewhere off the graph.
But of these thoughts he never spoke a word
Unless his heartbeat could be overheard.
Therefore, he promised he would keep her near
Wherever orders said he must appear.
He'd make arrangements, then, to bring his wife
On billetings abroad. She'd share his life,
But every venture he was asked to lead,
Would be her rival—that, they must concede.
For she was not allowed to stay in camp.
She visited when she could cadge a stamp

From some official. Now and then that worked,
They'd also be together while they both were jerked
Around the confines of the Middle East.
She lodged nearby until each conflict ceased.
But this time, army bases where she stayed
In Pakistan weren't close as she had prayed.
Before she was allowed to go to him
She had to be precleared, by a quite prim
Official, who checked all her documents
As if she posed some threat to the defense.
It made their marriage tricky to sustain,
Even before the dark influence of Kane.

On meeting him, she seemed to stay aloof—
Polite, of course, her grace beyond reproof—
But Zeke could see the set cast of her smile
That seemed to say, *I'll stop and think awhile*
Before I let this perfect stranger in.
Her look he saw, but not the origin
Of his dear wife's unease. He thought her shy!
Not that she needed space to rectify
The stirrings that the sight of Kane awoke
Down deep within, before he even spoke.
Zeke loved his NCO just as a son
And wanted Madison to know that none
He'd served with ever could be quite as close.
He told wild tales, well chosen to engross
The listener in Kane's feats of derring-do;
And there were stories—more than just a few
When Madison looked off, as in a trance,
And went to bed when she could get the chance.

But now, Zeke's old report of Kahn's attack
Had finally hit the leadership like flak.
It took nine months, but when thought sank in,
Then Pakistan took action, with a spin

That no one in the US could have planned.
The orders came down from the high command
That Zeke should travel to a forward camp
Where others' hatred of him would not cramp
That comity the allies strove to keep.
Then no one need be murdered in his sleep.
Besides, the General added with aplomb,
It would be neater—if there were a bomb,
And US troops were dead or badly maimed,
The incident could blandly be disclaimed
As some wild detour by a maverick force
That had no link to Pakistan, of course.
Zeke tried to reach his patrons at the Pentagon;
Their answering machines were not turned on.
So he was moved across the Khyber Pass
To an impromptu base in a crevasse.
Naturally, Kane followed him, as did a group
Of trusted aides who thought themselves a troop.

The camp was located outside Jamrud,
On Pakistani land—if in the mood,
A terrorist could blow it to Afghanistan
With light explosives and a well-laid plan.
It was the equivalent, Kane loudly swore,
Of being left outside a stranger's door
With a pinned message begging, "Take this child;
"It has not eaten and it's somewhat wild."
No wives, of course, could travel there:
A rutted airstrip, steeped in disrepair,
And long abandoned, ran along the rim,
Its tarmac coping laid there on a whim.
The band of brothers saw with sinking hearts,
How close they were to Kabul on the charts,
Almost the ash on some foul Soviet cigar,
And close, too close, to fragile Charikar.

The colonel never got an inkling who
Abdullah Khan had somehow gotten to
But that he'd paid off someone was quite clear.

Meanwhile, Zeke told Madison good-bye
And not to worry. He would rectify
The situation and be back so soon,
She'd think that she had slept an afternoon
And found him by her side when she awoke
With every worry vanishing like smoke.
Still in Peshawar, at a guarded place
She was an hour by road from his new base.
A mountain range divided them, it's true,
But there was a pass that they could travel through.
He had no notion that Abdullah Kahn
Had set the board and moved him like a pawn.

The incident occurred in August, when
High temperatures killed cattle in their pen.
It was his fortieth birthday—such a laugh
If that coincidence should be his epitaph.
Kane and two companions had gone out
By Humvee to check in on some redoubt
To which they might fall back if worse turned worst;
They could not leave such options unrehearsed.
For hours Zeke watched the high road from Kabul
And squinted at each peasant cloaked in wool
Who ambled down the way on daily chores,
With some good reason to be out-of-doors.
The coded message, when it came, was short:
"Assault on pass. Two soldiers dead. Abort
"All traffic" then GPS coordinates
The colonel knew the soldiers were his own.
Was it an IED? No more was known.

As horror wiped all other worries clean,
Zeke and his aide-de-camp rushed to the scene
And found what was Kane's Humvee near Jamrud,
Crushed like a soda can. Onlookers stood
And murmured near two dead men pooled in blood.
Neither was Kane, but Zeke had known them well;
There were no other dead that he could tell.
The bomb was hidden in a pile of rock
Beside the road. The detonation's shock
Had hurled the rocks in chunks across the lanes,
Shattering glass and bones and ripping veins.
The dead had sat on top, to tend the gun.
Where was the driver? Had he lived to run?
Zeke turned back to the car to look for clues
And there he found a pair of women's shoes.
Her shoes. And as he stood in growing fear,
A nightmarish scenario grew clear:
A secret birthday visit from his wife
To bring some pleasure to his hellish life.
His Pashtun enemy had laid a trap,
His great revenge: to terrorize, to slap
His longtime enemy, but let him live
While Kahn took everything that life could give.

A call to base confirmed that she was gone.
His men had signed her out, just after dawn.
A Pakistani colonel was in charge,
In bulk and also ego rather large.
He told Zeke right away to leave the scene
And go back to his post, not intervene.
Some choppers *huffled* in to whip the dust,
The dead were put in body bags and trussed,
And Zeke stood motionless until a ghastly moon
Began to pick through scraps of wreckage strewn

Across the road. And then, his strength at end,
He left the Pakistani squad to tend
To the littered roadside and the flashing lights,
That signaled nothing could be put to rights,
And with his solemn soldiers, he went back
To lie down in their retrofitted shack;
But not to sleep. He worked the comms to reach
Somebody whom he might implore, beseech,
Coerce, or failing that, reward or pay
To help him scour the pass the following day,
To look for clues, to brace the Fellahin.
No luck. A week of fruitless days
Brought only promised help, and then delays.
His local efforts found no one who'd seen
The tragedy or strangers, even been
In the vicinity. All suffered from
The same impassive blindness or had doubts
That anything amiss had happened there.
They shrugged: who knows, for death is everywhere!

Night fell after another fruitless day.
The colonel fought off pain the old-time way,
With whiskey from an olive-gray canteen,
Alone in bed, his mind an empty screen.
He'd led his men in tearful prayers for those
Who died, and wished them sweet repose,
And now, as cicadas ground their single note
And wore their females down with tuneless rote,
Zeke lay in sweat and wished that he himself,
Could be an urn of ashes on a shelf.
Some quiet knocks brought him to full alert
As did the voice, quite low, but tense and curt.
They had a bogey on the starlight scope—
Lurking behind some boulders on the slope,

Watching the camp and hiding in the rocks,
So well concealed it could have been a fox
Or jackal that was sniffing for its prey.
But nothing moved, and animals don't stay
So motionless. Zeke took two men and slipped
Into the dark. They crept by inches, gripped
Their rifles, sifting in just as the night
Removes so quietly day's dying light.
Five feet away, Zeke signaled them to creep,
Two paces further, then, as one, to leap,
Focus their scopes and rifles and to shout
At the intruder as if heaven has lashed out.

But guns were soon forgotten. They had found
A woman, wrapped in blankets, on the ground
Silent and unmoving as a stone.
Dead or unconscious; certainly alone.
There was no doubt that it was Madison;
Beside her was a knapsack, clasps undone:
"Wait!" cried a corporal, "that could be a bomb!
"Abdullah's favorite way to say 'salaam.'"
But Zeke picked up the knapsack and his wife
And carried them inside. He felt the life
Still in her as he took her to his room
And laid her on his bed. The faint perfume
Of her limp body was a precious scent
That he alone took as a sacrament.
Removing her torn clothes, he looked at her
And saw a body scratched and scabbed as per
A week of hiding in some thorny brush
Down in a wrinkle of the Hindu Kush.
"Darling, you're hurt. We need to go
Into Peshawar!" But she whispered, "No!"

And after that, she never said a word.
They gave her water, but she never stirred
Even to drink. She took no kind of food
Her eyes stayed closed, her lips together glued.
So, as she slept, Zeke took the knapsack to
The common room, where he could view
Its contents in the light. In going through
The papers in the mildew-scented bag,
Smelling of sweat enough to make him gag,
He found two pieces of a dried baguette,
Kane's ID, papers and a small cassette
Like those that Kane would carry in the field.
He also found, by paper scraps concealed,
A silver bauble that he'd seen Kane wear
Around his neck. He wore it everywhere.
A high school sweetheart gave it in his youth,
And said it would "protect him from the truth."
It was a woman, this small figurine
That verdigris had rendered black and green.

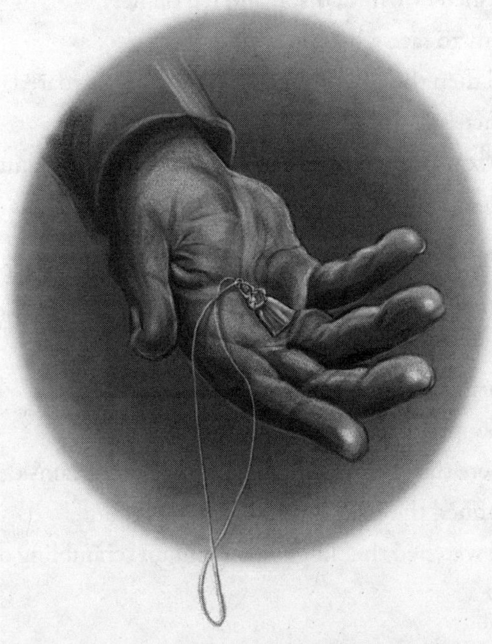

A sense of dread fell on our colonel then.
He did a little roll call of his men
And made sure they were in their beds or posts.
Then turned to a tape player and its ghosts.
He fumbled with the mystery cassette
While staring at Kane's little statuette,
But finally heard the voice he knew so well
Begin to weave its melancholy spell:
"When you hear this, I'm hoping I'll be dead,
"Or good as, if I'm still alive instead.
"She'd be up in Peshawar, not Jamrud,
"If I had used more care and understood
"The risks the way you always stop to do,
"But then, I proved, I'm certainly not you.
"I thought I'd bring a gift for you, my friend.
"And did not think of how all that could end.
"Just as we reached the bottom of the pass
"I saw anomalies up in the grass:
"A flash of whiteness on the scrawny slope,
"A glint of light off of a rifle scope.
"I pushed down Madison and fell on her
"Ready to face whatever would occur.
"And then the day turned dark, the hillside roared,
"Concussion hit us like a burning sword,
"The seats ripped from the floor, and we were slammed
"By rocks and shrapnel, jerked and jammed.

"*The whole scene plays* again each time I sleep—
"Pulling your lady from the damaged jeep,
"Seeing my soldiers lying on the road,
"Hearing the nearby killers, as they crowed,
"Whooping and praising Allah from the hide
"Where they had watched, far up the mountainside.
"I scanned the road for trailheads all around,
"And watched the thugs up-mountain scrambling down.

"Somehow we crossed the road to get away
"As rounds caromed and sparked but went astray,
"We writhed like snakes beneath a roadside rail,
"Stumbling, crouched, onto a rocky trail.
"Your wife was pale but terror made her spry,
"She made the first plateau as fast as I,
"And on that ledge, we paused to catch our breath
"And see if we could hear approaching death.
"Untrusting, we moved on ahead and climbed
"Forever, muscles on fire, dust-begrimed.
"We came into a place I thought I knew,
"From months before, when I was passing through.
"It was a hole, too small to seem a hiding place,
"But leading deep into an inner space.
"It lay some yards behind a sheltering ridge
"Across a stone that formed a narrow bridge,
"It was a cleft I'd noted long ago
"And, pulling Madison and crawling low,
"We snaked into cool air. The rocky bluff
"Above our cave was barrier enough
"To keep heat signatures from being seen.
"So there we starved, and rationed my canteen.
"And heard the helicopters far away,
"Grieving of what you'd think and what you'd say.

"*But every time* we tried to leave, we heard
"Search parties pass near where we lay interred.
"At last, at night they came and brought a dog.
"He and his handler had a dialogue
"Outside the narrow cave: "'Good boy!' 'Woof, woof!'
"While we lay there like fresh steak on the hoof,
"Till, as it snuffled in, I cut its throat
"And then its handler's—quietly, I'll note.
"Madison never looked at me again
"Without eyes full of fear, not even when

"I carried her along the trail before
"The dead team's loss was noticed by their corps.
"The rest is not worth telling, how I flagged
"A farm truck down, paid all I had, and dragged
"My paralyzed companion to the back,
"And lay her on some turnips in a sack
"Until we came within a mile of here.

"*I know that I have* ended my career
"With this outrageous breaching of our code,
"And I will make amends for what you're owed.
"Please let me make one last request of you:
"Spare Madison and keep her close. Be true!
"The danger and disgrace were all my own.
"And where I'm going, I must go alone."
Then there was nothing more on the cassette,
But what he'd heard left Zeke wan and upset.
By dead of night, a squad convoyed his wife
Up to Peshawar, where the doctors saved her life.
Zeke stayed with her for days; she would not speak.
She was in shock, they said. Could be a week
Before they'd know if she could interact.
Meanwhile, they counseled quietness and tact.
But three weeks passed, and then a month, then two.
As he surmised, the Jamrud base's crew
Were shortly brought back to Peshawar, now
That death and blood had satisfied Khan's vow,

Madison now could open both her eyes,
But simply stared ahead. Under the guise
Of stimulating a response, they tried
To talk and called it progress when she cried.
But as days proceeded, she grew sick again—
Nauseous and vomiting, seemingly in pain.

Zeke had an urgent meeting with the staff,
And gasped when their reaction was to laugh.
"Congratulations, Sir," guffawed an orderly
"I hope a healthy boy is what you'll see
"In seven months or so." Zeke stroked her hand
And whispered that she now was in command
Of all their happiness. But he could see
She lacked the disposition to agree.

Meanwhile, an officer arrived from base
To catch him up on rumors face-to-face.
It was well known that Kane remained at large,
Declared AWOL, now facing a discharge.
But then they got intelligence reports
Suggesting he had launched a fight of sorts
Against some warlord in Afghanistan.
For weeks, Kane picked off every partisan
That found or exited Abdullah's gate,
Until he fell before enormous weight
Of men and arms. How sad that vulture-bait
Was what this legendary man became,
His visitor opined, "So much for fame!"
When he had gone, the colonel put his head
Into his hands and grieved the cherished dead.
Then he got up, walked out the clinic door,
And soon was seen in Pakistan no more.

Some two weeks later, as Abdullah Kahn
Sits down one night alone to feast upon
A lamb shank, cooked with lotus roots and herbs,
A servant's cry outside the door disturbs
His peace. A minion bowing nervously.
Stammers that a man has come to see

The lord, some kind of foreigner, although
He would not give his name, but said, "He'll know."
No one was with him, so guards walked him to
The *mehmankhana*, lacking else to do,
For guests arriving at Khan's fortress door
Were searched then taken to the lower floor
In which the audience room was tucked away.
Warm with the smoke of charcoal fires it lay.
Abdullah entered, and he saw the man
Who'd broken faith with him and all his clan.
The warlord had the presence to sit down.
He pierced the villain with an angry frown.

"*You dare to come here*, walking to your death."
He cried, "You should not take another breath
"In this land that you ruined with your words.
"I'll feed your headless body to those birds
"That clean the world of vermin such as you."
The stranger answered: "I believe you're true,
"To Nanawatai: to the Pashtun code.
"This law from the Koran itself has flowed:
"That those who seek your help on bended knee
"And fling themselves upon your clemency,
"Without a thought of safety, must be spared,
"For power without grace is power impaired."
Abdullah Kahn sat back: "All that is true,
"But that was meant for Pashtuns, not for you.

"*Still, I am mystified* why you would come
"And put your neck in danger. I think some
"Would say you're trying to provoke
"Grave injury and death for Pashtun folk."
"My lord," said Zeke, "I have no enmity
"Against you or your people. You will see

"I'm only striving to uphold the oath
"I took to defend my land and people both.
"I did not choose this place, the war, the clime,
"But swore I would defend us for all time.
"The reason I have lodged my fate with you
"Is that I deem you honor-bound and true
"To those same values that have driven me.
"I've come to ask you, very humbly,
"That you release to me the body of
"The wild man who attacked you. For the love
"He bore me and his comrades whom you killed,
"He came alone for vengeance. For he willed
"That only he had cause to fight with you
"To vindicate his honor, as was due."
Around the smoky hall a silence reigned.
The one-eyed warlord pondered, unconstrained
By power, but considering what he'd heard.
At length, he spoke again. "You have my word
"That you and your dead comrade both may leave
"And find a place that's safe in which to grieve.
"Bury your dead. But know that if you dare
"Come back to these my lands, I hereby swear
"That we will flay the flesh off of your bones.
"And cast your corpse to dry out on hot stones."
With that, Abdullah Khan rose from the floor,
And his attendants saw Zeke to the door.
And then, a body, in a canvas shroud,
Was tossed out after him, as was allowed.
Unwrapping it, he saw by lantern-light
It was his friend he'd carry through the night.

He sat with Madison when he returned
And told the silent room all he had learned
About Kane's death, and how he'd brought him back
For burial with honors. He had a plaque

Pinned to a boulder on the Jamrud base:
He bore himself with dignity and grace
And gave his life so that his friends would live.
He hoped Kane's spirit would someday forgive
A monument in this ungrateful space.
But what, he thought, could be a better place?
And then, he gave his all to his dear wife
Hoping that he could coax her back to life.
And actually, it happened, on a day
Like any other, that he heard her say,
"You are the only one I've truly loved."
Before he could constrain himself, he shoved
A chair next to her bed and kneeled on it
To kiss her as if he would never quit.
She was by this time round with child, and he
Delighted her by guessing "he or she?"

Zeke was released from tours in Pakistan
And Germany received them with the yawn
It always gave the ins and outs of those
Recycled in from where-whoever-knows.
But they were happy, and in time they had
A gorgeous little girl, a blond-haired tad
Who woke them up and challenged them to smile
At three or four a.m., drill sergeant–style.
Before her birth, Zeke's partner took his hand
And gazed into his eyes. "I have not planned
"A way to tell you something that I must.
"During our long escape into the dust
"After the bomb, I lay inside a cave
"With Kane, hurt and pretending I was brave,
"As all those awful people came around.
"We lay so still and did not make a sound.
"The cold of night became a piercing chill
So like death's intimate embrace until

"It robbed me of my mind. I was insane..."
He stopped her. "There's no reason to explain.
"Long, long before this trauma came to be
"I had a test that proved at last to me
"That I would never father any kids. No child
"Would ever be my own. However wild
"The passions I might bear, I cannot make
"A child, for love nor mercy's sake."

He laid his finger on her lips and said,
"This child will be our memory of a time
"When strength of love enabled us to climb
"From shadows of betrayal to the sun.
"Without our friends, it might not have been done.
"So I will love as ours for evermore
"This child whom friendship, trust and honor bore."

He stayed with her until she fell asleep
And thought about the secrets he must keep.
Abdullah told him he respected Kane,
As did his men, for who, unless insane
Would fight an angry tribe all on his own.
And when Kane's last defense was overthrown,
And he himself was hit by mortal rounds,
His enemies crept close to hear the sounds
Of a great warrior going to his rest.
They sat with him and watched his heaving chest
Attempt to lift the weight of blood-soaked clothes,
Sharing the crisis of his final throes.
At last they saw him stare up at the skies
And breathe his final words. They memorize
Such things, if they respect the dying one.
Abdullah told Zeke that his men had run
Up close and heard him say, as if to kin:
"Sweet heaven full of stars! I breathe you in!"

And so he died. And with him dies this tale.
I hope this story has not seemed too stale.
Battles and soldiery are not in vogue
In this new age. They'd say Kane was a rogue
And Zeke perhaps a fool. I couldn't say."
Then, shaking his head, he slowly walked away.

With muttered thanks, his captive audience
Called quick good-byes. The tale had been intense.
The captain, Julia, fresh from jogging 'round
The decks, sprang indoors with a bound
And swept him off, to rest up from his chore.
But as they left, I stopped him at the door.
He'd done what was requested—told a story
Full of action, poignancy, and glory.
But I was drawn to ask him if he thought,
Outside of tales, a husband who had fought
So many battles, would remain so true,
So faithful to a faithless wife and crew
That he'd not try to right a carnal wrong.
No real-life people, surely, were that strong.
The General paused and looked me in the eye
And took my hand in his, gray head held high:
"Madison and Kane may both be dead.
"But they still gave me Julia," he said.

2

The Welder's Tale

The next day, I was skeptical that any
Members of our group, at least not many,
Would linger after breakfast to give ear
To our next storyteller. It was clear
That he who drew the second straw was rough
And somewhat angry. Then, it would be tough
To follow the high tale the General told;
The idea of a contest was still cold.
So I'd assumed that few would linger there
To hear a Welder letting down his hair.
I had not reckoned on our cruise director host,
Who, while our company still nibbled toast,
Went all around the tables with a bounce
And told us all he'd come round to announce
The story would begin on time, as planned
Did people want more coffee beforehand?
The Welder stood, and scowls played through his face.
Then, suddenly his words began to race.

Now listen, you entitled saps and sassies.
For years and years I welded school bus chassis—

Honest labor, skillfully performed,
To keep steel solid if it froze or warmed.
I figured if I worked under the bus
I'd not be thrown there by some ugly cuss
Who'd gone to college but still couldn't weld.
I'd worked near forty years and never held
A different job because I took such pride
In making buses that small kids could ride
In thoughtless safety, borne on faultless seams,
As they rode forward toward their brightest dreams.
At the assembly plant, where every day
I brought my lunch pail in and earned my pay,
Such as it was—and it was not a lot
To compensate for giving all I got.

But, in the end my loyalty and care
Did nothing much to keep me working there.
While I was turning out each perfect bus,
The world was making me superfluous.
You see, our owner's son bought a machine
Of silicone and polypropylene,
With circuitry so gol-durned convoluted
That, once set up, this thing, it was reputed,
Laid down a weld as clean and strong as mine.
It also worked from five a.m. to nine,
And then to three p.m. and then till dawn
Without the need to nap or even yawn.
It didn't pile up benefits, vacation days,
Or overtime, or ever want a raise.
They flattered me into teaching it and then,
Of course, the thing could do the work of ten.

One afternoon they said, "We've let you go!
"This check's your severance. Just sign below."

And, quick as quick, I found myself outside.
My wallet and ID were still inside.
I was refused reentry, as though forty years
Of sounds and smells and sweat that dripped like tears,
Were just a daydream. Kicked onto the curb,
Betrayed, fucked over—that's the verb!
I couldn't even bank my severance check,
Because my credit union, despite my trek,
Had just closed for the night. I tried to use
The ATM. It ate the gol-durned check,
And now it really had me by the neck!

It canceled the transaction, telling me
I hadn't entered my identity!
It kept the check, of course. I tried to call
Customer service. Someone in Nepal,
Who was quite new to English tested me
On who I was, but neither I nor he
Could fully comprehend the other's words.
I think I might have understood two-thirds.
I wish you could have heard him. I'll just say,
His attitude was that I'd spoiled *his* day.
"*Please give me the last four digits of*
"*Your social, please.*" There was no love.
"*That number does not match our records.*" *Click*.
Now I was really truly up the crick,

Without a job or anything to eat.
The unemployment office down the street
Had staff who might know what to do.
But when I reached it, there were only two
Poor frightened staffers facing down a mob
Of desperate people who had lost a job—
Each trying to submit an application.
Never was there such an aggregation:
Sentenced souls, lined up, as if they stood
To wait for the ferryman to cross the flood.
I saw a sign that said how long I'd wait
To reach the clerk's desk. At this glacial rate
I calculated it would take six hours.
The office closed in three. No magic powers?
Then you'd be standing till your muscle-tone
Shrank with disuse to skin stretched over bone.

In front of me in line a gaunt, old man
Stared blankly into space, gray as a pan

Of porridge. "You been waiting long?" I asked.
"Forever!" That was all he'd croak. I masked
My irritation with a hopeless sigh.
He was, of course, as penniless as I.
His head was stubbled with what once had been
Dark hair. Some missing buttons now and then
Would let his trench coat gape and bring to light
A shirt that once had been described as white.
I couldn't coax him into one more word
He stared ahead as if he had not heard.

I waited hours for the line to crawl
Till Jesus came again, then thought I'd call

From home. Once home and dialing from my chair,
I found it really didn't matter where
I was. By phone or on the internet
I heard an auto-bot: *"No job? No sweat!*
"You've reached our toll-free Public Service Line.
"Think you might have a jobless claim? Well, fine.
"Be sure you have your number, then press One.
"We'll mail the paperwork that must be done.
"If you don't have a number, then press Two.
"In just a few weeks, we'll get back to you.
"Press Three if you are waiting for our check.
"We don't control the mail, but what the heck.
"Need news of job availabilities
"For folks elsewhere who have advanced degrees?
"Press Four. More questions? Well, don't have a cow.
"To hear this list again, just press Five now. . ."

I woke next morning, phone still to my ear.
Music was playing now. It would appear
I'd been on hold for close to seven hours
Listening to a tape of "Hearts and Flowers."
From time to time a voice would stop the sound:
"Please key in your account, and then press pound.
"If you don't have one, please stay on the line,
"Your number is two thousand eighty-nine.
"You'll get a human on the phone within
"Four days. Now don't hang up and call again,
"You'll be behind a line that's even greater
"And moves as fast as a stalled elevator!
"Due to a call volume that's very high,
"We are experiencing delays. But please stand by,
"Our agents are assisting other clients
"Aided by the best computer science."

It was too early to go by the bank
Or to my workplace where my prospects stank.
So, hanging up, I went once more to join
That snaking line of people short of coin.
And there I found the gray man, still in place,
Just as I'd left him, staring into space.
I slipped behind him; no one seemed to care,
He'd hardly moved a single foot from where
I'd left him. So I told him how benign
He was to wait in this dissembly line.
How long had he waited? Again he croaked, "Forever."
"Well," I said, to pass the time, "I'm Trevor—."
He seemed to listen as I told my cares,
The job, the robot, and the banking scares,
And finally, the guy began to speak.
Hoarsely, as if he'd not talked for a week.
"I'm a historian," the geezer said.
That startled me. I looked him up and down
And shuffled my perceptions with a frown.
"What kind?" I asked. He looked annoyed then.
"I study dead economies and men."
He'd made a joke! I laughed, "Yes, I perceive.
"That we might be deceased before we leave."

He did not crack a smile, just said, "Could be."
Then turned. "Oh come on," I said, "seriously."
"Why stand around in an unending queue
"For days and days if there's no reason to?
"It's field research," he said. "That's why these clothes.
"I come disguised as someone no one knows,
"A down-and-out old feller. Smelly, too.
"But no one's got real close to me but you.
"I've learned a lot about the unemployed—
"The old ones desperate, the young annoyed."

I hit my forehead then. "The government!
"You're auditing this office! You've been sent
"To give an expert's view of what is wrong
"And why this process takes so frigging long!"

He sadly shook his head. "Efficiency
"Is what you suffer from. You think proficiency
"Outweighs humane concern. Now, take health care.
"You see that worried-looking man up there?
"A pediatrician, whose job of healing tots
"Was bought out by investor auto-bots.
"They're quick with answers, less concerned with curing
"Than with the knack of sounding reassuring.
"And there's a statistician. He looks quaint.
"His rivals are computers that don't faint
"When chasing algorithms 'round the clock.
"And now he's just been fired—a laughing-stock.
"Accountants and old members of the bar,
"Have thrived on their monopolies so far.
"But now computers download legal rules—
"There's little need to pay for fancy schools."

He lapsed back into silence. Then a voice
Behind us in line broke in. "You have a choice,"
A woman said, "Don't even lift a finger.
"Our government will rescue every swinger
"Who sits back long enough to ask for help.
"All you have to do is whine and yelp."
She stood behind us, dressed in a tailored suit
That she felt gave her standing to refute
Any suggestion that she might be on the dole.
She had been listening and lost self-control.
"A mind-reading philosopher," she smirked.
"I'll bet you've never, ever really worked.

"And now you're unemployed, with zip to do
"But make predictions of some cyber-coup.
"We've lived past the millennium and will
"Live on with our machines for centuries still.
"That's progress, friend! Why can't you see?
"Convenience and efficiency have set us free."
The old man looked at her with rheumy eyes
That somehow had the power to mesmerize.
"You do not understand a thing," he said.
"You might as well go home and get in bed.
"Nobody's 'free,' you're too split to unite
"And fix the fundamentals that aren't right.
"You've given your machines the power to drive
"The systems that keep all of you alive.
"You've let your tools design new better selves
"That humans have no hand in. Call these elves
"You've loosed to run your world for short-term gain.
"No trace of your ascendence will remain."
The woman was distressed by this harangue
And stepped back in the line from which she sprang.

I thought he had a point. Why not feel
Dark anger when a cyberforce can steal
Your livelihood—and call it "Progress," too!—
As if that term fits everything that's new.
Where the blazes was my severance check?
Stuck in a machine, my life a wreck.
Where were my wallet and my credit card?
Down at a factory now locked and barred.

I can't afford a house, I have to rent,
No doubt I'll soon be living in a tent.
I really need a fortress to protect
The little I have from blows I don't expect—

Catalogs and order forms and ads
That tempt the poor to fund expensive fads
And chase them through the mail and internet
So bankcards can rack up high-interest debt.
The algorithms work right through our slumber.
You're easier to process as a number,
Or so commanders of our prisons say.
You might as well go there to hide away.

While I was struggling with this reverie
The old guy had stepped back, to stare at me
With eyes that sparkled with some inner light,
As if he were most happy with my plight.
"Yes, every time," he said, "you give the job
"Of living to machines, you let them rob
"You of that much control. Eventually
"You'll ascertain that true equality
"Can come from being totally enslaved,
"Without the slightest chance of being saved,
"To systems so essential and so rife,
"They finally have usurped the power of life."
I hissed to him, "Who are you anyway?"
He answered, "Told you earlier today—
"Just a historian from a later time."
He waved in total silence like a mime,
Pulled off and swirled his coat and limb by limb,
A pale blue light just up and swallowed him.
What an unbelievable thing to see.
I clutched my heart and looked for company,
But all around looked vacantly ahead
If they'd not seen it, then they all were dead.

3

The Preacher's Tale

The next day, we were all so out of sorts
(The ocean being rough) that news reports
And coffee did not help a single bit.
We hardly ate our meal; we let it sit.
The sky outside the galley was dark gray.
The soggy flags flapped every which-a-way.
We hunched over our plates and hardly spoke
As damp lay on us like a muddy cloak.
We looked like spirits drenched, in just the fix
Described in the *Inferno*, Canto Six,
Unable to rise out of our chill despair,
Afflicted by the pestilential air.

Then, just outside our doleful view, we heard
Loud shouting—could not understand a word
Until the door flung open—then we saw
The preacher and the widow, jaw to jaw,
Bellowing with a verve you seldom see
Except in lovers who debate inconstancy.
"You are the Devil's spawn!" the preacher cried.
"Then you must be my father!" she replied

In no less volume. Then glancing our way,
They saw the room in silent disarray
And quickly walked to their respective seats.
Just like a couple who had split the sheets.

"How now!" our host exclaimed. "We can't have this!
"Let's fix it, if there's something gone amiss!
"Dissension on a ship will lead to grief,
"For tight confinement offers scant relief.
"Yet passion can give truth creative force—
"It happens that, in just the normal course
"Of our agenda, I was going to choose
"The preacher next to call upon his Muse
"And entertain us with some little tale
"That might distract us from this ugly gale."
The quickest glance showed that our reverend
Was not enthralled, but hoped not to offend.
He shifted in his chair and gave a sigh,
Tried on a smile and rose to testify.

"Brothers and Sisters," said this man of cloth,
"To fight the chill outside, the healing broth,
"Is our dear Lord and Savior Jesus Christ!
"If you come bid, you'll find he's bargain-priced!
"Jesus will love you, if you're down and out,
"Or if you've cut some corners round about.
"To Him, each one of you is next of kin:
"If you are locked outside, he'll let you in.
"Just look at what he did in Bethany,
"He raised dead Lazarus with alacrity
"From his befouled and rumpled beggar's bed.
"How much more readily will He instead
"Bestow Salvation on such souls as you!
"Look into your hearts. You know it's true!

"Salt of the earth, your salaries proclaim
"You've striven to excel and bless his name.
"Jesus will know each thought you have, each want
"You'd never tell a human confidant,
"As quickly as the check from you will clear.
"He'll set a Heavenly course that you can steer.

"*Imagine God* in all his majesty,
"The vast dominions he must oversee,
"The choirs of angels, throngs of cherubim,
"All bidding for some private time with him.
"Will He not love the folk who pay their way
"And do not worry Him or go astray?
"Will he not celebrate the Christians who
"Reflect so well on Him in all they do?
"My dearest friends, I hope you will rejoice:
"That God has given you an awesome choice:
"To serve him with your life or with your wealth,
"For each will win your soul eternal health!
"Consider advantages of offering
"A portion of your wealth to God our King.
"There is no other way that we can tell
"A righteous Christian from a ne'er-do-well.
"If God has blessed you with an ample purse,
"You are exempted from our primal curse
"By which man came, through Eve's unbridled lust
"For sinful fruit, to compromise God's trust.
"Consider how that tragedy began.

"*Soon after God on high* created Man,
"Adam took issue with the Heavenly plan.
"He wanted a companion, who could be
"His constant soulmate through eternity.
"So foolish! Was it not enough reward
"To stroll in conversation with our Lord!

"But God took Adam's rib and made a mate,
"To walk with Adam and participate
"In all of Eden's never-ending bliss.
"Wouldn't you think Eve would be fine with this?
"But she could tell the worth of every hug,
"And every romp on Eden's verdant rug.
"Man yearned for her, she found his missing part,
"The rib, could be restored by her soft art,
"While she, in turn found all that he desired,
"Could be exchanged for things that she required:
"A better tree, a sweeter meal, a bed
"Of softer moss to pillow her fair head.

"*And if her husband* was too slow to rouse
"From slumber or too idle to espouse
"Her errands as he should, she made him pay
"By finding an excuse to stay away,
"And if he questioned where she'd been
"She'd pout awhile, so prettily, and then
"Come up with stories about fairer fruit,
"And softer glades, new animals to boot.
"Then this first man would try his best to please
"And plead with her, from down upon his knees,
"To show him all the lovely things she'd seen,
"The fruits she'd tasted in each forest green.
"And that was the beginning of the end.
"As Adam gave his knees that fatal bend,
"Mankind fell with him down onto the grass
"Where serpents lurk, and sins can come to pass.
"But Jesus ransomed Adam's seed from sin
"With His own life. And though we can't begin
"To pay our debt in full for all He gave,
"We are obliged, before we reach the grave,
"To make amends as fully as we can
"And glorify what Jesus gave for man.

"*So, Brethren, heed* the Word of God through me.
"Consider that you owe Him your prosperity,
"And Sisters, make amends to God for Eve
"By showing our dear Lord that you believe!
"It's not too late to prove you're meant to go
"Up to the Heavenly realms, not down below!
"God will be gracious and accept your gift.
"His goodness and his mercy will be swift.
"But those of you who show you are just talk
He pointed at the widow, "You who balk
"At opening your purse to praise the Lord
"Who disrespect his messenger on board
"This ark! who'd feed him to the very fish
"That swim beneath us, you'll not get your wish—
"Convincing proof that your priorities
"Lie here with feminist sororities
"Not with your Savior and his Holy Church
"Whose Holy Name your guile and greed besmirch!"

The target of his wrath, as we would see
Was the poor widow, who sat quite near to me.
She looked composed, stared, smiling, at her hands
As if she gazed afar to distant lands.
And that just energized our speaker more,
For now his volume rose into a roar.
"You see that our Bathsheba does not speak
"Although she's married more men than a week
"Has days and sits on their collective wealth.
"I'd say this was inheritance by stealth.
"She's fabulously wealthy, but you see
"She turns up her nose at opportunity
"To give a portion to immortal God
"From her dog-eared, unmeritorious wad.
"It's hard to give this voice, even for me
"Because her acts so ring in infamy,

"But I will try, for our Salvation's sake
"To tell a story that should make you quake."

There was a minister in our fair town.
He did not posture or affect a gown
As many clergy do, in hopes to claim
Some status for repeating Jesus's name.
A holy man who lived for sacred things,
Transported by his faith as if on wings.
The object toward which he set a course
Was gathering the funds from every source
To build a temple to our sacred cause
Of praising God without one doubt or pause.
All of our earthly wants, you see, distract
The foolish from Salvation's purest fact,
Which is that God himself knows how to serve
Our needs. For instance, would you have the nerve
To tell our Lord, as bureaucrats all do,
The social causes that He must pursue?
Satan is quick to seize a wayward helm
Delighted to pervert and overwhelm.
This is the foremost reason why God's needs
Are best served first with money, not with deeds.
Our Lord and Savior puts the truth this way:
It is far easier, the Gospels say
"To thread a camel through a needle's eye,
"Than for a wealthy man to wend on high."

"***What are you preaching***, Friend?" I hear you ask.
"Didn't you just say that our foremost task
"Was making offerings from our weekly haul?
"How can we, if we lack the wherewithal?
"And didn't you just say God loves the rich
"Who pay to pull their oxcarts from the ditch?"

Brothers and Sisters, listen carefully:
The moral of this teaching is, you see
That by the time you die you must have spent
Enough on offerings to pay your rent
Eternally in Heaven. You'd better start!
You'll find it far too late when you depart.
That camel was disfigured by a hump.
He carried all his riches on his rump.
How could he get to Heaven with that thing?
The needle's eye, indeed! The offering
Of what he had on board, and he'd be svelte
When resurrected in his tawny pelt.
"Store treasure up above," said our sweet Lord,
Don't try to get to Heaven with your hoard!
"And don't fear poverty," the Savior said.
God will provide for you until you're dead,
Just as he does the lilies of the field,
Whose beauty is an act of God revealed.
Although their innocence inspires us all,
They still can be corrupted, shrink and fall.
Consider now, a tale of what is true;
Parsons themselves can sticks in Satan's glue.

In Sunday School, one sunny April day
This reverend chose as his subject "May"—
That month when Satan's powers are at their peak,
Disguised as Spring to snare the poor and weak.
The preacher told his crowded church that he
Had set his compass by Eternity,
And they should do the same, not fall for looks,
But keep their focus on the Holy Books.
He happened at that point to pause and think,
Look out across the crowded pews and blink,
And saw a sight that knocked him off his perch,
And left the congregation in the lurch.

A seraph of a woman whose bright eyes
Were locked on his as if he were her prize.
Both Common Sense and Piety essayed
To turn his gaze back down. They were dismayed
When he proved spellbound, looking at her hair,
Cascading amber under his blank stare.
Not Semiramis, with her wanton ways,
Nor bold Delilah better held the gaze
Of her intended victim. He was struck
As if infernal magic ran amok.
Had not this fey enchantress dropped her eyes,
He would have lost all power to improvise.

"Dear Friends," he cried, "Your pardon I implore.
"The Devil sent a draft in through the door.
"Our words are causing him severe distress,
"Destroying spells before they can possess."
Then with apparent zeal he went right on
To quote from Mark and Matthew, Luke and John.
And all the congregation was impressed
When he gave Thessalonians his best.
But finally our custom that we greet
Departing churchmen led to his defeat:
He met her at the door at sermon's end
And learned her name, attempting to pretend
That nothing had occurred in the last hour
Which might impel a man to shave and shower.
If only it were such a simple thing.
Her charms were far beyond imagining.
She came the next week and again the next.
Her presence left him senseless and perplexed.
He'd hide behind the baptistry until
His struggle with his feelings made him ill.
He memorized just where she sat each week
In hopes he'd see her turn the other cheek.

At length strict pastoral duty made him send
A simple note that asked her to attend
His "Seminar of Faith" down at the church.
I later saw that note, but our research
Never discovered any such event
In bulletin or other document.
There was no "Seminar of Faith," it seems,
Excepting in our reverend's restless dreams.
We would have cast him out, demon and all,
Following the sacred precepts of St. Paul,
But he was gone on an extended trip
To Belize, in a sinful partnership

With her: and, worse, on leaving, they'd withdrawn
The Church's Building Fund. So "Devil's Spawn"
I call a woman who promotes such sin
And wakens such a lust in Christian men.
Beware, I tell you! Never trust a girl
Whose soft lips set your senses in a whirl.
Beware the maiden ladies and the wives
Whose innocence pure devilment contrives.

And even widows hold their wealth so tight
They will not even offer God a mite.
Just shun them, Brothers, and ye Sisters, too!
Don't let Eve's ancient fraud unfold anew
On this, our modest little pleasure boat.
Redeem yourselves and keep the Church afloat,
Resist the sweet complicity of sin
And think of all the things you'll win
Through prayer—a bigger house, a car, a truck
A better job than that in which you're stuck!
So open up your hearts to Him. Believe!
You'll never count the treasures you receive.

The Congregants—that's us —were stricken dumb.
Our eyes were wide, our self-possession numb.
We stared around the room, and then we saw
The small Los Altos widow set her jaw.
Walking up front and, waving off the host,
She claimed rebuttal's necessary post.

4

The Widow of Los Altos Hills's Tale

She stood before us in a golden gown
That gleamed as if she'd meant to go to town,
Her arms akimbo, challenge in her eye,
Defending her own right to testify.
Instead of hanging with the likes of us,
She was prepared to make a royal fuss.
In light, she was a pantomime of truth:
Upheld by lacquer, seemingly, not youth.
She did not speak at first, but looked around,
An audience too surprised to make a sound.
She pushed her wavy hair back from her eyes
And said, "My friends, it comes as no surprise
"That you would hear a lengthy calumny
"From our evangelist. But who is he
"Whose views of sin are so completely odd,
"To casually presume to speak for God?
"Elijah tells us, God's not in the wind.
"There's no exception when you have been pinned

"To shelter by some preacher's blathery gust
"That leaves you wondering whom you can trust.
"At first I wondered if I should respond
"To claims that I am of the demimonde.

"***I am, in truth***, amused by that depiction,
"Which, at our age, requires a taste for fiction.
"Sadly, I think he saw me as a mark!
"Some widow who'd been walked around the park,
"More apt to give in to his clear intent
"That I should give my virtue up for Lent!
"Of course, he'd help me to reclaim my worth,
"By dunning me for all I have on earth.
"How could he think I'd pledge my final sou
"As if I were some silly parvenu!
"Vest all my assets in some stupid church?
"And on his word alone, without research?
"Not on your tintype, bub: go fly a kite!
"I did not leave the turnip truck last night!"
We were so shocked by everything she said
That we just sat and stared, our senses dead.
And then, remarkably, she waved and smiled
Perhaps she knew her words seemed rather wild.

"***I know I may seem harsh***, but that's required
"When men believe your decency retired
"The day you chose to wed a second time.
"We know each graceful line should have a rhyme,
"For, life, like verse, would otherwise be blank.
"But then, we have religious sorts to thank
"For messing up the rhythm out of spite.
"Have they ever had a joyful night?
"So, claim the poetry of life, my friends,
"And don't let anyone suggest you make amends.

"One simple couplet may be hard to beat,
"But many more will make a poem complete.
"Handsome young men, it's true, were my baptism,
"And after that an earnest catechism.
"Should I regret a day spent in my youth
"For liturgy that masquerades as truth?

"*I must give credit*, where some credit's due:
"Our reverend is not some ingenue.
"He lines each pigeon's nest with angel's plumes,
"Pretending they weren't plucked from witches' brooms.
"I heard his little diatribe just now,
"And thought that I should answer it somehow
"But could not find a way to make it real.
"My own life's prime objective is to feel
"And live and love, before I lose all breath.
"What fun can people have after their death?
"My first husband, a work of art named Jim,
"Was flat of stomach and so broad of limb
"You'd think you had embraced a classic torso
"Mounted over loins even more so.
"He was an athlete, my beloved first.
"And ran me round the bedroom till I cursed.
"Albert, my second, was a quiet man,
"And worked in earnest the entire span
"Of one whole decade after Jim's demise.
"I worshipped him, especially his thighs,
"Which were God-given, I acknowledge now
"(I hope that does not trouble you somehow!)
"But death, that carries all good things away,
"Took Albert on an unexpected day.
"And I was widowed twice, within ten years,
"I hardly had a chance to shed my tears.

"***My third life-love***, Edgardo, was a stud
"Who turned my insides into churning mud,
"But had a venal itch, and thought that I
"Could not resent what I would never spy.
"'If you possess the horse,'" he often said,
"'That does not mean you cannot ride instead
"'The pony, or take out a seasoned nag.'"
"Clearly, he thought that, in his nether bag
"He held some precious gift to womankind.
"I think his hormones colonized his mind.
"With infinite regret, we were divorced.
"His parents saw he promptly was re-horsed,
"And I got alimony that has served
"To keep me in the lifestyle I've deserved.
"But you are owed a story, not a list
"Of my accomplishments. I will desist
"From this biography and tell you now
"What comes of toying with a holy vow."

There was a preacher of great enterprise
Who founded a church of such enormous size
He should have paid a premium to berth
Its hulking presence on our burdened earth.
You had to give him credit: needy souls
Rushed in to enter the huge church's rolls
At such a rate, his church would shed its skin
Each year to find the space to put them in.
The people came in droves to hear him speak,
Not just on Sundays, but throughout the week,
And he coaxed money from his swooning flock
As Moses drew the water from a rock.
At last, by mortgaging the world-to-come
He bought ten acres of suburban slum.

He rid the place of vermin, trash, and narcs
And cleaned out the adjacent trailer parks.
He then installed vast parking lots instead,
A church school, where progressives feared to tread,
A station of one hundred megahertz
To broadcast urgent scriptural alerts,
And finally came a soaring Church of God,
A Christian stainless steel and glass *jihad*
That arced toward Heaven like a massive bow
With seven mighty arches in a row
On each curved side. And not a thing was straight
About this temple, as I will relate.
But let us say, few campuses could match
The size and splendor of this preacher's patch.

Within the walls of this pomposity
Near eighteen hundred sat each week to see
This Reverend Derwent Smith call down the Lord
And put the Devil's teachings to the sword.
This preacher found that if he amplified
God's Word at volumes that exemplified
The peals from Sinai that the Lord once spoke
Within his mighty, thunder-ridden cloak,
Then even when the congregants filed out,
God's echo followed them, His distant shout
Ringing as tinnitus along the garden path
As though they never would escape His wrath.
Our Reverend would seldom go outside.
He disliked nature and could not abide
The woods; he hated bugs like anything
And harbored doubts about the need for Spring.
His forest was of arc-lights, never trees,
The buzz one heard was lawnmowers not bees.
He was an inside man—a person who
Was happiest with his internal view.

In cool recesses of his church, he'd page
His volunteers to come to help him stage
Receptions for the persons sure to be
Church donors to the maximum degree.
He worked this program , from his tall, proud tower;
Soft schemes and machinations came to flower,
Lulled by the humming escalators that
Moved offerants upstairs in nothing flat
Into the foyer of the stainless nave,
Where he'd watch closely how they would behave.
There, offering boxes stood like slot machines,
Awaiting guilty gamblers of means.

The preacher was a powerful man these days,
A golfing friend of presidents. He'd gaze
Intently at the presidential drive
And lay the Prez short odds at ten to five
That he would reach the green in just one stroke.
He'd say a benediction if the bloke
Had gained the green; and if somehow he'd not
Would offer absolution on the spot.
The Reverend Smith was sought by cable news
To comment on religious people's views.

Like every creature short of God Himself
The preacher had a fault—the love of pelf.
But, after that, he had a second flaw.
He looked at women with obsessive awe.
Whenever youthful girls would come to him
For counseling, upon whatever whim,
He'd seldom let them go without a trial
Of virtue, set with secrecy and guile.
In an adjoining chamber, like a den,
He'd catechize them in the ways of men,

And I would bet my weight in kruggerrands
That this involved The Laying on of Hands.
A pattern had emerged over the years
That those who sought his help to wipe their tears
Were women quick to show their gratitude
And pay in cash for each beatitude.
In short, these privy pentecosts were wrought
Of greed and passion, for the bold who sought
To hazard their all on just a single throw,
The kind who'd ride bareback, everything on show,
Or just forget to close the bathroom door
To tantalize a likely paramour.

The Preacher never entertained a qualm
About these sessions. With a cool aplomb
That might have served Caligula, he styled
The meetings "Charity", which the Apostle Paul
Had named the highest virtue, after all.
The preacher harbored not a doubt that he
Would be exempted by such Charity
From any charge against his soul's net worth
When God reviewed his actions here on earth.
For did not Jesus spend three days in Hell
With every kind of crook and ne'er-do-well
Then rise again, His character intact?
The preacher found the parallel exact.

This morning his last visitor was one
Whose grace and beauty were designed to stun.
She was a study in convexity,
Which caused the preacher great perplexity,
For, he'd resolved to pull his horns back in,
And try some rectitude to balance sin,
But there was such advantage in her case
He felt his fickle heart begin to race.

She was an orphan girl, a child of wealth,
Who struggled to regain her mental health
After her parents' premature demise.
(They'd melded with a tractor twice their size
Out on a winding, foggy country road.)
The preacher knew the mother well, which showed
He was a family man, in his own way,
Inclusive as to whom he led astray.
But this was some years back, and now the girl
Had grown to set his senses in a whirl.

At eighteen, Sarah had survivor's guilt,
Her image of herself was all atilt.
He spent some weeks persuading her that she
Should not consider it infirmity
That she was irresistible to men
Whom she would fight off, time and time again.
She was just fourteen when her mother died
And had a boyfriend whom her folks decried.
It did not help that she was off with him
When both her parents' lights went dim.
In this our reverend thought he saw God's hand
Decisive, and too clear to countermand.
While musing, deep thoughts passing in a whirr,
He almost missed an opening from her.

"Do you believe in demons, Reverend Smith?"
The living hymn now asked, "Or are they myth?"
"I sure do," said the reverend, whose gaze
Was going where an actual demon's strays.
"I sure do, dear. In Revelations, it is clear.
"No question! Demons are always near."
His idol shuddered then. "So will you laugh,
"Or say I'm crazy in my epitaph,

"If something comes and I do not survive?"
He dimly heard this, thoughts in overdrive,
"What are you saying, darlin'?" he inquired,
He leaned in toward her, "Are you overtired?"
Her eyes were full, her dulcet voice was fraught;
Something was wrong to make her so distraught.

A pregnancy! he thought. *Of course, that's it!*
Boys can be demons when the hormones hit.
That could destroy all the pastoral work
He hoped to do with her. Some stupid jerk,
Some pushy boyfriend waited in the wings,
With no idea of how he threatened things.
But he was shocked when she went on
To whisper earnestly, her sweet face drawn.
"My sister is a devil," the child said,
"She hates me and won't rest until I'm dead."
"Sister? Sister?" asked the clergyman.
He thought he'd really known her entire clan,
Secretly, he felt sincere relief:
Devils and sisters were within his brief.
"Lamia, my twin. She's just not right.
"When we were babies, she was such a fright,
"Trying to cut me with a piece of glass,
"So she was sent off to a mental home.
"But now they've finally let her loose to roam
"And do the harm she's planned for fifteen years."
Young Sarah's cheeks were glistening with tears.

"*And now she's stalking me*. She comes at night.
"To scream and screech at me! It's such a fright.
"Oh, can't you help me?" begged the ingenue.
Well, what else was a priestly man to do?
"Of course," he told her, patting her sweet hand.
"I'll come to you tonight to understand

"What we are up against. She sounds possessed—
"But I am not that easily impressed.
"If demons are there, I'll drive the rascals out!"
More likely, give some orderlies a shout
And have them take the sister off again,
Quick as a deacon's child can say "amen,"
But let that pass. . . . Her blond hair's real, he thought;
But I'll know soon enough. She's good as caught:
Fisher of Men, this one is in the boat!
"I'll send the car," she said, "but bring a coat.
"We'll sit out on the terrace first; you'll see
"With your own eyes the things that trouble me."

The tryst was set for six o'clock that night;
As soon as his fair guest was out of sight,
He quickly canceled Confirmation Class
And gave his round of nursing homes a pass.
All afternoon, he showered, buffed his nails
And scraped the stubble off that roughens males.
He poured on body wash and rinsed it off.
He gargled acrid mouthwash till he coughed.
He scrubbed his armpits, for, he thought, her nose
Might nestle sweetly next to one of those.
His strategy was forming; it was sound.
He was quite sure no sister was around.
Lamia? Poor Sarah's reason was undone.
He checked the church's registry, just one
Of the family's two children was baptized,
And that was Sarah, as he had surmised.
After he'd freed her from the Devil's power,
He'd baptize her again in her own shower.

At half past five, clean as a holy man,
He waited blocks away, as per their plan,

Until a car with tinted glass drove up
All burnished silver as a loving cup,
And soon a liveried driver, in a snap,
Had come around the car and doffed his cap,
Then opened up the heavy door in back.
Promptly the priest was swallowed like a snack.
He felt like Jonah in this giant car,
But poured himself a whiskey from the bar,
And then another, as the city streets
Changed into fields and willowy retreats.
And finally they came up to the gate
He'd known when Sarah's mother sat in state—
The covered drive, the colonnade of trees,
The stately portico: he knew all these,
As well as how to find without the lights,
The mother's bedroom door on certain nights.
And he reflected, as he walked around
The well-known garden path, he might have found
A way to give that apple one more bite—
He'd certainly retained the appetite.

Cool dusk lay on the terrace; early Spring
Was not yet fully up to lingering,
But one small candle lit the mossy night
And at its table sat his heart's delight.
But not the vision that he hoped to see.
In fact, she looked bedraggled, as if she
Had singed her wings around a candle flame
And could not flutter back the way she came.
She had not even changed her clothes, but wore
Just what he'd last seen at his office door.
"Sarah!" he cried. She barely raised her head.
"Now Lamia is here!" was all she said.
A crystal bell sat on the tabletop.
The reverend picked it up and rang nonstop

Until, some moments later, lights came on.
The back door swung wide open, and upon
The lintel stood the driver with a tray
On which sat champagne glasses, an array
Of hors d'oeuvres, and a bottle of fine Brut.
The preacher beckoned him to fill a flute
For Sarah, and he made her drink it down.
She coughed and spluttered as if she would drown
But rosiness came back into her cheeks.
She cleared her throat, and he smiled back: "She speaks!"

But she would not be jollied. With a look
Of dread so earnest that her body shook,
She said, "What if the snake and Eve contrived
"To lie with each other, and their offspring thrived,
"Concealed within our flesh during the day
"But out at nighttime, having their own way.
"God does not tell us all His mysteries;
"Can we be sure that she's not one of these?"
"Who?" smiled the preacher, "Lamia? This sis
"Who's jealous of your every stolen kiss?"
He poured them both champagne and gulped his down,
Then tried his disapproving-cleric's frown.
"Why would you let a daydream make you sad?
"Isn't this just the type of myth you add
"To campfire stories, to make children quiet?
"Evil twin? Well, I, for one, don't buy it."
Rejection filled her eyes: "I was prepared
"For you to doubt me. That's why I am scared.
"You see, I'd hoped not to endanger you,
"A Man of God, so innocent and true.
"But I must know that someone understands."
With that, she rose and took his hands,
Kissing him deeply, murmuring his name.
And as she did, out of the woods there came

A scream of anguish rising to a pitch
That would have petrified the Endor Witch.

He leapt up, feeling shivers on his skin,
"Was that an owl?" he asked. "We should go in."
"All right," she sighed, "but she will come in, too.
"She'll find our room, whatever you may do."
Once safe inside, attempting not to run,
He locked the doors and windows, checked each one.
Then took her hands, remembering his role:
"God will protect your everlasting soul.
"If that's indeed a demon you will see
"The power the Lord God has given me.
"It will not get us, that I promise you."
"Then stay with me," she cried, as if on cue.
"You need not worry," said her reverend.
"I will be with you; I am your best friend.
"Let's go up to the bedroom. We can lie
"Beside each other. That should mortify
"This so-called Lamia. What have we to fear?
"She screeches in the woods, but we're in here."

Indeed, surrounded now by walls of brick
With stout oak doors, secure and over-thick,
He felt a thrill of conquest. He had gained
The fortress, only the sacking still remained.
There was no scratching on the windowpanes,
No tapping at the door, no rattling chains,
No further noise of any kind was heard.
It must have been, he thought, some kind of bird.
Now was his chance to move events along.
And she, as if to prove he was not wrong,
Slipped fingers in his belt before he spoke.
"Then I will take a bath, a good, long soak

"To wash off sin before I come to you
"And learn from an angel how to sin anew.
She pulled his belt and led him up the stair,
"Just lie down in my bedroom over there."
With that, she gave him one more lingering kiss
And left him to his prayers of stolen bliss.
He was ecstatic, knowing he would see
The awful sentence of mortality
Suspended just a little while for him.
While he explored her body, soft and slim.

He would not mention that he knew the room,
Or when it was he'd been there and with whom.
He stripped down to his underwear, and through
The inky dark, reached up to where he knew
The ceiling switch would be; it was his quirk
To leave the lights on as he did his work,
So he could marvel, and his prey could peek
At God's enormous gift—his fine physique.
He clicked the switch; the light did not come on.
And so he lay down with his head upon
Soft satin, closed his eyes, while good champagne
And whiskey sang soft gospels in his brain.

In dead of night, he woke up with a start.
A sinking sense of loss crept through his heart.
The window was open; linen curtains waved;
The moon looked in to see if he behaved.
And he was gratified to see his trim
New lover's body lying next to him.
She lay beneath the covers, just beyond
His touch. To prompt the young thing to respond,
He slid his hand under the satin sheets
To stroke her stomach. But for several beats

Nothing made sense. For something cold and scaly,
Writhed at his touch. A gargoyle lurched up palely,
Hissing and lunging, as a rancid smell
Issued, as from the bottom of a well.

He screamed and jackknifed backward out of bed,
Fell down the stairs, as if he were a sled,
Hit the front door tearing off the chain
Twisting the deadbolt knob, ignoring pain
From broken nails and lurched into the night,
All ghostly in his boxer shorts—for fright
Made clothes a matter for another day.
Soon even this thin remnant fell away
As underbrush and thorns conspired to tear
The wet and insubstantial underwear,
Leaving him naked as the fabled jay
Or Adam, just before he lost his way.
Two figures in the doorway watched him go;
The driver and a strange young woman so

Entranced by the sight that she stood there awhile
Smiling a devilish, knowing kind of smile.
"Pee-yu, I stink. My makeup is a sight.
"After it took an hour to get it right."
She smiled at her accomplice, with fond eyes,
Though blackened sockets in her pale disguise.
"And how'd you find a fish-skin that immense?"
"A giant grouper," he said, "Big expense."
"Well, golly," she said, "did it have to smell?
"I think we'll need to burn the sheets as well."
She paused as from the forest rose a yelp.
And intermittent fading cries for help.

"When I first saw it lying in the tub
"Just looking at it made me want to scrub,
"Not wear the nasty, awful thing to bed
"With plastic fangs and fright wigs on my head.
"What really did it were your sound effects.
"Without those, he'd have quickly moved to sex."
She shuddered at the thought. "That Banshee scream
"Was so horrific. That I won't forget."
He shrugged: "A boom box and the internet."
"Thank you, Cousin Dave," she sighed. "I think
"Of finding Mother's note behind the sink
"When we redid the kitchen. . . I believe
"It's providential, but it makes me grieve
"To know the only way that she could stop
"That creature's blackmail was to tell my Pop.
I hope that letter never saw the light of day."
"Me, too," said Dave. That's all there was to say.

The Preacher finally found the road to town
And was arrested, for he lacked a gown
Or trousers or a fig leaf at this point
And so, they had to throw him in the joint.
Every square inch was badly scratched or bruised,
Nor did he make much sense. He was confused
About what happened earlier that night
Except that he was paralyzed with fright.
It seemed to please him greatly to be safe
Behind some bars, because he did not chafe
At the restraint or even offer bail.
The reasons why a fully adult male
Might choose to walk buck naked into town
Caused ceaseless speculation up and down.
And soon his congregation bailed him out
And said it was the Devil's work, no doubt,

They sent him on an ocean trip, for those
Might not require one's wearing many clothes.
And after that, they all would vote as one
To send him on a mission, just for fun,
Preferably in places where a lack of fuss
Might make the naked less conspicuous.
Whatever the deal, at least he'd never go
Back to that dank and demon-filled chateau.
And so, friends, to your principles be true:
Don't flirt with your demons; they might flirt with you.

That night at dinner I was pleased to see
The farmer rise to face the company.
"Dear friends," he said, "it is very well
"For those of us who worry about Hell
"To talk about redemption, guilt, and such.
"But most of us don't bother very much
"About salvation and the life to come,
"When this life's tough to handle, and then some.
"Let's go to bed. My inner plowman's clock
"Still thinks I rise at dawn to feed the stock.
"But I'll be here at eight to tell you all
"A story that has held me in its thrall
"And made me think about the here and now
"Before I've let the future take a bow.
The lawyer and the lender shot a glance
At one another. Here's the hayseed's chance,
They seemed to say, to make himself a fool;
He should be in a corner on a stool.
But they joined in the faint applause that went
Around the room, and signified assent,
Or so our host determined: "Be it so!"
He called, as some had turned around to go.
"At breakfast stories will commence again!"
And so we left with an unvoiced "Amen."

5

The Farmer's Tale

The morning came, with fairer weather then.
The sea was blue, the sky a perfect ten,
Except on the horizon, where dense crowds
Of cumulus had formed a reef of clouds.
We were still shaken by the verbal war,
Between our speakers on the day before.
Some tiptoed into breakfast on eggshells,
Led on by the intriguing coffee smells
All wondering if we'd be witness to
A Salamis, Mylae, or Waterloo.
The lender took a seat next to the door,
In case he could not stand what lay in store.
The lawyer droned, as if his listeners hung
On every word that slithered from his tongue.
As I got closer, I found out that he
Was mad we weren't in Charlotte Amalie
By now. The cruise director kept his smile
On hand, reminding counsel that a boat
Must cruise through water, keep itself afloat
And could not just sprout wings and ailerons.
To satisfy some wealthy put-upons.

"Well," responded counsel, "at this rate
"I'll tell you that we're certain to be late!
"Charting the distance we have come instead
"Of time, we've gone less far than you had said.
"It should be morning on the second day!
"You owe us discounts, if we have to pay
"At all." The cruise director called out, "Whoa!
"Enjoy your time aboard. And if we're slow
"According to your calculations, you should be
"Delighted by a longer time at sea."
"Not hardly!" said the lawyer, "GPS
"Cannot be fooled. You didn't guess
"I'd have it, did you!" We were mystified
At what the lawyer meant, or why he cried
To Heaven there was something very wrong.
We hoped that we could jolly him along.

The farmer welcomed us when we came in,
As if we were his nearest, dearest kin.
He'd dressed as if he lacked all self-respect:
A cotton sweatshirt, clean but saggy-necked
Sat under well-worn dungarees; a cap
With some store logo sat next to his lap.
And much as we tried to hide our furtive glance,
You could not miss the oil-stains on his pants.
So, after an hour of clinking fork on plate,
Dabbling in coffee just to mitigate
The sunshine's jolting of each tired brain,
We saw the farmer rise to speak again.

"Dear Friends," he said, "I know that it appalls
"A few of you to see some overalls
"Stand up and tell you tales. One field of hay
"Is like the next, I seem to hear you say.

"But not so hasty! Life takes many turns,
"You cannot judge a man by what he earns,
"Nor know if his denim's worn for honesty:
"Or as some body armor against snobbery.
"Better to be thought a harmless hick
"Than be the pocket someone wants to pick.
"You see, my tale's about the way we look,
"And how that shapes our fate, by hook or crook.
"Will people make an effort to be fair?
"If you look like you don't come from there?
"I doubt it, but let's put it to the test.
"Let's see who rates me on the way I'm dressed."

I was real young the day I left the farm—
Or it left me—for good. The bank's alarm
When five bad harvests and expanding debt,
Plus forecasts that the winter would be wet,
Brought out the sheriff's men with bolts and locks,
Big boots that shook our porch and thunderous knocks;
Then, just like that, we had no place to sleep.
Our crops were left for other folks to reap.
Our lifeline flickered out—no other way
To state the fatal impact of that day.

Though only ten, I left for Illinois,
And hitchhiked to Chicago, where a boy
I'd heard, could find his way to fame
With luck, endurance, and a decent game.
But things were very different than I thought.
I could not get a single job I sought:
Although I lied about my age (I mean,
There's just no way you'd think I was eighteen).
I found soup kitchens, had my backpack stolen
Was almost raped, and tramped till feet were swollen.

I did not find a solitary friend
To bunk with when my cash was at an end.
I could not steal. I'd had no food for days,
And so, at last, I learned the desperate ways
Of folk who pick through dumpsters in their plight
Or raid the trash of houses late at night.

I found some favorite dumps, including one
That, after I scored a moldy hotdog bun,
Began to offer up uneaten meals,
Unopened cans of soda, little peels
Of shaven coconut on ice-cream cones
That dripped down on the mortared cobblestones.
I ate those first, of course, and then the meal—
Warm french fries, once ground beef, a cheddar wheel.

I should have known the bounty was a trap.
One evening, wiping yogurt off my lap
I sensed that I no longer was alone.
The man who blocked my route away was grown.
He seized my upper arm as I ran by
And held me with a tight grip, I won't lie.
"I didn't mean it, Sir! I meant no harm!"
"Sh-h-h, you'll wake the neighbors," said the Arm.
It dug into my collarbone and caused
A pain that grew enormous. Then it paused.

"Come in," my captor said. "It's time I knew
"Who I've been feeding for a week or two."
We staggered through the back door to a place
That seemed to be a temporary space:
Spare furnishings—a lamp without a shade.
A sofa and a single bed, unmade.
And he himself was thirty-ish and gaunt,
A Black man. "Is there something that you want?"

I quavered, "There ain't no cash on me!"
And shook all over with the urge to flee.
He smiled, "Why don't you tell me who you are,
"Treating my dumpster like your salad bar.
"Why are you out here? Why are you alone?"
At that, fatigue sank through me like a stone.
And so I told him how I came to be
An urban rat-kid without family.

All this was forty-something years ago.
Details are covered as by drifts of snow.
I don't remember what he said to me
That made me set aside uncertainty,
Or why I took the glass of milk and sat
In a tattered chair, as docile as a cat,
Nor why the stranger was so kind and calm
Rather than spraying me with an insect bomb.
"I'd like to help you," said my strange new friend.
"Just like you, I'm somewhat on the mend.
"But you need rest. If you feel safe with me,
"You'll have a bath and place to sleep and pee
"Maybe just overnight. More milk?"
I shook my head and sank into the silk
Of pillows that he tossed down on the floor.
And wondered if I'd reached the Heavenly shore.

"*You take me back,*" he said, "two dozen years.
"When I was young, and had no wants or fears.
"My parents, unlike yours, could care for me.
"They filled me full of things that I could be.
"I went to college and to business school
"And graduated feeling super cool.
"In Dallas, I became an analyst,
"And then a broker, with a client list.

"I traded anything that could be sold—
"For millions altogether, I am told—
"Commodities, options on currencies,
"And any instruments that were not sleaze.

"*The firm took notice*: youthful innocence
"Struck major clients, not as ignorance,
"But honesty and candor. They were charmed.
"Senior management was quite disarmed.
"Too soon some fat promotions came my way.
"So then, I found a tony place to stay
"In a small neighborhood, but ultra-riche,
"Called 'Wrenhurst'—just a little moneyed niche
"Close to downtown, but far enough apart
"To drive and never hit a shopping cart.
"This was two years ago. It seems an age,
"But that is how I know I've turned a page.

"*I leased a cottage* from the widow Steele,
"Presented by the firm of Cochineal,
"And moved in with my expectations high!
"So wrong! Within a single fortnight I
"Was writing to her agents to complain."
"At night, raccoons emerged from every drain
"And culvert that lay in the neighborhood.
"Now, I am used to thinking nature good.
"But these were large as chow dogs, and more bold,
"And apt to carry rabies, I was told.
"An access lane divided every block
"Behind the houses, paved with graveled rock,
"Lest garbage cans left out at the front curb
"Our high-class sensibilities disturb.
"The back lane was the raccoons' country club.
"They came each night to steal their favorite grub.

"At first, I kept mum, but the nasty things
"Would raid my garbage cans. As if on wings
"They scaled the backyard fence; barbed wire on top
"Did nothing in the least to make them stop.
"A mulch pile just behind the garden fence
"Served as a launchpad for their air offense,
"Flinging the cans around with a huge clang
"And rending the garbage bags with claw and fang.

"*They struck in early morning*, when my sleep
"Was at its tenderest. When I would leap
"Out of my bed to challenge their assault
"Dashing downstairs to bring it to a halt,

"I'd find the backyard empty, but destroyed,
"With cans askew and contents well deployed
"Across the yard, and out into the lane.
"Where trash streams led into a concrete drain.
"And then, as soon as I was back in bed,
"A new attack would try to wake the dead.

"I got some sympathy from Mrs. Steele:
"My landlady mistook me for genteel,
"Because I was young to live in such a place,
"And I was someone of a different race.
"She gathered plaudits from progressive friends
"For being in the fore of social trends.
"She lived in a large, Gothic style of house
"Across the lane. Long widowed from her spouse,
"She was a haughty lady, but quite kind
"To shrimps like me; in fact she was inclined
"To give me every benefit of doubt.
"And soon, I was invited to 'come out'
"In her back garden, for some snacks and drinks,
"One evening, with her dear friend, Mrs. Finks
"And Mrs. Woolley, both from 'down the street.'
She told me these were people she should meet.

"The date arrived; I entered from the lane
"And joined the three old friends out back. A mane
"Of fluffy white, sweet Mrs. Woolley's hair,
"Stood upright, like the product of a scare,
"And as I learned, she had the same inside
"Her head, a problem she had learned to hide.
"I later was informed by Mrs. Finks,
"After a long succession of strong drinks,
"That 'Dear Clarissa cannot get things right.'
"Just last year, on the trick-or-treating night

"She absolutely terrified some kids
"By squinting her eyes up tight behind their lids
"And ranting at them—how they looked a mess,
"And didn't their mothers teach them how to dress?

"*I found the three* companions that first night
"Like the Weird Sisters in the fading light.
"The table sat beneath a portico
"Of scented vines that let their blossoms go
"From time to time to spin into our hair,
"And large camellias, flanking a curved stair,
"Like Bishops deep in some official rite
"Consecrating battles or a knight.
"The ladies seemed to like my youthful view
"And asked me to cocktails every day or two.
"Our hostess rang a bell and in two winks
"A tall Latina maid brought out our drinks;
"The maid would never speak, just cleared and served
"With silent gravity. I was unnerved.
"She seemed to act as if I were not there.
"She might as well have served an empty chair.
"But worse than that, she had a racking cough;
"I had to lean away to feel well off.
"'Felicia' was her name, an irony
"For such a sickly sourpuss as she."

I yawned at my host. This was way too much
For me to process. I felt out of touch
With the strange man's bizarre, obsessive tale.
He saw my struggle and, as pure blackmail
Offered more ice cream, which I quickly took,
And, more alert, gave him a grateful look
That drove him on. "After a month," he said,
"Events then turned the world upon its head.

"*One evening there* was no server there—
"No bell-ring called Felicia down the stair.
"Instead, our hostess brought the drinks herself,
"A tray of glasses dusty from the shelf.
"'Felicia's gone,'" reported Mrs. Steele,
"'Back to Colombia. She did not feel
"'The need to tell me that she'd pulled up stakes.
"'Of course, she could not speak a word. It takes
"'Great patience to get help of any kind
"'These days. Her lack of talk I really did not mind,
"'And gave her the garage apartment, free. . . '"

"*She waved her knobby* hand dismissively.
"The garage, of course, opened onto the lane.
"On top of it, shabby and somewhat plain
"A small apartment perched, brick painted white,
"And round the side, securely out of sight
"Rose iron stairs that climbed up to a floor
"Above the place where, in the days of yore,
"Augustus Steele would stable his Rolls-Royce.
"And I remember saying, in a quiet voice,
"'Why would she leave? This seems an ideal place
"'For someone to live and work in any case.'"
"'You'd think so,'" Mrs. Steele said, "'but today
"'You can't depend on anyone you pay.

"'*I let her go to church* with her own kind
"'And acted absolutely color-blind
"'At least I've had the garage apartment cleaned.'
"Then fluff-haired Mrs. Woolley intervened:
"'But Zelda, doesn't your great-niece come tonight?'
"'Won't she stay up there?' 'You are quite right,
"'Clarissa dear,' said Mrs. Steele, "'Pure chance
"'But all in all, a lucky circumstance.'

"Quick as a conjurer, out of her pocket,
"She pulled a little chain on which a locket
"That she opened for us gave a view
"Of a quite beautiful young girl. It's true,
"I stared too long at her. Touched up or no,
"Her photograph showed life and health aglow.
"'Wow.' I murmured. 'She is really hot!'"
"My exclamation brought a crimson spot
"To Mrs. Steele's well-powdered, withered cheek.
"It was a signal that our little clique
"Should go and let our hostess greet her niece
"Sans audience, in privacy and peace.
"And so I plodded down the lane as though
"I had a long and lonely way to go.

"*Next day, at work*, I paddled in a slew,
"Of projects that I had to muscle through
"And came back home just after six o'clock,
"To find police cars up and down our block.
"Down at the curb in front of my brick walk
"A knot of uniforms engaged in talk.
"They leaned against their cars, whose winking lights
"Looked garish in our neighborhood—by rights
"A spot where things were never out of place,
"Where even burned-out lightbulbs spelled disgrace.
"Police, they make me nervous, always have,
"Though nothing on my conscience needed salve
"I parked and ambled to my door, as though
"It was a place I had a right to go.

"*But as I slid* my key into the lock,
"Behind me I heard heavy knuckles knock
"Against my porch's wooden balustrade—
"A bit aggressively—I am afraid:

"'Excuse me, are you Jackson Moore?'" The sound
"Of my full name caused me to whip around.
"I saw credentials on a plastic card
"Quite near my nose. I said, 'Yes, it's my yard.'
"'Detective Sergeant Reilly!' he said. 'And,
"'You've just confirmed to me you own this land?'
"He was a terrier, with an attentive face:
"'I only rent,'" I said, "'a quiet place
"'To live that's near my work. But hey,
"'Why are my lodgings on your mind today?'
"I thought, *Aha! He's here for the raccoons!*
"*They called it in. I should have brought balloons*
"*And party hats*. He studied me: 'You're new
"'To this particular neighborhood. That true?'
"'Oh, yes, I called about the garbage here.'
"'Garbage,' he repeated, with a sneer.
"'Let's walk around the back, Sir. You'll see why.'"

"*I gave up on responding*, with a sigh.
"We walked around the house and toward the lane,
"The raccoon-haunted locus of my pain.
"'A place like this,' he said, 'Must cost some dough.
"'And I'm recording this, just so you know.'
"'So tell me,' I said. 'What's this all about?'
"He indicated that I'd soon find out.
"And, rounding the corner, even I could see
"That crime scene tape was spread from tree to tree.
"A gurney held a corpse beneath a sheet.
"Medical technicians made the scene complete.
"He said, 'Perhaps you'd like to tell me why
"'A murder victim would be left to die
"'Under a mulch pile heaped up by your gate?'
"Suddenly, I could not concentrate.
"I stared at the sheet. 'Is it the maid?' I said.
"'What maid would that be, Sir?'" My head

"Was spinning now. 'How did you know
"'This was a "she," Sir? I did not tell you so.'
"'It was a guess," I said, "a maid's gone missing!"'
"He brings his face so close we're almost kissing.

"*I can smell tobacco* on his breath:
"It's strange the things you notice around death.
"At the gurney, he said simply, 'Take a look,'
"And pulled aside the sheet. It only took
"A minute, but the sadness of the sight
"Has never left me since that awful night.
"I moaned. 'Her grand-niece. Mrs. Steele's.
"'I never met her, but it really feels
"'As if I have. I saw her photograph
"'Last night.' My lawyer said my epitaph
"As 'citizen' was written at that point,
"And I was lucky not to end up in the joint.
"The local papers gave the story play
"And former friends contributed their say
"I soon was infamous. I got details,
"In nasty notes arriving through the mails,
"And warrants to search my rented home
"Revealing nothing with a fine-toothed comb.

"*Had I been married*, I would be divorced.
"My best friend was a lawyer I was forced
"To hire at the time of my disgrace
"And for my wrongful termination case.
"Meanwhile, my landlady, dear Mrs. Steele
"Told everyone she'd asked me to a meal
"And in return I'd gone and killed her niece,
"A harmless beauty, pure as virgin fleece.
"Police found no new evidence that I'd
"Done anything but rent the place she died.

"And so it went for some months. I stayed free,
"Avoiding former friends and colloquy,
"But living in the deepest disrepute,
"With untrue charges I could not dispute.
"And, with no job now. Severance seemed to flow
"Into that sump that only lawyers know.
"My landlady called the whole world to insist,
"That everyone should strike me from their list.
"She went before a justice of the peace
"In vain, to seek rescission of my lease.

"*But no one told the raccoons* I'd been shunned,
"They came by every night, and I was stunned
"At their boldness. Now I was a different man
"With little to lose and ample time to plan.
"In fact, I was tired of being pushed around
"By Fate and forced to give up ground
"I mapped the raccoon ruins in detail,
"The bags and wrappers they left as a trail
"Across the lane into a culvert's maw.
"I shone a flashlight down the pipe and saw,
"Or thought I saw the other end was blocked
"By a thing or things that hid and mocked
"My efforts just beyond the flashlight beam.
"I left some food. It was my foolish scheme
"To draw the creatures out. To my surprise.
"One day I thought I saw some glowing eyes.
"I called the police to report the raccoons' lair.
"The person at the front desk did not care;
"Said they'd look into it—a pat response
"Assuring me that all my needs and wants
"Would be ignored with all their energy,
"If they even possessed that quality.

"*I called the detective*, my antagonist.
"Promptly, of course, he came out to assist
"And brought two young recruits; for well he knew
"That troubled men betray themselves. His view
"Was that he might as well come humor me
"And take the chance, this opportunity
"Might lead to arrest if I let down my guard.
"His terrier eyes gleamed as we left the yard
"And came up to the conduit and trail
"Of slimy remnants from my garbage pail.
"I shone the flashlight, and they saw the eyes,
"Agreed that some raccoons of record size
"Were lurking in the pipe, and Reilly said,'"
"'This isn't Pest Control; call them instead.'"

"Then, deep within the pipe they heard a sneeze.
"Which made all three draw guns and shout out: 'Freeze!'"
"This the mysterious thing was glad to do.
"'Come out of there!'" made more sense, in my view.

"***The sergeant shook*** his head, and with a grin
"Pulled something from his belt and tossed it in.
"There was bang, and smoke, and then a din,
"As, with a roar the culvert's darkness surged,
"And through the smoke and acrid smell emerged
"A thing of enormous size, human in shape.
"Masses of greasy hair hung to its nape
"And blended with a beard so scraggly
"That it and its suit of rags merged seamlessly!
"A rookie cried in terror at the sight
"Of this thing rising to its awful height
"Of seven feet. Fierce eyes, a snarling face,
"Long arms, huge hands, too tall a brute to Mace
"Or choke or pepper spray, it stood astride
"The culvert, great head swinging side to side
"Roaring a thing that sounded like a word
"But in a tongue that I had never heard.

"***It sprang at me*** and quickly knocked me down—
"A six-year-old, tossing a toy clown.
"'Stop!'" cried the sergeant. "'Hands up, you! Stay back!'"
"It turned on them. I heard their pistols crack
"So loudly, with so many bullets fired,
"That when the bang of guns at last expired
"The giant thing lay silent on the ground.
"Now heavy breathing was our only sound.
"An ambulance rolled up, and we, quite shaken
"By events, were treated. Photos were taken,

"Measurements were made. Six orderlies
"Could hardly raise the creature to its knees.
"Then everybody left. I was alone
"Beside the mulch-pile where the corpse was thrown.
"I could not shake a notion that precluded calm:
"I thought the thing had called out for its mom.

"For three full days and nights I did not sleep.
"The story brought reporters by the heap,
"But neighbors did not call about the news.
"I hung up on the press. I had some views
"That troubled me about the incident.
"Raccoons now left my trash cans quite alone,
"So I inferred the monster had, unknown
"To residents, been scavenging remains
"Of rotting dinners thrown out in the lanes.
"Sergeant Reilly, on the other hand,
"Dropped by the house to make me understand
"That Mrs. Steele's great-niece was surely killed
"By that same creature. Bloodwork made that clear.
"I waited for 'We're sorry!' to appear
"In his small speech, but he just drove away.
"Still, it was good of him to come and say
"I now was innocent again. But things
"Remained to do. They say that real truth stings
"When people try to pluck it from the air.
"So I was left unhappily aware
"Of certain facts that simply did not fit.
"Why did the 'monster' stay here? Surely it
"Was better off not sleeping in a drain?
"Why did it kill the girl? And why remain
"In the vicinity of such a crime?
"The truth began to crystalize with time.

"'*I let her go to church* with her own kind,'
"Said Mrs. Steele. Was that where I would find
"The truth? I called up every single church
"Near Wrenhurst, and focused my research
"On city bus lines serving populations
"Of immigrants from Spanish-speaking nations.
"At length, I found the San Antonio parish—
"Bright as a santo on the inside, garish
"To a non-believer's eye. An office stood
"Just off the narthex, with a screen of wood
"That bore the caption: 'Immigration Station.'
"Behind it sat the cure for my frustration,
"Bianca Domenica Marcos, known
"To her friends as 'Bella,' told me on the phone
"She'd known Felicia who never talked,
"Plus other family members; but she balked
"At saying any more. I knew right then
"She'd not say much to non-Latino men
"Who might get deportation orders filed,

"*But when we met*, she saw me as a child,
"I'm sure, for she was sixty, if a day,
"My mother's age is all that I can say,
"With heavy spectacles that she took off
"As I announced myself with a shy cough.
"She quickly frowned when I said who I was
"And stood, but listened as I pled my cause.
"I told her how Felicia disappeared,
"The death of Mrs. Steele's grandniece, the weird
"Appearance of the hairy monster-man,
"The officers who shot him when he ran
"Up screaming. How I thought I'd heard him say
"'Mama, Mama!'" as he passed away.
"Listening, I found my story quite absurd.
"I wondered if she would believe a word.

"But she was deeply moved. She smiled at me
"Over the lenses that I now could see
"Were fogged. She told me she would take a chance.
"'Felicia is dead,' she said. 'The circumstance
"'In which she passed away is not well known.
"'She had pneumonia. Refugees are prone
"'To that disease because they hide and pray
"'That their condition will just go away.
"'You see, she had no papers. She was scared
"'To tell a doctor, even if one cared.
"'And much was riding on continued health.
"'She had a boy, smuggled in by stealth
"'In hopes that she could get a doctor's help
"'In treating him. Indeed, that giant whelp
"'Had more things wrong with him than she could mend.
"'Down in Colombia, such cases end.
"'*Acromegalia* had made him grow
"'To giant size. His brain was really slow,
"'But all in all, he was a child so sweet—
"'A hug from him would sweep you off your feet.
"'And he was gentle, and, I think, afraid
"'Of all things harsh. She kept him where she stayed.

"'When Mrs. Steele was drunk, and in her bed,
"'Felicia saw her giant bathed and fed,
"'And every night she slept down on the floor
"'So he could take her mattress. Furthermore,
"'She kept from him all knowledge of her health,
"'Still praying she could earn sufficient wealth
"'To treat his problems and to ease his mind.
"'But life is a hard taskmaster, we all find.
"'One night, her body was retrieved outside
"'A hospital that always has denied

"'Treatment for those without insurance cards.
"'They found Felicia's corpse a dozen yards
"'Outside the institution's "Urgent Care."
"'But we don't even know who brought her there.
"'I'm sure her son the giant then ran wild.
"'We've never seen a vestige of the child.'
"I'd heard enough, and all now fell in place:
"A needless murder and a dark disgrace.
"I thanked her warmly, for we each had cried
"Before the other. Now, disqualified
"From all pretense, we shared a common goal:
"To try to understand the human soul.

"*The ladies all were* there when I walked through
"The backyard gate and strolled into their view.
"They were surprised to see me. It had been
"At least six months since we'd sat chin to chin.
"'So who invited you?' asked Mrs. Steele,
"'Don't stay and make us hear your spiel.'"
"I laughed and told her that I would not stay.
"And very soon, I'd really go away
"For good. But if she truly wanted me
"To leave without some more disharmony
"She'd listen to a story I would tell;
"And then I'd gladly leave and go to Hell.
"She nodded her assent, uncertainly
"Because she'd thought that she was through with me.

"*Felicia had become* a liability—
"Not only was she paperless, but she
"Was sick with something that was killing her.
"You noticed, Mrs. Steele, and that would stir—
"Your instinct for survival. So a plan
"Was hatched and put into the can.

"You figured that your maid was very sick
"To an extent that jeopardized the slick
"Expedient you used to hire her—
"Paperless immigrants cannot transfer
"Their service to another, better job,
"And she'd forever stay to clean and swab.
"When it was clear she could no longer serve,
"And she was nearly dead, you lost your nerve,
"You and your girlfriends planned to drop her off
"At some facility that, when they heard her cough,
"And found out that she had zero means to pay.
"Would contact Immigration right away.
"You waited till Felicia was so sick
"She could not fight back when you came to pick
"Her up and walk her outside to your car.
"The nearest health facility was not too far,
"So when you sat her down outside the door
"And vanished quickly through the night before
"Security came out, you thought you'd won,
"But then, you never knew about her son.

"*You had no inkling* private healthcare firms,
"Riding on xenophobia, changed their terms
"So that no uninsured could be admitted
"Without employer guarantees that fitted
"All the requirements for a legal stay.
"So others were abruptly turned away.
"The private hospital that you left her at
"Would not admit her. That was that.
"And she was, at that point, so very weak,
"She couldn't hail a cab—she couldn't speak.
"And so, she finally crawled away into
"A corner of the building, where a crew
"Next morning found a corpse that no one knew.

"When you two, in an act devoid of love,
"Drove up and thrust your servant with a shove
"Through that perverse and unreceptive door
"You did not know she'd left behind a spore,
"A giant son, half-grown, who did not know
"His mom was gone, or even that she'd go.
"That night, he climbed up the apartment stairs
"And gently slipped inside, while unawares
"A young girl slept upon his mother's bed,
"And screamed as he slipped in with her instead.
"You have to think that mutual panic lies
"At the root of your niece's quick demise.
"And afterward, a child of giant shape
"Would drag her down the stairway and escape,
"But only after trying to bury her;
"He was a good boy with his life a-blur.
"Two months he waited for his mom's return,
"Ate trash, drank slops, but always tried to earn
"His mom's approval, just by acting right.
"Each evening, he thought, this will be the night
"When she comes back. And so time passed
"And the police came in to kill at last."

"*I looked at them*, so frail, so elderly,
"And found the sympathy to let them be.
"I finally said to them: 'I hope you know
"'I'll think of you wherever I may go,
"'And wait for any chance to make amends
"'For all these errors, and my taste in friends.'"
"With that, I drove off into welcome dark.
"And after traveling, I chose to park
"In this dark city, where I thought I'd find
"The chance to do good works and save my mind."
He stopped and looked me in the eye and said:
"I also swore that, in the days ahead,

"If chance allowed, although I could not mend
"The fate of that poor child or change his end,
"I would make sure his death was not in vain.
"If ever I found another one whose skein
"Of life was tangled, kinked, or rotten,
"Whose right to happiness had been forgotten,
"Abandoned by their family or friends.
"I'd do my level best to make amends.
"So, if you let me, my can-diving pal,
"We'll start rejuvenating your morale."
True to his promise, he adopted me
And gave me every opportunity
To work and learn from him and his career.
And that's the only reason that I'm here.
I'm now in charge of the world's largest farm:
And may God keep all of us safe from harm.

The story ended, and the speaker sat
At once, thinking his tale had fallen flat,
And I saw resignation in his eyes.
I'm sure he thought his truthfulness unwise.
Then, one by one, much of the audience
Came up to shake his hand; it was my sense
That everyone saw past the overalls
Except for the finance professionals
Who pecked at cell phones as they tried to get
The man's credentials from the internet.

Meanwhile, our host announced another tale:
"Ladies and gentlemen! It seems a gale
"Will hit this morning. You've been charmed
"By the scary story, not the least alarmed
"At how the blue sky has now turned to black.
"It will be hours before the jolly sun comes back

"And passengers can once more go outside.
"So I propose we stay right here and ride
"The weather out with food and drink and lore.
"I'm told that Mrs. Flake is next in store. . ."
At that, this worthy lady jumped upright
Hugging her lapdog in a grip so tight
It yelped, and she said, "No! You said, 'Tonight!'
"I am not ready to speak to them just yet!"
The good host frowned. "I thought we were all set."
Fiona brightened up: "Ernest can do it!
"If there's fat to be chewed, I'll make him chew it!"
She turned back to a short man, pale and plump:
"Ernest, tell them the tale of Broken Pump."
Ernest demurred. "I'll need a night to think"
"About that story. And I'll need a drink."
He asked the cruise director, "Can we wait
"Until tomorrow? Will that be too late?"
The cruise director smiled. "Only for some."
He shot the lawyer a look. "It would be dumb
To make this game a chore." So we adjourned
Until the morning, as the lawyer burned
With indignation. "We'd be there,"
He shouted, "if these crew members played fair."
So most of us went to bed. I wondered why
The lawyer was such an irritable guy.

6

The Scientist's Tale

Next day, the scientist expediently
Walked to the podium obediently,
As if he were a show dog in a ring
Well trained for just this very sort of thing.
He cleared his throat, and took his glasses off,
Sighed deeply and began, after a cough.

I am a scientist. My specialty
Is research phytopharmacology.
I study the effect of drugs from plants
On us and on themselves. By happenstance
As I was working for the government
Obsessing, as was my usual intent,
On ways to combat toxic algae bloom,
I found myself inside a conference room
With a man of science who had real-world skills
For turning red-tape mountains into hills.

His name was Bartram Rodgers, and he was
A person born to take on any cause

And raise it to a calling. There was never
A champion more genuine or clever.
An ornithologist whose love was owls,
He fought all threats against his favorite fowls
From logging, real estate development,
Pollution and the rest. So eloquent
Was he that he was a keynote speaker for
Conventions of researchers by the score,
Societies, foundations, wildlife groups:
The ones developers call "nincompoops"
Whenever disputes on land-use may arise.
He was among the first to recognize
The warming of the earth and in his field
Developed data sets that he could wield
To show the impact, year-to-year, on birds
And insect populations. As his words
Reached further into the community
Of scientists who work on public policy
He gained an eminence that would have led
A lesser man to have a swollen head.
And yet, no matter how renowned he was,
He happily would put his work on pause
To keep in touch with those of us who knew
Him better than the world could ever do.

We worked for years on panels to review
Research from scientists relating to
The science of climate and ecology,
And kept our standards high without apology.
Yet, even the good and brilliant aren't immune
To Fortune's bent for changing with the moon.
New leaders took the helm of government,
And started to assert that money spent
On issues such as global warming was
Poured down a liberal rat-hole. Soon the laws

Were changed, the funding fell away,
With scientists discharged from EPA
For saying PCBs weren't good for soil,
Or speaking disrespectfully of oil.
Those still with jobs grew quiet and concerned
That they'd be shit-canned if their views were learned.

My old friend sat one weekend at his desk
And pondered this political burlesque,
And then, without even a note to me,
Resigned his posts in Washington, D.C.
And disappeared as fully as a man
Sick with disgust and indignation can.
For seven months we did not even know
Where he had gone, nor why he chose to go.
Then one fall afternoon, I carried in
The mail and sat to read it in my den
And found a letter posted from Duluth—
A place I'd never visited, in truth,
And in the envelope, a single sheet
Said, in his hand: "You must come up. We'll meet
In Broken Pump, Cook County, off Sam's Road.
As soon as possible." The postmark showed
It had been mailed to me three days before.
Besides that sentence, there was nothing more.

I went online, searching for Broken Pump,
And finally found a reference in a clump
Of unincorporated townships near the tip
Of Minnesota's jutting upper lip
Quite close to Lake Superior's icy shores.
I packed my bags and went off to the wars.
Since I was sure Bart's simple note to me
Masked a deep and unvoiced urgency

I packed the SAT-phone that I always brought
For fieldwork, almost as an afterthought.
That very night I flew to Thunder Bay,
Ontario. It was an hour away
From that remote and wild peninsula
To which my friend decided to withdraw.
But it was now the middle of the night,
And rental cars were booked, and so, despite
My wish to drive straight down to Broken Pump,
I took a room there in some local dump,
Like every other place in town half full.

At 6 o'clock a.m. I rubbed the wool
Out of my eyes and found a rental car.
I drove to the south along the bright lake, far
Into the woodlands flush with October light,
But pillared with conifers as dark as night.
Once over Pigeon River, commissars
From US Customs kindly checked all cars.
Mine had no notion where Sam's Road might be
Nor whom to ask. "I'm not from here", said he:
"All this peninsula is Indian lands,
"Reserved by treaty for Ojibwe bands."
"Why don't you drive to Grand Marais and speak
"To someone local about what you seek."

So I had reached one goal, but just the first.
My hopes of finding Bartram had just burst.
I drove Route 61 to Grand Marais,
Only some few dozen miles away.
It was the metropolis of the Northern Shore
With thirteen hundred residents or more.
I passed a tourist center on my left
And U-turned in there with a squeal. Though deft,

I thought, I drew derision from a man
Who leaned on the wall out front, so he could scan
And comment on the automotive skill
Of every driver who rolled down the hill.
Annoyed, I walked right past him toward the place,
A tacky little strip-mall of a space,
With a clerk who made quite sure I would not leave
Without a bundle I could barely heave
Of brochures, coupons, advertisements all
In color—a touristic free-for-all.
But as for Sam's Road, though she knew that well,
She said of Broken Pump, she'd not heard tell.

"I'd ask that feller there." She pointed out
At where my driving critic lounged about.
"Old Joe has lived here for a hundred years,"
She smiled, "and knows far more than first appears."
Reluctantly, I thanked her for the tip
And went outside to meet the silly drip
Who'd sneered as I attempted to turn in.
He was a scrawny fellow, with a chin
Of stubble. There were jagged scars
Across his face, like those you earn in bars
Or jail—the biggest ended at his eye,
Which did not close and seemed to cry.
His hair was reddish, but too thin to say
For sure. What he had left showed streaks of gray.

"Well, hi," he said, before I'd said a word.
"You look like you are lost. I overheard
"You ask Amelia all about Sam's Road.
"It turns out that I have my own abode
"On a small parcel just off that same track—
"Although the road goes on to hell and back.

"I'm sure the bugger's forty-five miles long,
"You're in Canada, before you know you're wrong."
"I'm visiting a friend," I said, "but did not get
"The address straight. I've tried the internet
"And friends who know us both, without success,
"So I've come up to look for him, I guess.
"'Well, what's his name?' my new friend said. "'I bet
"'I know him. If I don't, then someone's met
"'Him recently in town. We'll go from there.'"
"His name is Bartram Rodgers! 'I declare!'
My new friend hollered, slapping his knee,
"'That fellow lives just up the road from me!'"

"I see him every day!" he said, but frowned,
"He didn't say that you might come around!
"In fact, he said that he was going out
"To spend a few days on a walkabout."
"He's like that," I observed. "A quiet man
"Who always says as little as he can.
"But what's your name?" I asked, "Ernest is mine."
He took a moment to respond, "That's fine,"
He said, "I'm Esau, but folks call me Joe.
"Now come on, you can follow. I'll drive slow."
I got into my car and followed close
Down forest corridors, until the dose
Of dust his Jeep kicked up left me so blind
I dropped back fifty feet or so behind. . .

"Ernest!" interrupted Mrs. Flake,
The tone of voice snapped all of us awake
And made her snoozing bulldog give a yelp,
"Let's take it as a given you had help
"And much as we've loved the drive, the reason why
"You're speaking is the story." "Sorry, Fi,"

Said Ernest, meekly, "It's just my memory.
"Every moment of that trip is real to me."

After half an hour, when we had stopped
Some miles up dusty Sam's Road, my guide hopped
Out of his Jeep and led me through the trees.
And there, in a little clearing by degrees
I saw a trailer, of the kind that tucks
Behind and half-atop big pickup trucks.
What truck there must have been was ages gone
For decades, the trailer that had ridden on
Its back had hidden in a skin of rust.
Its tires were dead, its roof looked hard to trust,
Piled under withered twigs, spruce cones, and leaves
And branches forming artificial eaves.

The back door squealed hard when I opened it
And stepped into a musty, dimly lit
Compartment. Startled, I saw a feathered fan
Which, eyes adjusted, was a great wingspan
Some five feet wide, flanking a sculptured head,
With yellow eyes in oval scoops, a red
Beak ringed by feather clouds of brown and gray.
"I've never seen an owl that large!" I say.
My guide, old Joe, still at the trailer door,
Has seemed to keep his eyes fixed on the floor.
"Yep, that's my great gray owl right there;
"I knew Bart loved 'em, so I thought I'd share.
"It's not a bad protector, in a sense..."
"But where'd you get it?" I said, "It's immense!"
"Well, this one tried to mess around with me
"When I was counting owlets in her tree
"Up in Tamarack. I came too near
"Her nest of babies, which I thought was clear."

He waved a hand over his battered face.
"Blind in this eye as well. It's just a trace,
"A nasty relic of that awful time:
"Never ask scientists how high to climb.
"For now, I thought this owl could stand its guard
"And scare off any creatures in the yard."
"Was Bart in danger, too?" I asked.
Joe's good eye showed a gleam, as quickly masked:
"No more than any of us," he replied.
"Out here, you get no second chances. I'd
"Be crushed to lose a friend like Bart, so I've
"Done all I could to keep the guy alive.
"He does not think of safety, when he's on
"Some scientific mission here and yon."
I looked around the trailer, saw a bed
A table, kitchen, and a way ahead.

"I think I'll stay here," I said, "I would hate
"To miss Bart. You don't really have to wait."
Joe seemed uneasy, then he shrugged. "All right."
"It's pretty cramped, and it gets cold at night,
"But suit yourself. I'm up about a mile
"On Sam's Road, I'll be up there for a while.
"I have a little shop there, where I strip
"Old furniture. Come see. It's worth a trip."
When he had left, of course, I poked around
Sniffing through the trailer like a hound,
Exploring, next, the boggy, naked woods.
At noon I stopped, and carried my few goods
Out of the car. Things I saw bothered me:
The top was off a half-full tin of tea;
Bart's boots were sitting just behind the door.
A lantern full of fuel sat on the floor.

Worst of all, his SAT phone, which he'd take
On field trips lay in pieces, for godsake.
He'd left no note or clue of any kind.
Wouldn't he leave at least a note behind?
I searched around, I pulled the mattress out,
I looked on shelves and tossed some clothes about.

One thing that Joe had said bit like a flea:
Why would my old friend try to summon me,
Then go out on a camping trip? I've learned
Enough to know that, if I get concerned
About a situation and don't act,
I will not sleep until I face the fact.
So calling in a favor, I placed a call
From Broken Pump to near the D.C. Mall,
Tawana Moore, an honorary niece,
Now superintendent of the park police.
We'd worked together on a task force that
Did not address its task or issue scat
For its report, because the winds of change
Nixed the whole project. That was nothing strange.
But I had met Tawana—she was great.
Compared to her, I felt quite second-rate,
But we became close family over time
And went to lunch on schedule or a dime.

To my surprise, she soon picked up the phone
And listened as I told my fears. Alone
Among my friends, she'd cast a somber eye
On every stratagem that folks might try
To sway the disposition of their case.
She'd long since given up the need for grace.
Tawana took my call and, for a while,
Listened in silence as I dumped a pile

Of theories about Bart and Broken Pump,
The trailer scarcely better than a dump,
My sense that something really was not right.
I knew that she was listening despite
The fact that I bore all the symptoms of
A crank whose rantings were his only love.
And then a call came in, she had to go.
Disconnected, I thought that must show
How quickly civil servants fade away:
Give up your title, and you've had your day.
In Grand Marais I ate and bought supplies
Like bottled water, garbage bags, and ties,
And then, as evening made to settle down,
I drove on Sam's Road back away from town
To where I'd marked the roadside with a stake.
I'd flagged it with a clip-on necktie, a fake,
But useful if I had to show respect.
Yet in the deepening twilight shadow-flecked,
I found no stake. So, tired and morose,
I pulled off on a shoulder that felt close
To where Bart's ugly trailer should have been,
And cut the engine. I was not prepared
To walk into dark woodlands that were shared
By every sort of creature, tooth and claw,
That might want human sinews in their craw.
But after bouncing off each sapling there
In the vicinity of Bartram's Lair
(As I'd begun to think of it) I found
The trailer with the squeaky door whose sound
Should scare off interlopers from the brush.
Once in its musty confines, in the hush

Of owl wings, I found the lantern and
With my new matches, lit the wick and fanned

The flame till the whole space reeked of kerosene.
The lantern light conveyed a ghastly sheen
To glassy eyes and feathers. I was stumped
By why my new acquaintance, Joe, had dumped
His giant taxidermy on my friend
And why my friend had taken it. The end
Of this inquiry would not come tonight.
At length, deep in fatigue, I doused the light.
I ran through all the problems that were posed
By bits and pieces that had been disclosed,

And there in the dark, I did an exercise
To calm my mind: dear Bart would realize
When he returned that I had just sacked out
In his small forest home because of doubt
That everything, including him, was fine,
Not desperate or in some deep decline.

That night would be the worst I've ever spent.
The trailer made a bathysphere's descent
Into the darkness, wrapped in sounds so strange
And nearby that they seemed to interchange
Themselves with fears already in my head.
I could not tell if I had made my bed
Outside, or if the noises were internal.
Fear was the only constant. An infernal
Snuffling around the ruined trailer wheels,
Snapping branches, little, startled squeals:
Composed a nocturne of dystonic woe.
I never was more glad to see night go.
Although I'd scarcely slept, I felt profound
Relief that, somehow, I was still around.
I even chuckled as I looked upon
My trailer-mate, the owl, who had gone

A little brown with daylight. I dry-shaved
And dressed to go find breakfast. "You've behaved
Quite well so far," I told the bird of prey,
"I think we'll live to scare another day."

Whistling, as I strolled out to the car,
I stopped, on seeing something quite bizarre:
Bright as a scarlet feather, near a stone
My clip-on tie lay raddled and unsewn,
Chewed to a skein of fibers that, had I
Not known better, would not have thought a tie.
While I looked at it my SAT phone rang
It was Tawana's office. "Hi there, gang.
"Need a break from making tourist rules,
"Let kids wade in the reflecting pools."
But it was Tawana herself, alone. No laugh,
A longish pause. Hoo Boy, that was a gaffe.
Her voice was hoarse, her tone upset.
"I don't know just what to tell you yet.
"But in 2001, a ranger died,
"Near Broken Pump—an expert, bona fide,
"In avian breeding. Disappeared that fall,
"And we all thought he'd simply gone AWOL—
"Met someone else and we had been upstaged,
"Or his commitment dwindled as he aged.

"***Next springtime***, in a muskeg, he was found
"Half sunk in sphagnum, near a breeding ground
"For owls. Within a year another person died,
"Whose name was Emily Belariszeid,
"A fine zoologist whose field was owls.
"Renowned, esteemed—with mustache and some jowls
"She might have even won the Wiley Prize.
"Now, when a person of such import dies,

"We never share particulars of death,
"Or compromise their research in one breath.
"We only share the news that they're deceased.
"And point inquirers toward their parish priest."
"The records that I accessed were abridged,
"So heavily redacted they were ridged
"With pen-strokes and crosshatching, quite a chore
"To look at, wasted effort to explore.
"But," she said, "these two belonged to us,
"And both died in or near that village, plus
"They both were studying owls. I've made a call
"To Emma Little Bow. I don't recall
"Exactly who she is in Minnesota,
"But there's not a detail, not even an iota,
"That she would know. So she
"Is likely to help us solve this mystery.
"See if you can get her on the phone.
"Perhaps the life you save will be your own.
"And very funny you are, by the way
"We'll save a special pool where you can play."

I called Ms. Little Bow and asked if I
Could come to talk to her sometime, to try
To find out why this owl thing was so queer.
Just come on over, she said. I'll be here.
When I arrived, I found she worked alone:
No sleek assistant for the telephone,
Or fetching coffee for their visitors,
Much less for out-of-town inquisitors.
An ancient Mr. Coffee, with an inch
Of grounds down in the bottom made me flinch.
In sum, she seemed not all that much impressed
By me or by information I possessed.
She only thawed a bit when I portrayed
The weird and wild discoveries we'd made.

She steepled her fingers as she sat and thought,
And then, I guess, decided that she ought
From a metal cabinet, tall and badly dinged,
She pulled Manila folders, coffee ringed.

"***Before you read,***" she said, her face a mask,
"What's up with all these questions that you ask?
"What do you know of Indians or owls?
"OK," she sighed, reacting to my scowls.
"Then, let me summarize before you read
"The part of these murders that provoked the need
"To hide the details of several murder scenes.
"The victims were interred, like kings or queens,
"There on the muskeg floor, in coffin cloths
"Of fibers, webbed like pupae of great moths.
"Inside, police autopsies found remains
"All broken and dissolved. They took pains
"To try to find a working theory,
"But all they could say with any certainty
"Was that the deceased were human. Here, we knew
"Of course, the cause of death. Owls don't chew
"Their prey, you see, they swallow each kill whole.
"Digestion makes the prey a casserole,
"And then they upchuck a package of remains
"Onto the forest floor. Before the rains
"Destroy them, students collect them, and they are
"Important. They're a sort of guiding star
"For raptor study. When dissected, they reveal
"Not only what the bird had for its meal,
"But how it hunted, and how much it ate.

"***And that is what now*** moves me to relate
"How greatly these crime scenes disturbed our bands.
"They looked like owl kill. No one understands

"How pellets like those in which the dead were found
"Could be four feet at least, and two feet round.
"Because that means the predatory owl
"Was twelve feet long at least. There is no fowl,
"Needless to say, who'd ever reach that size,
"Or seize an adult human as its prize.
"And yet, the giant pellets were just what
"A bird that big would carry in its gut.
"Here, look at these," She handed me a stack
Of glossy 8 x 10s. There was a sack,
But long and blanched and furry, pierced with sticks.
A close-up of it showed my eyes played tricks
And that the sticks were splintered bones, all napped
With shreds of cloth and hair enwrapped,
The dried-up remnants of a grisly feast,
A churned autopsy at the very least.

Successive photos showed dissection of
The grim cocoon, the buckles, scraps of glove
With little bits of fingerbone inside,
And underclothes be-wadded, stiff, and dried.
"I've seen enough," I said, and handed her
The grisly photos, "when did this occur?"
"This one three years ago; spring before last,
"For the other, just as winter rains had passed."
"Suspects?" I queried. "None that we could find,
"And yes, there was an inquest; agents mined
"The sites for samples, analyzed them well,
"And walked the scene. As far as they could tell,
"The pellets looked authentic; these remains
"Had been digested. Scientists took pains
"Down at the state lab; but they can't tell how
"A killer could pull this off. So even now
"You won't hear anyone describe the scene
"Or what they found. Behind the painted screen

"That's headquarters, they've got the perfect ruse—
"Preventing public panic—to excuse
"Their nontransparent action on these cases.
"Regardless, they'll have owl egg on their faces."

I sat and looked at Emma Little Bow
And where I found the courage, I don't know,
But I burst out: "So what about the stories
"You folks tell, about these territories
"And some Great Owl. My friend Bart told me
"Once, long ago, in Washington, D.C.,
"When he had drunk too much, that you believe
"A spirit owl preys on those who grieve."
She stared at me, and then picked up the phone.
"Eddie," she said, "Come help us pick a bone.
"To me she said, "Eddie's the best.
"Among the Ani-shína-abeg. The rest
"Forget their culture; Eddie is the store
"For knowledge of our ancient lore.
"Also a techno-whiz, as you will see—
"He has an advanced computer science degree.

I'd been expecting some wise, leathery chief,
Wrinkled and expressionless, belief
In secret ancient ways baked in his face.
But Eddie was a very different case.
His hair was graying, but his step was spry,
His handshake firm, some humor in his eye.
He came in from the back and in one hand
Were circuit boards and springs tied with a band.
He said, "You've met my wife; if she called me
"That means we can't invite you in for tea."
"Oh, Eddie," said his wife. "Now drop that crap.
"This man has lost his friend; he sees a trap

"Laid everywhere for him. So let's be kind.
"Yes, he's white, a *gichi-mookomaan*, and blind
"Without our help, but not an enemy
"Who comes to cheat us, far as I can see."
The rest was in Ojibwe. Therefore, I
Was grateful when at last I heard Ed sigh:

"**Your kind dishonors** every guarantee,
"But Emma thinks you come respectfully,
"And I don't sense you've got some trick to play.
"The things you're really asking me to say
"About Gookooko'oo—the great gray owl—
"A spirit bird who's always on the prowl,
"May violate our deeply held beliefs
"As handed down for years by all our chiefs.
"You people call her 'Phantom of the North.'
"She is the messenger that Death sends forth.
"To tell a person that the time has come.
"Whether they're a noble or a bum,
"She flies to them and calls them by their name,
"To let them know that, soon enough, their flame
"Of life will flicker out. We may not love
"The owl, who calls us from the dark-above
"To let our families prepare their tears.
"And yet, it's good to know when darkness nears
"As willed by the Protectors of our band
"Who watch on high, and then, one day, command
"The silent shadow of the woods to drown
"Our final scream within her fluffy down,
"To float down softly till her awful claws
"Dig deep and bring us our eternal pause.

"**Some find** in the Great Owl our tribal sense
"Of how alone man is in this immense

"Impermanence that we call life on earth.
"They say we start to die upon our birth
"And one of our writers says that solitude
"Will break you with its yearning. I'd conclude,
"That you, perhaps, should let the owl alone
"And leave her in the realm of the unknown."
"I am a scientist," I answered, "who
"Attempts to prove conjecture to be true.
"So what I'm asking is: Is there an owl
"That measures twelve feet long and comes to prowl
"Around these woods at night—some ancient one
"That comes and goes its way without the sun?"
He smiled at me, "You people seem to like
"All answers to be certain. When you hike
"You ask us, 'Do you see any bears up here?'
"Well, yes, but that may really not be true.
"In your case. It depends on what you do.
"And how you do it. We may all believe
"The Great Owl haunts these woods and calls our name.
"But I can't show her to you all the same,
"And if you find her, we won't know she's found,
"Because, you will no longer be around."

I left the building and drove back to Bart's,
This time I did not need explorers' arts
To find the trees the trailer lay behind.
Still empty. Eddie's tale ran through my mind.
But as a scientist, I had to think
That ghost stories, at which adults wink
And tell to wide-eyed children are not real.
I called Tawana and said: "Here's the deal.
"I'm in Bart's place, and he is missing still.
"But now I'm making progress with this drill.
"The murders are related, you were right.
"The State is keeping evidence from public sight.

"These agents were both victims of foul play.
"We'll need to know what other DNA
"Besides decedents' was recovered by
"The state technicians. If they ask you why,
"Then have the FBI call State Police
"And get the inquest samples, or a piece
"Of every bureaucrat that they might need
"To chew to bits to get them to concede
"And share the unredacted lab reports.
"If needed, you will take things to the courts."

I had to smile that I was overheard
By an enormous reupholstered bird
That, with its musty wings so near my face,
Encroached upon my soul and half my space.
I had no wish to touch the thing, but now
The thought of Eddie's warnings made me vow
To look at how it moved and might have felt
Sinking those lethal talons in your pelt.
Around the legs I grabbed and lifted it
Then set it on my knees for just a bit.
For all its bulk and span, it was so light
And soft—the body underneath was quite
A small part, overall, of its great size.
I stared into the golden, glassy eyes,
And at its talons, curved and needle-sharp,
And thought, this should be kept under a tarp,
Not left to scare adults out of their socks!
And then my fingers felt a tiny box
Above its tail, concealed in the deep fluff,
And held to the body by a wire cuff.
The thing was somewhat smaller than a dime.
I've seen enough transmitters in my time
To know that I was on the air. But why?
Was this man Joe some kind of backwoods spy?

I stepped outside; and then, not trusting that,
Walked over to my car, got in and sat.

I placed a call to Emma Little Bow:
"Oh, hi!" she said. "Now whatcha need to know?"
I asked for information on the man I'd met
On Sam's Road, how he seemed to know folks, yet
Was lonely. He restored old furniture.
Ensuing silence made me feel unsure.
Then she said, "Joe's a bad 'un, bitter and
"He's had some warrants, too, I understand.
"Why do you ask?" Now, it would sound absurd
To tell her I thought Joe had bugged a bird.
So I just said, "He played a little fowl
"With my friend Bart. So I am going to growl
"At him and find out what it is he's done."
And she said, "Won't you let us do that, hon?
"Leave it to us. I think that guy's bad news."
I was beginning to hold the selfsame views.
"How up is Ed on spyware?" "He's a whiz."
"Of course," I said, "Well here's a little quiz. . ."

Later I missed, a dozen times or more,
The almost hidden place I'd driven past before.
Close to the ground a small sign said, "Old Chairs
"And Other Junk Made Just Like New." No airs
Put on out here! Bare branches scraped my car
As I drove through the trees and up as far
As there still was a lane, there were some stairs,
A little shack, a few decaying chairs.
I knocked at the peeling door a dozen times,
But heard no one inside. No doorbell chimes.
Making my way through dead leaves to the back,
I found a Quonset hut, all painted black

And anchored to a cracking concrete floor.
A fan was buzzing through the open door,
And noxious vapors made me gag and squint.
Inside, some pipe-like Bunsen burners sent
Up orange flames that made the shadows dance
Like devotees in a demonic trance.
And there Joe stood before a length of chain,
That held a dripping chair above a drain.
A radio played Motown; he was all
Into the music, having quite a ball,
Prancing and jiving as he held a brush
With rubber gloves and scrubbed away some slush.

"Oh, hey!" he called out, as he noticed me.
"Hey, good of you to come! Long time, no see."
He pulled a glove off, as he walked around
A three-by-five-foot opening in the ground,
Filled with a murky liquid. As I stared,
Joe smiled at me—a jagged grin that bared
Uneven teeth. "Oh, that's there's just my lye—
"You dunk a chair in there, and, my, oh, my,
"Does it strip paint and varnish off the thing!
"It stinks a bit, though, and you can't just sling
"The stuff around 'cause it will really burn.
"But I am sure you didn't come to learn
"To make your living cleaning up this crap.
"Tell me what's up. Whatcha got on tap."
His attitude was friendly, though his face
And damaged eye seemed from a different place.

"You know," I told him, "I am Bart's true friend.
"I came here thinking I could put an end
"To his seclusion, get him back on track,
"Help his depression, maybe bring him back

"To Washington, D.C., I planned to show
"How much his voice was missed back there, you know,
"That things are not all politics and strife.
"But I know nothing of his recent life.
"You do, I think. So tell me where to find
"A man who'd hike, but leave his boots behind."
The damaged man just looked at me and smirked.
I'd tried for sympathy. It hadn't worked.
"This little thing was on your owl's neck.
"I'm sure that Bart would never think to check

"On whether the wildlife used technology."
I held up the device so he could see;
But he just put his hand upon his hip
And laughed, "That there's a tracker, with a chip.
"It tells me when the artifact is moved!
"It's a museum piece whose value's proved
"To be about four hundred fifty dollars.
"That's not much to hifalutin scholars

"*Such as you*, but it's a lot for me."
So, money was a trigger, I could see.
"Now you," I said. "A different pew, same church.
"A science guy who says he's done research,
"Instead, you're stripping varnish off of chairs.
"Who are your customers, the local bears?"
At that, the little smirker came unglued.
He showed his teeth. "Now that's just goddamned rude,
"Coming from someone who's a denizen
"Of that foul god-forsaken weasel's den,
"Refuge for ninnies who profess to lead
"But really spend our money as they feed,
"Out of the shallow pockets of the poor.
"Bring them all out here where raptors soar!
He threw his gloves aside. I heard them slap
Against the wall. "You had to make me snap,
"Dintcha you squishy little queer?"
To my surprise, his eyes began to tear.
But when he got back in control he said,
"So, welcome to the kingdom of the dead."

"*You can't remember me*, I bet you can't.
"You turned down my proposal for a grant.
"Bartie was the 'expert' that you used
"When any grant for owls was refused.

"In truth, I was beneath the notice of
"You scientific grandees high above.
"You just returned my papers, said to try,
"To validate this thesis, reapply;
"You had to know the field work couldn't wait:
"I had to start work by a certain date.
"The permit would expire in half a year.
"So I spent all I'd saved on science gear—
"The effing school had cost me all the rest.
"I came up here; for months I did my best
"To draft a piece on owl intelligence
"To send to you. But Bart said, fold your tents.
"This abstract does not cite authority.
"By which he meant, I'd no seniority.
"In short, encouragement had been a lie.
"Your message was, just go away and die.

"*By then, of course*, I'm so much in the hole,
"I had to live on what I caught or stole.
"And do odd jobs and sleep in any lairs,
"That weren't already full of frigging bears!
"I strained the water out of slimy pools
"And learned some skills that lay outside the rules.
"A dozen times, I almost passed away,
"For all I know, I did just die one day,
"For death became, between me and the owl,
"A bond of two forgotten things that prowl.
"Escaping this place wasn't a real choice:
"The wilderness had took away my voice,
"I wrote for help to you and other gents
"Who'd set me on this sequence of events.
"But I desisted when I finally got
"The message you would never give me squat.
"Eventually I found this place to stay.
"Not even crazy folks will live this way,

"Without electric lights or any heat,
"Still catching half the stuff I have to eat.

"*But as for Bartie* turning on his heel
"And moving up here? He just came to steal.
"He had forgotten me, but not my work.
"You must have thought I'm just some stupid jerk
"Who never followed up on his ideas at all.
"But Bart was a clever one. He paid a call
"On all the tribal bands, to sell his 'dream'
"For owl breeding grounds, a little scheme
"To let the Feds move in and take the land.
"They'd leave the Indians, you understand,
"But me, I'd lose the chance to ever see
"Me recognized, for my discovery,
"And win the merit I so well deserved!"

Was it his words that left me so unnerved?
Thunderstruck, I simply stood abashed
As this strange, horrifying madman gnashed
His teeth and claimed to share humanity.
For moments I was too surprised to see
The knife that he now held in his right hand.
Some worn dissecting tool, I understand.
Now talking is not stabbing, so I'd say
I talked in earnest as he stepped my way.
"Where's Bart? I know you may not care,
"But please, just tell me if he's here somewhere."
He rolled his eyes and giggled like a child
"Let's say he met the Owl, out in the wild.
"You follow me, I'll show you just the spot
"Where they hooked up, as like as not.
"Out in a muskeg, where the tamarack
"Is broken and the spruce is thick and black."

"I'll tell you what I think," I finally said.
"I think that you're the reason that he is dead.
"I think you killed him, and you rolled him in
"The lye pit. Then when all his bones were thin
"And all the flesh was flensed away by lye,
"You fished out the remains, wrapped them to dry
"In his own clothes, sprayed the whole mess
"With acid, till at last you made it coalesce
"Into a giant pellet. Before a storm
"You put it where it would winter and deform
"Into the pellet of an owl, to terrorize
"The credulous, come spring, and foster lies."
He gestured with the knife and jerked his head.
Inviting me to lead the way. Instead
I asked one question, in a humble tone:
"So this discovery that you made alone,
"Can you describe it now, before I go
"To be with Bart. I'd really like to know
"As much as he does, since I'll share the space
"With him in some remote, forgotten place."
I thought to put a quaver in my voice, but it
Was there already, I will just admit.
Joe slit his good eye, and I saw that he,
Like any inventor wanted to show me
His genius, and at last that thought prevailed.

"OK," he said, "I'll show you what you failed
"To see when I first asked you for your trust."
He reached into his pocket, and he fussed
Around awhile, then drew an object out.
"What is it?" I asked. "What is this about?"
He held it up. It was some kind of bone
Inset with holes, a chanter or the drone
Of some old set of pipes. Upon its end
An owl's claws were tied, as if to lend

A spirit of aggression to its sound.
The pipe was etched with symbols all around.
And, from the talons, looking newly shed,
A small gray feather, striped with brownish red.
It hung and twirled as Joe laid fingers out
Along the ridges of the bone. Devout

As a shaman, he then blew a line of frost,
Tones that were cold, that rose and wandered, lost
Into the woods, as if all hope had died.
"Great Jesus, what the hell was that?" I cried.
"I've called the Owl," he said. "It won't be long."
But all that I heard coming was a throng
Of stumbling footsteps, howls and shouting, and
Into the hut crashed the Ojibwe band.

I had no time even to feel relief.
"That whistle's ours!" yelled Eddie. "Stop, you thief!"
He kept on shouting, Emma drew a gun,
And crazy Joe took off then at a run,
Slipped and swore, and hopped and staggered off,
A torch tipped over, flames ran down a trough,
And bullets whined, and rusted iron squealed,
A door swung open that had been concealed
Back in the darkness. We ran gingerly
Trying to dodge mantraps we couldn't see.
I barked my shin on ironwork, stubbed my toe.
When we emerged, there was no sign of Joe.
So Emma said brusquely that we might as well
Go back and search little slice of hell.
"Where's Eddie?" I asked, as we went in.
Emma smiled grimly. "He's just gone to pin
"Joe's ears. Joe stole the thing, the Owl Claw,
"An instrument of ancient tribal law.
"To us the claw is such a sacred thing—
"A whistle carved from a gray owl's wing,
"For centuries our band had kept it safe
"Until one day, we helped a human waif
"Lost in the forest, had to take him in.
"A thirsty, starving bag of bones and skin.
"And for our mercy, he soon paid us back
"By stuffing our sacred treasure in a sack

"And selling it, we thought. We could not prove
"That it was him, and he stayed on the move.
"Of course, we cursed him, and we searched around
"The usual stores where pilfered goods are found.

"But nothing ever turned up till today.
Eddie at last returned. He would not say
Where Joe had gone. He said that, luckily
Joe dropped the Owl's Claw beside a tree,
When I would ask if Joe had met the Owl,
He'd smile as if to say, "Throw in the towel!"
Go home to where you think in black and white
And leave us to our world of second sight.

I stayed in Broken Pump a day or so,
But drove out just ahead of their first snow.
There'd be no sign of Bart until the spring,
When to the surface thawing peat would bring
Cocoons of bones and clothes to analyze.
But as for now, we only could surmise.
So I spent all the winter with a dream
Of giant owls, noiseless as the stream
Of Lethe, drifting like the snowfall, light
As a single snowflake in the dead of night.
I thought of my theory that the maniac
Had turned his victims into spongy wrack,
Then dried them into pellets of such size
That scientists might ask him to advise
On giant spirits of the wilderness
And how one might control them, or address
The finer points of owl intelligence.
So fame and fortune would at last commence.

Remembering I had asked Tawana to
Get the lab to run some work anew,

I called her one day and asked about the test
For DNA she'd done at my request
To find what human DNA besides
The victims' showed up in those homicides.
But over the phone I almost heard her scowl.
"No human DNA," she said. "It all was owl."

The boat was pitching and that left us pale;
Not to mention import of the tale.
Even the bulldogs seemed a bit perturbed,
And lay there, passing gas, as if disturbed.
But from the back, a jocular "Whoo! Whoo!"
Proceeded from the character named Stu,
The talent scout for college football teams.
"Stuffed owls and academics? In your dreams!
"You eggheads couldn't tell a decent tale
"After three quarts of India Pale Ale."
Though standing up, the scout was truly plastered.
But functional drunkenness he'd really mastered
From the age of sixteen, when he tried
To score a touchdown for the other side
But circled back before he actually scored
And ran the field-length while all praised the Lord.
Now inside he may have been a shaking ghost.
(He'd drunk all day, according to our host).
But though his hair was dirty, and his face
Looked puffy he still trudged to take his place
As Ernest left. Once up in front he stopped
A moment, to suppress a belch, adopt
An air he might have thought urbane,
And launched into a story in this vein:

7

The Sports Recruiter's Tale

I know I've had a little much to drink,
But that's my normal state these days, I think.
Our egghead friend has told a gruesome tale
And yet, it could have been a lot more male.
There is no love or romance in that yarn,
So I would say; we do not give a darn
Or care even a little bit about
Who murdered Bart, or how the bird turned out.
I know I'm soused, but that has lent me strength
To cut the story time to modest length
And tell you that the finest tale is love—
And not the noble sort, but push and shove.
I've seen you snobs inspect the way I dress
And then avoid me, either more or less.
But I'll surprise you, since you didn't ask
About the man that lies behind this mask.

I was a jock in college, one who could
Try any sport and end up more than good.

I had a body that made rivals grieve,
Grown women stare and girlish bosoms heave.
So if you want a tale that is correct
And proper in societal aspect,
Stop listening. I'll give it to you straight
And tell you how young animals relate.
If it offends, well, I will never see
You in the future, nor will you see me.

I'd won a scholarship in basketball
And gotten funds from football down the hall,
And played some rugby and some hockey, too.
My talents were possessed by very few.
So at my college, even freshman year,
The scouts would take me out and buy me beer,
And tell me they could guarantee
A full ride and a place on varsity
At one of the Big Twelve. By second term
I'd transferred out, as records will confirm.
Now, you might wonder why a jock like me
Chose plasma physics as my specialty.
Well, I will have to say I landed there
Because I goofed up on the questionnaire
That asked me what I'd like to major in.
I really thought I'd give PhysEd a spin,
But couldn't find it on the form and guessed
That "Phys." was the same course with its name compressed.
And that was wrong, but it turned out all right,
As you will see—until one fatal night.

I had Professor Stubbs that sophomore year.
An academic fossil, who could hardly hear,
But he'd been central to experiments
Back in the early nineties, which, though dense

As things in physics are, made him quite famous
Even to me, a youthful ignoramus.
Professor Stubbs and others on his team
Thought they had figured out the long-time dream
Of fusing hydrogen without the heat
That stars employ to bring about that feat
(At several hundred millions of degrees,
A thing not many people do with ease).
And yet, the fusion of those nuclei
Releases so much power by and by
That all our planet's needs could be supplied
By fusing the simple atoms that reside
In plenty all around us. So the thing
That motivated Stubbs was reckoning
That he could cause this fusion without heat,
Through chemical reaction. Very sweet!
Or would have been! But it was hard
To get the science worthies to regard
His work as more than crackpot. Then he found
That excess calories would hang around
The elements he used—palladium
Immersed in dishes of deuterium
And charged with electromagnetism or
Some piercing lasers. Colleagues might deplore
That no one else could replicate his feat.
Or find even a modicum of heat.

I did not care a fig about his chemistry
Or physics, for that matter. I could see
One way that Stubbs was special—his young wife
Or girlfriend was the quintessence of life!
She'd been an undergraduate the year,
I transferred, and the sight of her could cheer
A saint out of his oath of chastity.
(And I can tell you "saint" did not mean me.)

Cara was why I never missed a day
Of physics class, the thing that made me stay,
Once I had learned it wasn't quite PhysEd.
She kept me from giving myself up for dead.
Her eyes would find my own when she came in,
An arc of things electric would begin
To close the space between us, till it broke
When old Professor Stubbs began to croak
His lecture. Such an awful thing to hear,
Except that nothing said was very clear.

Without her I'd have dropped the class at once
Instead of courting failure like a dunce.
She was a dewy, soft-skinned thing, so sweet
To look at that you melted in your seat.
Her brunette hair fell thick around her neck.
Her eyes were deep and brown. I was a wreck
When one day she just dropped our physics class.
I was informed she'd given school a pass
To live with the companion of her dreams.
And that was our Professor Stubbs, it seems.
The sheer incomprehensibility
Of such a thing sparked my hostility.
I was appalled she had no better taste
Than letting all her beauty go to waste
On such a withered root as Old Doc Stubbs.
In all my life, I've felt a lot of snubs
But none has ever given such offense
As Cara's utter lack of common sense.

A girlfriend in her group reported that
The physics prof had helped her fix a flat
One day on the expressway, and then called
A dozen times to say he was enthralled
By her maturity, her pluck and sense.
She did not really offer much defense.
We were outraged, for reasons not quite pure.
Compared to Stubbsy, we weren't that mature,
But knew that teachers should not put the moves
On students, even if the school approves.
And somehow Stubbs had fooled the chancellor
(The school's illicit-romance canceler),
And snatched up Cara. Eventually, we were stumped
So now she'd go and fix *his* flat, we grumped.
Quite disillusioned, I now vowed to drop
This awful course. I'd find a way to stop

The agony and take an Incomplete,
Go concentrate on football, use my feet.

Imagine, then, my very great surprise
When Stubbsy raised his ancient, hooded eyes
One day, and with that voice that gave me gas,
Said "Please come to my office after class."

An hour later, I was running free
Around the college track in ecstasy.
I'd judged from the professor's awful frown
That I would get a formal dressing down,
Or maybe the old guy would just suggest
I give the plasma-physics gig a rest
And take up volleyball or gardening.
Not so. There was to be no reckoning
About my grades or aptitude. He sought
To hire a lab tech for some work he thought
Would suit me. Since the university
Had cut off his research in chemistry
And fusion, his new lab was in his house,
Down in the cellar; his prospective spouse
Pinch-hit as his assistant. But now she,
Had urged him to hire another (that was . . . me!)
Who could be more objective and opine
If any little thing was out of line.
He saw her wisdom and embraced her love
And promptly set his mind on the above.

There was no salary involved, but room
And board; then slowly, with sepulchral gloom,
He said I'd have to drop his course. Conflict
Of interest could make us all derelict
Of duty, for, if we did our jobs well
Critics would make our reputations hell.

I'd get course credit; he would not delay
My path through physics doing things this way.
(The least of my concerns, but still good news;
My sponsors would not get the bad reviews
About my aptitude for one year more.
By then, on-field or off, I knew I'd score.)
We shook on it, and I said I'd report
To his address, Two Hundred Willow Court,
The next day. As I ran around the track
I thought of Cara, and her utter lack
Of scruple where I seemed to be concerned.
At least, that's how I saw it. I had learned
Some things about real love, and I'd surmise
I'd seen those things in my beloved's eyes.

Two hundred Willow Court, a cul-de-sac
A mile from campus, off the beaten track,
Seemed perfect for whatever wizardry
Might change the future for the likes of me.
It was of mossy brick, with slate-tiled roof,
And backed onto a glen. It hung aloof
But looked as if it might just tumble down
If passing vehicles backfired, or a clown
Set off a cherry bomb out on the lawn.
I'd brought a suitcase and some books withdrawn
From the library. But my intent
To make a good impression came and went
When Dr. Stubbs came squinting to the door.
He acted like we'd never met before;
Though when I said my name, he moved away
And let me enter. On another day
I might have stammered thanks; but I perceived
That some cerebral problem had him peeved.
Without a word, he shooed me up the stair
And up again into an attic where

A narrow door admitted us into
A space that might have boxed a woman's shoe.
But there, a bed, fresh made by my beloved,
Kept me from feeling the least bit pushed or shoved.
I checked the bed, and thereupon I lay
As Dr. Stubbs went silently away.
A hint of perfume toyed with my nose,
And underneath the sheets I found a rose.

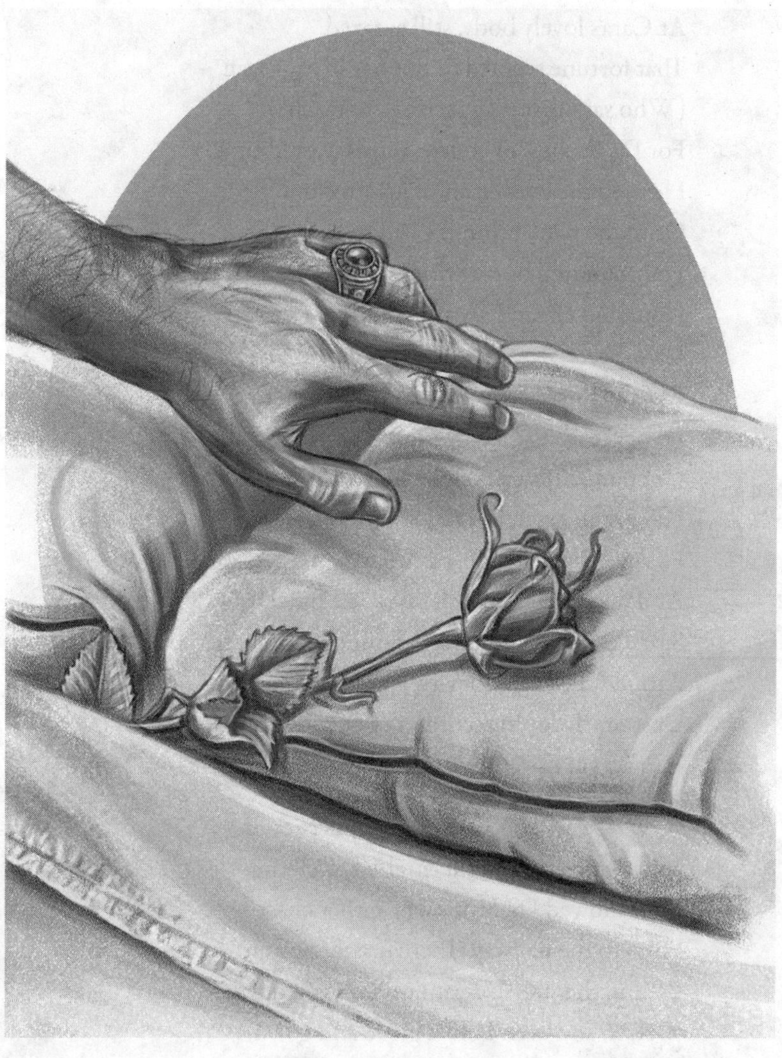

That night at dinner, I beheld my sweet
Who served up food delicious to eat.
More satisfying, though, was that she'd shown
Their "Smart Home" system access to my phone;
The lights, alarms, and heat responded to
My call. I don't think Stubbsy even knew,
And had a feeling that he'd not approve.
It seemed irrelevant at this remove.
I only picked at dinner, as I gazed
At Cara's lovely body, still amazed
That fortune seemed to put her in my reach.
(Who says that it's a sacrifice to teach?)
For Dr. Stubbs, of course, meals wasted time.
He used the conversation just to climb
Onto the pile of things I had to know.
Four hundred boring things lined in a row:
Coulomb effect, Lawson criterion,
Muon-catalyzed confusion—on and on.
Remarkably, at one point, I heard him say,
I'd never see the lab by night or day.
Contamination risk was far too great.
I'd have to listen to Doc Stubbs relate
His every step on closed-link video
And take notes on each test performed below.
Small cameras and microphones were spaced
Around the lab, and with equipment placed
Upstairs, I would record my notes.
"Let's try it now!" he said, feeling his oats.

Cara said she was going to her room,
And I, accordingly, succumbed to gloom,
But followed Dr. Stubbs, or rather chased
Him, to the hallway. There he stopped and paced
Behind the stairs. "I cannot have you down
"Below, and even I must glove and gown,

"But I will have transmitter downstairs,
"So you can hear and watch each step that bears
"Upon the outcome we desire, and I
"Will furnish a narration as I try
"To prove cold fusion, a phenomenon
"As monumental as the Parthenon.
"Tonight, you'll watch and I will fill you in
"On what you need to know as we begin."
With that, he opened an adjacent door
And disappeared down to the lower floor,
Then, in another moment, flickered on
My screen. I watched him struggling to don
His gloves and gown and wondered what on earth
Had led my Cara to this awful berth.

"*I have another athlete* in this stadium,"
Joked Dr. Stubbs, "it's called Palladium."
He seemed to wave a wire. "This is the champ
"Of hydrogen absorption. If we clamp
"This wire onto a generator and
"We run electric current through the strand
"Into a bowl of heavy water—that's to say—
"Water which has taken on, as prey,
"An extra H1 neutron, in deuterium
"Which has a neutron. . ." I had grown quite numb.
Back at "Palladium". I wondered how
I'd live to disembark this turgid scow.
But then, out of our camera range, I saw
A figure, nylon-clad without a bra,
Her finger to her lips, slip in and whack
The console, turning mic and camera black.
Her shapely tush that made her nylon sheath
Drift up like water from a spring beneath,
Slid down beside me, as Professor Stubbs
Went on about his heavy water tubs.

"Hot fusion," he explained, "has neutrons that
"Degrade in reaction, and convert to fat."
"*Let's be degraded.*" I sighed. *Cara breathed.*
"And then the hot reaction must be sheathed
"In one magnetic system, every inch,
"Creating what is commonly called "Z-Pinch."
"*Zee pinch," she giggled. "Ow!" But slammed her lips.*
On mine. "So many," said our prof, "enhance
"Hot fusion with technology's advance,
"A thruster with the Hall-effect device
"Will push a spacecraft out of orbit. Nice!"
He said, rubbing his hands together,
"In effect, the thruster slips its tether.
But Cara had her arms above her head
"*The hall effect," she moaned. "To orbit!"* she said.
"Between the thruster where propellant's lit
"And where electrons go, produced by it,
"Our energy potential. . ." droned our host
". . . trapped within magnetic fields, then, most
"Electrons are extremely energetic,
"Ionizing atoms in frenetic
"Bumps. . ." "*Ex . . . tremely . . . energetic.*"
Cara panted, and we heard no more,
Creatively absorbed upon the floor.
When we came to, Professor Stubbs had moved
Along to muons, which he said improved
The fusion process, though one surely must
Be careful that one's measurements adjust
To gauge the "alpha-sticking problem" here—
The small chance that some muons disappear
Into an alpha particle, moving it
From the catalysis. *My girl had bit.*
Her lip, but smiled. "You've definitely got
"An alpha-sticking problem, you hotshot.

"*But you'd better turn the camera back on.*"
With that, in just a moment, she was gone.

And so it went, for weeks of stolen love,
Cold fusion down below and hot above.
Professor Stubbs would notice that I'd failed
To turn the camera on, and that entailed
Excuses that eventually led me
Into a burst of creativity.
For Stubbs became concerned that his success
In masterminding fusion splaced a stress
Upon the gas, causing a tensor field
That, once set up throughout the house, could yield
A force intense enough to cause the lights
To flicker on our more industrious nights.
In fact, I had begun to fiddle with
My Smart Home access, and to pith
The system's lights when insobriety,
And a fair measure of my own anxiety,
Made such stage management a thrill.
It was a signal that I'd turned to ill.
And over time, Professor Stubbs grew wan.
He missed some classes, and his pep was gone,
But nightly he was down inside the lab;
He came up tense and snappish as a crab.

It seems that, to enhance cold fusion, he
Now messed with radioactivity
By using tritium, an isotope
Of hydrogen that offered lots of hope
Of making faster fusion, but was "hot,"
Creating radiation on the spot.
This put a crimp in Dr. Stubbs's stride;
I sensed he'd put security aside.

That might be why he'd grown so querulous.
It was not that the gas alone was perilous—
For tritium is what makes the numbers glow
On timepieces or your clock radio—
But even Professor Stubbs admitted that
Few folks had pushed the substance to the mat
And tried to fuse it into energy.
I saw in this some opportunity.
For Cara's sake, I tended to enhance
The flickering lab lights almost every chance
I got. But then a devious twist of fate
Played right into our hands as I'll relate.

A doctoral candidate named Algernon
(Lank-haired, with the charisma of a prawn),
Had fancied Cara after it came out
That she was the professor's roustabout.
Unlike the prof, this Algernon was sly
And realized that she'd weary by and by
Of her December romance—and I knew
That this definitively was most true.
The oily fellow frequently was seen
Walking alone through Willow Court. He'd preen
Out on the sidewalk, and he'd wave
As if he had some reason to behave
Like one we loved, some closest, dearest friend.
By instinct, we were quick to comprehend
That strange repeat appearances foretell
An ending that won't suit us very well.

And finally, one day, while we ate lunch,
Before the usual plasma-physics crunch,
The doorbell rang, and Cara went to see
But ran back in and said, "Dear Ernst, could we

"Have you go answer it? It's Algernon."
Stubbsy looked surprised, and when he'd gone
We both gaped, bug-eyed at his empty chair,
While from the doorway we became aware
Of mumbled words and nervous giggles that
We heard with apprehension as we sat
And waited for Professor Stubbs's return.
He came and said, "Now, Cara, fetch an urn
"Or some container for these marvelous flowers.
"I've never, in innumerable hours,
"Had students ever thank me quite like this."
Cara and I knew then something was amiss.
"He told me I had been his guiding star
"Through all his courses and his life, so far."

Quick thinking, Algernon! I told myself,
As I retrieved a pitcher from the shelf
And stuffed the flowers in, and took the card
That said "To Cara, Heart's Desire!" My guard
Was down when I exclaimed, "That hopeless dork!
His mother sent him back and kept the stork."
"What's that?" Professor Stubbs asked, looking up.
"I said his mom had loved him from a pup."
He smiled. "You know, I've never heard that said,
"But yes, he's gifted; he will get ahead."
The next few weeks we lived in total fear
That any day young Algernon would veer
Into our snuggery. Once a candy box
Was melted on the porch; and once some lox
And fresh-baked bagels, packed in Styrofoam—
With a small card, unsigned, that said "Shalom!
"But I'm not Jewish," she said. "Nor is he!"
"He's covering bases," said I, "Let it be."
At last, we knew that something must be done.
Our very way of life was being overrun

By this dumb suitor, who eventually
Would wise up Dr. Stubbs to some degree.
And so we thought, and we devised a scheme,
Requiring powders and cosmetic cream;
A friend of Cara's in dramatic arts
Would share some makeup for our scripted parts.

The next day, Cara went off to the school
And sat in the department vestibule
To watch the students pour in, till she spied
Our Algernon, his book bag at his side.
He sloped on through the doorway, late for class.
Then stopped, as if some paralyzing gas
Just reached his nervous system through his snoot.
Now anyone who was the least astute
Would recognize his shock as nothing more
Than hormones concentrating in his core.
"Dear Algernon," cooed Cara, "You have been
"So sweet to send me gifts. So many men
"Would just as soon have left me to my fate
"Once I took an old man as my mate.
"I don't have time to talk just now, but we
"Should try to get together soon and see
"Just how compatible we are. My spouse
"And I are seldom together at the house
"After, say, nine o'clock at night. If you
"Drop by tonight, we'll talk then—just us two.
She left him sitting dully on a bench,
Unable to free his muscles from the clench
Of those desires he now felt all at once.
I almost pitied the conniving dunce.

It was a gentle night on Willow Court.
But I'd had errands; time was getting short.

I'd given Cara's drama friend her list
And had a bag closed tightly in my fist.
I synced with Stubbs, already in his lair,
And found him tense and grumpy as a bear.
But then again, I had, for several nights,
Employed the Smart Home grid to flicker lights
At crucial moments in his testing place,
Restoring power just as Stubbs would race
Out to the stairs. "Are you recording this?"
My boss would cry. "Yessir," I'd hiss
As if so stressed I hardly could respond,
Given the weakness of the fusion bond.
Tonight he meant to test his awful theory
That cold collisions manufactured eerie
Tensor-field effects that we should note.
He found the whole conception less remote
Than he had thought before he played with tritium.
If he'd not been a jerk I'd pity him.
But then he settled down, content that I
Would measure any force that went awry.
I kept an eye out as cosmetic cream
Was mixed with things important to my scheme.
The salve smelled wondrous in a flowery way,
And Cara had just put it all away
When came a quiet rapping at the door,
And Algernon, still liquid at the core,
Called in a husky whisper, "Darling, I'm here."
Oh, how wished I'd thought to bring a beer.

She let him in as I slipped out of sight
Into the door that opened on the right,
A step or two down the descending stairs
That led to where Stubbs labored, unawares.
The next ten minutes were an agony,
As Cara played her part with sophistry

I never would have thought was possible.
"My love," she sighed. "As irresponsible
"As this must make me seem, I need a feel
"Of your dear body, which is my ideal,
"But cannot violate my husband's house.
"The most that I can do is, like a mouse,
"Nibble and scamper over your sweet frame.
"But you will be delighted that you came.
"I have this lotion," says she, "that, if you
"Will let me, I will pour on like the dew.
"Take off your clothes, my darling. Let me start."
And Algernon, infected to his heart
With aching lust for her, complied at once.
Massaging cream into his backs and fronts
She quickly made him voiceless, but for grunts.
I listened to the groans of baritone
And wished I had him somewhere out alone.
But timing now was everything. We'd planned
A code word for "the endgame is at hand!"
That code word, she had said, was "Pooky-poo"
(A soubriquet I had objected to).
But nonetheless, when "Pooky-poo!" rang out,
I doused the lights and gave an awful shout.
And turned my camera full on Algernon.
Fluorescent cream was spread on that Don Juan,
And made arms, chest, neck, face, and forehead flair.
She'd even run her fingers through his hair.
And so he flamed in phosphorescent light:
His hands on fire, his face a ghoulish fright.
But most dramatic was the scene on tape
When Dr. Stubbs burst in, his mouth agape
And my GoPro used "automatic zoom"
As Stubbs chased Algernon around the room
And howled for an ambulance, medtechs, and such.
We filmed the neighbors gathered in a clutch

Down by the sidewalk while the strange pair rolled
Over the front lawn in a stranglehold.
The local TV was appreciative
Of this wild view of how professors live.

Earlier, Cara packed for both of us,
Knowing that this was going to cause a fuss.
And so we quickly conjured an escape,
But first we copied and mailed in the tape.
For years, I've been a little bit contrite:
I could have barked at Stubbs, yet chose to bite.
But then, Romance has faded from my heart.
Cara, it happened, played no lasting part
In my life story. Always younger jocks
Were there to charm her feet out of her socks,
And move on to the rest of her wardrobe.
And so our love life blinked much like a strobe.
We ran to California, stayed a month or two,
Then I lost touch with her at CSU
Where she had gone to finish her degree
And fascinate some younger men than me.
I lost it all, and yet, believe me men,
For that first night, I'd lose it all again.

We were astonished by this stranger's tale,
We knew a sleepless night and too much ale
Could make a careless person uninhibited.
Despite his braggadocio he exhibited
A pitiful compulsion to explain
These youthful exploits that still caused him pain.
As we debated, Stu went to his seat;
His eyes closed soon as he was off his feet.
But as we stretched and rose to go outside
A good look at the window would decide

Most people that wet decks were not much fun.
The lawyer wanted rebates for no sun.
Our host announced that coffee and light brunch
Were on their way to take us through to lunch.
And soon an alto voice pierced through the hum
Of indecision that had left us glum.
It was the CPA who took the spot
And called for our attention. "This is not
"A long tale," she began, "an anecdote
"That aims to strike a slightly truer note
"On love and youth than what came just before."
The scout responded with a snarfling snore.
"With that last comment," laughed the CPA,
"Let's talk about young love a different way."

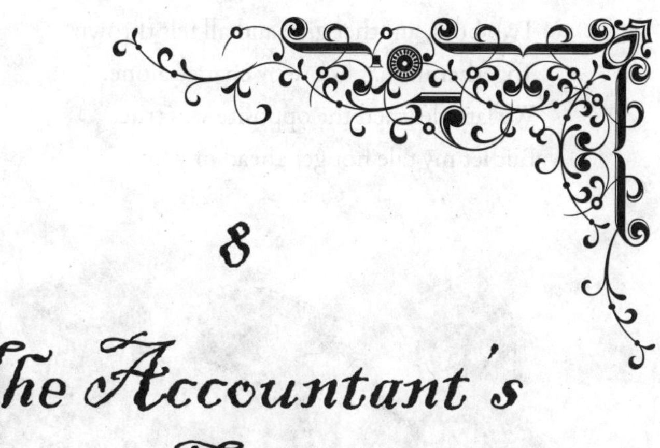

8

The Accountant's Tale

Male beauty and physique are passing things.
Life's ecstasies all fade to sufferings.
It's only virtue that can make a mate
Outlast their normal expiration date.
Although my story may to some seem dull,
And some will leave and others may annul
The moral of my tale by drinking hard,
Listening could prevent the fate of Abelard,
Pyramus, or Romeo or others who
Have lost their loves in thoughtless rendezvous.
It is your fault if you choose hot romance
That dies as certainty replaces chance.
Far better you expect a little more
Of future mates than beauty at their core.
Internal worth will keep love new for years
Till Death brings sorrowful, not bitter, tears.
My senior year at university,
I shared a tiny rental house with three—

Two boys, another girl: and all felt thrown
Together in that house by chance alone.
We later learned the opposite was true,
But let my tale not get ahead of you.

I got an advertisement for a place,
Off-campus, but convenient, with the space
For me to have a bedroom and a bath.
It was a bargain, when you did the math.
I did not quite believe my fortune or
The fact I'd got my foot into the door.
I am a Jew—as creeps anticipated,
I majored in finance, though seldom stated,
To be Jewish in this goyish school,
Was to be outcast—certainly uncool.
Someone was pulling strings: that thought occurred
The moment the return post brought the word
I'd been approved and all. And then I read
A message slipped inside, no letterhead

Or signature, just script: "If you'll consent
"To pay utilities and taxes, then your rent
"Will be forgiven, and we will advance
"Amounts you pay, so nothing's left to chance.
"What do you say? Just sign the lease, and that
"Can be our contract." I signed in seconds flat.

This landlord certainly could mean no harm.
There was no earthly reason for alarm.
Obviously, I had qualified
To receive a benefaction: that implied
Perhaps my synagogue was pitching in
Anonymously lest pride make it sin.
So that is what I told myself to think:
There was the offer, down in pen and ink.
Now I will introduce the other three,
Who rented this peculiar house with me.

Titus Brand was muscled like a god,
Blond-haired and tan, though somewhat lantern-jawed,
A college jock, who often just for fun
Chewed unmixed protein powder, then would run
Nine hundred stadium steps in half an hour;
And often then, he would forget to shower.
His parents were not of the bourgeoisie,
For each had been at different times trustee
Of this same school. His dad, named Hamilton,
Gave loud paternal lectures when his son
Forgot the glory of the Brand forbears
And failed to claim his right to put on airs.
Or did not ape his father in some sport,
(Or such, at least, was gossip's ill report).
A failing grade or bedding a woman who
Was not deemed qualified in Father's view

To marry into wealth and privilege
Was deemed a sin as dire as passing gas
In company, or knocking up a lass.
In fact, both Hamilton and Mary Beth,
Ty's parents, were inexorable as death
About the goals their offspring should achieve
To qualify as worthy to receive
A full familial blessing (which entailed
Some trust funds, that would vanish if he failed).

Now, Titus, luckily for him, had not
Been born disabled, corpulent, or squat.
Quite fair of body, capable of mind,
He was expected to leave peers behind.
In fact, he had been coached from birth to win
A scholarship to Oxford. Thick or thin,
His parents had their hearts set on the Rhodes.
They groomed him well in all the social codes,
Political maneuvers, and the verve
To qualify him. Yet, I must observe
In looking back: that regimen was why
He sought out gin and tonics on the sly.

Still fairer far than he was Stephanie.
Her body was a peerless symphony
Whose every movement played in perfect tune!
Only an aged, introspective prune
Would not be pulled into those eyes that shone
And highlighted each delicate cheekbone.
Her flowing hair was just the shade of red
That gives boys secret fantasies in bed.
We studied in what we called the library,
Which she made Eden, and we found that we
Would spend our time just memorizing her,
While our assignments passed us in a blur.

Titus especially stared at her, entranced,
But she seemed not the type to be romanced.

Paul, the third of us, was simply poor.
He lived for Greek and Latin; furthermore,
And came, of course, from a parochial school,
For which he was the butt of ridicule.
And that distance continued. Deathly shy
Too thin, and the antithesis of spry,
Paul ate his instant ramen from a dish.
While Ty romanced more girlfriends than you'd wish,
Paul sat with Homer and Herodotus,
For hours up in his room, the silly wuss.
To get a date with someone in this century,
He'd have to give up friends from BCE.
His study habits had us all in awe.
We hardly could believe it when we saw
Cradled in his lap, a five-pound lexicon.
Liddell and Scott sat open. Thereupon
Would sit some volume of Greek poetry
That would convey no joy to you or me.
And, after a time, his legs and back would ache,
Suggesting that he stop and take a break;
But he was so intense and unaware,
He'd simply twist and stay there in his chair
Defying gravity, his seat rocked back
His thin lap balancing a tipsy stack
Of books diverse in weight, but such a mix
A sneeze could turn his furniture to sticks.
Thus, six or seven months into our lease,
Paul was reading of the Golden Fleece,
And for that length of time had sat quite still,
Bending his concentration to his will.
A sudden beating on the parlor door
Startled him into jumping to the floor.

Though twisted like a pretzel, up he got,
Not knowing that the large Liddell and Scott
He'd cradled in his lap had put to sleep
Both legs and feet, which dead-dropped in a sweep
From high up on the bureau to the floor,
And snapped both ankles. And this was before
The chair broke up and stacks of books
And table lamps crashed down. The Buddenbrooks,
Were all their plenty thrown into the hall,
Would not have faced a greater ruin than Paul.
It seems the one who knocked was Stephanie.
She found her key in time to hear the agony
That issued from our poor Paul's garret room,
She found him on the floor within a tomb
Of books and lampshades. Ankles had begun
To swell. Soon after calling 911.
As sirens shrieked and ice bags were applied
Stephanie looked at him doubtfully and sighed:
"Oh, Paul," she said, "Whatever do we do
"To make sure your worst enemy's not you."

Slit trouser legs that would admit a cast
Were Paul's sad lot for months, and as he passed
On crutches with a bookbag on his back.
I wish that I could tell you that his knack
For breaking legs while reading ancient Greek
Had gone unnoticed; but within a week,
Titus had told his friends, and belly laughs
Resounded from the burly riffs and raffs
Who'd hang around the locker rooms and plan
Humiliating lessons for the little man.
Did that teach Paul to get outside a bit
Or take some time to get a little fit?
No, the experience just confirmed him in
His idée fixe that exercise was sin.

Now Titus and Paul were outwardly good friends:
At least, they shared class papers, odds and ends
Of gossip, prepped for tests and did a few
Question-and-answer sessions for review.
And so things sat, until, one winter day,
Paul had a toothache. It is safe to say
The pain had grown for weeks, but he was shy
Of telling anyone the reason why.
Not till his swollen jaw turned puce one day
Was he inclined to give the news away.
It looked like someone kicked him in the face.
So clearly had he learned to fear disgrace,
He'd kept the growing torture to himself,
Till pain dropped off the continental shelf.
He choked down aspirin and he gargled salt—
I think he was afraid we'd find some fault
With any weakness after the broken legs.
We found him moaning, swishing the last dregs
Of some clove anesthetic, with his jaw
Distended by infection. Quite in awe,
We rushed to campus healthcare and were told
That oral problems so advanced and old
Required an oral surgeon's expertise,
At clinics that could take emergencies.
He'd two cracked molars—Paul maintained from stress;
Infection had rushed him with a full-court press.
They gave him pills for pain, but nothing strong,
And talked of sepsis if some things went wrong
With the extraction. And he'd need two crowns!

Although our tiny little college town
Boasted a dental clinic; that was booked.
The college nurses dialed around and looked

For clinics with some openings today.
They found one in Manhattan, miles away.
He'd have to catch a bus, and do it soon.
For most of us, the far side of the moon
Was easier to reach and just as cheap.
The fares from here to Midtown were quite steep.
Besides we thought that one of us should go
To minister to Paul in all his woe.
Ty was against it. I just wasn't free.
We dithered, but at last just Stephanie
Would bundle Paul onto an inbound bus
And get on with him, managing the fuss
Of dealing with the schedule and the cost
Of two round trips, and with no time lost.

They rolled away. For mile on ugly mile,
On through exurban New York's garbage pile,
They picked their way. Time took a seat beside them.
At length, with any scenery denied them
They started a small drip of conversation,
That moved to freshet and then inundation,
Mostly about the curious circumstance
Of rooming together. Was it all by chance?
"So, what about the rent? It's very low
"Amy stays there free, for all I know!
"She pays utilities in lieu of rent,
"With money that she's regularly sent.
"But she has no idea who owns the place,"
Said Stephanie. "I've tried to find a trace
"In city records. Zip!" Paul tried to feign
A fit of drowsiness brought on by pain,
But feeling her eyes boring into him,
He hung his head. "I have arrangements, too.
"Somebody pays me, but I don't know who.

"A cashier's check arrives. It doesn't say
"Who sent it, only that it's last month's pay."
"Gosh!" Steph said. "What do you have to do?"
"Write essays, but beyond that, I've no clue."
"Who for?" she asked, "for one of us?"
Paul looked unhappy. "Some unlucky cuss.
"A girl. Dyslexic. Famous, by the way."
"Ty's a slow reader, too. He does OK!"
Said Stephanie, and thought, *This isn't right.*
"How do you know, since she stays out of sight,
"She doesn't hand your work in as her own?
"Have you even spoken on the phone?"
"They say that this is just to help her learn—
"We're only doing someone a good turn."
Steph shook her head: "I think it's got to be
"A phony deal of some kind. Let me see
"If I can solve this puzzle by and by."
Paul winced and sat up straight then asked, "But why?
"You can't let on I told you! I'm a fool.
"But I need what I earn to stay in school."
"OK," she said, remembering how spare
His meals were, how he did not seem to care
For going out to have a beer with friends,
Nor fries or films toward which the young heart tends.
His eyes were closed. She thought she saw appear
Beneath the lids the welling of a tear.

She thought then of the secrets that she knew
And that her own apologies were due.
"You know," she almost whispered to the boy,
"I have a story similar to yours,
"But more embarrassing to one like me.
"I've known Ty. We were both in senior high
"And he was captain of the this and that. My, my,

"How he chased me through those years and would not stop.
"He tried to pin me on a tabletop.
"'Quit stalking me,' I begged. I think the lout
"Turned off the brains required to figure out
"That I would never lie down for his charms.
"Trust me, I saw the sculpture of his arms
"The rippled flatness of his stomach and
"The chiseled face, the flawless skin so tanned.
"He was quite perfect; but beneath Adonis lay
"A Dragon looking for a nymph to slay.
"As his intended prey for all those years
"I only held off rape through threats and tears.
"Finally, I wrote a lengthy letter to
"His parents, the enablers, and I promise you
"They read it, since it put them on alert
"That all would be public if ever I were hurt.
"I let my father read it; he was proud,
"And gave it to his lawyer, and he vowed
"That he would publicize it to the skies
"If ever any trouble should arise.

"But when I got to college, I found he,
"That's Ty, had come there also, just for me.
"And so, for three years, I have stayed away
"From parties, alcohol, and sports buffets,
"And somehow kept clear of my nemesis.
"I dated, met some guys that I could kiss
"Without too many worries, at least not
"The kind I could not handle on the spot,
"But I became too confident, you see—
"I truly thought I got away scot-free.
"This year, I answered this advertisement
"That promised subsidies on monthly rent,
"If I would help a student in remedial math.
"My major puts me on that special path,

"So I said, yes, of course. And here am I
"Put up off-campus in a house with Ty!
"Who lately, has implied—that massive ghoul—
"That, if I hold him off, I am a fool.
"For if he claimed I hadn't even tried
"To help him with his math or to provide
"A single bit of solace or support,
"I'd face a breach of contract suit in court."
"My god," cried Paul, the thought of tears long gone.
"We have to find a knight to take his pawn!"
To which his friend, though ignorant of chess,
Loudly answered, "Yes, yes, yes! Yes, yes!"

A little later they were in New York
But let off somewhere so they had to walk.
Though it took time to find the right address,
They got there when they should have, more or less,
And squinted up a canyon wall to see
How high up level sixty-six might be,
For, that was where the dentist had his suite.
Now Paul, as cautioned, had declined to eat.
Long elevator rides made him unsteady;
Though he'd arrived, he said he was not ready.
He told the nurse he could not tolerate
Most anesthetics. Did his records state
That opioids could make him lose his mind?
She said, her tone professionally kind
While handing him eight slips of legal murk,
"Of course, dear, now just sign this paperwork."

The operation, when it came to pass,
Would use both lidocaine and laughing gas,
And afterward, seeing that Paul looked
A lot like a squash severely overcooked

Steph stammered to the nurse, "Is he OK?"
"Of course, my dear! Now would you step this way.
"The co-pay and consent forms for discharge
"And aftercare are simple, by and large. . ."
Paul was tacking toward a door marked "Men's,"
Squinting, as if peering through a lens.
"He should not drive a car or operate
"Machinery while he's in this mental state. . ."
Stephanie grimaced while the nurse droned on;
She thought Paul moved like an automaton
When he came back into the waiting room,
As if he'd risen from a moldy tomb.
"We have to go," she told the prattling nurse,
Who said, "Put this prescription in your purse."
She heard a "ding" as Paul left through the door
Of an elevator headed for another floor.
But which floor? Stephanie assumed the Ground,
But when she reached the lobby, all she found
Were sidewalk crowds and noise; no friend in view.
Back in the elevator, Paul came to.

The car was full, and it was going up.
His mouth was dry. He had to find a cup
Of water. Looking around the crowded car,
He spotted no one that he knew so far.
Five men wore suits. A woman, stout and pink,
Flaunted a floor-length coat of long-haired mink.
He barely had room to breathe. He'd like to run,
But blushed to find his zipper was undone.
Desperate to escape, he slipped behind
The massive fur-clad woman. In the blind
Of her luxurious coat, he zipped his fly.
He got it halfway on the second try.
The elevator bell chimed. He saw her peer
And say, "Excuse me, but I get off here."

Walking behind her, frog-legged, so did he,
Zipped at the crotch to mink hairs solidly.
It did not go well, security arrived
And heard his explanation. They "high-fived"
The capture of another lowlife scum
And made him sit until police could come,
The woman had quickly cast aside her mink.
Screaming at high volume, "Who would think
"Such perverts lurked on public elevators
"Mid-town condos should be safe from satyrs."

And that's how Stephanie discovered him,
(His lap aflow with mink) confused and dim.

Jail was, of course, the boy's next destination.
He got a free ride downtown to the station,
And soon was booked and locked into a cell
With thirty cellmates. He looked so unwell
The tattooed, flexing jailbirds all hung back,
And there he waited, on the slowest track
Toward counsel and arraignment. Stephanie
Was sent home by police. She wasn't family
So had no prison visitation rights.
Paul had two grim days and scary nights
Till she returned one morning with a man
Young and fresh-scrubbed, bespectacled, and tan,
Who had the common sense neither to laugh
Nor smile at Paul's recounting of his gaffe.
This lawyer, Jack, for so he proved to be,
Turned out to be a friend of Stephanie,
And he was just the man to set things right.
Paul would not have to stay another night.
And then they left, and several hours later
Came back to pick up Paul, the ersatz satyr.

It seems his accuser, with some time to think,
Quailed at allowing someone humped her mink.
She would not make a statement on the crime,
So Paul was set free till another time.
They were all shaking hands outside the door,
Discussing what more process was in store
When Paul went ashen and reached for the arm
Of his newfound lawyer. His extreme alarm
Was taken first for weakness after jail.
So when they saw him tremble and go pale,

They hustled back inside, where a canteen
Sold sandwiches and five forms of caffeine.
They fed him, sat him on a plastic chair,
And brought a cup of water. "Not all there,"
Said Stephanie: "Hey Paul, what's going on?"
But Paul just sat there, shaken, pale, and drawn.
"It had to all come out, I guess," said he.
"I saw a man I never hoped to see
"Outside the precinct house." "What man?" they asked.
And when Paul spoke, all mysteries were unmasked.

For the months she'd known him, Steph had had no clue
Of all the awful things Paul had to do.
It started way back, when he first applied,
To college, without money set aside.
A person with such grades and scores as he
Could get a four-year ride, tuition-free.
But while his quick admission was a cinch,
On cost of living they'd not move an inch.
Paul was an orphan, and his parish school
Lacked assets other than the Golden Rule.
Loans from a bank, as far as he could see,
Quite seldom went to those in penury.
To go to college and remain alive,
He'd have to find employment to survive.
He wrote the college asking for some aid
To help him while he searched for jobs that paid.

A few days later he received a call—
"This is Ms. Pool, sub-dean of protocol.
"We might have something for you." In a smooth
Slow voice, she continued then to soothe:
"We have a patron who will undertake
"To pay your room and board—more than you'd make

"From several student jobs, if you'll agree
"To tutor an unnamed celebrity.
"This famous student is extremely bright,
"But finds it difficult to read or write.
"She never will keep up, without a hand
"From someone smart, like you, who'll understand
"The need to keep her eminence from shame,
"Which will result if people link her name
"To special education needs and such.
"Whatever care we take is none too much."
She went on, while Paul listened, and his hope
That had so long been tethered, slipped its rope.
He heard that he would never meet his ward.
He must agree, before he came on board,
To type, not write, all tests and essays out
And leave them at a drop along a route

They'd pick for him. She sounded rather bored,
But when she named the price, he praised the Lord,
And indicated, with unseemly speed,
It sounded perfect, he could fill the need,
"In that case," she responded, "we are done."
He'd really thought he'd have some time to run
Things through his mind before his final say.
But paperwork arrived without delay—
A contract and a cashier's check. My god!
He never had imagined such a wad.
The courier, a lawyer so he said,
Had long ears bracketing a lumpy head,
Well scented with patchouli oil and rum,
He strolled into the room as if he'd come
With Paul's permission. Didn't even knock.
Though Paul was certain he'd engaged the lock.
"Sign here and here!" this apparition croaked.
As Paul complied, The strange man lit and smoked

A small cigar—no talk, no sign of haste.
Before he disappeared, as if erased
While Paul was rubbing at his smarting eyes.
Cigar smoke hung around, like dirty lies,
As Paul essayed to read the documents.
He knew he failed to make sufficient sense
Of them or glean much meaning as he read.
He'd signed on with a group called Thunderhead.
Their terms of confidentiality
And nondisclosure were quite long, but key,
They said they'd take their money back at once
And seize his bank accounts if he was dunce
Enough to violate a key provision.
A lawyer had advised on his decision?
No way. All that just made him go to bed.
But he sat up and thought through things instead.
Someone had signed as "Agent" with a scrawl
Quite indecipherable. No address at all,
Or contact number he could try to phone.
He'd never felt more utterly alone.
He should have turned them down, right on the spot.
It was just weird, celebrity or not.
But he had never seen a check so big.
Just looking at it made him dance a jig.
So he had signed on with true gratitude
And silently deplored his attitude.
When he arrived on campus, he went by
The Office of Admissions, just to try
To thank Ms. Pool, sub-dean of protocol.
He found no trace of her. No trace at all.

At school he found the stipend served him well.
He could buy books sometimes, relax a spell.
But scheduling his life to do his part
And keep his bargain, was a work of art.

The job was tough, and every other night
He picked up from the person-out-of-sight,
The new assignments and left at the drop
Some finished essays. It would never stop.
And by his third year, he was very tired.
How had he ever gotten so enmired?
The fourth-year summer, health began to fail.
He got an unsigned message in the mail,
Saying that he now could stay rent free
Because the project went so flawlessly.
But the fat stipend he'd received at first
Would be reduced. That made him fear the worst.
Then he met Titus, Amy, and Stephanie,
All doing well, and Ty especially
Was being nominated for the Rhodes,
An athlete-scholar without episodes
Of misbehavior that might set him back.
He had the things that other people lack,
Including smarts; young Ty was very bright.
Paul thought the opposite at first, but right
As his own future life was being spent
On some celebrity's entitlement,
He saw that Titus would grow great through life.
He doubted he himself would find a wife.

Finally, he realized what he had to do.
He'd put aside some cash to see him through
The rest of senior year. He sat and wrote
His benefactors a sweet good-bye note
And left it at the drop. He was not well,
It said. Best wishes to the clientele.
He'd kept his bargain and would keep his health.
Without a heartbeat, what's the use of wealth?

Stephanie and his new friends listened while
Paul wove his spell. They did not frown nor smile.
He rubbed his face and took a drink
Of water, as he closed his eyes to think.

"***But I've discovered,***" he said, "to my sorrow,"
"That people steal the things they cannot borrow.
"A week ago I had a visit from
"That selfsame fragrant lawyer who had come,
"To have me sign the contract years ago.
It was a shock, an unexpected blow.
"My housemates, all of them, had gone to class,
"But I had questions on atomic mass
"To finish up for my discreet Unknown;
I sat hunched over, working quite alone.
"I smelled patchouli quite a bit before
"The man came through my open bedroom door,
"But couldn't place it. I was sniffing when
"He hit me hard, and I was down for ten.
"'I'm gonna tell you something, so we're clear.'"
My teeth were loose, my lip was split, the fear
Of Lumpy Patchouli, as I'd christened him,
Was pouring concrete into every limb.
"'I'm hearing that you've gotten very tired
"'Of being paid. You say, that you've *retired*.
"'You seem to think you might just up and quit.
"'Well think again, you stuck-up little shit.
"'It ain't our problem that you're feeling tired—
"'That's crap. You'll quit when you are fired!
"'What you've been up to here is known as fraud.'
"The lowlife showed his yellow teeth and pawed
"My shirt to pull it up and lift my head
"Then, bringing his ugly face down close, he said:
"'You wrote things to be passed by someone else.
"'They'll lock you up and take your ties and belts,

"'And turn you over for your hour in court.
"'You rat us out, we'll drop a hot report
"'Right to the state's attorney. Play it cute,
"'And you'll do time; we'll shove you down the chute.'
"With that, just to be certain that I saw,
"His point, he hauled up and kicked me in the jaw."
"That's why," cried Stephanie, "your teeth were cracked!
"That's why we're here!" "It's how those people act,"
Paul told her. "I'm afraid there's more
"That makes this story far worse than before.
"When I had left my note, I hung around
"If that's what you call 'flat on the ground
"Behind a bush'. I watched the drop, with dread—
"An empty planter near a garden shed.
"For several hours I watched with well-rubbed eye.
"And then, as I was drowsing, I saw Ty.
"He brought the note I'd left up to the light,
"Read it, and cursed and ran into the night."

He sighed. "And so the man I glimpsed outside,
"Who turned his knobby head and tried to hide,
"Was Lumpy Patchouli! He's been sent for us.
"I'll bet he followed close behind our bus.
"Maybe they think I came downtown to squeal."
Jack smiled: "Then why not make things real.
"Let's find the state's attorney, go ahead.
"And let *them* worry for a while instead."
Now Stephanie, while the lawyer made a call,
Found that she was holding hands with Paul.

SO it was Ty the whole time, and his folks,
Who used the four of us as sorry jokes.
The Brands were cool customers, the three of them,
Affecting nonchalance through haw and hem.

The charges of extortion, hungry press
Baying outside their door about duress
Of young adults. The Brands decided they
Would make their summer house their getaway.
They both dismissed the charges as "uncouth,"
And mixed a bit more gin with their vermouth.
One shouldn't be surprised at all, I guess.
Ty had a gilded pathway to success.
The story soon got out he'd won the Rhodes,
And, though untrue, that caused some overloads
Of indignation in the Oxford set
Who deemed it the meanest degradation yet
Inflicted on that namesake founder Cecil,
Builder of the most prestigious vessel
Bound for Oxford, the Rhodes Scholarship.
The origins of that we'd rather skip.

Titus's father thought it up to Ty
To shape good news before he'd testify;
And so, he booked his son for interviews
In call-in programs on the nightly news.
They did not go so well. In fact, his mom
Called in to rescue him. She showed aplomb—
She called as several people, and the line
Stayed clogged with her until things stopped at nine.
Paul marveled how her voice was her tool,
And then it hit him: "That is sub-dean Pool!
"No wonder I could not find her!"
Ty was raw meat for journalists: he cried,
Which both his parents afterward denied.
In fact, so deeply were they in denial
They hardly bothered to prepare for trial.
They had their lawyers, feigning apoplexia,
Ask if the Court gave weight to Ty's dyslexia,

Implying the jurist had discriminated
Against a disabled man so celebrated.

Soon after Ty's surprising TV scene,
He met the academic guillotine.
He was expelled, all scholarships revoked,
All honors stripped, all past connections cloaked.
There were now front-page stories on the Brands
Both in the US and in other lands.
Lumpy was put away, not having learned
That Wealth will always let The Help be burned.
His testimony was what earned a ride
For both the Brands of several months inside.
And we were all right, but called to testify
In several trials, as witnesses for Ty,
The senior Brands, and for the state; and so,
Besieged by press, we found we had to go
Away from the house, fan out and separately
Take rooms in other places. Stephanie
Defied the lawyers' wishes that we stay
Apart and never talk about the way
The legal case was going. She had found
She wasn't happy without Paul around,
And so she would not use her new address
Except for stating it in court or to the press.

And Paul was even happier than she.
He seldom thought of all the nights when he
Felt pride he'd eased the disability
Of someone famous who relied on him.
His satisfaction with the law was rather slim,
Except he was not charged with felonies,
Nor did he have to go down on his knees
Until, a few months later, he proposed
To Stephanie, which could not be disclosed

Until the trial was over. So they talked
In Paul's apartment, and they never walked
Together, except sometimes, after dark,
They'd take a moonlit stroll around the park.

Amy, the accountant, gazed across the room.
Her fevered eyes held lamplight in the gloom.
"So that's the story," she said tenderly.
"Stephanie won her beau, as you can see.
"Titus was not imprisoned—at least not
"By any legal process—but the rot
"Within his soul grew dark from injuries
"By family; for he'd learned at their knees
"That lying was the quickest way to please,
And so efficient. Now he turned to meth
"For comfort while alone, and met his death
"A few years later. Both the elder Brands
"Had moved abroad without him. Though their hands
"Were noticeable in investment schemes,
It just was not the lifestyle of their dreams.
Lumpy became a Christian missionary
Ministering to the downcast and unwary
Who could tolerate patchouli oil.
As for myself, I've farmed this fertile soil
For guidance. Now, when I rectify accounts
I always recommend prevention's ounce.
"Well that is good of you," a loud voice said.
The broker of insurance scratched his head.
"I could have sold those people policies
"That cover every reason for unease.
"This Tyson did not have to cheat to win.
"Nor should this Paul have ever grown so thin.
"Engaged mink stoles and false arrests are so
"Preventable, if people only know.

"Insurance bought to cover such a loss
"Will calm the nerves as well as applesauce.
"You didn't know that, didja! Never mind,
"Just stick with me a little and you'll find
"That what I sell is peace of mind, and then
"Some iffy coverage for those gals and men
"Who just don't fit the normal risk profile.
"But let me talk to you good folks awhile."

"Wait!" It was the cruise director's voice.
"We've had three tales today, and my own choice
"Is to carry on again another day.
"Nine tomorrow morning's what I'd say."
At that, the Lawyer leapt up to his feet,
"Good ploy, Director. Wouldn't that be neat!
"Keep us all talking and you'll never have to tell
"Our group that we've been kidnapped for a spell.
"According to my GPS, we've gone
"Around in circles for the last few days
"And you are adding even more delays.
"So now, we all demand to meet the captain
"To learn how much intrigue this voyage is wrapped in."
To my surprise the cruise director laughed.
"Right before we strand you on a raft."
"Well then," the lawyer said, "I aim to learn
"All records that in any way concern
Delay of our arrival in St. Thomas
"Or I will make you rue the day, I promise.
In answer the director walked away.
Postponing the squabble till another day.

9

The Insurance Salesman's Tale

Next morning, we came dutifully back
To our "arena," as one jokester's crack
Would have it. Soon the salesman took his stand
And spoke as if he had our fates in hand.
"Risk! A word of terrifying strength!
"Experts like me can talk at tiresome length
"Of how completely unexpectedly
"Risk happens when a limb falls from a tree.
"Our modern culture is devoted to
"Eliminating risk from all we do,
"Shifting the costs to others if we can—
"You got a beef—just go and see that man.
"We feel we have a right! Life's hard enough
"Without the chance that something off the cuff
"Will make our carefully constructed plans
"Crash down just like a stack of pots and pans.
"But crash they will, unless we keep aware
"Of the contingencies. You can prepare

"With just a little budgetary drain
"To blunt Fate's force and ease Fate's pain.
"If not, whenever some affliction strikes
"You'll panic as the mass confusion spikes.
"Maybe tornados in a thunderstorm
"Or fire from atmosphere grown warm.
"My briefcase holds the very policy
"You'll need for any new uncertainty.
"Come see me after this. I'll gladly sell
"You contracts to stave off a living hell.
"Annuities, fixed or variable, will see
"You through a long-term disability,
"And fraud insurance fit for any scam,
"And life insurance, term and no exam,
"And wellness to address health's every quirk,
"And burial coverage if that doesn't work,
"But first I'll tell you that you're never safe.
"However much you grumble and you chafe.
"Even if you put on triple locks,
"Destruction enters, and it never knocks.

"*Hold on!*" the builder gave an angry shout.
"I've got two dozen housing tracts about,
"The locks are strong, the windows good and tight;
"The doors are stout, the owners sleep at night.
"You have no right to try to waken fears.
"My residents stay safe and sound for years.
"So don't start trouble when there's none around!"
"Ah, yes," the salesman said, "I'll now expound
"On why insurance is of greater need
"For housing units built with undue speed.

"*Builders are businesspeople*. Deal in bulk.
"Not spending months perfecting one great hulk,

"Prefabrication is the game if you are wise.
"You purchase premade walls of standard size,
"Dormers and gables, windows, all prefab.
"The only custom part's the concrete slab.
"Pour *that* a standard size, and off you go:
"The home's erected in a day or so.
"It's plumbed and wired up to standard specs
"All pre-allotted for the whole complex.
"You'll make a lot, if units look the same,
"With nothing different but the buyer's name.
"Because the builder buys the housing parts
"In preassembled bulk. The building arts
"Become a matter, then, of cut and paste.
"Until the entire project is defaced
"By dreary sameness not so far from that
"Which bees construct as larval habitat.

"Outrageous!" yelled the builder, now quite red.
"You're just repeating slanders now instead
"Of giving builders credit when it's due.
"Not everybody earns as much as you.
"Affordability's what we provide,
"So struggling folk have some place to reside
"Besides their car. That's first, elitist prick!
"And democratic values, laid on thick—
"That's number two. Every house of ours
"Looks just the same—no columns, walks, or towers
"To send the message 'I'm worth more than you.'
"No, every home presents a simple view
"Of every other home. They're all alike.
"Except for the wading pool or little trike
"On some front lawns. And everyone, you see,
"Has benefit of extra privacy
"That pundits call 'herd anonymity.'

"It's hard, if you don't occupy that space,
"To find your way to any name or place.
"And only snobs would venture to profess
"You can't identify your house unless
"You've tied a ribbon on the front porch door.
"You have equality, why ask for more?"

"I take your point," said the insurance man.
"But life so very seldom works to plan.
"Prefab components may well bring some ease
"But also multiply deficiencies.
"Just one mistake in a component truss
"Repeated by machines one hundred plus
"Can cause the whole development to fail.
"So if you please, I'll get on with my tale."

There was a lady named Eliza Jane,
A gentle soul, who liked both sun and rain,
And idolized her father growing up,
So meek and good, not everybody's cup
Of tea, too careful not to give offense,
Even with idiots devoid of sense.
Such shyness set her back when she was young,
For when the teenaged set she ran among
Were pairing off, she only watched, and prayed;
And thus, at sixty, she was still a maid.
She had no money, but she was so sweet
No one could bear to put her on the street.
She worked as a telephonist in those
Establishments that sell sheer underclothes
To women (and some men) who want this cheap
Mail-order lingerie to give or keep.
And then she was retired. As quick as that
She had to find some other welcome mat

That she could cross, or sit on if need be,
While waiting without rancor for eternity.
It happened that an old acquaintance who
Kept up with her at times—like me or you—
Found her employment at a housing tract.
That waived her rent in lieu of pay, in fact.
This prefab suburb was named Village Green,
After a grassy meadow that had not been seen
Since the bulldozers scraped away the grass
To make way for cement and fiberglass.
The units were small townhomes, vinyl-clad,
With little stoops and tiny walks that had
The look of having once been clean and new.
The siding had now bleached into a hue
Designers might have named "Despair," a tone
Of ecru very close to dirty bone.
At one time, people owned these, she would bet,
But now she thought that all of them were let.
Some homes had lost their numbers, some had not.
While some were tidy, some had gone to pot.
Some may have had no occupants at all,
Or needed a comprehensive overhaul.
But otherwise, each was as like the rest
As chicken eggs laid in a single nest.

Hers was the "Model Home" where couples came,
To take a peek and let salespeople take their name
And told them this was just the house they'd sought.
Now it was just run down. *Like me*, she thought.
But it was furnished, in a sixties style
(Gold fridge and range and avocado tile),
And on the counter lay an envelope
Of cash for groceries and bathroom soap.
The bed was no more than a little cot,
But all in all, this was a tidy spot.

Her house was not far from the office where
She'd earn her keep by sitting in a chair
That swiveled, though it squeaked, from files to desk.
Before her stood a couple from burlesque:
A bald man built to win the caber toss;
the short one in a plaid suit was her boss,

And he was saying in a nasal whine,
"Now, Boyce ain't spoke two words since he was nine.
"But he's a genius when it comes to heavy work.
"He makes his living bein' a big jerk."
He snarfled at the thought; she must have winced.
"I get the feeling that you're not convinced.
"You wutten' unnerstand." She wished she could.
There was so little that she understood.
"But one thing in particular, just one thing,"
He dropped his voice: "Just watch out for a sting."
"What is that?" she whispered very low.
"Forget it," said her boss. "You shouldn't know."
He smiled at her—a mirthless kind of grin:
"So, just look busy, file stuff to begin.
"I'll give you papers. Start up a routine.
"If anybody new comes on the scene
"They oughta see an office that is busy."
Pointing to a nameplate that said "Lizzie,"
"We changed yer name. 'Eliza' is a bore.
"So if they ask, yer Lizzie. Nothing more.
"When people call, you'll make a note for me,
"So I can call them confidentially."
He bent down close and whispered, "There are things
"That you report to me at once." "Like 'stings'?"
She whispered back, not knowing what those were.
"She's funny," he told Boyce. He stared at her.
"If someone walks in, tells you that he's come
"With cash to buy a unit, act all dumb

"And tell him that you only can take checks
"Drawn on a local bank. If he objects
"Or makes a fuss, you ask to see ID
"And write the number down and call for me.
"And don't forget one other little thing—
"Don't ever—EVER—mention the word 'STING.'"

They brought her stacks of paper. She complied
With his instructions to look occupied.
Yet almost every day she simply sat,
Watched motes of dust or tidied this and that.
She bought a begonia for the windowsill
And watered it until it grew to fill
The window with its red, serrated leaves.
She wondered if she'd gone to work for thieves.
But she had other things to fill her mind,
Or wipe it clean, or some of both combined.
One day, she felt her head was in a spin.
She couldn't name the season she was in,
What year it was, or who was president.
Such vagueness regularly came and went.
She wrote reminder notes, and for each call
That came in now and then, taped to the wall
Behind the desk the things that she should say.
Some days she stayed quite lucid. In this way,
She got along just well enough, she thought.
She hoped that her employer never caught
Her when she was at work but quite impaired.
That was the only thing that got her scared...
Well, another symptom gave her a fright.
Some evenings when she hadn't slept all night,
She'd lose her way while trying to get home.
The houses looked the same, you see. She'd roam
Along the curving streets and cul-de-sacs
Until she found she'd doubled her own tracks,

Or sometimes found that she had lost the plot
When, on a porch, her front door key would not
Let her inside. Very occasionally
A resident would look with sympathy
On this old soul who looked so tempest-tossed,
Washed up upon another's stoop and lost.
A ride back home, some tea to clear her head
Were almost always what she got instead
Of angry words, slammed doors, and clicking locks.
Once back inside her sparsely furnished box,
She'd lie in bed, repeating her address
Over and over to relieve her stress.
Telling herself to get back on her game.

And then one day in June, young Stanley came.
She's never seen a man who dressed so well,
In silk ties, Harris tweed, the slightest smell
Of eau de cologne of a designer brand,
An earnest face, so angular and tanned
His head of blue-black hair close-cropped, his mouth
A thing of fascination. After a drouth
Of twenty years, she felt her feelings stir.
But did not want him to think less of her.
"I live just down the street," the young man said,
"And came to visit. Things have gotten dead
"Around here, and there's never anyone
"To talk to. You're as quiet as a nun
"Each day when I come walking past your door,
"So I thought I should say hello before
"You moved to another place, like all the rest."
She'd put his age at twenty-nine, she guessed.
He was a friendly young man. Though on guard
At first, she was so bored that it was hard
To be unfriendly, when he came each day.
She found she loved to chat the time away.

He asked about her life, and listened well
To all the little things she had to tell.
As time went by, she opened windows in
The little office. Fresh air was no sin,
She thought. He voiced approval of the spunk
With which she'd met hard times. She'd never slunk
Away, he said, but kept her head on straight
And always managed to alleviate
Misfortunes that would "crush a lesser girl."
She blushed at that and fiddled with a curl.
But, one day, through the window flew a bee,
Attracted by his aftershave, you see,
And all intent on finding such rare fruit,
It buzzed ferociously around his suit
Until he flapped it, and it stung his neck,
He modeled an impromptu discotheque
And scared Eliza Jane like anything!
"Oh, no," she cried at once, "Is it a STING?"
He had not heard her, busy with his hurt,
Rubbing his neck, unbuttoning his shirt.
"I have no ice," she said. She saw a welt
Low on his throat, and thought how ice would melt
And trickle down his collar, and below;
"Put something on that!" croaked Eliza. "Go!"

When he had left, she sat and closed her eyes.
Then woke up suddenly. To her surprise
She saw her boss stood glowering in the door
One hand upon each frame, "It is a poor
"Performance on your part, Eliza Jane."
"I'm sorry sir . . . so sleepy. I'll explain."
"No need," he snapped, "I know about your trysts!
"Agent Walker from the FBI insists
"On dropping by to chat with you alone
"Most afternoons, I find. And you have shown,

"That we can't really trust you with this post. . ."
"No, no," she cried. "I think I've done almost
"All of the things you've asked of me. I've tried
"To do this job. I knew that you relied
"On me. Whatever could it be that I've done wrong?
"I've followed your instructions all along!"
He answered, by holding up a small device
Which whirred and hummed. He clicked it twice.

She sat there for a moment. FBI?!
Stanley, her sweet companion, was a spy?
"It was a bee that stung him on the neck.
"Just look!" She pointed to a golden wreck
Of exoskeleton down on the floor.
"You see?" she cried. But he said nothing more.
He turned and left the office. She just sat.
It made no sense. Then, feeling like a rat,
She gave up thoughts of working more that day.

Her basic instinct was to get away.
Shrugging on the cardigan she wore,
She slammed and double-locked the office door,
And rushed away from there so very fast
She took the wrong direction out and passed
Five streets before she saw how far astray
She'd wandered from her customary way.
Retracing steps did not move things along,
Because each turn she took was taken wrong.
Had her house vanished? That disjointed thought
Made her walk faster when she really ought
To have slowed down and tried to clear her head,
But simmering panic pushed her on instead.
When finally she stopped to catch her breath,
She gazed upon a street as still as death—
Chipped houses boarded up along the row
Like ill-patched broken teeth. She did not know
If this could be the same development
Where her peculiar boss had waived the rent.
It looked the same, but she had lost the gist
Of where to go and what to do. A mist
Of doubt descended. Was she now asleep
And in a dream so terrible, so deep
That all the world had aged a hundred years?
Was this house, falling down around her ears,

Her own home, gone to ruin while she slept?
It was the spitting image of her house, except
For all the others that looked just the same.
There was no number by the door, no name
Upon a letterbox. But then she saw
The spavined door ajar. Despite the gnaw
Of fear, she pushed it open. All was dark
Inside, damp and chill, empty and stark.
She hugged her cardigan against the dank,
And turned to leave. But then, she heard a clank
From deep inside the house, and next a moan.
A somewhat empty mindset, reason flown,
Can make it hard to concentrate on fear,
Murmurs and metal clinks now pulled her near
An inner door outlined in dimmest light.
She turned the knob and saw the strangest sight.
A row of half-dressed girls chained to the wall?
Dog dishes full of mush to which they'd crawl
On hands and knees. She could not take it in.
Then massive hands fell hard upon her thin
Neck from the dark behind her and she heard
A snarl of hatred, rage without a word.
She twisted in the hands and felt them pull
Her sweater from her shoulders. Flimsy wool
Was all the ogre held. He tipped and crashed
Unbalanced to the floor, and as she dashed
Out of that house, she heard howls, yells, and screams—
That was herself, running from horrid dreams.
She did not stop to breathe until a part
Of the development came into view. Her heart
Alone made noise as she stood and panted.
But then a car rolled up, stopped, and decanted
A spruce young man, well dressed and redolent
Of aftershave. Now Stanley wore dark glasses
As agents do, to signal to the masses

That, if the eyes are windows to the soul,
Their own reveal a bottomless black hole.
He opened the back door and palmed her head
And pushed her down: "Get in the car!" he said.
"No handcuffs yet," he told her, "that will keep."
She did not answer, being fast asleep.

Later, when she came to, in a cell
She had not fit their profile very well.
They'd bargained for a lower-level dunce,
Who'd rat out her superiors at once.
But even when they questioned her at length
To break down her resolve and test her strength,
They found she did not know a single thing
About her boss's money-laundering,
Or empty houses that took in as "rent"
Criminal acts in kind and not a cent
Of their own money. All were absentee,
Subletting their small houses for a fee
To other criminals with other crimes in mind.
As for Eliza, there were no facts to find.
And so they took her home, although she said
She thought that several men might want her dead.
They took her statement down on endless tape,
The women and the chains, her close escape,
But in the end, she gave them no address
Or clues to the location. Her duress
Was not believable or competent;
They'd bigger fish to fry, so home she went.
The black sedan stayed idling on the street
While Stanley walked her up, and took a seat
Down on the stoop, until she found her key.
Then waved and walked back down to his Grand Prix.
For reasons he afterward could not describe
He idled by the curb. There was some vibe

That made him look at windows to the house,
And one was smashed. Eliza in her blouse
Was in the living room. He saw her pass,
Unsettled in the frame of window glass.
And then he saw her bend down, and she screamed.
He heard it from the street, as if it beamed
Directly from a satellite. He burst
Out of the car, fearing all the worst
That could be happening; he beat the door,
Then threw it back. He saw her on the floor,
Clutching in one hand a knitted thing
Disheveled and fraying like a pile of string.
"My cardigan," she sobbed, down on the floor.
"Look what he did to it!" Four hours more
Of questioning were necessary to
Decide if her strange story could be true—
A criminal whom she had seen do wrong,
Was warning her to hush and move along.
That version was a hard sell to the brass,
Who did not want to give her tale a pass.
She was unhinged, his supervisor said,
Unstable, clearly crazy in the head.
She no doubt ripped the cardigan herself
And put it at the bottom of a shelf
Where she could "find" it and could then distract
The agents from the evidence they'd tracked.
Local police were called in to reseal
The broken window, and to hear her spiel.
Then everyone departed around two
Or maybe three, discovering nothing new.

At dewy four a.m., there was a click.
As pins turned in a lock inclined to stick.

Bat ears might have heard, but there were none
To catch the tick of tumblers one by one.
The door moved in, as gentle as a breath,
As silent as the dagger of Macbeth;
A rush of bootsteps then, aimed to surprise
And slow the focusing of sleepy eyes;
A sash cord, too, to catch the scrawny neck,
Pull it back and snap it. Not a speck
Of blood to stain his clothes, no DNA,
Only a job well done for ample pay.
Her little room was dark, and he thought *Hey,*
It's like she has already passed away.
He found the cot; his fingers found the cord...
To his surprise, the victim simply snored.
With clawlike hands, he reached to grasp her head,
And found a federal agent there instead.

Boyce sat blinking in a crowd of cops.
His wrists were cuffed. Stanley was "the tops"
According to his shoulder-slapping band
Of Fibbies. Over and over he had to stand
For fist bumps and high-fives, and then to tell
Again just why the takedown went so well.
They all agreed that what had made it work
Was Stanley's willingness to risk a dirk
Between the ribs by feigning careless sleep—
He later got the nickname, "Sleepy Peep."
Eliza came in to identify the perp,
And after that heard not a single chirp
From anyone. Once Boyce was dragged
Out to a van, she felt she might be tagged
As evidence herself. And so she sat,
A stranger in her living room, and that

Was that. After two hours or so when all
Was done—the photos for the precinct wall
All taken, the doorknobs dusted; her poor sweater
Bagged as evidence, she thought she'd better
Try to get some sleep; but as she stood
And moved off to her room, thinking she could,
Her one-time buddy Stan got in her way.
"I'm sorry," he told her, "but you cannot stay.
"This is a crime scene now. I'll help you pack."
"But this is MY home," she cried. "You get back!"
He shook his head. "I know what you've been through. . ."
She snapped, "I'm not so sure you really do—

"I'm clear, you've never been deceived by me.
"But here you are, not who you said you'd be.
"Is this the way you gain the public trust?"
"Listen to me," he shook her. "Now you must!
"Your boss, whose name is Sammy Delaware
"Is missing now. And you must be aware
"That, when we've caught him, only little you
"Can bring him to the justice that is due.
"This tract development is just a shell—
"A waystation that's on the road to hell.
"He traffics foreign minors through this place,
"It's so anonymous that none can trace
"To any certainty where girls were held.
"He launders money, too. Of course he does.
"It gives him close to a delirious buzz
"To undermine the federal government.

"*But what you need to know*, in the event
"That we can't catch him. There is only one
"Who ties him to the wrongs that he has done
"That's you. The first thing you should take from that,
"He'll stop at nothing just to lay you flat.
"Here's what I'm authorized to offer you.
"You'll be our witness now, against these two,
"And we will now protect you. That will mean
"We must remove you wholly from this scene.
"From here on out, you really won't exist.
"We'll 'disappear you' into trackless mist.
"But first, you'll be obliged to testify
"To things these criminals cannot deny."
She hung her head and said, "And how
"Am I pulled into this and made to bow
"To gods of state, when all I did was try
"To live my life out of the public eye.

"I've never asked for anything, and yet
"You tell me that I'm under some dark threat.
"Does that threat really come from them, or you?"
"Eliza Jane," he said, "now I will tell you true.
"Despite the noble things our government
"Pronounces, when it has to have consent
"Of citizens, it does not like the poor.
"But for a witness, we can find a door
"Through which you can escape once and for all.
"Let witness protection lift you from the brawl
"Of this combative world into a place
"That, though it may not be perfume and lace
"Will nonetheless be better than you've had."

And so Eliza testified. So glad
Was she to win emancipation from
Her former life, that she was, in the sum
Of all that folks like her had ever given,
The most effective witness. She was driven
By hope, by fear and outrage, just a little,
To give the answer to a legal riddle.
And once she'd done so, happily
She disappeared into eternity.

"What a witness!" the sleek lawyer snorted.
"I'd just love to see how she comported
"Herself up on the stand!" Jumping up
He did a little skit holding his cup
As if it were a brief: "Who grabbed your neck
"Eliza Jane? Oh, it was dark? Oh, heck
"How then can you be sure it was this Boyce?
"Oh. You just know it was? Well let's rejoice—
"But how are you sure, it being so dark and all?
"His hands were very big, so he was tall?

"Ladies and gentlemen of the jury. No man
"In our group of suspects is quite tall. Plan
"To bring in every beanpole in this town!
"Then try to cut the list of suspects down!
"And, where did this dark battery occur?
"You can't remember? Everything's a blur?
"Didn't you make a note of the address?
"I see! You were experiencing distress.
"Well, so's my client, Boyce; he knows well
"He wasn't there. None of it rings a bell.
"Chained teenaged girls? No such were ever found
"Despite a long forensic runaround.
"In truth, dear lady, you don't really know
"A human slaver from a buffalo. . ."
"Excuse me, mister!" roared a baritone.
"You act like it's up to you and you alone.
"Too bad your knowledge of the human race
"Is like an alien's from outer space."
"And who the hell," the lawyer sneered, "are you?"
"No one you haven't met and stared straight through
"A dozen times," the union steward said.
He smoothed some thin hairs over his bald head.

It seemed that what had once grown on his dome
Had moved to forearms, thick enough to comb.
"I'm just a guy that you would never meet
"For conversation, long as there's a street
"For you to scoot across. A union man,
"Plain and simple. Organize and plan
"Collective action, so that folk like you
"Don't help the corporations and their crew
"Grab wages, benefits, and overtime,
"Whenever the stock price wants another dime.
"The government has helped with every scheme.
"But then again, they're on the corporate team,

"Hiding behind well-compensated suits like you
"Who make your living finding folks to screw.
"It makes sense, don't it? I don't make the pile
"Of gelt I'd need to live the life of style.
"No, no, they scalp a bit from here and there
"Each quarter till one day, there is no hair.
"But I can see my lawyer friend's turned red.
"I hope it's shame, but bet he's mad instead.
"So I am volunteering now to tell a tale
"Of folks, whose day-old bread gets stale
"And too-warm milk grows sour and still they live
"With far more joy than your stories give."

10

The Shop Steward's Tale

The last time I laughed was 1981.
After that year, nothing was much fun.
I backed a total jerk for president.
He won; I lost my job as punishment,
Along with any references I'd need.
He was a gamecock; I was chicken feed.
And he was charming, as he forced us out:
For skin-deep charm is what D.C.'s about.

I was ex-military, out of Nam,
Took shrapnel and was sent to rest in Guam.
Back stateside, I went months without a job
Until a buddy from our discharged mob
Helped me to find a gig controlling flights—
Mostly daywork, though there were some nights.
You'd say "Bye-bye" to dusk and "Hi" to dawn,
And leave the airport with your brain half-gone.
The job itself was stressful—that I'll say.
So many flights came in both night and day,

You'd just as well control a swarm of bees
With words like "thanks so much" and "pretty please."
So, on the whole, the work paid pretty well,
But soon as I started, things went straight to hell.
We worked for Uncle Sam, and that, at first,
Meant steady pay. The work was not the worst,
Though, trust me, staring at a thrum
Of radar blips, until your lids grow numb,
Or blinking at green radar streaks, that each
Denote an aircraft struggling to reach
The runway takes its toll, caffeine's required,
Despite the fact that you are deeply tired.
And yet the traffic just grew greater
While promised raises were deferred till later.
It's not so crazy that, day after day,
The stress would lead to worries about pay.

Pilots were paid much better than were we,
Who kept them from crashing in downtown D.C.
And, meanwhile, unpaid overtime increased.
Sick days and vacation time just ceased.
When it got worse, our union called a strike.
But rather than discussions of a hike
In wages and conditions, we soon found
That governments are vicious on the ground.
Whatever their lah-dee-dah pretense,
They'll always break their word. It's common sense.
And so our federal union struck for pay
But lost eleven thousand jobs that day
Including mine. Moreover, Reagan's ploy
To cast us all as moochers would annoy
No one but us; the rest thought we were nuts!
The scabs that took our jobs were patriots.
While our federal bosses thought, "How grand!"
"The White House fired the whole bunch out of hand

"And minus benefits. Let's hire some folks
"Who are not unionized; then, when one croaks,
"We won't owe his survivors anything.
"So show them all the door! Let Freedom ring!"
Well, after this disaster, I was sick
Of government, the Congress, and the prick
Who cared far more for pollsters than for us.
I packed my bags and hopped onto a bus,
Headed toward a township way out west
That I picked blindfolded, called "Virtue's Rest."

Now, Virtue's Rest was just a little place,
Maybe two thousand people, with a pace
Of life even a tortoise would find slow.
They grew about as fast as oak trees grow.
Their enterprise and atmosphere both stunk.
As other towns expanded, this one shrunk!
The farmers all around raised giant hogs
That wallowed in their pestilential bogs
And bubbled methane fit to set alight
The stratosphere and make bright day at night.
A sister industry, the other op
The town supported, was a tanning shop
That processed hog hides into fancy purses
(Though not the ears you read about in verses).

And that was it. The founders of the town
Who, after the Civil War had settled down,
Expecting that a railroad would lay tracks
To Virtue's Rest, found that, behind their backs
A more aggressive township without qualms
Went out to Washington and greased some palms.
The railroad curved away from Virtue's Rest
And brought rich produce from the Middle West

Directly east, on tracks too distant from
The cheated township, leaving not a crumb
Of easy transport within reach. And then,
In every war that called up local men,
The ones that left to serve, if they survived
Refused to come back home. And when deprived
Of native sons to marry, most girls found
There wasn't any cause to stick around.

In Eisenhower's time, when multilane
Hubs and highways opened fields of grain
The town again was bypassed. You can see
Why people gave up on prosperity,
Why people came to be a little down,
And took the nearest wagon out of town.
And yet, almost as soon as I had paid
A monumental fare to be conveyed
From the last bus stop (over ninety miles
Away!), I found a job that promised piles
Of cash for simple work that I could do
Without the fuss of learning something new.
It happened this way. I rolled into town
Near noon—The empty streets were brown,
Not from a drought, but from a lack of care.
Great lines of potholes led from here to there
Most everywhere I looked. There were some shops—
A five-and-dime, a laundromat, some flops

With window signs that promised "Rooms to Let";
It looked as run down as a town could get.
I thought at first that I would take a stroll,
But up and down I could not see a soul
As I stood staring in a waking dream
I could have sworn I heard a kind of scream,

The gargled hissing sound a man might make
Whose vocal cords were cut, or some large snake
That held a moaning victim in its jaws.
Though not yet close, its strangeness gave me pause.
I heard an engine rumble then, not far,
And up rolled an extraordinary car.
I have to say, by this time I was tense
And what I saw before me made no sense.

It was a classic car from decades past,
A white-walled red convertible, quite fast
And finned, top down, and on its curving hood
A turkey vulture of enamel stood,

With hooked bill, sable feathers, naked brow
As bold as the figurehead upon the prow
Of some great warship of an ancient fleet.
Just as the car approached me on the street,
I saw the little buzzard open wings and beak
And once again emit that garbled shriek.
I'm sure I jumped and paled because a howl
Rose from the owners of the robot fowl.
"How did you do that?" I found strength to ask.
The passenger, still laughing, raised a flask
And took a lengthy swig. "You're big and fit."
He held his stare and took another hit.
"Well thanks," I said, "I think I ought to be.
"After two hitches in the infantry.
"I just came into town." "I know," he said.
"What brings you here?" I shook my head.

"*I am not really sure*. I lost my job
"Through no fault of my own." He chirped "No prob!"
He was a little fellow, I observed;
Although the strangeness had me all unnerved,
I did not show it. I'd seen things more weird
And would see dozens more, I feared.
"So, I'm the mayor of this place," the small man said,
Stroking the gray-black stubble on his head,
"This here's my lawyer, Silas. He don't talk a lot,
"But he does what I need. I call him "Spot."
"And as for me, my name is Danny Whee.
"When You Say "Whee!" you're calling me.
"I been the mayor for seven terms or more
"And I got lots of future terms in store,
"'Cause people know that I take out the trash
"And give 'em value for their hard-earned cash.
"I clean up after people, and that's why
"I buzz my buzzard here when I roll by."

He reached under the dash and grabbed a handle
"I love this little guy. His name is 'Vandal.'"
He jerked a wire and Vandal, who had napped,
Gurgled his sepulchral hiss and flapped.
"I got a job for you: Security!
"I'll pay to keep creeps away from me.
"There's nothing much requires you to be rough.
"You mostly have to stand there, looking tough,
"So no one will attack the lawful mayor
"If they are just a little bit off square."
I thought it over. "So! What does it pay?"
The sum he whispered to me made my day.
"You're on!" I cried. "So where shall I report?"
"To Town Hall, three blocks down, next to the court—
"I'll see you there tomorrow, bright and early!"

So it was, attempting to look surly,
I stood for several weeks, arms crossed and hat
Pulled low over dark glasses: simply that,
For Town Hall turned out to be little more
Than a converted red-brick corner store,
Civic credentials painted large in gold
Across the storefront, letters big and bold.
It would have seemed official, if the door
Were not a screen door, onto which a corps
Of flies was plastered, every single one
Was drawn by something rotten, and undone.
I never found the courthouse. Just as well.
It likely had been vacant for a spell.
And when I entered the mayor's place of work,
Expecting some paint or plush or other perk,
Once through the vestibule there was a door
That, when unlocked, revealed a vinyl floor
Chock-full of metal cabinets for files.
But more surprising was that, stacked in piles,

On graphite desks were towers of currency
So thick there were no desktops left to see.
But I had very little time to gawk
Before some minion came over to talk.
Today, he said, my big boss had a chore:
A small delivery to a nearby farm; no more.
He gave me a manila envelope
Containing a legal notice. Like a dope,
I did not even ask him what it was.
Then again, I s'pose I had no cause.

Silent Silas drove me out of town
Across some foothills, bare, dry, and brown
Until we tipped down to a valley floor.
And there, amid a distant mountain's pour
Of snowmelt, sat a sprawling, weathered ranch,
Looking deposited by avalanche.
Sunstruck and gray, like all the hills around,
It stretched its crooked porch along the ground
And sloped its steep-pitched roof up toward the sky
As if, did it aspire to, it might fly.
Around this settlement were livestock pens
That forty days of rainfall could not cleanse,
And scattered in them little fluffs of white
That could not be identified by sight.
"He raises turkeys," my companion said,
"But he ain't paid the taxes on this spread."
"Taxes for what?" I asked. "He's not in town!"
His answer back was just a deepening frown,
But one that chilled the heart. "We have a lien,"
He finally said, "And that in time will mean
"His tax protest will end up in defeat."
He then leaned back, and stretched out in his seat.
"The township limits moved five years ago
"And annexed this whole place, just so you know,

"And he ain't paid a tax." "What could he owe?
"So far from town, what services or care
"Do you provide?" He fixed me with a stare.
"You got a lot of questions for a guy
"That just rolled into town. I wonder why
"You need to know so much." And my reply
Was silence, but I shrugged, as if to say,
"Whatever!" Then I quickly looked away.
"Let's move it!" said my caustic chaperone,
He stepped on the gas. We rolled off like a stone.
As we approached, I learned what "nervous" is,
For once again I asked my friend what services
The township might provide, and he said, "Fire!"
"Surely if circumstances were that dire,"
I said, "You'd be too late to get out here
Before the ranch burned down." I saw him leer.
"Well then, with luck, the bastard might be dead.
"So that would be a doggone shame," he said.

A man strolled down the muddy path to meet us,
Grinning, with open hand to greet us,
Smiling as if we were his next of kin
And he was ready to invite us in.
"Silas," he called, "what brings you so far out
"Beyond your jurisdiction? Jacob Stout!"
He said to me, and shook my hand, right through
My open window. "I'll just bet you two
"Would not come all this way to say 'Hello.'
"So, what can I do for you before you go?"
I noticed then that smile was pretty forced,
In fact, from feelings pretty well divorced;
His eyes might kill one hundred as he smiled,
And yet, he kept his manner kind and mild.
"Bubba here's got papers for you, Jake,"
Croaked Silas, pinching me, for goodness' sake.

"I asked him to come witness our transaction
"Lest you claim you weren't served in this action."
Jacob took the envelope and said
He needed space to read and clear his head.
And so my grasping friend and I sat still
And watched Jake amble up a gentle hill
Until he reached a pen where turkey hens
Mobbed the fence, thinking a palate cleanse
Might be in store within the envelope,
Some greens or grain or slice of cantaloupe.
Jake stayed there, reading for a little while,
Then jammed the papers in his jeans—his file
For everything important, I surmised,
And came back down. "I've been advised,"
He said when he came back, "Never to sign
"A document that is quite this asinine.
"This bullshit says that I am in arrears,
"In fact, it says I have been so for years.

"**But I can't figure** how I owe, because
"I don't live in the town or by its laws."
Silas just pulled back like a striking snake
And hissed, "You're making a severe mistake!
"The town of Virtue's Rest annexed this land
"Five years ago. It's on the books as planned."
"For this here tax," Stout asked, "What do you do"
"For me?" And Silas smirked: "We're serving you
"This second, ain't we? Get off that high horse
"And sign before we come back with brute force.
"Bubba!" he snarled, though that is not my name,
"Go rescue Mr. Stout there from his shame
"And get his signature upon these summons
"So he can put an end to his short-comins."
It must have been the sorrow on my face
That lifted the corner of Stout's mouth a trace:

"You got a pen, son?" Yes, of course I did.
He took it and he signed, as he was bid.
"There goes my flock," he said, "I'll have to sell
"And in this market, that's a funeral knell.
"So, guess I won't raise turkey poults no more.
"Thank god I got the ranch, so I ain't poor."
Silas said, "We always have next year.

"*See that the flock's tax* value free and clear
"Is down at city hall within a week."
He drove away then, with a smile so bleak
That it would turn your stomach inside out.
"You'll get 'em when I give 'em," called old Stout.
But we were on our way then back to town,
With Silas yielding nothing but a frown.
But when we had arrived at city hall,
He pushed me roughly up against the wall
And hissed, "Don't think for a minute I won't tell
"You made excuses for that ne'er-do-well.
"You're out of here, as far as I'm concerned,
"And for His Honor, that will be a lesson learned.
"You don't hire scruffy riffraff off the street
"And hope that they will make your life complete.
He handed me an envelope of cash
And snarled: "Your back pay! Coulda been a stash,
"Well that ship's sailed. You hear me? You are done."
At that, he reached behind and pulled a gun.
"If you are gonna argue, think again:
"I've punched the pink slips of some better men."
Maybe it was fortitude that made me smile;
More likely, it was thinking of his trial.
I went back to the flophouse, ate and drank
And thought how much the whole tax levy stank.

Next day, when I woke, I found my mind still set
On Jacob Stout and predatory debt.
So I decided that I'd have to try
To stay until I helped him rectify
The gross extortion I believed I'd seen,
In serving Silas's spurious tax lien.
About ten miles is what I made the road,
And dust fought back with every mile I strode.
At somewhere close to noon. I found the rise
That looked down at the turkey ranch. Its size
Was vast but empty. I did not see the flock
That formerly filled up the wire-fenced block.
Instead, I saw a giant semitruck
Blocking the tiny entrance, looking stuck.
Around it paced my new friend Jacob Stout,
Walking a cup of coffee round about.
He saw me and stopped dead with sheer surprise,
I said, "I'm here to help you beat those guys!
"I'll stand beside you; you are being wronged."
He put a hand on my shoulder. I belonged
As quick as that. He said, "Can you drive these?"
And I replied, "Oh, yessir. That's a breeze."
The truck had long been loaded, Jake explained,
Before dawn all the turkeys were restrained
Not harvested, he said. "Sorry they had
"To go. Do you like animals? I love 'em bad."
It was a gentle conversation, till he checked
His watch and braced himself, and stood erect.
"This here's my Trojan Turkey, in reverse,
"It's holding the whole flock, for better or worse.
"You're driving," he said, "And that helps us take
"Advantage of the morning! So let's wake
"The town before the trailer gets too hot."
I thought of hauling heat-struck birds for squat,

With no fulfillment of the lien. So I
Released the brake and chugged up toward the sky
And into town, in just about an hour,
Ready to take on the civic power.
As we rolled in, Jake signaled for me to stop.
He talked to men with duckbill caps atop,
Beyond my hearing, they decided something grave.
And then we rolled on, feeling somewhat brave,
At least in my case. All those guys were in
On whatsoever sticky we'd begin.
It was late morning, and the streets were bare,
But Jacob said, "We'll have some people there
When we release the load." And, sure enough
A crowd had gathered, looking mad and tough.
They held some signage up: "OUR LIVES, OUR LAND!"
And Spanish signs I did not understand.
Directed by my friend, I beeped the truck
Backward to the entrance doors. We stuck
Into the portal as if it were made
To handle truck deliveries in trade.
Now Jake slid from the Trojan Turkey's cab,
Walked back, and gave the roll-up door a jab
So that it rattled up its squealing tracks,
And Jake began to unload burlap sacks.
Meanwhile, more folks had gathered in the street—
Thick and silent as a field of wheat
Awaiting the combine in the bright sunshine.

I stood and listened for the vulturine
Approach of Mayor Whee's car, and soon enough
It rolled up through the crowds now looking tough.
"What the hell do you think you're doin', Jake?"
The mayor yelled. "What's the fuss, for goodness' sake?"
"Just payin' my taxes, Your Honor," Jake replied.
"You wanted my flock, so here they are, curbside!"

"You FOOL!" Mayor Whee yelled back, "What kind of stunt
"Is this?" And, in a rage, he reached in front,
Under the dash and made the buzzard scream!
At that, the truck's load like a flapping stream
Of living pillow-innards rushed the door
And poured inside to ruin the hall's decor.
Some freedom-fighting gobblers caused a rout
By rushing the crowd, with feathers all fluffed out,
And jumped up, beating wings in their attack.
I knew the mayor would not invite them back!
The rest sought safety in the tottering piles
Of sacrosanct, most confidential files
And flapped until some airborne contents sailed
Around the room and out the door. They scaled
The stacks of currency with grabby feet
So loose one hundreds flew into the street.
The human crowds then elbowed their way in,
And, dodging irate fowl, took a spin
Around the premises. Men soon emerged
With bales of greenbacks banded into stacks. They urged
The others to go in and check it out.
Meanwhile, official papers sailed about
The street, with loose banknotes of many kinds—
The product of a multitude of fines.

And, in the aftermath, the turkeys sat
On cornices, in trees, and sent the splat
Of white-green droppings to the city street.
Some strangers in the crowd walked up to greet
Mayor Whee, and Silas, and a dozen more
And put them all in handcuffs, while a roar
Of thanks arose from people all around.
I smiled a lot, but Jake just stood and frowned.

"Listen!" he told me, "Go! This ain't your fight!
"Get outta here. Let others make it right.
"Just know that you will be my friend,
"If you're unfortunate enough to end
"Your days in Virtue's Rest. Now scoot,
"And find a better elephant to shoot,

"Since that's the stuff you're made of!" So he smiled
And turned me by the shoulders, and I filed
Away behind a line of turkey hens
Who seemed at least to have the common sense
To walk away from power and save their souls.

After a mile or so of swales and knolls
I reached a road, and by some crazy luck
I thumbed a ride with some old pickup truck
That had behind its wheel a union man,
Heading for the Dakotas. As we rolled
Along the country roads, I found I told
Him all about the stint with Mayor Whee,
And he discoursed on workers' dignity.
He said the bosses counting on their work
Were never going to give a raise or perk
Unless they had to, and how even then
They'd fire you and find some other men
Who'd work for less. Unless a union had
Your back. He said I was a likely lad,
Why didn't I come fight for workers' rights
Instead of things that kept me up a-nights?
He said that my experience talking turkey
Would help me deal with bosses tough as jerky.
I smiled at him and said, "Sounds like a plan!"
And that's how I became a union man.

11

The Builder's Tale

The builder had been stewing through this rant
And glaring at the salesman whose descant
Upon the ills of look-alike townhouses
Left him sore. Among his bitterest grouses
Was that the insurance man over-appraised
Before the joists and frames were even raised.
So, taking the next speaker's place in line
He glared as if the salesman were a swine:

"*You of all people ought* to know how much
"You save in underwriting costs and such
"When we develop—we appraise one home,
"We've done them all. Burglars won't come roam—
"Property's distributed in small amounts
"Around the suburb. Thieves would have to bounce
"From house to house down an entire street
"To justify the wear and tear on feet.
"And don't make fun of anonymity!
"It's worth pure gold if your proximity
"Is rife with life-insurance salesmen or
"Political campaigners door-to-door.

"*You say you'd like* to have a getaway
"Out in the country, where you'd keep at bay
"The soiled and ever-hectic urban life,
"And live in peace and quiet with your wife
"Beside a stream, perhaps, whose gentle flow
"Would soothe your sleep and keep your heart rate slow.
"You'd see your distant neighbors, smile and wave,
"And know each other's names, and you would save
"The mail for them if they left home to travel.
"Of course, bucolic visions will unravel.
"Just as real life can and always does.
"Small townships with a charming face still buzz
"With tensions, feuds, and envy. You're exposed
"To boredom and small talk. Their minds are closed.
"You still won't be safe. Though you have property,
"Pneumonia won't respect your privacy,
"Nor accidents your wealth. A little slip
"Resulting in a badly broken hip
"Will be your death without a neighbor near.
"Such casual mishaps are the things to fear.
"A short tale will suffice to illustrate—
How idylls all at once will dissipate."

After some years, a young insurance man
Was able to retire ahead of plan.
He traded options and he sold stocks short.
Through foresight and dumb luck, his friends report,
His gambles earned returns that were enough
To keep him and his spouse out of the rough
And on the fairway for the rest of life.
But riches can be boring, and his wife
Grew tired of the perpetual request
Of friends to give a handout, to invest

In their lost causes, charities, or schools.
They were less easy to dissuade than mules.
Let us enjoy wealth just awhile, she thought,
Without becoming quite so overwrought.
So, at the end of one long, trying day,
She told her husband they must move away.
"Just for a while," she told him, "just us two,
"Where no one knows us. Somewhere with a view
"Of mountain ranges." She seemed so distraught
He would have promised more, and so he caught

Her in his arms and kissed away her tears,
Then told her he had thought just that for years.
He'd get right on it (not intending to,
At least, not yet). He'd far too much to do
To be retired. He secretly was sore
That she herself was not a whole lot more
In sync with what he did in his career,
That, after all, was what had got them here.

And so he bought her gift spa treatments that
Purported to calm nerves in nothing flat
And leave one in a glowing state of health,
While he'd be free to go increase their wealth.
And so they lived, till late one autumn night
She asked him what he'd done to set things right
About their mountain home. He hemmed and hawed!
(*Of course*, he thought, *her reasoning is flawed!*
How could I ever really get away
With markets in flux, and not just day-to-day,
But hourly, by the minute—I could miss a cue
And lose a bundle. Then what would we do?)
She looked a little sad, and then she said:
"I knew you'd never do this, so instead,
"Of waiting, I just went online and found
"Our dream. With Smoky Mountains all around."
She swept her hand, "High up, the perfect place."
He stared at her as if she'd dropped from space,
Or risen in her graveclothes from a tomb.
"It looks out over parkland—breathing room,
"My Love, for you and me." His blowup, when
It came, burst like a Brahma from its pen.
Hurtful words and spiteful, rough and loud
That, had they been outside, would draw a crowd.
But she just sat there, waiting for the pause,
And when it came, began to plead her cause.

The gist was this: she wanted him to see
The place she'd picked. If he would just agree
To spend two nights there with her and to wile
Away a weekend, she would only smile
If he said no, not mention it again.
She'd settle for vacations now and then.
"The leaves are turning now. It has Wi-Fi
"Because the cabin's almost in the sky."
"Cabin?" he snorted. "Just for now," she said.
"We'll build a little chalet home instead.
"Till then, there is a cabin on the lot,
"Refurbished, insulated, just the spot
"To wake and see the sunshine on the leaves
"As they turn red. The woods come to the eaves,
"And from the porch you see the mountains run
"Into the distance in the morning sun."
He did some calculations in his head.
She'll really owe me, his addition said.
Three days of cold with nothing much to do
But loiter and pretend to like the view.
If that is all it takes to never hear again
About this kind of waste of time, I'm in.
"OK!" he said, and was embarrassed by
How quickly his agreement made her cry.

They came out on the third week in October
By plane and then by taxi. None too sober
At the airport, he was sleeping soundly
In the cab's back seat. He cursed her roundly
When she patted him awake to pay the fare.
She was the one who brought a cooler there
And threw in beer, some champagne, and some steaks.
She carried in the bags, for goodness' sakes!

But all around the mountain air smelled clean
As if light rain had cooled and washed the scene.
She was intoxicated by that air
And filled with joy while just standing there.
The cabin had a sloping porch in front,
So dogs, she thought, could cool off from the hunt,

But otherwise its large gray timbers sat
Upon the ground. And underneath a mat,
She found a key that slipped into the door.
Inside was everything she'd hankered for:
Wood floors, high windows, with a bath and nook
That held a modest little place to cook,
In front of the old hearth was laid a stone,
The perfect size to kneel on or lie prone
Next to the crackle from a hearty fire,
And warm up until the time came to retire.

The stone looked ancient, polished smooth, but worn,
One corner broken, and she could have sworn
The air came through it from the soil below,
Adding some interest to the fire's glow.
Across the room, a rustic bunk bed stood,
Fresh made, both top and bottom. Very good!
The smells of knotty pine, clean linens, air
Had wafted in from open vents somewhere.
She ventured back, up to a windowed door
And saw, as promised, mountain peaks galore,
Then spun around to see her husband gaze
At her and smile just as in olden days.
"The lights don't work too well, except the kitchen.
"Instead of standing around and bitchin'
"We'll have to make a roaring fire tonight!"
"You're right!" she whispered. "We'll make fire all right!"

They spent the afternoon hiking around,
And taking in the wonders that they found:
The trees ablaze with scarlet, orange, yellow;
Calls of birds, a forest floor so mellow
With rotting leaf fall of a hundred years
It cushioned footsteps. All moved her to tears.

They talked about a deck, with sliding doors
That opened silently upon great stores
Of plants and creatures that their woods must hold—
Foxes and deer and other things untold.
He found an axe and several cords of wood
And laid a fire he thought looked pretty good,
Considering the years since he was a Boy Scout;
And when she said she'd never had a doubt
That he was a survivor, he just glowed,
Despite himself, and hoped that nothing showed.
They tried the bunk beds, both on top of one,
And slept until the day was almost done.

At last, the evening came. They had the steaks
And then champagne, and lit the fire. It takes
But just a little while until your will
Succumbs to a warm fire and at length is still.
So she lay dreaming of the miracle
That he was hers. Nothing empirical
Had proved this to her, but the change
In his affect when he viewed the mountain range.
And he, too, holding her hand before the fire
Felt satisfaction and acute desire.
She'll come to stay here frequently, he thought,
And lessen the chance that maybe I'll be caught
In my adventures with a younger girl.
I'll come from time to time, but blame the swirl
Of work. A sensible excuse! He bet
This all would work out fine. No sweat!
And so, this loving couple went to bed,
She top, he bottom, soon as good as dead.
They locked the doors up, being city dwellers
Much more suspicious than these country fellers.

But in the dark of night she came awake,
Quite startled. Had she heard some branches break?
Some popping in the fire? The fire was out.
You idiot! she told herself *What's this about?*
Today has left you really overwrought.
And then she heard a sliding sound, she thought,
Like fingers moving slowly over wood.
Then nothing. *Oh*, she thought, *This is not good.*
She told herself: *Don't let some little fright*
Destroy this absolutely perfect night.
The fire had died away; there was no light.
It seemed the very nadir of the night.
Her fingers found a lamp clipped on her bunk;
But it clicked uselessly, the piece of junk!
All was now silent, so she tried to sleep,
But thought she heard a swish and then a sweep,
Both gentle sounds, as if the habit of a nun
Were moving over tiles at rising sun.
"Donald!" she whispered. Soon her husband woke.
"Do you hear anything?" He groaned and spoke,
"What . . . hear?" "Wake up and pay attention!
"Something is in here with us!" Apprehension
Made her shake, she heard him sit in bed.
But he surveyed the dark and scratched his head.
"No, I don't see a thing." And then a snore.
He did not give responses any more.
So he'd gone back to sleep. It made her seethe!
And she was lying there too scared to breathe.

She thought she saw the shadows twitch and slink.
"Donald!" she hissed. "Wake up! Wake UP! I think
"There's something on the floor. What should we do?"
Cursing, he sat up in his bunk. "Damn you!

He yelled, "You finally got me to embrace
"The idea of a second home, your 'perfect place.'
"And now you're here, you're having scary dreams?
"If joy leaves you fraying at the seams,
"How will this place ever make you happy?
"Be quiet. Go to sleep." He sounded snappy.
"Go back to sleep! But take this as a warning.
"I don't expect to wake up until morning."
Confused, she settled back into her bed
And pulled the covers high above her head.
Somehow, she drifted off to sleep,
But in the pre-dawn darkness came a deep
Bellow from nearby. "Ow! Ow! A nail!"
"I'm stepping on it! God!!" And then a wail:
"No! I'm being stung by wasps. They bite
"My legs every step." A scream. "The light!"
She leaned out of the bunk and stretched out her arm,
Grasping at darkness, waving it in alarm.
"Can you climb on the bed?" she shouted.
He was a thrashing shadow now. She doubted
He had heard her. "Turn on the light!" he yelled.
She tried it again. "It doesn't work!" Tears welled,
Throat tightened. "What can I do to help?" she called.
He'd fallen now. She heard him as he sprawled.
Then silence. Straining to penetrate the gloom,
She just could see a body in the room.
And as the dawn crept in, saw his head
Bent at the neck, and knew he must be dead.
Then, as the morning lit the cabin floor,
She saw the room was clean and bare. No more
Dangers seen anywhere. The floor looked swept,
Just as it had when they arrived. Well kept.

She found no pulse, no movement in the dead.
His legs and arms were swollen, puffed and red.
The rest of him looked green as washed-up kelp.
Should she have jumped from the bunks to try to help?
He had been right about her all along.
She was entitled, selfish, in the wrong.
So, in the chill, dim early morning air,
She went to summon help that had no prayer
Of doing anything but stand and stare.
When she and the state troopers had arrived
Back at the scene, authorities contrived
To make the tragedy a bigger deal.
Red blinking lights made everything unreal,
Especially in daylight. Did they think
The passing deer might crash without the blink?
Technicians and a group of crime-scene men
Were mapping their turf. A lady with a wen
Turned out to be the coroner, and she
Stayed deep in conversation with a deputy.
The victim's wife was sleeping in a chair
Brought out for her in that excess of care
Which indicates she was potential prey,
A trooper woke her up, so he could say
"Forensic teams are coming in. Who is
"The landlord? Where's the lease?" The quiz
Went on until she found the paperwork,
And gave it to the bureaucratic jerk.
Then all at once, the body was rolled out
As if it were a drunken roustabout
Bagged, atop the gurney, and she wept
Because that ending was so damned inept
For someone like her husband, who would try
At least to exit with a grand good-bye.

In latish afternoon an expert came—
A full professor with a lettered name.
He was a scientist, asked by the state
To come in, as a person of some weight,
And help with complex cases. A short man,
Some hair grew from every body part hair can,
But his affect was gentle and his face
Was crinkled with laugh lines in every place
That's called upon to laugh. He took her hand
And asked her to repeat events that spanned
The date on which she'd married, to the night
That left her in this agonizing plight.
And then, he made her go back over all
That had elapsed inside after nightfall.
When she was done, he said he'd like to start
By taking the old fireplace apart.
Listlessly, she waved him on, and then

Immediately, there entered several men
With long steel bars, who plunged them in the grout
Around the hearth-fire stone and pried it out.
"Stand back!" someone cried out, "Stand back!
"Quick, quick, come here! And grab a sack."
"Come on, you'll want to see this," said the Prof.
Leading her by one arm toward the trough
Where moments before, the damaged hearthstone lay,
They edged in baby steps; then, "Light!" she heard him say.
He clicked a Maglite on and shone it in the pit.
And then she heard the crowding folks cry, "Shit!"
She opened her eyes onto a dreadful sight:
Below floor level, at the end of light,
She saw the pit floor move. A writhing ball,
A knot of things untied itself to crawl.

"So cover it!" her prop and expert cried.
They dropped a tarp and shut the things inside.
"Come here, my dear," the old professor said.
"It's quite a shock to know why he is dead."
"I *don't* know," she exclaimed. "What did I see?"
He looked up at an overhanging tree
That flared gold-crimson in the dying light.
"This time of year, our fast-encroaching night
"Signals to some animals a pressing need,
"To find each other, and to pay good heed
"To the approach of ice and bitter cold.
"It says that, if they reckon to grow old,
"They'll stop their hunting and go find warm beds.
"These native vipers, dear, called 'copperheads,'
"Have slept decades of cold beneath that stone,
"Knotted to form a kind of temperate zone.
"Crisp weather, like we've had, will drive them in.
"Your fire awoke them and their next of kin!
"Some came up through the flagstone's corner door,
"To cool themselves down on the cabin floor.
"So I must tell the coroner who writes
"The autopsy, there were three dozen bites.
"It is a freakish thing. The copperhead
"Is our least poisonous snake, so it is said.
"But I am rather sure the sudden shock
"From all of these attacks ran out the clock.
"At least his death was merciful. He fell
"And broke his neck. You should not dwell
"On how he might have suffered. It was short,
"As I will say in my police report."

And then, after a while, the troopers left,
With writhing sacks that they could barely heft,

And promises to come back very soon
To check on her. In bed, she watched the moon
Climb its immortal stairway through the sky,
As if it dared her to pursue a reason why.
His grim tale told, the builder sat back down
And left all of our faces in a frown.
"Call it a day!" the cruise director said,
"We'll find no nest of serpents in our bed."

12

The Businessman's Tale

Next day, we all were restless, and we sensed
Something was off. As this day commenced,
The serving staff were looking rather glum
The lawyer busy gnawing on his thumb.
The cruise director was late getting there.
And no one seemed to have a smile to spare.
A blushing man was pushed out front by friends.
He wore some pins recording time one spends
In civic clubs like Lions, Elks, or Moose,
Stuck to a blazer that was colored puce
And clashed with the bright crimson of his face.
He'd always look completely out of place,
In any scene in which he played a part.
You'd say that he made artlessness an art.
A colleague on each elbow hustled him
Up to the rostrum, while he, weak of limb
Was almost dragged quite nerveless to the fore.
This transport scared the poor man even more.

His lips moved as he grasped the microphone
And once he realized he was there alone.
He jerked and twitched, as if he had the bends,
To vigorous cheering from his several friends,
With sideways glances at them, he began:

All five of us, like hash out of a pan,
Come here from Bumph, in eastern Arkansas.
A town of timber and tobacco chaw.
Now, you elite folks with your education,
I'm sure you think you represent this nation,
And I've heard lots of high and mighty things,
Like some of you have been the pals of kings.
So what I think I maybe ought to do
Is tell how attitudes can ruin you.

A college lady in our little town
Would bring out her old dusty cap and gown
Whenever you would stop in for a visit.
That ain't too far from high and mighty, is it?
Lou-Ellen was her name. She'd oversell
A pot of turnip greens by hurrying to tell
You how she'd studied with some famous chef.
How did her husband stand it? —He was deaf.
But anyways, she had a son, who was
Engaged to a lady close to menopause,
Nor was he much younger, based on looks.
They were a pair of aged, unread books.
But he worked for the fire department, she
As a clerk down at the water company.
Lou-Ellen wrote their wedding invitation—
Words that, engraved, provoked a mild sensation:
"Surely, in all the history of our town
"There never was a match of such renown.

"He, with Fire attendant on his will,
"She, who a thousand empty baths can fill.
"Water and Fire, essential faculties
"Attested by the Greek Empedocles—
"Others may take the mud and empty air,
"Those two last elements—plebian fare!

"This bride can release her waters in a rush
"To make his hose and fire hydrant gush,
"Until all flames are quenched and die away.
"So come, dear friends, and watch this couple say
"The words that will complete their blessed bond.
"He'll be promoted now, to captain, or beyond,
"While she will be acknowledged as the key
"That winds clocks at the Water Company.
"This marvelous event begins at three
"With Sunday coffee after, in the Rectory."

To say the invitation caused a stir
While factual, might not be kind to her.
It made the corkboard down at city hall,
Outside the mayor's suite on a plaster wall,
And caused a cataclysm that Lou-Ellen took
As praise. The whole town came to have a look
That Wedding Day. The church was full of flowers
Unlikely to survive as fresh for hours.
And then, as if to draw things further out
Lou-Ellen booked a full choir. 'Round about
Five dozen souls would form two lines and sing
Sweet wedding songs as they were entering,
And, when they reached the chancel, they'd abide
Till it was time to croon "Here comes the bride!"
The choir at St. Erasmus was a mix
Of pros and those who did it all for kicks.

The reigning queen of the entire throng
Was Julie Jump. She brought the rest along
By leadership, but mostly through her charm.
Her voice was wondrous, and her face was warm
With smiles and dimples under sparkling eyes
That made men grin and struggle to surmise

What lay beneath the billowing choir robes,
And think wild thoughts of nibbling earlobes.
It wasn't a surprise that males all gawked
At her stiletto heels, for as she walked
They made her body bobble where it was not taut,
Suggesting the sensation that men sought.
The choirboys of course had seen her vest
Through empty keyholes, as she primped and dressed.
They all matured in only half an hour,
And should have left to take a chilly shower.
At Christmas, when she sang "O Holy Night,"
Flashing her teeth through a sweet overbite,
And got to the command, "Fall on your knees!"
The adolescents toppled like felled trees.

So at the wedding, as the choir processed,
Young Julie Jump, ahead of all the rest,
As was her due, sang beautifully, until
Nemesis intruded with a will.
In center aisle, there was a heating grate
Designed of old for different shoes. It ate
Her new stiletto heel, held it alone
As if it were Excalibur in stone.
Young Julie was a woman of great sense.
She slipped her foot out, so to recommence
Her walk, in tempo, up the aisle—unevenly,
I must confess, but bravely, as you'll see.
Two rows behind her marched a tenor, who
Was just as sweet on her as I or you.
His Walter Raleigh moment had arrived.
Sweeping gallantly down, this hero strived
To pull the missing heel out of the grate.
But it was wedged too tightly and, by fate
As he picked up the shoe, this suave Don Juan,
He pulled out the whole grate, and bore it on

Holding the grate and shoe close to his robe.
But then, as if embracing the ill luck of Job,
The bass behind him, nose in music, stepped
Into an unexpected void and swept
With gravity down to the depths of Hell,
(That is, a heating duct bent in an ell

Some eight feet underneath the center aisle).
Limp as a noodle, after falling half a mile,
Or so it seemed, he shot into the bend
And stuck, with flaccid arms and legs both penned
Within the sloping duct, beyond our reach,
His hips and buttocks plugging up the breach,
His head and shoulders upright in the chute,
Leaving him free to holler and to hoot.
And that's what he did. Quite naturally: he howled
Like a sacrificial victim disemboweled.
Because the flowing choir robes had concealed,
Specifics of the accident weren't revealed,
Half of the congregation simply saw
The basso disappear, sucked down the maw
Of the netherworld. The others heard the sound
Of some demonic spirit underground,
Weeping and wailing and gnashing all his teeth
Summoning spirits from the world beneath.
Neither half remained to see a Rite
Of Marriage brazenly performed despite
Such metaphysical forebodings. Some
Were spooked enough to say they'd never come,
While others, with less superstition, stayed
To watch the township's little fire brigade
Come in to rescue the poor swallowed man.
They tried to reach him from the top. That plan
Was thwarted by his distance down the duct.
And so, after a dozen plans were chucked,
They brought a cutting torch—acetylene,
I think—and, taping off the sorry scene,
Proceeded to cut modern Jonah out.
It took around two hours, just about.
And thus, Lou-Ellen's best-laid plans were naught.
Her children, still a little overwrought,

Wed privately, before a justice of the peace.
She and her husband planned their own decease,
But found it, in the end, much easier
(Though, given the publicity, queasier),
To move across the county line. They did.
Sometimes it's better not to overbid.

13

The Cruise Director's Tale

The queen of charity gave such a snort,
Her dogs both whined to have their naps cut short.
"You're such a condescending little man,"
She spread her caftan's arms into a fan
And glared at the poor man across the room.
"It's disrespectful of your mother's womb!"
The storyteller froze in disbelief.
His smiling face now drooped with grief.
The lady was intent on shaming him.
Her face was flushed and her expression grim.
"Why shouldn't women have the right
"To gain due equity without a fight.
"How can you laugh at one who tries to rise
"Before some husband cuts her down to size?
"Just let her have her moment in the sun
"And stop pretending that it's shameful fun."
As if to emphasize how deep he was in poo,
Her bulldog tinkled on the bad guy's shoe.

It took the cruise director to undo the harm,
And turn the fire from four- to one-alarm:
"Be Lady Justice and hold out your scales:
How many heroes feature in these tales?
Male grifters, grafters, gangsters, sneaky kids,
And men whose working lives have hit the skids,
Predatory priests, rogues on the lam.
But women are the flim to every flam.
No gender's better when you're telling tales,
And everyone's repute in lockstep fails.
That's all because the world does not exempt
You from its law that all will be unkempt
To some degree, or not be dressed for life.
I'll tell you of another kind of wife."

There was a lady back in my hometown
Who seldom got out of her dressing gown,
Unless she had a person in for tea—
And there weren't many whom she cared to see.
When she went out, she always dressed in tweed,
With scarf and cane, of which she had no need;
But in her stately house, de temps en temps
She lounged *en déshabillément*.
For when she was young, she had been told
Her creamy satin skin would not grow old,
"But should remain," cried one ecstatic beau,
"Unsmothered by clothes, eternally on show."
Of course, he had a motive, said Ms. Prue
(For that was the lady's name, or it will do).

The mansion that she lived in was Beaux Arts,
And more secluded than its counterparts.
So, inside, she was apt to let the air
Have access to her almost-everywhere.

Glass cabinets were filled with antique Sèvres
That guests would gawk at, mid-*fromage de chèvres*
On small *gaufrettes* brought all the way from France.
Her evenings did not leave one thing to chance.
Besides her china, she was very keen
On bichons frises, and her child, eighteen.
And so, she kenneled both, to some degree,
In runs or bedrooms, as the case may be.
Guinevere, her daughter, "Gwen" for short,
Was boarded at a school, with child support

Furnished by Mr. Prue, of whom no trace
Could otherwise be found about her place.
(She kept his name, of course, which was the key
To shares in quite an ample legacy.)
She knew what children of Gwen's age would do
If not watched carefully and kept in view.

Ms. Prue could track their ancestry to Noah
And probably could name some protozoa
Who figured early in her family tree.
In truth, she liked things with a pedigree
And would not risk her own on teenage whims.
So Gwen was a "her" kept far away from "hims."
But those precautions could at least be shared
With schools. To keep the bichon unimpaired
Required an army of attendants and some wit,
Lest some stray dog might chance to take a hit
At compromising Madame Eglantine.
That little dog was whelped by "Dame Pristine"
And sired by "Mauffrey's Gallant," so renowned
That his *cojones* weighed in, pound for pound,
At more than truffles, if you went by price.
Now, our Ms. Prue would never roll the dice
On such a prize as future breeding rights.
Therefore, the bitch was always in her sights.
Snow-white and fluffier than eider-down,
With a corona flaring from her crown,
This pup projected innocence and love—
The canine version of a snowy dove.
The problem was, the dove was now in heat!
She had to stay a virgin to compete
At Kennel Club events, and own the ring,
And win a "Best in Show." The merest fling,
With some streetwise canine Lothario
Would ruin it all. If she should have a go,

She'd lose her honor and her value, too.
And that gave anxious nightmares to Ms. Prue.

She dreamt her fallen dog had given birth
To half-breed litters colored like the earth.
So, while in heat, the dog was kept upstairs,
And vets and groomers made to bring their wares
To Chateau Prue. And why not? Costs of all
Required to raise her champion were not small.
From puppyhood, the dog learned to say "Ah-h"
For various doctors at the doggy spa,
And now had trainers, and a handler, too;
Five veterinarians, of which a few
Were specialists in blood, from out of town,
And knew the kinds of flaws that bring dogs down.
The groomer was handpicked by this new team,
A young man, and his styling was a dream,
His name was Tzefanyahu, but his charm
And youth would never ever cause alarm.
And since bichons frises were hard to groom
Ms. Prue would let him use the spare bedroom
In which she quartered Madame Eglantine,
Just down the hall from where she lay serene.
The little dog slept on a queen-sized bed
But often seemed to use the floor instead,
Contriving oftentimes to leave some stool.
The room was Gwen's until she went to school,
But smelling it on break, the girl refused
To share and moved upstairs, quite unamused.

It was now summer and Gwen soon would go
Off to a women's U. deemed *à propos.*
To bide the time, Gwen stayed up in her room
Lost in a teenage existential gloom.

Since Gwen was out of sight, Ms. Prue relaxed.
With less to think of, she would feel less taxed.
There were the dog-show applications and
Certificates she had to have in hand,
Attesting to her little dog's good health,
Plus many other things requiring wealth
That she and her accountants must discuss.
No wonder that she did not want a fuss.
And so, she spent the summer paying bills
And going through the necessary drills
To qualify the dog. And in the fall,
When she kissed Gwen her good-bye in the hall,
Her daughter hugged her and with tearful eyes,
Said, "Mom, I'm pregnant. It was a surprise."
So Tzef and I . . ." Ms. Prue said faintly, "Who?"
"Your groomer, Mom. His name's 'Tzefanyahu'.
"I'm dropping out of college. We'll groom pets.
"And that will be as happy as life gets!"
With that, her daughter walked out of the door
And left her mother prostrate on the floor.

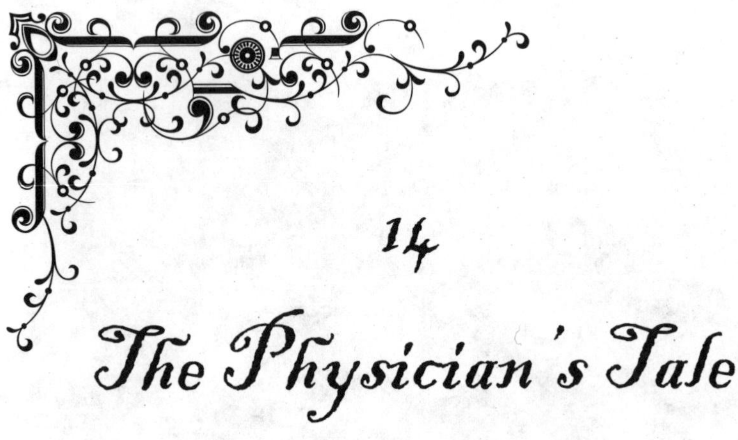

14

The Physician's Tale

The ship's physician, black bag at his side,
Would regularly roll in like the tide
"To check on you," he said. He always wore
A white lab jacket and his pocket bore
His stethoscope; but the Hawaiian shirt
He donned beneath that outfit could divert
The eyes, the widow said. Out of the loop,
But always on the fringes of our group,
He'd learned, it struck me, over many years
Never to treat his patients as his peers.
Though affable, he would not sit and talk.
And if you went to start a chat, he'd balk.
I think, at parties, many folks had tried
To tell him what was wrong with them inside,
And where they hurt, and how their feet were sore,
Though he had not caught sight of them before.
I thought he was a stage prop, not a doc.
If you would find his cabin door and knock
He never would be there. But if you'd check
The golf mat at the far end of the deck,

You'd often find him working on his putting.
It made you want to shout out something cutting.
But then, you thought, physicians back at home
Were just like this but had more room to roam.

Then my opinion changed. He cared, in fact,
But did not have much chance to interact.

Today he came to our table and sat down.
"To what do we owe this honor?" With a frown
The lawyer challenged him to conversation,
And I expected to see hesitation
On the doctor's part, but he was quick
To answer: "I could treat you, were you sick,
"But rudeness has no cure." At that, we all
Sat up and looked at him. He'd had the gall
To take on our pet lawyer, and he'd won
With one remark. And yet, he was not done.
"I've come to warn you of a situation
"That's apt to put an end to your vacation.
"Four days ago, we got the word that we
"Might not be able to come in from sea.

"For Charlotte Amalie has radioed
"To tell us we could not, as planned, unload
"Our passengers. It seems that while we've cruised
"From New York toward St. Thomas and amused
"Ourselves, an unknown pathogen has come
"From China, spreading fast. Headstrong but dumb,
"Elected leaders have already made
"Decisions that most certainly delayed
"Containing this infection. All around
"The world now worried scientists have found
"New cases well before they've got a grip
"On whether they're pandemic or a blip.
"No treatments or prevention yet. This rate,
"Of spread has led me to anticipate
"Worldwide infection. We are safe for now
"Because we beat it out of port somehow,
"But we will risk infection if we dock.
"We'd have to quarantine until the clock

"Runs out on time for symptoms to manifest.
"That could be weeks or many days at best.
"Although the ship's speed was reduced for days
"Down to a crawl, in hopes, that we'd not raise
"St. Thomas till the pestilence had passed
"We've finally had to face the truth at last.
"It's here to stay; we will not be allowed
"To disembark and join the tourist crowd."

He looked at all our faces and took stock
Of our surprise, bewilderment, and shock.
"Why didn't they tell us this before we paid?"
The pilot groused. "I'll bet we're just delayed
"A little while. It happens all the time
"You're waiting at the gate, you hear a chime,
"The intercom then tells you that your flight
"Has been rescheduled as a fly-by-night."
The doctor shook his head: "A shame, I know,
"But cancellation is the way to go.
"A bug so fast and fatal will outrun
"Our boat. There seems to be no starting gun
"You can rely on. But aboard this ship
"You're safe for the duration of your trip.
"The captain says he'll try some other ports.
"No passengers are feeling out of sorts;
"But I've advised him not to even try.
"Nowhere is safe. To say so is to lie."

We sat and stared dumbstruck as time uncurled.
"So who elected you to run the world?"
The lawyer snarked. "Where is your evidence
"Of this apocalypse? It makes no sense
"To give up such a well-planned holiday
"For risks that are, essentially, hearsay."

"No, wait!" The salesman suddenly broke in.
"Can't you see he's trying to begin
"His story! Go ahead!" he told the doc.
"You've got a half an hour by the clock."
We all applauded. The physician sighed.
"Quite soon, more evidence will be supplied
"Than you might hope to see. If you've denied
"The truth of this contagion, you will find
"That one day you will sit and cry how blind
"You were, when those you love are carried off.
"It may now seem permissible to scoff
"At something 'too invisible to harm.'
"I only hope you have a good-luck charm,
"Some anodyne medallion 'round the neck,
"For when you find an unseen viral speck
"Has flattened you, your spouse, and children, too,
"You will regret your lack of follow-through.
"I want my money back," the lawyer said.
"And damages for being kept in dread,
"Aboard this ship. I call it false arrest!"
The doctor laughed: "No, you've been blessed.

"Once you would have had no choice. You're lucky.
"Not to live in earlier days. Though plucky
"You might be, if trussed up like a pullet
"And made to bite down on a leaden bullet
"As I sawed off your left leg at the knee,
"You'd lose the attitude, and possibly
"Consider what it means to be alive.
"Or, more than that, you might begin to thrive.
"New maladies like this fast-spreading one
"Will not be finished with us till they're done.
"We might be in an age of pestilence,
"With germs against which we have no defense.

"New medieval plagues rode stealthily
"Among vast crowds who lived unhealthily
"And coldly slaughtered almost half of them—
"A tide of random violence none could stem.
"Why think those days were over long ago?
"We've had contagions since that time, you know."

"Bananas!" cried the lawyer, fists closed tight.
"Exactly," said the doctor, "You're quite right!"
Scrambling the peevish counsel in mid-thought.
"Lowly bananas," said the doctor. "Bought
"For many decades in your local store.
"They're not even the same fruit anymore.

"The first ones fell to blight a century back
"And quickly died completely out, for lack
"Of human prudence. They were all one plant,
"Cloned in volume, overcrowded, scant
"Attention paid to factors of disease,
"Until it was too late to save the trees.
"They all succumbed; and now a cultivar
"We hybridized from species near and far

"Is fast succumbing to a different blight.
"Effective remedies are not in sight.
"To test the truth of what I'm telling you,
"Look at our natural scourges like the flu.
"We are abundant and so closely packed
"That we are vulnerable, and that's a fact.
"But unlike clones, we all have different genes,
"So will not be wiped out by any means,
"Just cut back like a rosebush, leaving sun
"And air for those whose growth has just begun.
"So our survivors, as this plague expires,
"May be more likely to fulfill desires
"Without the struggle of so many peers.
"That's consolation, if this peril nears,
"Meantime, however, get what help you can,
"And always try to aid your fellow man."

We sat in silence when he stopped. A lapse
In conversation made the lawyer's claps
Echo, as the doctor left the room.
I thought I saw his cheeks begin to bloom
With indignation at the rudeness, but
He gave no sign until our legal nut
Breathed "Loser!" when Doc stopped to wave good-bye.
At that, the doctor looked him in the eye
And summed up all our feelings at the slight:
"You think you're top banana? Hope you're right."

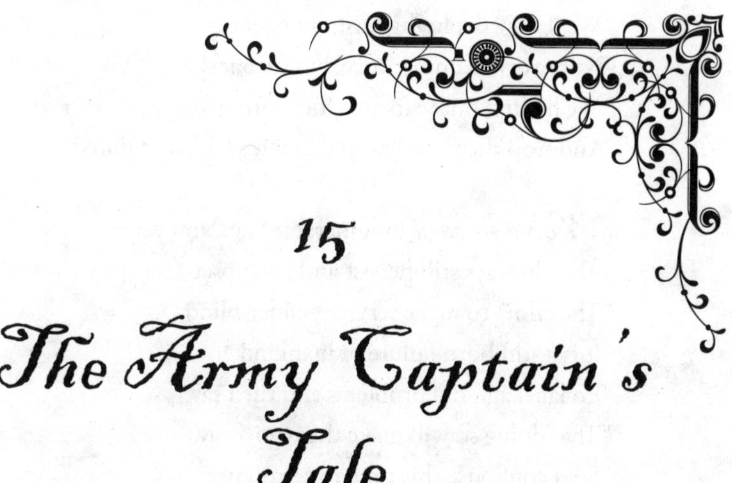

15

The Army Captain's Tale

That afternoon, and at the urging of
The queen of charity, who did not love
The cruise director's observations on her sex,
A woman, truly proud in all respects,
Stood up to speak. Julia, the General's daughter.
She spoke forthrightly, as her service taught her.

I am an army captain. I command
A handpicked ninety-seven-person band
Of fit combatants, every one of whom,
Whatever race or gender, I must groom
To be outstanding infantry, equipped
In mind, physique, and spirit to be shipped.
I am a woman. If you're getting on
In years, you probably are thinking, "Brawn
"Is what our army needs, not women's charms!
"They put some girl in charge? Sound the alarms!

"We'll now deploy against our enemies
"Not overwhelming force, but niceties!
"We'll blind our fearsome foes with powder puffs
"And stop them in their tracks with frills and fluffs?"

"We've passed innumerable laws, and yet,
"The old ways still persist and still upset
"The effort to make service gender-blind.
"It is a stubborn failure of mankind
"To label age-old problems and then say
"That doing so will make them go away.
"So, I could use this time to sermonize
"And cite each race I've won, and each first prize
"I've racked up for endurance, skill, and pluck.
"But I am well aware that, without luck,
"You'll just decide that I've exaggerated
"Or maybe that the test results were weighted.
"You don't think so? If you're on the fence.
"I'll share with you just one experience.

Some years ago, my very first command
Was leading a platoon. Please understand
That I was only a Lieutenant then,
Commanding somewhere close to thirty men
And several women. We were infantry,
So one-in-seven men and close to three-
In-four young women could not make the grade.
It's true that men and women are not made
Alike in strength and stamina, and yet
An enemy will kill all slackers on a bet.
High standards of the infantry apply,
Whether your chromosomes are x or y.
To pass, each gender has to throw
A live grenade one hundred feet or so,

Drag a man fifty feet with their own power,
Run five miles in three-quarters of an hour,
And march a backpack seventy pounds in weight
At least twelve miles and not come back too late.

Women and men are trained together in
Mixed-gender squads. They both lose nails and skin,
They practice the same raids, and both endure
Ice, sun, wind, rain, and feeling like manure,
When extra push-ups are imposed for being slow.
But, back to my platoon: I had to show
The brass that I was capable and smart
And more than likely to fulfill my part
Of the equation. To keep us on our way
Toward the role that officers must play,
The army gives officers an NCO—
A platoon sergeant trained so long ago
That he's seen everything (except what's new,
Like women soldiers, or two sexes who
Are sure to violate the old taboo
Against confusing military duty
With subjugating tempting hunks of booty).
Getting along with Sergeant Weatherby
Required a person I will never be.
Our meetings were respectful, and I knew
He'd be in charge of chores and schedules, too,
And tasks and exercising of the troops.
But I knew that my type were nincompoops
To him. You'd have to put him on the rack
Before he would confess it, but my back
Was not his first priority. He swore
By things that went back decades in the corps.
Coveting validation, I admit,
I took him in my confidence. A bit

At first, but as my understanding grew
I leaned on him more often than I knew.
Now, this is not an easy sort of thing
For me to talk about, but everything
Important to this story must be told.

A soldier, maybe twenty-one-years old,
Saluted at my door, just after mess.
She seemed hysterical, and I confess,
At first, I took in every other word
She said and made no sense of what I heard.
"Private Lopez," I said. "Now have some water.
"Calm yourself. At ease." I barely caught her
When she misjudged the seat and almost slid
Onto the floor. I got her settled and amid
The sobbing asked if she were hurt.
She shook her head, and soon was more alert.
I said, "I'll call First Sergeant Weatherby
"And get you help!" "No! please!" she said to me.
Fresh tears. I had no choice then but to say:
"Soldier. You know that this is not the way
"We're trained to handle problems. Chain of command
"Requires that what you can't solve out of hand
"You bring to the leader to whom you've been assigned—
"Not to platoon command! No one will find
"You acted rightly to come straight to me.
"Unless this is a true emergency."
"It is! It is!" she cried. And so I said,
"I'll give you fifteen minutes. Go ahead."
"I came because, when I was seventeen
"I was assaulted. I was pretty green.
"It was a soldier that a former friend
"Had introduced me to. And in the end
"He hurt me pretty bad. And we had gone
"On several dates. He was a real Don Juan."

She needed surgery to hide the scars,
And psychiatric help, before the stars
Would shine down as before. He was long gone,
To fight in Asia. Alone and overdrawn,
With doctors telling her to face her fear
The girl enlisted, and that's what brought her here.

She'd chosen sniping as a specialty
Because she could shoot nuts off of a tree
And conjure up the rapist's pretty face
On targets when she trained there at the base.

She had a favorite bunker at the edge
Of our best rifle range. Saltbush and sedge
Concealed its ports, which, on a scrubby hill,
Provided fields of view and men to "kill."
She trained there, by permission, with a squad
Of soldiers and their noncommissioned god
Who was, by reputation, said to be
Of preternatural ability.

Today, the base post office had for her
An envelope she handed me without demur.
Anonymous and brown, with no return address,
It carried two old clippings from the press.
The first reported a "suspected" rape
In West Virginia. While it hung black crepe

Over the prospects of the victim, I could see
She had survived and sat across from me.
The second one, quite old, dealt with a crime
That happened on this base before my time.
A local was assaulted in a spot
Out by the training fields, remote and not
Much used, except for training infantry
In long-range rifle fire, a specialty
That takes only a few high-skilled recruits
Possessing military attributes
Of nerve and patience to kill far away.
The girl, this clipping struggled not to say
Was raped and mutilated, case unsolved.
And all civilian protests unresolved.

This mailing clearly was a threat, and I
Used pace military guidance to reply:
"Yes, quite disturbing, and this case will be
"High on the list of things I oversee.
"Go to your sergeant. Be assured, I'll brief
"Him on the threat, and he'll secure relief
"From any other menaces. You'll see
"How we protect the members of our infantry."
And so I said good night. She left,
But not without a face that looked bereft
Of hope or comfort. I filed the report
Required for all encounters of this sort,
And then I went to bed myself, but vowed
That I would speak as soon as time allowed
With Sergeant Weatherby, before staff meeting
Carried us off to matters far more fleeting.
I'd copied Weatherby on my report:
It was his job. Let's keep the process short.
But then, of course, I thought that first I must
Create a record that the matter was discussed.

I'd raise it in the meeting and then say
That staff should follow up the normal way.

And so, that's what I did. To my surprise
The three squad leaders present rolled their eyes.
We sat in the command post at a table.
The little conference room was scarcely able
To give up space for Weatherby and me
And random gear, much less the other three.
I knew Staff Sergeant Pound, and he had brought,
A woman, Corporal Billings, who had taught
Half the platoon to drill, and then, as well
Another sergeant, name of Ben Odell,
Pleasant, big and blond, but also new,
And more than likely not to have a view.
He'd transferred to my unit from the 4th Platoon,
But could as well have transferred from the moon,
For headquarters had still not sent his file.
The three of them stayed mute for quite a while.
I had to wait them out, and though I glared,
The NCOs sat 'round about and stared.

The room was hot and stuffy as a tank.
Wherever these guys hung, surroundings stank
Of canvas and cigars, but now a whiff
Of sickly sweetness added to the sniff,
Somewhat like urinals in the latrine—
The smell of porcelain we had to clean

In boot camp. I scanned the room until I found
The B-Squad sergeant, Jeremiah Pound,
Lounging against the wall and chewing gum
As if he'd ride it into Kingdom Come.
Could chewing something make that awful smell,
Or was it aftershave from him or Ben Odell?

"Sergeant!" I cried, "Unhinge your jaw.
"Chewing that loud should be against the law."
So Sergeant Pound put fingers in his mouth,
Took out the wad and almost tossed it south
Down to the floor, but caught himself in time.
"Yes, ma'am," he snarked, "I'm sorry for my crime."
"OK," I told him. "So, now back to work—
"And Sergeant Pound, shitcan the smirk—
"Tell me about this Lopez, who is she?
Pound sneered and then he shrugged elaborately.
"Attention-seeking. That's her strongest suit.
"She needs another ninety days of boot,
"Or she'll wash out of here, it's guaranteed.
"Let Corporal Billings tell you what you need."

Billings was a hard-faced woman who
Could stare the shiny polish off a shoe.
She croaked, "The odds she makes it? One to ten:
"Don't get on with the others, if they're men.
"The other day she almost went stark mad.
"Some slick sleeve in the captain's office had
"Made passes at her. I'd-a just up and decked him:
"Lopez tried to make us all suspect him
"Of attempted stalking." "She has issues,"
I agreed. Pound said, "Then buy her tissues.
"Sorry, Ma'am, I think that she's unsuitable."
I looked at Weatherby—he was inscrutable,
Hunched at the table, playing with a pen,
Twirling the thing across his fingers, then
Tapping its top down on a paper stack.
"We don't want made-up charges coming back,
"Let's see the little sweetheart gets some rest."
"Sergeant," I protested, "She's depressed.

"It's real important not to patronize!
"Let's do this by the book." His hooded eyes
Said, "This is stupid!" but his mouth expressed
The promise that he'd honor my request.

My day was busy, but that afternoon
I walked to company headquarters and soon
Was entering the captain's door,
Though not to see the captain. There was more
That I could learn from talking to the staff,
Who handled routine chores on his behalf.
A dozen aides were working in a space
Too small to hide a fondle or embrace.
I saw one file clerk who looked qualified
To be the one that Lopez said had tried
To steal her virtue. He was a looker,
But, unless perception quite forsook her,
She could not think he tried harassment here
With oh-so-many witnesses so near.
We had a chat, this well-made man and I,
Till I discovered that he was so shy,
He blushed and dropped his eyes when I was hot
And took my jacket off. No, he was not
A predator, but who else could it be?
Back at the platoon, I tried to see
The sergeant, but he was not there. I checked
The log he kept and, as I would expect,
He had a meeting with some new recruits.
I left a note: "Talk Lopez? When it suits."

I did not hear from him till after dark,
And even then I couldn't strike a spark.
"So what has happened with her, Sergeant Weatherby?
"You followed up with her?" "Well no, not me.

"I asked First Sergeant Pound to take that on."
"Pound!" I exclaimed. I heard a stifled yawn.
"Well, look," said Weatherby, "he's her superior.
"Chain-of-command says clearly I'm inferior
"To his responsibility. If I
"Would interfere, I'd harm his rank and my
"Own reputation. Lieutenant, Pound's on first!"
I said, "I hear you, but I fear the worst:
"Is there a log of what she's doing now?
"Or does it matter to you anyhow?"
He volleyed back, "With all respect, of course..."
"Well, I'm responsible," I said, "the source
"Of your own responsibility. You understand?"
"It's not about you or me but chain of command."
"OK, I'll track it down," he said, "Then you
"Will realize you've done all you can do."

In fifteen minutes he called back and said:
"I tracked down Sergeant Pound. He went ahead
"And gave her leave to go off-duty when
"She wanted to, as long as she checked in."
There was a pause. "He passed the job to Billings."
I felt nerve-endings throb, like foil on fillings.
"But she's got conflicts. So he passed the ball
"To Ben Odell." "Whom we don't know at all!"
I said. He checked his log, "She's on the rifle range.
"She took a night scope. Seems a little strange,
"But may be par for this particular course."
"She ought to have been watched," I said, with force.
"It's disappointing that we're all so slack:
"Is she a danger? Someone who might crack
"And harm our own, or someone we don't know?"
(Like a suspected clipping-mailing beau,
I thought.) "OK, I'm going out to get her."
"Wait! I'll go," said Weatherby. "I'm better-

"Suited for this kind of . . ." I clicked off
Before I could reprimand or maybe scoff.

A half hour later at the range no threat
Was visible as I crept along to get
To where the final bunker stood. No lights
Inside or out. No rifle shots for sure. No signs of life.
For all I knew, she trained her scope on me,
A juicy piece of walk-on targetry.
The tension made me home in like a shark,
Attuned to every ripple of the dark.
But with the sense of some vague fear dispersed
So finely through the shadows that they cursed
A silent oath of possibility.
Darkness will give you bats' ears finally.
Creeping silently into the inky black
And up the hill that rode the bunker's back,
And past a pisser window, sweet and sour.
I heard thin gasps of crying without power
To shriek its fear, and then a creepy voice.

"Girly-girl," it trilled. "This is your choice.
"Put down the gun. Who needs that anyway?
"I will protect you. Hold you. Let us play."
That seemed to amuse it, "Let us play!" it laughed.
"L-leave me alone!" her voice a candle in a draft.
"Naw-w-w. I think it's Karma, little thing,
"You can't escape your destiny—its wedding ring
"Is on your finger. When my friend Bobby Joe
"Took that wild ride with you, you didn't know
"That was rehearsal for our here and now.
"Under the light of stars, we'll dig and plow
"And plant our seed and then we'll leave the field
"To nature, till one day you are revealed,

"A goddess lying on a couch of dew.
"You'll be discovered! It is your debut.
"Fortune will never let you go. You'll be
"A public icon through eternity."
There was a rustle as her body slid
Through brush, a warning click as rifle bid
It stop. "You'll want to put the rifle down.
"I loaded blanks while you were on the town.
"Just drop it, girly-girl, and take my hand
"So I can take you to the promised land."

I was atop the bunker now, and there
I saw two shadows: one seemed unaware
Of just how close the other was to her.
But I could name that shadow now. The myrrh
I'd thought had come from a latrine
Was unmistakable. The scent was keen,
The same aroma I had smelled,
While NCOs told less than they withheld.
"Sergeant Odell!" I yelled. "Move! Step away!
"Now! If you want to live another day."
The bigger shadow quickly bent and grabbed.
"Give me that gun!" it hissed, and had it nabbed
The weapon I'd not be here saying this,
I'd be endlessly adrift in the Abyss.
But Private Lopez suddenly resisted.
She came alive, she kicked and jerked and twisted
The gun, and I yelled, "Get off her I'll shoot!
"And I won't miss. On three, two . . . don't be cute."
I crouched to jump. In fact, I was not armed.
The bluff I had to run was charmed,
For, when I threw a rock and broke his nose,
He wavered till I caught him by the clothes

And threw him to the ground, where he lay still.
Until I checked the one he tried to kill.
Then he was up and scrabbling through the brush.

I ran to the young woman in a rush
And held her tight, and spoke some soothing things
And wrapped her in my jacket against swings
Of temperature and chills brought on by shock.
We stood there for a moment, taking stock.
Behind us, on the field we saw twin lights—
Weatherby coming to put it all to rights.

He sent MPs to look for Ben Odell,
Wrapped Lopez in more towels, then gave me hell.
"Why did you do this? You could have gotten killed!"
But I was tired, not ready to be grilled.
"Sergeant," I murmured, "all of us can fight.
"All of us will give our lives for right.
"If you had cared a bit for this poor wretch
"You'd not have shown an hour late to kvetch."
"You had the information that I had, yet you
"Prejudged the situation through and through.
"And had it been some guy who was both fit
"And inexperienced, likely to be hit
"On by some nice-looking, seductive guy,
"You'd start the Inquisition, or you'd try.
"Listen," I said. "I'm confident in you.
"You are experienced, brave, and true.
"I feel you are a friend, which causes me
"No end of worry when we disagree.
"But I think you have both the judgment and
"The perspicacity to understand
"That dealing fairly with these new recruits
"Sometimes takes running shoes instead of boots.

"We all are products of enlightenment,
"Which some of us accept and some resent.
"But I would say this troubled kid—this 'she,'
"Is still entitled to the equity
"And process that we furnish to the men.
"We know this as gospel, but in practice when
"The soldier is a woman; we are all
"Both male and female, very apt to stall.
"What that does is cause us to avoid
"Engaging with the female troops employed
"To keep our country safe. No overkill
"Or special treatment but, for good or ill,
"We treat our charges fairly and no more.
"They have to learn what they enlisted for."

Weatherby listened, to my great surprise,
Saluted and cracked a grin, and I'd advise
No one to underestimate the love
That soldiers have, when push has come to shove,
For their profession and esprit de corps.
This is the love that gets us through a war.
When I was raised to captain, Weatherby
Was foremost as an advocate for me.

16

The Business Lawyer's Tale

The business lawyer was on deck. He made
Some fuss because he was not being paid.
He claimed attorney-client privilege,
Was needed just to keep a civil edge.
Professional advice might be delayed
If there was not a chance of being paid.
The cruise director was not having any—
He spoke of oral contract and how many
People did not take to legal lore
Or know a pleading from a plesiosaur.
But after adulation and attention
And grave assurances he need not mention
Any secret data he might know,
He strutted to the front, as if on show
And gave this talk—of course, on how he rose
To prominence, striking a courtroom pose:

Many a year has gone by since the crash
Of 'eighty-seven, when folks ran for cash

And left stocks on the floor for me to buy.
At bargain basement prices, by-the-by,
I was a fledgling lawyer then, but knew
That although market panic might hurt *you*,
If your investment strategy was unsound,
Because I kept my ear close to the ground,
That could spell opportunity for *me*.
I had these contacts on the street, you see,
Old school friends mostly, clubmates, sidekicks, such
As care to keep old wealthy friends in touch

Most academic things I learned I soon forgot.
Compared to friends I made, they weren't worth squat.
No one rises to the tops of trees
By majoring in so-called humanities.
Extracurricular courses in "Connections,"
"Private Wealth" and "Social Intersections,"
Were worth more than a thousand normal classes
To keep us apt and different from the masses.
Summer visits to each other's houses
Produced liaisons that turned into spouses.
When after graduation contacts slowed,
Alumni rosters were the motherlode
Of business referrals. Letters of support,
Flew like the arrows around Agincourt.
And I was not self-conscious when I wrote
Encomia on behalf of some dumb scrote,
Who might attribute his success to me,
If not out loud, at least internally.
To gain a happy life of realized dreams,
Squeezing each dollar till the eagle screams
Is not the avenue. You've got to know
The people and events that make wealth grow

And cultivate them, as you learned in school.
Send birthday greetings, keep them in your pool
Of sources. Join a well-heeled legal firm
And give your time to mammon for a term,
Or join the government in some position
That leaves you with insight and, in addition,
Yields contacts that will translate into fees.
Take either path, you'll pave your way with ease.
Once you have established your own shop
With your name on the letterhead, don't stop

Telling your friends you did it all for them,
To help them gain, and wear the diadem
Rich people make from assets they acquire.
You'll be their favorite legal gun for hire,
And each transaction that you conjure up,
Will mean a smorgasbord in fees. Hup! Hup!

Of course, a number of these ventures won't
Succeed—you'll help acquire some firms that don't,
Or cutting-edge securities that fail
Because they're based on values that entail
A seamless modeling based on belief
Their own assumptions cannot come to grief.
They'll swamp the purchasers with information,
Technical terms whose object is sedation,
Detailing every risk that might appear,
Disclosing even that such risks are near,
But all in terms no one can read without
Advanced degrees in calculus and clout
Gained from probabilities and when
The azure sky eventually falls in,
A few years down the road stockholders find
Despite the obligations left behind
There is no smidgeon of an asset there
For the invested vultures to pick bare.
In Zeno's paradox, as you go half
The total distance every time, they'll laugh
At how you'll never reach your goal.
But that's the secret of this little stroll
Through high finance. Proceed by lesser steps
As you approach diminishing returns.
No one can object to twists and turns!

I don't apologize for funds I take
From random dolts whose lives are a mistake.
I have no sympathy for those who fail
To use God's gifts and therefore land in jail.
I am successful. That's been my desire,
And, as I'm growing older, I aspire
To nothing more than showing I am right
To profit from those folk whose skulls are tight.
You'll think me arrogant, but you may go
And screw yourselves. I'm not the least bit slow
To castigate you for your humbleness.
And that is now the end of my address.

He smoothed his camel jacket and sat down.
Every listener now wore a frown
Save one—the sly-eyed, bushy-bearded lender.
Either his colleague's candor made him tender
Thanks that he'd have a spotlight of his own
Or, watching how the other's pride had grown
He thought the attorney's drop-jaw pride-montage
Would offer his own sins some camouflage.
At any rate, he ambled to the fore
And without introduction took the floor.

17

The Private Lender's Tale

Were I a king, I'd have this flag unfurled:
"Here stands the Darwin of the start-up world."
Young ego-sick time-wasters come to me
Seeking my imprimatur, for no fee,
On their half-baked and valueless ideas.
They've hypnotized some friends and family
And now they have moved along to wheedling me!
The ultimate irony is that I'm called
An "angel investor." I am appalled.
One angel is the messenger of Death.
So while I talk to folks, I hold my breath
And close my eyelids as I analyze
Whether their braincase seems a proper size.
If so, would their small business last two years
Or ebb away, borne on investors' tears?
Ninety-five percent who spin a tale
Of riches and success are doomed to fail.

But here's how I do justice—with a Midas touch.
I lend them money—I suppose, not much,
But heavily secured against default,
A black-and-white contractual gestalt
Of doom. When they come back to me for more,
I send them empty-handed from my door.
"You say you needed money and no bank
"Will lend to you? That means your credit stank!
"Repay my loan with default interest or
"I'll nail a writ of attachment to your door."
And so they learn the lesson, "Don't dive in
Unless you know the depth"; and don't begin
A process that you lack the wit to finish,
Or you will see your livelihood diminish.

I earn a decent living from this trade
And you are quite naive if you're dismayed.
Go visit poultry farms or livestock pens
To watch the calves and lambkins meet their ends.
I do no greater wrong than farmers do.
We cull our herds; we harvest what we grew.
Efficiency is one thing we've contributed.
The bottom line is: earnings are distributed
Among the capable, adept, and smart.
I am that system's servant. Call me pagan,
If you wish, or some financial "Fagan"
Preying on youngsters. I don't give a hoot.
Attempt to bully me with threats of suit,
I merely laugh. I have a lawyer on retainer
Who makes winning cases a no-brainer—
Totally as vicious as sure-handed,
She's never hooked a case she hasn't landed.
I've brought her in and haven't paid a dime,
It doesn't even take her that much time.

But what if they exceed all expectation,
Hit all their targets and escape purgation.
If they survive somehow to tell the tale,
They'll just be swallowed by some corporate whale
That files their products, gripes it overspent.
And if they bargain for the management
Of their old business, they are soon forced out,
For lacking smarts and hustle, say. No doubt,
Next, they'll haunt the halls of companies
Known to hire folks approaching on their knees
And if that works, they end their lives as minions
Fearful to voice their ideas and opinions.
It's all a waste of time and management.
Far better to pull the weed before you've spent
Scarce capital, good will and inside power
Trying to make it grow into a flower.

You see, the country's changing, running out
Of wealth and capital and using up the clout
It wielded once to pacify the world.
Could the US do that now? Past leaders hurled
All prudence out the window, to expend
Remaining assets for no better end
Than holding onto power. First, they'd borrow;
Then put off accounting till tomorrow,
Giving their President a second term,

Whether he's an ass or pachyderm!
We have lived through decades of such perfidy.
The business world's response to piracy.
Is to build far taller ships to dominate—
Snap up competitors and grow so great
That rivalry is nipped off in the bud
And money circulates inside of them like blood.

Then, as Leviathan, the slightest motion of tail
Will send their rivals under. These are whales,
Remember, and consumers are their plankton.
Small business rivals, if they have yanked on
A sales lead in Leviathan's domain, will be
Reduced to shredded protein in the sea.

That's just to say, when taking all with all,
You'll find no innovation by the small.
Start-up firms, my clientele, are stiffed
In the market soon, they're fish food set adrift

For some behemoth to suck idly in,
Shaking the bloody remnants from its chin.
So, Darwinism we can disavow:
Survival of the fattest is the watchword now.
To understand, just look at what we are:
Eight billion fireflies trapped inside a jar,
All lacking purpose, comity, and joy.
Is there some stratagem we should employ
To find ways out of our collective fate?
Well, if there is, we'll think of it too late
To get us anywhere. Say you're savants,
What would you list as your essential wants?
Full bellies, entertainment, and no cares?
To synthesize our food, stage sports affairs,
And maybe bet on them while out carousing.
Offer free health care, subsidize cheap housing!
Wait! You're doing some of that; what more
Can you do to make this nation soar
As high as its antecedents? Here's my spin—
The how-to books say that you'll never win,
If you accept the facts. So turn a page.
Why not adapt our genomes to this age!

We form our products in a common mold;
Parts are assembled after they've been sold.
The buyer gets a less expensive chair;
The maker saves the cost and wear and tear.
So we put modularity in brands.
Some products are untouched by human hands,
Stamped by machinery from a softwood stock
And covered in a hair-thin, hardwood frock.
This modularity alone will seal our fate.
If all's the same, why bother to be great?
Your jobs and livelihoods will fail one day

There'll be no opportunity for pay.
So while you can, your function is to buy
The things that are for sale. If you or I
Do not do our self-effacing parts
By loading up our personal shopping carts,
The whole of our frail commerce will collapse.
But buy online the slightest thing, perhaps
Something that you won't need and soon will trash,
The trackers will be on you in a flash.
A few at first, then squadrons, and then scads
Tagging you for a plethora of ads,
When money's earned in bits and paid in bytes,
Who will bother about privacy rights?

Long since, all individuals have become
Commodities of commerce for some.
You now must think of something else to do
Reclaim the pursuit of happiness from the few.
Technology, you know, is here to stay.
It rules our lives, no matter what we say.
Despite our will, it follows its own laws.
So we must find a way to clip its claws.
Let's take the next step. Let's compete!
Let's bulletproof our lifestyles, to defeat
This social and commercial anarchy,
Use pseudoscientific mastery
To minimize the death-grip of "the Some."
Already, work in health care has become,
A hyper-costly anodyne for woes.
No longer must we take off all our clothes
For physical exams. A vial of blood
Unlocks the secrets of our hardihood.
Monthly we block inherited diseases,
Fooling with genes until each sickness eases.

Discoveries are made most everyday,
As we manipulate our human clay.

So why not use this new ability
To lend our species more agility
Through genomes we revise. It's bound to take
Some time to redirect the current stake
Of corporations toward the common good.
Could we not invent some brotherhood
Of equals saving money and esteem?
Women could then attain their ardent dream
Of shapeliness; their husbands would be
Muscular and tall. Wives would look warmly
On their mesomorphic spouses. Think
How often partners can create a stink
Not just because we leave some things undone,
Because we fail to pick up cues and run
To carry out their wishes and demands.
Let's get spousal relations off our hands.
Let ladies flounce their fashionable plumes
Without concern about shop fitting rooms
And alterations. Men could all play sports
Quite unconcerned at how they look in shorts.

My point is this. If we're no longer needed
In business matters, can it be conceded
Salvation lies in efforts close at hand
Which could restore our mastery of the land?
The possibility is there, if we will use
The science of genetics to infuse
Our weary selves with cellular renewal,
Passing new chances on by family jewel.
I have a little offering, for just
A favored few investors, and there must

Be several of you here who qualify,
To get in at the ground floor. You can buy
A front seat at the metamorphosis
Of human life. Test this hypothesis—
We cannot stop the world's disintegration,
Or the commandeering of our nation
Or our own contraptions run amok.
But still there's one recourse that doesn't suck.
The path lies in the special shares I'm selling to
My dearest friends, and no more than a few.
Believe me, I don't sell them willingly
To people who have funds but no esprit.
I want them to be bought by special friends
Who comprehend my means and like my ends.

I will not sell to those I don't respect
Or those with whom my mind does not connect.
I'm tired of supporting people's dreams
And buying into other people's schemes.
I'm not a proud man, but I draw the line
At people who pretend they're friends of mine,
Or intimates who want the things I've got,
My three apartments or perhaps my yacht,
Rather than wanting me to be their friend.
True loneliness is what you've purchased in the end.
I had to pay my wife an extra fee
To climb into the marriage bed with me.
I gave her trips abroad and lavish meals
All financed by my seed-investment deals.
But when she went off of our balcony,
Her final flight was totally for free.

18

The Pilot's Tale

"I am an aircraft pilot," said the man
Who took the rostrum next under the plan
Worked out among reluctant people who
Had hoped to skip their places in the queue.
We were still frozen with the shock
Of our last speaker's casuistic talk
About his role in finance and his wife,
Who obviously jumped to take her life.
Having a pilot next in line was shivery,
After gravitational delivery.
The pilot cleared his voice and pulled the knot
Of a tie no longer there. And then he caught
His voice and said: I'll tell you why,
Although a pilot, I don't choose to fly.
The turning point was a charter flight.
The memories still keep me up at night.
I'd known Lewinski for a dozen years.
He was an OK guy after some beers,
And not so bad dead sober, though he'd stay
Less often in that state, I have to say.

Lewinski was the short straw you would pray
You'd never draw. And yet, it seemed
No matter how his fellow pilots steamed
And put in bad reviews he still remained
A pilot, with his résumé unstained.
His aunt, a vicious woman, short and stout,
Still led the charter company. Her clout
Explains Lewinski's almost bomb-proof path—
Also the lack of any aftermath.

He looked the pilot with his aviator shades,
His slicked-back hair and 2X shoulder blades.
His expertise in aircraft was superb.
Defective instruments did not disturb
His calm assessment of the airplane's needs.
The office talk was full of daring deeds
Lewinski performed in adverse circumstances—
Gossip like that promotes a person's chances.
In spite of that, he was co-piloting.
No senior friend would take him under-wing.
So let's admit it—he was really odd.
He practiced magic and, I swear to God,
Would come aboard with dozens of new tricks
To entertain the flight crew, just for kicks
But most of the staff he flew with thought,
His conduct puerile. The strictest sought
To have him grounded, claiming he'd no care
For all the people he dragged through thin air
Holding their lives at ransom. Surely, he
Should take his in-flight duties seriously?
At last, I have to say, he only flew
On flights with crews who liked him. They were few.
I later learned most would not let him use
The bathroom in the galley, lest he choose
To stage a "show" and render travelers dumb.
He'd done it and caused pandemonium.
And so I had him frequently beside me,
Piloting my aircraft, woe betide me.

Most of his repertoire was quite routine,
But he was a ventriloquist. I mean,
He worked at it: I watched him overtax
The shoddy dummies he'd named Sal and Max.

His vision was a Punch and Judy show,
But his falsetto grated and his lips were slow.
Still, he was born a carney barker, and
If carnivals were still alive, his brand
Of prestidigitation would be cause
For gasps of wonder, followed by applause.
But he was here instead, and so was I,
Speeding aloft, five miles into the sky.
My charter from Duluth to Montreal
Was full of tradesmen lit by alcohol,
Getting in shape for Mardi Gras carousing.
I glanced at Lewinski, who was drowsing.
"OK," I said. "The autopilot's on;
"The weather's great. Let's see some tricks."
He brought out decks of cards and did a mix

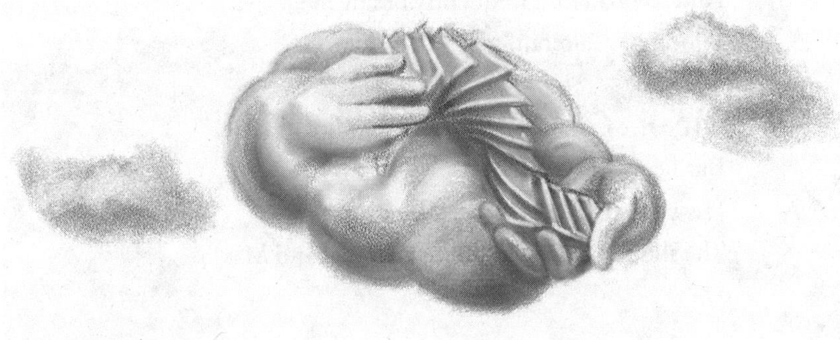

Of coin illusions and, as an afterthought
Produced a magic rope that wouldn't knot.
The most entangled snarl that you could tie
Would always pull apart at the first try.

I was quite stunned. But then my awe and doubt,
Took backseat when he pulled a pillbox out
And popped two capsules, swallowing them dry.
"Prescription," said he, daring me to pry.

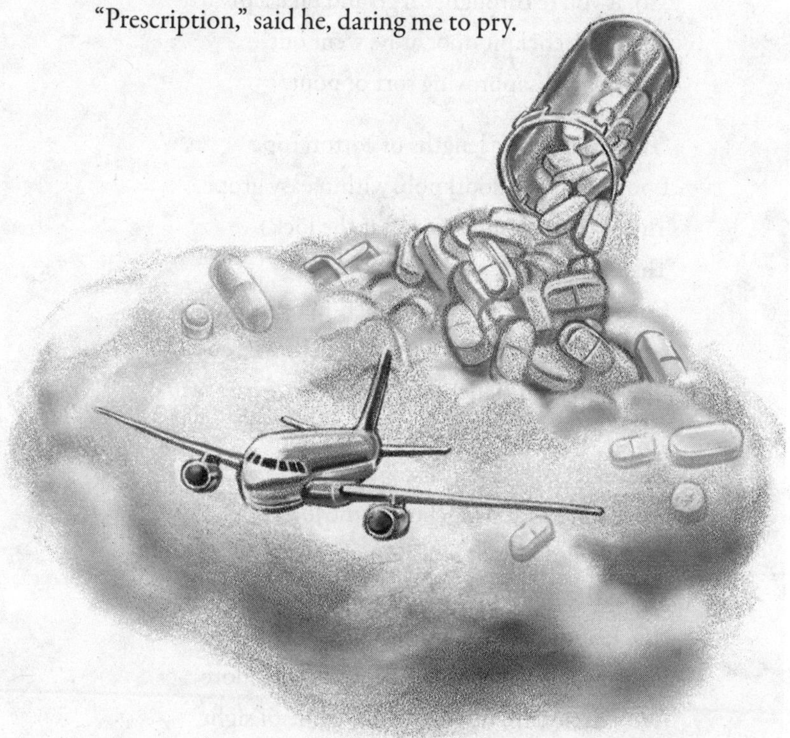

"What for?" I asked. "It's nothing bad I hope."
He yawned and stretched and finally said, "Nope,
"It's something that I need to stay aware."
He put the pillbox back beside his chair.
"That's good, then! But you ought to tell me why
"You need it now. We're five miles in the sky."
He looked upset; he did not want to say.
"I have to ask," I said, "You know the way

"They've been since 9/11." His response?
"'Mostly just jangled nerves." This nonchalance
Was not what I needed: "Well, then, what's it for?"
"It's so that, if I nap, I will not snore."
"Why would you nap while piloting a plane?"
"I wouldn't," he said, "so, I won't explain.
"You're violating HIPAA asking this!
"So, if you're through, I'll go and take a piss."
I held the cockpit door as he went out
Wearing a disapproving sort of pout.

We had some lengths of cotton rope
Looped on the doorknob, within easy grope.
This was our system to defeat the locks
That, after 9/11, were a pox
On anyone who lost the punch-in code
And put the cockpit door in shut-down mode.
The door would lock until perdition froze
And you grew cauliflower from your nose.
That safety system was scant comfort to
A person headed quickly for the loo.
So we would hitch one loop of cotton rope
Onto the flight attendants' coat rack, slope
The length of cord down to the cockpit door
And 'round the handle. Seven years or more
We'd done this, just beyond the line of sight
Of passengers. Lewinski made his tight
Exit out of the little toilet room;
He elbowed my ribs, in humor, I assume.
As I pushed past and said, "My turn, I hope!"
"OK," he muttered, and he looped the rope
Back to the doorhandle as he went inside,
Lingering to make sure it was well tied.
I sat on the toilet, with my nerves becalmed
Until I cracked the bottle I had palmed

From where he'd put it down beside his chair
And read the little label that was there:
"*Pitolisant?*" I mouthed, "take with Tagamet
"At the first sign of paralysis or threat
"Of narcolepsis". *Oh my god!* I rose
Straight up like Dracula, tucked in my clothes,
And burst from the lavatory like a bomb.

Apart from me, the scene outside was calm
The cabin lights were dimmed; most were asleep
Or drowsing now. In something like a leap
I gained the cockpit door, and there I found
The little length of rope down on the ground.
He'd tied it with his magic rope, I guessed.
He'd think of all his tricks this was the best.
The door was shut tight. I declined to beat
Against it with my head and fists and feet,
But said, "Lewinski! Open up the door!"
I plied my ear and thought I heard a snore.
"Lewinski!" I shouted, loud enough to wake
The first three rows of passengers and make
A few of them sit up and stare with fright.
"Don't worry," I assured them, "It's all right.
"This is an exercise we're made to do
"To test the cabin's safety. We'll be through
"In just a bit." And then I saw the fear
That flickered in their eyes. "Lewinski, dear!"
I cooed. "This will be fine," I said, "you'll see."
I grinned at them quite unconvincingly.
"You're very loud," one lady blurted out.
"Can't you see we're sleeping?" "Without doubt,
"Madame! But it's the price we have to pay
"To make sure we are right with TSA!"
That did not seem to satisfy, or even soothe.
I'd have to come up quick with something smooth.

I had an idea. "Oh, Lewinsky," I called out.
"It's time for a show. There is a talent scout
"On board, who wants to see and hear
"The great Lewinski." I was in deep fear,
Of course, of no reply. Keep calm, keep calm!

Then came some crackles on the intercom.
"*They want a show?*" The high-pitched voice of Sal
Broke through the silence. "*Is this for our morale?*
"We've been living in a bag for years.
"So now you want us to believe our ears?
"You recognize us, eh? I doubt it, chumps."
Then Max broke in. "*This is the dumps!*
"Let's split this scene. We'll take this plane
"To Broadway or to Vegas! Drink champagne,
"Take these stiffs to Iowa. That's their style.
"Someone will scrape them up, after a while."
"*Hee-hee-hee-hee!*" came Sal's psychotic shriek.
"How high should we drop 'em from this week?

I looked over the cabin: every neck was craned;
Every eye showed panic; every voice was strained.
Faces were blanched, some had half-risen in fear.
All clearly thought the end of days was near.
Something must be done, before things blew.
"They're only puppets," I said lamely, "glue
"And sticks and cloth, part of a magic act!"
"We're being flown by puppets?" someone quacked.
"Here's my idea," I said, "but I need you
"To work with me on this. Here's what to do."
I spoke to them quite calmly, and, to my surprise,
They did not answer back or roll their eyes.
Upon my signal, they began to squall:
"Bravo, bravo, Now take a curtain call!"

Applause rang out, and voices yelled "Encore!"
And to my joy, out of the cockpit door
The puppet heads appeared and took a bow,
And then the puppeteer, oblivious somehow.
They came next to me for more applause.
I reached out and grabbed with hands like jaws,
Smiled at the audience as I dragged him back
Into the cockpit, scarce could forbear to whack
Him as I sat him in his pilot's seat.
"Consider your time with me to be complete!
"I honestly," screamed I, "Cannot begin
"To say how badly I feel taken in
"By your shenanigans!" But as I stared
Into his eyes I was still unprepared
To see them roll up in their sockets and
Shut down. So until we could land,
I used a roll of duct tape to restrain
Him, should he come awake. But now, his brain
Was on vacation till, in Montreal
We left him with the magistrate on call.

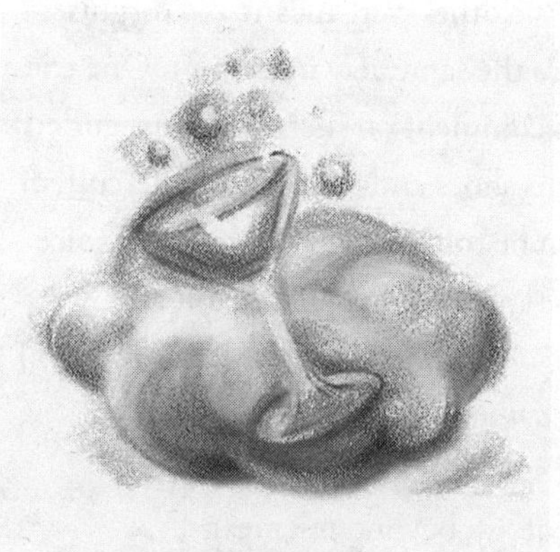

19

The Social Worker's Tale

I had not known quite what to make
Of our next storyteller. Through the ache
Of elder members on the downward slide
With more gray hairs than dye could ever hide,
This man shone forth as in the peak of health,
Although his fortune did not run to wealth,
Unless his clothes were meant as a disguise.
They were the same, day in day out. One tries
Never to comment on such things as scuffed
Old tennis shoes and pantlegs raddle-cuffed.
But when he told his tale, we saw his choice
Of modesty in manner and in voice.

I have an undergraduate degree
In social studies and philosophy;
Also theology, beyond my means,
But none of it proved worth a hill of beans.

Pythagoras once jotted in a scroll,
Beans are the only plant to have a soul.
Dissect a random bean and you will know
Its fatty seed leaves hold an embryo
That early scientists concluded was
A transmigrated soul that had the blahs.
But did this status help the little bean
Or gladden its brief time upon the scene?
No, not at all. The poor legume was shunned—
An instant "has-bean"—hobbled by a fund
Of superstitious drivel that its "soul"
Was actually the essence of a troll
Or something worse. They threw the beans away
Or kept them till the feral holiday
When all the starving spirits of the dead
That rise to feed on human souls, instead
Could sniff out all the beans throughout the night
And feed on them until the morning light.

Beans were the college students of those days,
With like trajectories in many ways.
Their cheerful résumés foretold a lot;
But still their destiny remained: a pot.
Most doors of opportunity are locked;
No one responds, however hard you've knocked,
Unless you've got some pull or privileged class,
(Meaning you'll never have to bust your ass).
But all's not lost. The gig economy
Creates new jobs for every wannabe.
If you have the gumption needed, and can drive,
You can deliver pizza till age sixty-five,
And any doctor of humanities
Can get a job, down on his aging knees,
Scraping a living out of clogged-up drains,
Alongside those who've never used their brains.

I was a social worker, minoring in Psych,
Well trained in wellness, guidance, and the like
But I, too, found no opportunities.
Employers thought my graduate degrees
Were much too fancy just for social work.
Awards and honors simply seemed to irk
Prospective bosses. They were looking for
A person they could train and underpay,
Then terminate before promotion day;
A licensed person who would certify
Deficiencies in treatment without asking why.
After some interviews, I was so stunned
That I was ready to demand refund
Of my tuition, fees, and costs of school
That fit me out to be a corporate tool.

I am retired now, and finally
I do the type of work (although for free)
I hoped to make a living from when young.
I've opened storefront clinics, and among
The services I provide is counseling,
And eldercare and help with forms. The thing
That galls me is it took me forty years
To pay school loans and interest in arrears.
The best work I could find was for the state,
Inspecting nursing homes—a modest fate,
But one that did not make me grovel or
Assist the rich in troubling the poor.
Pure chance was really all that got me hired.
It seems a health inspector'd just retired.
He'd worn a badge of sorts and had to tote
A gun concealed beneath his overcoat.
They made me take a class in self-defense
And pistol-training, though that made no sense.

I was bemused by their concern for me.
Just where in eldercare could danger be?
Eventually, I found my predecessor had
Been shot by a backwoods patient gone quite mad.
Meanwhile, I learned hallucination-calming
And every end-of-life skill but embalming.

When that was done, I found I simply sat
Around and waited to be called to bat.
My biggest task was helping answer phones.
Along with all the other office drones.

Most of the calls were health-insurance gripes,
Complaints about dry sanitary wipes,
Or other issues equally outside
The purview of my agency. I tried
At first to guide them to another place,
But they would call back with a new sad case.
On some days, my acrylic telephone
Sat silent; but on others, was a chaperone,
Connecting me with those who dropped a dime
To gain someone's attention for a time.
Since I was young, I felt I'd been ensnared
To give folks fantasies that someone cared.
As for duties, I read gray reports
From nursing homes and eldercare resorts
Submitted, as required, to the state.
This made me love my telephone. My plate
Was filled with helpings of long rosters that
An actuary could engorge in nothing flat,
But made my eyesight blur and temples ache,
My shoulders twitch, my upset stomach quake.
While, on phone duty, I'd relax my brain,
Pretending I was fishing in light rain—
I'd feel the bait, I'd let the line go slack,
Then stand there free until a bite came back.
Most bites were small, but every now and then,
You'd feel the line twitch from the gliding fin
Of some great hunter moving past unseen,
Daring you to let it cause a scene.

One morning, as I check incoming calls
From overnight, a frantic message falls
Upon my ears. A woman, drunk and sad,
Hinting at mayhem, slurring words like mad,
Ending with: "You're not there, so, silly me.
"Silly to even try this! Yes sirree!

"Cleaning up this mess requires a call
"To people far more powerful than y'all.
"So, why would I leave messages for you?
"I'm sure you got important things to do. . ."
And then there was a pause; I heard some ice
Fall down her glass, not once, but twice:
"They're murdering old folks—for the cash, okay?
"But you won't ever catch 'em. There's no way."
[*Click!*] The message ended and the line went dead,
Leaving a crowd of echoes in my head.
There were so many crackpots who would call
And gabble till they drove you up the wall.
It did not help that almost all of these
Were people isolated by disease
Or ostracized, perhaps, because they "weren't
Quite right." But when they had been burnt
By hostile neighbors or by families,
They'd call and call as if you held the keys
To Safety, Peace, and Justice. But this call
Was different. She made no offer to tell all,
She did not ask the agency to ring her back.
She sounded drunk and scared, but stayed on track.

It happened my probation time was up
In one more month. From being just a pup
I'd then transform into a full-grown hound,
With my own kennel in the office pound.
But I'd been told my one deficiency
Was field experience—an irony
For an inspector, but that kind of work
Was given to senior staffers by the clerk.
I'd been told that, if I wished to be
More than the filler of a vacancy,
More than someone seen as second-string,
I'd need to show initiative and bring

A case into the office on my own.
I had a caller ID on my phone.
We found the number easily, and then
Our tech supplied the rest. "Mae Beth LeGuin"
Worked for a private care facility
Called "God's Last Trumpet." I could plainly see
From the files that she had worked there many years,
As their controller—sunk up to her ears,
I'd bet, in all their recordkeeping work,
Keeping the financials clear of murk.

The next day, I was visiting her house,
Which proved to be a mansion for a mouse—
A threadbare bungalow—and when I knocked
I feared it was abandoned, seized, and locked.
It took three minutes for a latch to turn.
Then through the crack, and chain, I could discern
A tiny woman, hesitant and frail
Confused at a visit from an unknown male.
I showed her my credentials, but those seemed
To make her close the door—I thought she screamed
But it was a tiny sound, I was unsure.
And so, I wheedled through the cracked front door,
That I was just responding to her call
To me the night before, and that was all.
At length, the entrance door swung open wide,
My sleeve was grabbed, and I was tugged inside.
"Did anybody see you?" gasped my host,
Her back against the door, pale as a ghost.
"Like whom?" I managed. She did not reply.
"Is someone watching you?" I asked. "But why?"
She shook her head, looked down, then took my hand
And led me to a couch whose life had spanned
More than my own short time on earth, I thought;
I sat and heard its springs become distraught.

She perched on a stool and would not look at me
As if she'd lit there momentarily
And soon would wing again into the air,
It took awhile to feel a welcome there.
We chitchatted an hour, till she relaxed
Enough to take me through her set of facts.
But then, the bony sofa and the fug
Of ancient, curtained muslin, threadbare rug,
Slipped from my senses, as I heard a tale
Whose lightest word would make your courage fail.

God's Last Trumpet was a nursing home.
If you were to take a fine-tooth comb
To the surrounding woodlands, looking for
A place more sweetly set, you'd be footsore,
But empty-handed. Here were gentle porches
Lined with rockers, and ensconced gas torches
Chasing the evening shadows from the stairs.
The sheer lace curtains gathered in long pairs,
Floated on threads as frail as ladies' lashes,
Softening the rows of muntined window sashes.
Inside there were paneled sitting rooms,
End tables, porcelain vases, fragrant blooms,
Plush sofas, tall and firm enough in seat
To help you hoist your mother to her feet.
I let her reminisce and smile through tears.
She'd worked for God's Last Trumpet thirteen years,
Mostly for the owner, Harold Dove,
Who'd given it his fortune and his love.
He'd built it for his mother, whom a stroke
Had turned from someone who would smile and joke
At any hardship that might come her way
Into a waxwork, prematurely gray.
She was so frail, requiring constant care,
And he so skeptical of places where

She'd be beyond his sight, should ills occur
He'd be nearby the home he built for her.
And ran it like a genteel small hotel.
A Black man, Mr. Dove admitted whites as well.
No one who visited this lovely place
Was unaffected by its quiet grace.
You'd sit down on a sofa with your mom,
And whisper to her, through the evening calm,
Of Heaven and the merit of the elderly,
Who no doubt felt as close as they could be
To Paradise until they passed for good.
The paneled walls were finest cherry wood,
Exquisite inlays laced the hardwood floors.
But no one saw beyond the inner doors.

Two years ago, the nursing home was bought
By some opaque financial juggernaut,
Which had the means to offer so much cash
That any further bargaining seemed rash.
Within a week or two, the deal was done,
To the perplexity of almost everyone.
The new proprietors addressed them all
Over the intercom out in the hall,
Changes were in the works, they told the staff,
To cut unnecessary costs by half.
Swiftly, the long-time staff were canned
And those remaining brought to understand
That now strict confidentiality
agreements must be signed immediately.
The staff were told how much the reputation
Of the Home would suffer from false information
Released by someone who, to feed a grudge,
Might bring the enterprise before a judge
Who might impose huge penalties.
Considering the liabilities

For breaching patient privacy and such.
That did not scare the staffers overmuch.
The nondisclosures threatened huge expense
For anyone accused of the offense
Of telling people what went on at work.
As time went on, this drove the staff berserk.
Nurses and aides resigned and were replaced
With some less qualified. So then, she traced
The résumés of one or two and failed
To find the training that the job entailed.

This bothered her, and she began to look
At all the revenues she had to book,
And worried about what she should infer
From what short timers many patients were.
Many seemed only to reside three weeks
Before they lost all color in their cheeks
And disappeared from sight. Some trance,
She thought, had broken. Now she looked askance
At things she'd treated as a bit off-track:
A crematorium installed out back,
Part of the Home's new promise of full service;
Files kept under lock and key; how nervous
Managers became when she inquired
If someone was discharged or had expired.
"Where have these patients gone?" she asked a nurse
Who made her lips into a little purse
And pushed on by. So our Mae Beth LeGuin,
Even with the state her nerves were in,
Began to search through records on the sly
Whenever someone left some files nearby.
She noticed that the clientele were older—
Irrelevant until she found a folder
Full of deeds by which the elderly
Had transferred title to their property

To pay for their continuing care. The name
Of the broker who took charge of that whole game
Looked so familiar; in a moment she was sure:
She'd found and secreted a fund brochure,
And there he was, right on the partners list:
She looked them up. A gerontologist,
Named Bentrix, sent his patients to the Home;
An undertaker, who turned flesh to loam;
A lawyer, of course "Yes, he is always there
"Sniffing around," she said. "He's lost that hair."
She obviously was amused at that; then frowned:

"The board has five directors, but I found
"No record of the fifth one, who's the chair."
She'd looked for information most everywhere,
But in the process, she had tripped some wired
Alarms set out for snoops. So it transpired
Before she finished this important quest
She had a visit from a suspect guest—
The lawyer aforementioned, who dropped by
Her office at the Home to tell her why
Her job would be abolished in a week.
Before she even had a chance to speak
He plopped the severance papers on the desk,
And, just to show he'd earned the suffix "Esq.,"
He stopped at the door and said, "I'd sign,
"If I were you. The company, by design,
"Is turning over staff. It needs new blood."
He tried a smile on, but it was a dud,
Unnatural as crocodilian tears.
"In recognition of your many years
"We will continue for a while to contract you,
To keep books from your residence, in lieu
Of coming to the office. Take a day
To think about it and to sign the NDA!"

My head was in a whirl. I said, "So long,
Be careful." Then I hugged her, which was wrong.
I got permission to unleash a squad
Of agents who investigated fraud.
I won't bore you with everything they found,
But they ran each and every clue to ground.
It seems that no incoming sick survived
More than a fortnight after they arrived.
No one on staff showed curiosity
Patients accepted had few family,
Poor health. No one was surprised they died.
The doctor who referred them certified
The deaths as "in due course." The Home released
Instructions, duly signed by the deceased,
That they should be cremated, their remains
Scattered through the woodlands and the lanes
Where they had found such peace. The lawyer then
Would take his word processor and his pen
And sell decedents' real estate forthwith,
So quickly chain of title was a myth
Obscured by time and transfer, and the fund
Kept everyone well compensated. Stunned
By the intricacy of each twist and turn,
We got an exhumation order for an urn
That had been buried in the early days
Before the plot's refinement of its ways
And found the urn contained large cuts of beef,
Burnt, of course, to cinders. No relief
To weary sleuths would be provided by
Matched DNA or other ways to tie
The crimes to God's Last Trumpet, and much less
To owners of the fund. In great distress
I drove to town to see Mae Beth LeGuin,
Whom I'd begun to think of as my kin.

Her little house was quiet—no one there,
The porch unswept. I went next door, to where
Some lawn-strewn children's toys said neighbors were
And found a woman nursing a liqueur.
She told me that an ambulance had come
And taken Miss LeGuin to her new home.
Why, I asked, and who? She hit her head,
The EMTs and orderlies had said

They'd told the neighbor. For her loyalty,
They'd take her in and care for her for free.
"Who?" I exclaimed. "Who told you this?"
"A Dr. Bentrix from the Home!" How'd I miss
The danger that was now the centerpiece
Of all that had gone wrong? The state police
Responded when I called, and then I rang
My office, as I drove, and my harangue
Produced some pledges of a quick response.
But, as I feared, the words hid nonchalance.
When I arrived out at the Home no one was there
From law enforcement, and I saw nowhere
The members of my team. So I went in
And flashed my county badge. A knowing grin
Spread through the faces of the burly staff
That lined up in a human epitaph
Across the inner doors. I showed my gun.
And then a suited, balding man said, "Son,
"You're in a heap of trouble. There's no need
"To make it worse. Before you have to plead
"To felonies, let's try to work this out."
I said, "I want to know beyond a doubt
That my friend Miss LeGuin's OK."
"Oh, if that's all," he said, "then come this way."

He pushed a switch. The inner doors swung out.
Beyond stretched rows of tiny rooms—about
A hundred meters long, a catacombs
Of doors on each side paired like chromosomes,
And fifteen doorways down, I found my friend,
Sedated, but still conscious. To extend
Her custody one minute more than needed
Was reprehensible. So they conceded,
The lawyer and orderlies soon left.
My friend weighed only ninety pounds, by heft,

So in a chair she went, and I commenced
To roll her through the swinging doors and thence,
Out to my car. Once we were in, I swore
That I was done with "homes" forevermore.
I did not know how very true that was.
Back at the office, circumspect applause
Broke out when I walked in, and for a while
I told and retold the story with a smile
To toasts of office coffee and weak tea.
Mae Beth was with her next-door neighbor. She
Was still a little groggy, but at least
No longer was "on deck" to be deceased.

Next morning, when I'd taken off my coat
And checked my gun, I found a note
On my desk. The commissioner, it seems,
Sought to commend me. In my wildest dreams
I never conceived the highest brass would be
By any way or means aware of me.
When I arrived, up in the "Penthouse Suite,"
As we described it down on Hard Knock Street,
The secretary took me right away
Into the Inner Sanctum. "Just don't stay,"
She whispered, "You're only shoehorned in.
"He doesn't have much time to wag the chin."
Behind a massive desk a shriveled man
Was signing things. His features were so tan,
It looked as if the sun had baked his youth
Away. Or maybe vodka and vermouth.
He paused and looked at me with hooded eyes—
Scanning me up and down, as if to memorize:
"Are you the one who opened up a file
"On that old nursing home? It's been awhile
"Since we found anything that they'd done wrong."
"Yes, sir," I answered, moving things along.

I explained that it was not the place
Itself, but management that brought disgrace,
By treating patients as mere inventory—
Processed products of a made-up story.
I was going on to real estate,
When he held up a hand. "You may be great,"
He said, "at what you do, but you are fired!
"And we are sorry you were ever hired."

I did not take it in at first. The shock
Was so intense that I could not take stock
Of what he said, much less the reasons why.
"You pulled a gun, just like some crazy guy,
"On healthcare workers. You harassed
"The nursing staff and went on to miscast
"The owners of the Home as evil monsters,
"Though they all are large and frequent sponsors
"Of charities and local churches. And
"There's one more thing that you should understand:
"One of those monsters is the local mayor,
"My baby-sister's son. You have no prayer
"Of slandering that boy without a stretch
"In jail!" I felt his words hit home and etch
The message on my soul. The missing owner.
That is who he had to be. "A loner,"
He went on, "I took time to check you out.
"That's what you are, beyond a single doubt.
"No friends, no family that we've divined.
"So after this you will be jailed and fined.

A box with all my things was at the door
As I walked out and off the "penthouse" floor.
A squad car followed me as I drove from the lot
And out of town. As soon as I was not

Still in its beat, the cop car turned its nose,
So I went back to pick up all my clothes,
Then headed north to find some part-time work
And thank my stars no one had gone berserk
When they discovered I had smoked their game.
And I received a bonus all the same:
Mae Beth LeGuin would come along with me
To find a new existence, willingly.
She helped me open up my storefront clinic.
I think you'd have to be a total cynic
To deny how much she was adored
By all who sought our help and were restored.

20

The Charity Queen's Tale

The Queen of Charity stood up to speak
Although we had not seen her for a week
Since she'd huffed off, affronted by a tale
She found offensive coming from a male.
The cruise director had not scheduled her,
But he knew when to challenge or defer.
So when she said she'd talk of climate change,
He was so glad to cut and rearrange
The schedule and to let her highness sweep
Up to the front. Her dogs lay in a heap
Around her feet as she began to talk
While eyeing our reactions like a hawk.

I'm Chair of an environmental trust—
The Fjord Foundation. You're nonplussed?
Not heard of it? You're not alone! I hired
Some Wall Street weasels who had just retired
To overhaul the place and plot its course
Then I took over and canned all things Norse.

My hires brought dough and knew where to get more.
The first thing that we did was show the door
To all the staff, who'd thought their mission was
Saving small Nordic inlets in the cause
Of cleanliness. Well, I suppose that's nice
For donors with a tolerance for ice.
But crypto-walrus lovers, faux-Laplanders
Never would drink the Brandy Alexanders
That I pour down the folks who write fat checks
As soon as they can slither on their specs.
No. As the heir of oilmen, I know well
That serious money wants to hear the bell
Ring loud when they have given cash to me;
That means, you gotta have publicity
In media that can give your vision class.
That means your mission must be clear as glass
And popular beyond imagining.
Environmental warming's just the thing!
Over the last five years, we've redefined
The Fjord Foundation's mission and designed
A cause that brings us, every single year,
More money than the old outfit would clear
In fifty or one hundred years perhaps.
I won't say that it fell into our laps.
We entertained until we could not view
An hors d'oeuvre plate without the urge to spew.
But in the end, the climate's served us well:
Survival's such an easy thing to sell.

Let others whom the Fjord Foundation pays
Advise how everyone should mend their ways.
I just throw parties for my wealthy friends
And give them status that will serve their ends.
I've found that the progenitors of folks
Who sit on fortunes once gave righteous pokes

Right to the eyes of others who competed,
Blinding them perhaps; or simply cheated,
Robbed the public, or did other things
To make the hair curl. Pulling a few strings
I can provide respectability
Through seats on a benevolent facility;
Provide the atmosphere to get them placed
Within the very Pantheon of taste
Ruled by the top class of society.
Just furnish a few badges of propriety,
And history will be forgiving men
And women who will, every now and then,
Stop walking to peruse a donor's name
On some exalted monument to fame
May honor them with a familial smile
Or even stop to wonder for a while
Just who they were; what made their hearts so large?
Such pride of place gives swindlers a charge.

So, you may ask, what do I get from this,
Aside from obligations not to miss
Conventions, summits, interviews, and such?
Well, people are grateful, and I have the touch.
My efforts do some good, and there are perks:
E.g., my residence near Dallas works
As a control for our experiments
On residential energy and hence
I keep the air-conditioning on high
In summer, and I pour the oil on by and by
When temperatures get cold. My dark green lawn
Each day gets watered deeply before dawn
And makes the sprinklers sing from spring to frost.
That gives us certain basis for the cost
Of turning or not turning on the hose.
We are transparent: everybody knows

About the house, from state officials to
Progressive folks who otherwise might stew
Over the waste. But since it's all for science
We have no problems with the Green Alliance.
And no one worries that I drive a Rolls
That comes out at the bottom of the polls
For energy efficiency. We show
All types of waste that people ought to know.
And pay the state an ad valorem tax
For excess carbon: then the climate nuts relax.

And although beef's my favorite meat, I care
So much about the world I eat mine rare.

I also don't much use my jet, but go
By train or boat like this. Though travel's slow.
Climate activists cannot connect the dots
Specifically to us. It ties them all in knots.
As they consider how to understand
The impact of emergencies on hand:
My helicopter on the upper deck
Is poised to waft me from this bottleneck.
So I am going to take a nap. I hope
I've shown you lots of ways that you can cope.

21

The Teacher's Tale

That evening before dinner, we all sat,
And went back over tales and chewed the fat.
I have to say that we were not amused
To find ourselves on such an endless cruise,
With virus waiting to destroy us all
At every single dock and point of call.
We worried that stories still untold
Would be short because excitement had grown cold,
Or maybe our contest took a larger place
In our imaginations than we'd face,
As each of us conceived we'd messed up badly.
I was not to present a tale as, sadly,
The director needed me to keep these notes.
In part to clarify disputed votes.
That gentleman himself had not arrived
So we discussed whose stories seemed contrived.
Would people do the things the General said?
Attack alone and fight till they fell dead?
The lawyer, who had drunk a lot of beer,
Since lunch, deemed such men ignorant of fear.

He thought the General's story was all true.
The teacher quietly expressed her view:
All people are afraid, but tame their fright
If they are representing truth and right.

"Pooh!" said the lawyer. "How would you know fear?
"You've never had a terrorist appear
"To bomb your schoolhouse or just do you in!"
The teacher gave him back a modest grin.
She said, "Men think all danger is overt.
"They picture watchful troops on high alert;
"But women and children know how quietly
"The worst abominations come to be.
"They're social and political, I'd note.
"Folks smile as they put hands around your throat."
Our host walked in to witness this debate,
And chimed in, "Why don't you elaborate!
"We all would like to know what teachers say
"About the dangers lurking in our way."
With that, I thought he smirked at other men,
As if to say, "We'll hear some nonsense from this hen."
The cruise director came and took a chair.
He quieted us with one inclusive stare
And nodded to the teacher to begin,
As if assuring her he'd listen in.
The teacher blushed, but then she stood right up.
Swirling the tepid coffee in her cup,
Tossing it off quite briskly, she began:
My tale is of a teacher. Let's just call her Ann.
For thirty-seven years the lady taught
Fourth grade, in time whole families, and brought
Enlightenment to children—parents, too.
Some teachers think fourth grade's a witch's brew,
A trial of wills, pre-hormone rodeo,
Each boy a potential Romeo,

Each little girl a femme fatale in précis,
Wearing clothes too meager or too lacy.
But this good teacher never looked at clothes,
She only saw young people in the throes
Of growing up. She tried to make the grade
More of a challenge than an escapade.

Last year, she tried to teach a boy named Charlie
Who had two mood-states: petulant and snarly.
Also, he was small and prone to tears.
When he was teased, his funny little ears
Turned crimson as ripe cherries in a bowl.
He'd stand stock still as comments took their toll;
Then suddenly lash out when it was more
Than he could take. His classmates all kept score
Of who was best at making Charlie blurt
High shrieks of rage. They'd wager their dessert
On whether he would cuss, or sit and cry,
Or, even better, lunge at them and try
To scratch their eyes out, like a feral cat.
They loved it when he'd go and act like that.
In the middle of one pitched conniption
The teacher thought she needed a prescription—
A beta-blocker or some sedative
To make her headaches less repetitive.

Recess was over, kids were coming in.
Echoing off the cinderblock, their din
Almost obscured the sound of one thin wail.
She saw the troubled Charlie in mid-flail,
At bay among a hunting pack of boys,
Whose jeering added volume to the noise.
She couldn't stand it; entering the fray
And pushing antic juveniles away

She swept their target up and held him tight.
"Don't fret," she said, "they're far more bark than bite!"
Though Charlie still was growling like a beast,
Beneath his tears, she had him safe, at least.
But as she carried him away from harm,
To her astonishment, he bit her arm.
It was a savage bite, that clove the skin.
Then as she put him down, he kicked her shin.
She was not elderly, but still things bled
Through fingers as she gripped her arm and said,
"WHY?" The proper question, as they faced each other.
Over the sobs he tried so hard to smother,
He spoke, and what she thought she heard was sad:
"*Not* a boy! A LION! Ask my dad!"

Then, when the school's staff nurse had come and gone,
And warned her not to try to carry on
Without some disinfectant—stitches, too—
She sat and pondered what she ought to do.
The wound was bleeding freely, and she thought
This should have been a no-no that she taught:
Biting was something animals might do:
But not true human beings like me or you.
A substitute, Ms. Switch, who took no sass,
Came running at her call to take the class.
It had been rumored (none could prove a thing)
That Switch was not inclined to nurturing;
She grabbed unruly students by the hair.
The teacher walked five blocks to urgent care,
Pressing brown towels from the ladies' room
Hard on her arm, watching them quickly bloom.
They took her right away. The doctor said,
Once a tourniquet turned off the red,
The bite was deep and likely to turn septic.
Who was the child and was he epileptic?

No matter, he said, we'll sink a stitch or two
And dress the wound, said you'll be good as new,
But keep it covered so it doesn't scar.
(It did so anyway, and near and far,
Forever after, that arm bore a brand—
A large, segmented "U" that never tanned.)

The visit cost her two weeks' pay, or more.
She took the stitches out herself, therefore.
The principal was told of the event
But quickly made it clear the boy meant
No harm. He'd just been in a schoolyard fight;
And wasn't it lucky that he was all right.
(No mention of the deep bite on her arm;
It seems that was no reason for alarm.)
He did say children here were scions of
Top politicians and the constant love
Those parents learned to show this school should be,
Our guiding light. Unconscious of hyperbole,
He said that they'd put students' families first,
And since Ann proved she could survive the worst
Behavior that her little kids could brew.
He felt secure that she was of his view.

Later, with Charles's parents on the phone,
She mentioned his bite had almost reached the bone.
Mom was alarmed, but quite calm underneath.
She wished to know if he had hurt his teeth.
The father only asked what she had done
To cause such wild behavior in his son.
"He says that he's a lion," Ann remarked.
"Because you told him so." Her comment sparked
The angriest response she'd ever heard.
"You're making this my fault, you whirlybird?"
"No, not at all," she said. "I'm only quoting him;
"He's quite upset." She probed her aching limb.
"I've called to let you know the things he claimed.
"In no way was he saying that he blamed
"His parents. He was trying to be brave.
"By roaring like a lion in his cave."

The father spoke, "I told him to be a lion.
"Not a pantywaist. He shouldn't buy in
"To that bully crap. So what if he gets licked.
"He'll be a man, not some St. Benedict."
"No, he will be a boy," the teacher said,
Wishing the man could see her shake her head.

"They pick on him, you see, because he's small
"And sensitive. I thought you'd take this call
"To hear what happened, then come pick him up.
"We've given him a hug, a cookie, and a cup
"Of orange juice. We try, but he needs you."

The mother came back on. "I have a meeting,"
Over her husband's roar: "He needs a beating,
"Not a cookie. Coddling gets us nowhere.
"Too bad I'm out of town and can't get there."
Then to his wife, he asked "What's this appointment
"That you can't miss? Massage with herbal ointment?
"Perhaps it would be your mani-pedi-cure?"
"Fay's made the time for me," she sniffed. "You boor—
"Did you forget about that black tie function?"
The conversation now had reached some junction
The only sound she heard was heavy breathing.
She could just sit and listen to them seething.
Sensing they'd reached some verbal cul-de-sac,
She said a bus would take young Charlie back.

That would have been her last encounter but
Blind Fate would deal her one more savage cut.
Our "culture wars," in the vernacular,
Were raising storms of dust spectacular.
They made of former friends new foes,
As polarized as thick Antarctic floes.
Race and religion, politics and tribe
Were blared about, making a jarring vibe.
Loud as they were, the clashes failed to reach
The little classroom where Ann loved to teach.
Until one day a flyer went around
Reporting on school board races, and she found
That, after a long and mighty bitter fight,
Some newcomers, by some electoral sleight,

Had taken over every school-board seat,
Dealing the old board a profound defeat.

The new group cut some corners as they went,
But there were no incumbents to dissent.
In truth, these new folk were a zealous lot
Who claimed the former board was full of rot.
They'd clean it out and make sure social themes
Consisted only of nostalgic dreams:
Patriotism, firm belief in God,
Pilgrims living high on beans and cod.
No Indians, of course, except for kicks—
In this account, those meekly took their licks;
Stir in some gentle slaves for novelty,
Well cared for by their masters, then set free
To be Americans. . . Eyes misted over,
History became a field of clover.
George Washington again became a saint,
Uniquely lovable and boldly quaint,
Who, were it not for chopping cherry trees,
Would never spend a moment on his knees.
Though all of this surprised her, she was floored
To learn that Charlie's parents led the board.
She felt she should have done something to stop
That troubled pair from coming out on top.
But it was done, and they did not forget
Their sweet child's sassy teacher, on a bet.
Word got around. The hallway gossip said
Her days were numbered; her career was dead.
In fact, she quickly was removed from teaching,
The reason for discharge was "overreaching."

She sat back down and left us all distressed
Except the lawyer. It must be confessed

He would not lend a sympathetic ear
To anyone who had not hired him. Here
Was a teacher telling a sad tale that smelt
Of liberal fantasy. Though deeply felt,
It still had a pluck of heartstrings at its core:
"What you speak of," said he, "we deplore.
"But the new school board's message was not wrong.
"She should have learned to listen, get along,
"And she'd still have that job. She'd be OK,
"She'd live maybe to fight another day."
The teacher thought this through and then replied:
"I am not learned, and I don't reside
"Among the tabernacles of the great
"Or disregard the problems I relate.
"But I do know the things of which I speak,
"And also know this tale is not unique.
"Parents should teach their children self-control,
"Which they will need in life. That's not the role
"Of schools or teachers. We should reinforce
"The values that will keep the kids on course.
"That means we open eyes to issues that,
"If come upon too late will knock them flat."

"Dream on!" the lawyer said. "There is no chance—
"You might as well try teaching pigs to dance.
"Kids these days have other things to do
"Like spraying paint or getting a tattoo.
"Simplifying history's not so bad.
"They'll get the gist. That's more than they have had.
"And more important, they will feel allowed
"To venerate their country and be proud."
The teacher answered: "With all due respect.
"Pure certainty without the intellect
"Is far more apt to poison than to heal."
"More claptrap!" said the lawyer. "How we feel

"About our history's the only thing
"That keeps this country safe without a king."
The teacher smiled. "I'm sure you'd volunteer
"To wear the crown. Look, what we feel is fear.
"Fear of other races, fear of change.
"Caution is good, but fear will rearrange
"Your very values and your sense of place.
"What's more important, hearts and minds or race?
"If you conceal our real past, bad and good,
"You're just avoiding being understood.
"Children can always recognize a fable
"Even one served up at the dinner table."

"*OK, that's it!*" The lawyer pushed away
His chair so hard it squealed. "I'd stay,
"To be indoctrinated, but I'd rather
"Go and have a drink and ditch this blather.
"Since our 'fables' give me liberty
"To choose my own companions, don't you see?
"So I will go and take a tot of rum.
"I'm buying, anyone who wants to come."
The teacher smiled, although she must have known
The lawyer hoped we'd leave her there alone.
A few left with him that I'd thought would stay.
The preacher, for example, with his way
Of hating social issues. I'd give odds
He'd stay and rant. But he served other gods
Tonight, including Eros, I suspect,
And as he left I saw I was correct.
His friend the lobbyist was on his arm
Talking and walking with animated charm
In the direction of the lobby bar
Which, luckily for them, was not too far.

But I went over, as the others rose
And took the teacher's hand. "Nobody knows,"
I said, "What bravery it takes to teach.
To risk rejection, to be told you preach!
To take on children and their parents, too.
So I'm left wondering if your 'Ann' is you."
She stared at me with her appraising eyes
That barely managed to conceal surprise.
And then she slowly raised one sleeve.
There was the scar that a child's small teeth would leave.
"So, Charlie brought his father's gun to school
"And was caught waving it, the little fool.
"He was suspended," she said, "not expelled.
"It had no bullets. Still, his parents yelled.
She gently smiled a moment. "I should go."
I watched her leave and felt an afterglow.

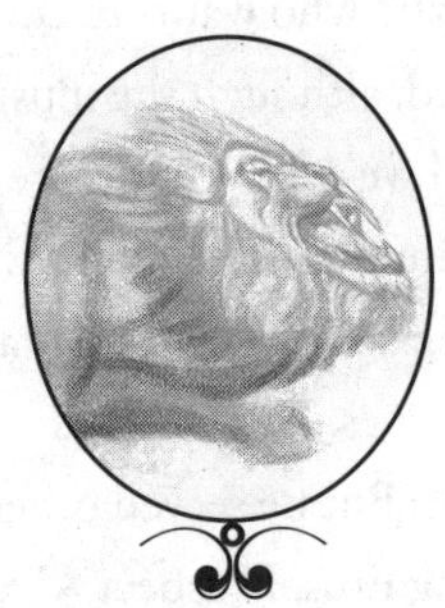

22

The Lobbyist's Tale

The lobbyist was next, we all agreed
And she seemed satisfied to meet the need.
She told us of her life in Washington
And why her role was lucrative and fun:

As junior senator from my home state.
I didn't know much, but my style was great
Among the corndogs, chili bowls, and dills:
I learned to dodge, but lacked survival skills.
So my election sparked a free-for-all
Among the well-dressed people in the hall
Who lined up just to get to speak to me,
I know now they were lobbyists, you see.
They cast an appraising eye when they came in,
Was I rich or poor or fat or thin?
Canny or naive? Suburban or
Should I write "rustic" on my outer door.
My staff—were they experienced or green
As I was? It was quite a scene.
I kept my mouth shut, lest I might reveal
How little I understood of every spiel.

I did not know what "cloture" was, in fact,
Nor, if it came to that, "bill" versus "act."
At least I'd learned that statutes did not stand
In parks or halls. Back in the hinterland,
My mentor, Alva Riley, said that she
Would fly with me to Washington, D.C.
And serve as pro-tempore chief of staff
To save me from the unintended gaffe.
She had been head of the party in our state
And intimately knew the good and great.
She dealt with press requests that struck me dumb.
In fact, she was the sole perennial mum
I'd met outside of garden catalogs
Or in the buttonholes of pedagogues.
But life ordains that nothing good can stay
And as I grew in strength, she slipped away.
I cannot blame her. Washington, D.C.
Will change the person that you thought you'd be.

The person she recruited for her job
Looked just like an enforcer for the Mob
And come to that, he acted that way, too.
A telephone receiver stuck like glue
Between his double-chin and rumpled shirt.
Because his conversations ranged from curt
To clipped, he must have talked to half the Hill.
His desktop, full of papers, bore a spill
Of ancient stew and countless coffee rings.
But he knew several hundred hidden things
About the delegation from each state.
And he had promised Alva to relate
To me the way that I should learn to think
About this world to save me from a shrink.
Angelo, my chief, rose to his name
Bought me a beer and then explained the game:

"You are a public servant. That's your life,
"To work in a place where treachery is rife,
"In service of the folks who sent you here.
"Despite their votes, you'll find that not a tear
"Is shed for you if you should somehow fail
"In health or reputation. They will rail
"And they will blame you, even if, at worst,
"Your sin was to put the country's interests first."

"*The people are a fickle* master, who
"Will, oh so quickly, pass the buck to you
"They will not understand reality—
"That you're one fish in this vast legal sea;
"They won't take time to learn the pros and cons
"Of policy. Your messages get yawns.

"But promises of better times result
"In raucous rallies that may catapult
"A lesser person up the lines to claim
"The title 'Honorable' before her name.
"I bet you think you've got six years to see
"If this place suits you, and you want to be
"Here for a dozen years, or for eighteen;
"You won't have time to sit around and preen.
"Right now is when you have to start to raise
"Your reelection funds. So who will pay
"To re-elect a freshman anyway?
"Well, that's where all those lobbyists come in.
"You drop a hint, I'll teach you how to spin
"In person and by phone. You'll need to lay
"Up sixty-thousand dollars every day
"Toward your campaign for reelection to
"Your current job. I have a list of who
"To call tomorrow, starting around five.
"Each day you'll need two hours to survive
"The fresh young face that's bound to challenge you.
"In six years' time when you're no longer new."
"But wait!" I cried. "They said I'd have to raise
"Some campaign funds, but not on all the days
"I stay in office!" Then my chief of staff
Looked long and hard at me, then gave a laugh.
"You may decide," he said, "you'd rather throw
"Your race than lose the honest self you know.
"If you decide this place is not for you,
"Don't wait too long to act upon that cue.
"I'll tell you what can happen when someone
"Lingers too long after their work is done.

"*D.C. is like* a garden full of flowers:
"Voluptuous, but toxic. It empowers

"A person who chooses it as their career
"To flit from flower to flower within its sphere.
"But two things happen as the time goes by:
"You grow old, and lose out to some younger guy
"With half of your experience, but a link
"To some important donor. Just a wink
"And nod, and suddenly you're out.
"Each year brings tyros round about
"Looking for jobs with power or something near it,
"Bringing connections and a youthful spirit.
"Many will fail after they stay awhile,
"Worn out and disillusioned by the guile
"Their seniors will deploy to keep their posts.
"They head back to their parents on the coasts.
"But plenty still get jobs, with greater pay
"And young ambition fueling their way.
"Second, the denizens of D.C. find
"The search for power has poisoned their mind.
"For they for many years have sipped so eagerly
"At toxic flowers and powers and meagerly
"Tried antidotes, that they cannot go home.
"The skills they've learned are all unique to Rome.
"They can't get jobs except as lobbyists
"And find they lack the know-how that exists
"In business, where they're looked on with disdain.
"And so they end as ghosts that drag their chain
"Of dwindling contacts till most links are worn.
"They die ignored; for Washington will mourn
"Only the famous mighty whose demise
"Leaves room for the nonentities to rise."

I stayed a member of the Senate till
My dossier swelled to bursting with each skill
A member could attain. Then I resigned.
I'd been there five years, wined and dined

By every industry that I could see
Might one day have a subcontract for me.
I'm very rich, but drinking from the stream
Of money that flows uphill like a dream
Does not disturb my sleep or make me sad.
I don't feel guilty or the least bit bad.
Could what I do be called immoral? Sure,
But so was what I tried to do before.
At that, the thick-skinned lobbyist sat down
And just ignored the group's collective frown.

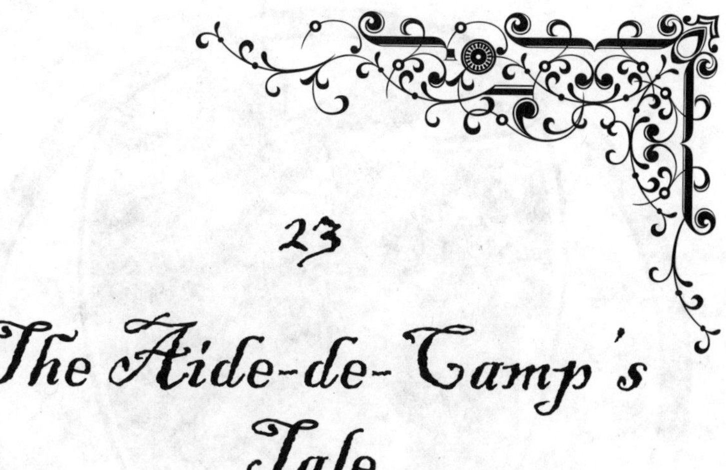

23

The Aide-de-Camp's Tale

At last the General's aide-de-camp stood up
He acted like he wished this bitter cup
Could pass him by. He was a modest man
Who did not like attention—often ran
From it, in fact. But he was also brave
And conscious of how soldiers should behave
Both in and out of uniform. He spoke
When spoken to and blew no smoke:

I have been a general's aide-de-camp
For many years. To some, that is a stamp
Of low ambition and poor self-esteem.
I beg to differ. Working for the cream
Of military service, the elite,
Is less subservience and more a feat
Of acrobatics. People of high rank
Aren't gods, but still as thick-skinned as a tank.

Entrusted with responsibility
That most of us will never have to see,
To that extent, they're very much alone.
It is a duty they must solely own.
As I recount this story, think of me
Not as a great man's gopher or a flea,
But as protector of a scarce resource—
Good leadership. You understand, of course,
I've served with only two men in this role.
I found the first, much higher ranked, a prole—
A cushion for brass pins. The second, though,
Was one who's never sought to be the fizz
On the champagne, the ooh-la-la,
The figure on the float at Mardi Gras.

I've been the squire of this amazing knight,
And followed him through every hopeless fight.
I've been respected, never bent the knee,
But I've been part of him and he of me.

Parse "loyalty" and you will understand
Not to reject my service out-of-hand.
Loyalty has fostered our worst acts,
The kind historic monuments and plaques
Are all too often fashioned to conceal.
If loyalty is unrepentant zeal
To carry out the misdeeds of the great
And gild in myth the crimes they perpetrate,
Then I want none of it, nor would my boss.
What is the safeguard to protect from loss
The honor that you've taken to be true?
Loyalty's no simple bond, like glue.
It gets its strength by stretching to surround
Each individual within the bugle's sound
But also what they carry deep within—
The knowledge that all humankind are kin,
And mercy, truth, and fairness are on call,
Not owned by anyone, but shared by all.
A loyal general will understand
Half-truths are not a part of his command,
And he would not insist his aide pursue
Deeds he could never bring himself to do.

My first assignment as an aide-de-camp
Was to a brigadier well up the ramp
To stardom in defense intelligence.
Which did not mean that he had common sense.
This General courted celebrity
Within the covert ranks, sat at the knee

Of great and near great, and his rise was fast.
His influence on the chiefs of staff was vast.
In fact, he was a relative of one.
But after everything was said and done,
He was the perfect cypher—hard to know,
But wise about which way the wind might blow.
Diplomats and chiefs of foreign corps,
New heads of state or old were little more
Than opportunities, and my main job
Was standing at the shoulder of this nob
In my dress uniform—an epaulette,
But functional and no collegial threat.
And so, attentive to his beck and call,
Made indispensable by acting small,
I learned the job and felt he valued me.

There was a conference on energy,
Held at a hotel that had lost its own.
This monumental lodging now had thrown
Its lot in with big corporate hosts like this.
The venue's tatty opulence brought bliss
To those who longed again for eighty-nine
When Berlin lost its wall and all was fine.
Now whispering oil men, waiting in the wings,
Hinted at new reserves and seismic pings,
While lobbyist-lawyers and geologists
Checked faces against photos on their lists
As VIPs moved though the human lake,
Drawing their aides like dinghies in their wake.

The president himself was there, and so
Fit, spooky guys were everywhere you'd go,
Lean men in long, light-tan overcoats,
Inches of coiled wire sprouting at their throats.

One of them checked off names and held out keys,
Bearing the General's name, and "Socrates."
"Who's this?" "That's you. A code name. You must rate."
The General called: "C'mon, you'll make us late!"
"Who's Socrates?" I asked him through the throng.
"Some random Greek," he said. "Now move along."

The ballroom was an otherworldly scene:
A crowd engaged in one collective preen.
Among the crowd of men in shiny suits,
Belts with enormous buckles, snakeskin boots
Were women driven by rivalry to wear
Formal dresses that they thought had flair,
But ended with a look that lay between
Coquettish and a little bit obscene.
The General pushed me like a riot shield
In front of him, forcing other guests to yield,
As if it were five hundred against two.
But just at the elevator quite a few
New weapons salesmen caught him unawares.
So I took both his suitcases upstairs,
Relieved by the elevator's closing doors
That cut the hubbub. I got off on floors
That once had been reserved for plutocrats,
But now were let to ordinary cats
Who could flash bottomless expense accounts
And pay quite inexcusable amounts
For rooms with a tad of grandeur; not that they
Would get a better sleep for that outlay.

The General's room was spacious, grandly set
With antique-furniture-not-antique-yet.
His clothes hung nicely in a chifforobe,
And after I was done, you'd have to probe

At length to find an object out of place.
He'll love it, I thought. *There is not a trace*
Of things to fuss about. I took his key,
And left to find the room where I would be,
Hoping it would not be too far away:
I would be getting up all night, I'd say,
From what I knew about the pains he took
To feel attended on. I took a look:
The key for "Socrates" led to a room
Just at the hallway's end, so I could zoom
Right to his side at any time of day.
He'd laid on me a verbal dossier
To execute tomorrow without fail.
And what did this imperative entail?
Well, going to the kitchen before dawn
To see that breakfast with his guest was on.
It was his plan to break bread with the mayor
Of this great city, so they must prepare
The eggs exactly as each liked them done.
Each had a different preference. What fun!
The breakfast was at six, so he could speak
At Conference Opening, then get a peek
In at the president, whose jet took off
At ten. I have to say, I had to scoff,
Internally at least, while saying yes,
For clearly he considered me as less
An aide-de-camp than personal valet.
But then I reckoned with my soul. I'd say
I bucked up and retired my personal self
From the equation. Was I ready for the shelf
With other burnt-out servicemen? God, no!
So if the General said go, I'd promptly go.
With that, I slid the key of "Socrates"
Into the latch, and opened it with ease.

As it swung in, I saw an awesome sight:
A suite of rooms whose spaciousness and height
Spoke of a grandeur passed away for eons
Last seen when great estates were built by peons:
Gilded, cross-vaulted ceilings, and a bed
That should have hosted Louis Quatorze instead;
Piled carpeting that gently laved your feet:
Palatial bathrooms, wet bars—a huge suite!
And just inside the door, there sat a cart
Bedecked with flowers, on which, composed with art,
A range of delicacies sat, heaped tall—
Caviar and chocolates, pâtés and cheese,
And oysters on the half-shell, if you please,
Fresh as if brought in by the latest tide,
Sitting on ice, with condiments beside.
Leaning on the vase of flowers I saw
A card, such nice calligraphy, my awe
And dread were multiplied one hundred-fold.
"Welcome, General! We have been told
"That you are fond of small delights, so we
"Are pleased to offer this miscellany
"Of delicacies that may please your heart
"And thus we greet you with this little cart."
I stared at it with horror. Had I messed
The reservations up? So, I'd confessed
To be new at this. What had I done wrong?
Was it a test of competency all along?
Mustering courage, I rang his deputy,
Who seemed to be enjoying TV
Just down the hall. "A terrible mistake!
"The hotel screwed this up, for goodness' sake!"
I cried. "They've sent the General's food to me!"
Sarcastically, he said, "Oh dear, let's see:

"Someone screwed up. So, why is that your fault?
"Let's check this out. Is pepper there, and salt?"
In a few minutes he was outside the door,
A short, thin man, who ate enough for four.
"He's tied up with the press till late," he said.
"Let's clear this up before we go to bed."
With that, he tucked a napkin to his chin,
Lit into a shrimp and said, "Dig in."

After he'd left, I thought that I should hide.
The rich food churned like queasy thoughts inside.
If strawberries had maddened Captain Queeg
What about oysters flown from Chincoteague.
I moved the ravaged cart out to the hall,
Hoping the hotel staff was on the ball,
And took the lift down to the kitchen so
Next morning I would know the way to go.
The crowds had dissipated now, so I
Poked around a while, as if a spy.
I hit the front desk to drop off the key
And tell them it was his. Then heavily
Afflicted by misgivings I walked back
Across the empty lobby, on the track
Of a spare elevator, heard a shout
And saw a frazzled desk clerk running out
And waving frantically at me. "Your key,"
"You mixed them up," he said, "You see?
"Go on, I'll give the General a spare—
"Good night, Lieutenant Socrates, take care."

There's only so much worry men can take,
So, hoping that this wasn't my mistake,
I went back to the suite, saw with a frown
That room service had turned the covers down,

And fell in bed; but not until I'd stood
Before the floor-length windows, livelihood
And prospects fading into vacant black
Of office windows in a glassy stack
Across the street and wondered why
My spring of intuition had run dry.
I set my alarm for four o'clock a.m.
To head downstairs and execute the whim
Of him to whom I was indentured now.
I'd slept uneasily, considering how
Dark waves of worry whispered all that night,
Seeping across the deep-piled carpet right
Up to my bed. Indeed, as I was headed to
The shower, I observed a lengthy queue
Of office envelopes that had been slid
Under my door that night. And, God forbid,
They all were for the General, and all
Were stamped at least with "SECRET." But my call,
If challenged at that stupid predawn, hour,
Would be "Nothing's more important than a shower."
I breathed in steam and, as I thought things through,
My innate sense of mess and wrongness grew.

The hotel staff weren't in on this burlesque
Except perhaps the man at the front desk.
The mailroom for the Pentagon also
Dropped SECRET mail under my door, as though
The General were here. I dressed at a rate
That would have left a racehorse at the gate,
And, taking the SECRET envelopes in hand,
With my demeanor absolutely bland,
I walked up to a spooky gentleman
Who stood considering a ceiling fan
As if it were a listening device.
I had to clear my throat not once, but twice,

Before he turned to look at my ID,
Which I held up so he could plainly see.
"I'm looking for Socrates. Do you know where
"To find him?" "Yeah, he's downstairs, with the mayor."
"I've got communiqués for him," I said,
"I can't just leave them sitting on his bed."
I turned the envelopes so he could snatch
A glimpse of SECRET stamps on each dispatch.

"Maybe I should just wait up here outside
"His room," I mused. The spooky man replied:
"He won't be back. There was a sniper threat!
"He switched his room with someone else. No sweat,
"But staying was too dangerous a call
"Even in a new room down the hall.
"So he decided just to walk away
"And find another, safer place to stay."

I was struck dumb. Just earlier that night,
The black and silver sparkle of the sight
Outside the windows drew me, like an ass,
To wait until a spark and hail of glass
Would leave me on the deep-piled carpet, sprawled.
The others in my troop would be appalled
At how, at just the wrong place and wrong time,
I'd stepped into the crosshairs of a crime.

Loyalty, I pondered as I flew
Back to the base, was not a plant that grew
In places choked with power and vanity.
I found a better spot eventually,
A combat leader's staff, exposed to threat,
But the most honest work a man could get.

24

The Bartender's Tale

"Well, here we are again, back at home port."
I sat with the farmer. This was a cruise cut short
By circumstance, but lengthened by red tape—
Ten days, in which we pleaded to escape
The ship, while cruise directors strove to get
A bunch of port authorities to let
The vessel dock. Our entry was denied;
They paid no heed, no matter what we tried.
"No one on board is ill!" we would insist.
"The doctor on our ship has made a list
And checked for symptoms of the new disease!"
But that put not one bureaucrat at ease.
At every port, the message was the same:
If COVID-19 struck, they'd be to blame
For letting us come in. There were no tests
Available to back up our requests.
We'd have to stay here on the ship, offshore.
Even in storms they would not let us moor.
And so, the cruise line poured free drinks
To salve the sting of failure and the jinx

That dogged the cruise. At last we turned around
And headed north while fuel could be found
To get us back to harbor in New York.
I thought the reverend would pop his cork.
Returning seemed to take a month of days.

We told our final stories, with our gaze
Perpetually on the rolling gray-blue sea,
The mighty confidante of entropy,
And played a game of guessing at the miles
The ship had traveled every story. Styles
Of storytelling that run slow are fine,
If burnished with a glass or two of wine;
They take your mind off of the moody deep.
Then one day we are back! But wait! A sweep
Of the horizon gives no sign of land,
We hear that our arrival might be banned
Because of measures that had been imposed
To quarantine the ill or indisposed.
We lay offshore for days while agents fretted
Over how thoroughly we must be vetted.
The rumor that was particularly galling
Was that officialdom was simply stalling
Until they had to let us off of the boat.
They thought it better if we simply stayed afloat.

Luckily, we had a well-stocked bar,
And alcohol soon put events on par
With rained-out baseball games and canceled shows.
Our stories done, we twiddled thumbs and toes
And strolled the deck in thought, so many times
That I was soon recalling paradigms
I'd learned in school. *"Amo, amas, amat. . ."*
A few more days, and I might have a shot

At bringing to mind the Gettysburg Address
And bits of the Constitution, more or less.
At last, as if returning from a spin,
The ship began to move, bow pointed in
Toward shore and word was passed among our group,
That we would dock today at last. A whoop
Went up from every passenger aboard.
And soon, ten dozen drinks were poured,
And those of us who still could see
Through foggy windows, toasted Liberty,
Whose statue, eternally without fatigue,
Banished with torchlight treasonous intrigue.
"We need some freedom here," I prayed to her.
"Please rescue me from this spar-varnished stir."
My prayer was cut short by my farmer friend
"Why won't they let us go?" he asked: "I tend
"To think no one's in charge. If it's a plague
"You'd think authorities would be less vague.
"We've sat four days on hold—a five-day trip
"Has turned to ten, and then another four,
"Without a single chance to go onshore."
"Hey, drinks are free, at least," the scout broke in.
"Best they could do." That beer shone on his chin.
"And hey, that champagne never came. Who won?"
"I did!" the widow breathed. "All judged and done,
"Except for the announcement." Her perfume
Purled through her voice and vivified the room.
"Buy you a drink?" I thought it well to ask.
"Of course," she cooed. "How sweet! Is there a cask
"Of sherry somewhere on this lovely boat?
"I'll need at least four shots to stay afloat
"On land . . . I'd ask for rum," she turned to me,
"But it's run out, we've been so long at sea."

I turned to the bartender. He had been
A silent member of our group, and then,
I came to learn he'd quietly been hired
To take the place of someone they had fired.
He was a handsome man, if dissolute,
But women seemed to find him rather cute,
Stubble-cheeked and tan and curly-haired,
The type my ex-wife hit on, when she dared.
A leather thong tied loosely on his wrist,
He looked to be the perfect hedonist.
I realized I had never heard him speak,
Which somehow seemed a part of his mystique.

He made great vodka tonics, with a squeeze
Of lime, but also rarer recipes
That suddenly were called for, as supplies
Of standard drinks ran out. He'd exorcise
Strange spirits from the dusty stores below
Brandy that went fast; gin that was sloe.

The widow sweetly trilled over the throng
Of gathering friends, at least a dozen strong:
"Now you! Yes, don't you stand and dry that glass
"And act like you don't hear me, bold-as-brass.
"You're a member of our group, the only one
"Who has not told a tale. So we're not done
"Until you do. I promise we'll tune in to you."
All conversation stopped, even some crew
Who lounged outside the bar doors listened in!
The scout, as if someone applied a pin,
Snorted awake and belched and scratched his ass
Then reached across the counter for his glass.
The bartender looked sheepish. First, he bowed
His head, as if he really disavowed
Any connection with our wayward group.
Finally, his shoulders seemed to droop.
"OK," the barman said. "I acquiesce.
"This galley's laden with forgetfulness,
"As Thomas Wyatt puts it." "Hold on there!"
The lawyer said, "First, just tell us where
On earth a barman learns that kind of stuff?"

"Ah yes," our worthy pourer then replied
"You'd be much happier if I denied
"My doctorate in English. Folks like me.
"Are not supposed to get a PhD.
"I guess we're all supposed to know our place
"Not wave credentials in a better's face.

"I studied poetry because it gave me gifts
"That I could share with others. Many rifts
"Society now faces could be healed
"By sharing inspiration from each field
"Of knowledge. Poems are intoxication,
"Bits of insight, paths of revelation,
"Lofty at times, and often indirect,
"Leading to feelings that we don't expect,
"Conducting us to deeper thoughts than words
"Express alone. But leave that for the birds,
"Some people say (who never would sit still
"For oral recitations of whatever skill).
"And so, to stay alive, I'm selling drink,
"To spread some momentary joy, to link
"My clients to the spiritual guide
"That they don't realize they have inside.

"Baloney," said the lawyer. "You're unreal!
"In real life, saying what you truly feel
"Requires just opening your mouth and talking,
"Not soaking first in drunken thoughts and squawking."
He snorted, "Now I'll have another beer."
He slid his empty glass across the bar, quite near
The edge. The barkeep caught and filled the glass.
The welder told the lawyer he lacked class,
To which that advocate responded: "Oh, shut up!
"Go stand on a corner and hold out your cup!
"The Men's is thataway: go soak your head!"
The welder cocked his fist; the farmer said,
"Just let it go! No bar fights. End of story":
We others muttered things "defamatory,"
Or so the lawyer said. But they were true.
The barman handed back the glass and spoke anew:

"I am a barkeep, so I have no tale.
"That's not poured out each night in wine and ale.
"Just to recount a worthwhile story here
"I'd have to remember more than last night's beer. . ."
"Come off it!" smiled the widow. "Go ahead!"
He thought for just a moment, then he said:
"One skill barkeepers have is we're invisible.
"To people like our lawyer. Oh, how risible—
"We are beneath their notice, they would say
"But we hear things that take our breath away.
"And we stand silently, don't say a thing.
"Or sometimes, usually alone, they bring
"Their troubles to the barstool. We'll deny
"We ever heard a thing that went awry.
"And this is pretty honorable, I think,
"Even if you hardly buy one drink.
"*In vino veritas!* I speak the truth,
"I hear things that I never dreamt in youth.
"Were I to speak of the romances,
"Squandered loves, and second chances
"I have witnessed right here every day,
"You'd wish for real that I would go away,
"And not tell any tales. But we're discreet,
"We publicans. The bar is a retreat.
"Where you can tell me that you're troubled at
"The way your Caribbean trip fell flat,
"You've all complained of that bad luck to me
"As if I specialized in therapy,
"And I've heard quite a few of you explain
"That you will never have this chance again.

"So let me ask you what you mean by 'chance'?
"The opportunity to cast a passing glance
"At isolated, humid plots of earth
"Out of a porthole window? What's that worth?

"From the time we disembarked, we would be guided,
"Around some places others have decided
"Are the most important things to see.
"Novel and strange, for sure! Yet memory
"Of all of it will fade, except the bites
"Of insects, sunburn, and hot, sleepless nights.
"Those who rush away to foreign parts
"Change only the constellations, not their hearts.
"The purpose of your trip you'd find right here
"In this same group, that's come from far and near.
"Look at it this way. What you will recall
"Is not the endless sky or ocean sprawl.
"By far our most momentous journey,
("Until our one-way trip out on some gurney,)
"Will be the one we take ourselves, inside,
"Or share with others. This huge ship will glide
"Across the ocean's surface, but the wake
"Lasts only minutes, and the sea will take
"No notice of its passing, nor remember you.
"And yet, for a certainty I know for true
"You'll think of those who put their tales on trial,
"And even when you're very old you'll smile."

With that, there was commotion at the doors
And then the cruise director yelled "Who pours?"
He rolled a case of champagne on a cart.
"Hooray!" he called, "You're ready to depart.
"Dry land's the destination, but before you go.
"We have unfinished business, and, so,
"I've brought the promised bottles of champagne."
A voice cried out "Who won?" And then again
"Who won?" came from the back. The cruise director
Stopped and thought. He was a born deflector—
Difficult decisions weren't his thing.
So I was not surprised to hear him fling

The judgment back at us! "Why, everyone!"
He said, "You're each so good that everybody won!
"And that is why I brought so much champagne."
I heard amid the grumbling, "I'll abstain."
A woman's voice—was it the widow?—miffed
Just because everybody won? I'm sure she sniffed,
But took a glass. The cruise director raised
His own and shouted out a lengthy toast.

And everybody drank or maybe most.
Quickly we said good-byes. The teacher
Told me all the ways that I could reach her;

The farmer tipped his hat to me and turned,
But quickly the festive meeting was adjourned.
Those with cell phones, who had griped and flailed
Because their Wi-Fi coverage had failed
Out on the high seas disembarked as though
Their phones had taken root and soon would grow.
Some were wearing homemade fabric masks,
Fashioned with sewing kits and whisky flasks,
While others, like myself, essayed the gangplank
Lacking all protection, with our minds blank.
Soon, a madding crowd were hugging those
Whom very soon most likely they'd expose
To pathogens. Our group was soon dispersed,
And thinking they'd survived the very worst,
Rolled luggage down the strangely empty streets
Or rested a moment on some bus-stop seats
Or fanned out, hailing taxicabs as they
Through New York made their solitary way.

Apologia

If you have read or listened to these tales
And found that wit flags or your patience fails,
Or you resent a tale that speaks less well
Of your profession than the one you'd tell,
Or makes too much of simple indiscretions:
Remember, you weren't present at these sessions
And, sad to say, I think you'll never be
Except perhaps by listening to me.
The *Ocean Froth* itself long since has docked,
Its gangway lowered and the gates unlocked.
The storytellers scattered with the wind,
Nor did they give me license to amend.

If there is any awkwardness, I hope
That you will let them have a little rope:
Not everyone's a storyteller. They
All told their tales to pass the time away.
While oceans billowed and pandemics raged
And we were blessed by inconvenience, caged
By circumstance. Sheer boredom made us sing
Of things not hoped for, but life-altering,
Or passions for achievement that were thwarted,
Or plans well laid that had to be aborted.

The ship we'd boarded never would arrive
At promised ports; but then, we stayed alive,
Crossing the cloudy mirror of the sea,
Like birds lost in forgetful fog. And we,
Instead of seeing novelty unfurled
By some far distant, more complacent world,
Discovered that to travel hopefully,
Is often better, thoughtful men agree,
Than finally reaching Edens that won't last.
Now, thank you for the time that you have passed
Among our company of lonely hearts,
For now we all have played our given parts,
And though we otherwise like to pretend,
We all are stories and all have an end.

Acknowledgments

I want to acknowledge and thank my colleagues and friends at Fulcrum Publishing. The vivacious Robert C. Baron, founder and chair, is in every way, one of life's singular achievements—intelligent, joyful, capable, and willing to take almost any chance for the sake of principle. Like Yeats's "Fiddler of Dooney," he can make folk "dance like a wave of the sea." Patty Maher, production manager, who designed the book, has been the best and most dependable of friends. A steady hand with occasionally flighty new authors. Senior editor Alison Auch has been a rock of patience and a clever and tireless aesthetician of language and its possibilities. Thanks also to Kateri Kramer, director of marketing, and her able deputy Kelli Jerve, who have advanced a project that is out of the ordinary for most publishers today. I am also most grateful to Sam Scinta, Fulcrum's publisher, who has thrown the force of marketing and support behind.

My colleague and illustrator, Cathy Morrison is a total gem, except, of course, without hard surfaces. She is talented, tireless, and flexible, but also perceptive, inspired, and fun—exactly the combination of qualities that were needed to shape this book.

I acknowledge, with joy, the teachers and friends who shaped my life many decades ago by challenging, empowering, and understanding my love of literature and cultures. These mentors and friends lie at the heart of any achievement of mine, and I am eternally grateful to them: Godfrey K. Bond, W. Robert Connor, Bernard C. Fenik, Benedict H. Gross, Alastair Martin, Donald John Mathison, and James C. Tatum.

Last, but not at all least, I have to express deep gratitude to my Southern coastal family of origin, especially my sisters, Malinda and Diane who taught me from knee-high things that have ever since lain close to my soul.

If I were to begin naming dear friends from the latter part of my life the text of this book would become an appendix. All of them are loved and appreciated, some beyond measure.

—Josiah Oakes Hatch III

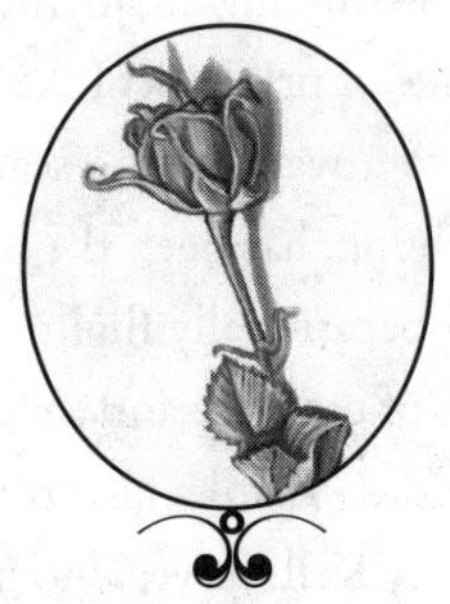

Bibliography

Baugh, Albert C., and Thomas Cable. *A History of the English Language*, 6th ed. London and New York: Routledge, 2012.

Bennett, J. A. W., and G. V. Smithers, eds. *Early Middle English Verse and Prose, 1155–1300*. Norman Davis, contrib. Oxford, UK: Oxford University Press, 1982.

Benson, Larry D., ed. *The Riverside Chaucer*. Boston: Houghton Mifflin, 1987.

Burrell, Arthur, ed. *Chaucer's* Canterbury Tales *for the Modern Reader*. London: J. M. Dent & Sons, 1913.

Chaucer, Geoffrey. *The Canterbury Tales*. Edited by A. C. Cawley. New York: Knopf, 1992.

Coleridge, Samuel. *The Rime of the Ancient Mariner*. Oxford, UK: Oxford University Press, 1930.

Dante, Alighieri. *The Divine Comedy*. Trans. Clive James. New York: Liveright Publishing, 2014.

De Weever, Jacqueline. *Chaucer Name Dictionary: A Guide to Astrological, Biblical, Historical, Literary, and Mythological Names in the Works of Geoffrey Chaucer*. Abingdon, Oxon, UK and New York: Routledge, 1988.

Donne, John. *Poems of John Donne*. From the text of the 1633 ed., revised by James Russell Lowell. New York: Grolier Club, 1895.

Gardner, John, *The Life and Times of Chaucer*. New York: Barnes & Noble, 1999.

Gilbert, W. S. *The Bab Ballads*. London: MacMillan & Co Ltd., 1897. Reprinted 1964.

Goldsmith, Oliver. *The Deserted Village: A Poem*, 8th ed. Gale ECCO, Print Editions, 2017.

Homer. *The Iliad*. Over 200 translations, including John Dryden and Alexander Pope.

———. *The Iliad*. A New Translation by Caroline Alexander. New York: Ecco, 2015.

———. *The Iliad*. Trans. by Robert Fagles. Introduction by Bernard Knox. New York: Viking, 1990.

———. *The Iliad*. Trans. by Richmond Latimer. Chicago: University of Chicago Press, 1951.

Longfellow, Henry Wadsworth. *The Song of Hiawatha*. Boston: Ticknor and Fields, 1848. Reprinted by Bounty Books, 1962.

———. *Evangeline*. Boston: Ticknor and Fields, 1856. Reprinted by Houghton Mifflin, 1986.

Milton, John. *Paradise Lost: Complete Poetry of John Milton*. New York: The Modern Library, 1942.

The Oxford Book of American Poetry. David Leitman, ed. New York: Oxford University Press, 2011.

The Oxford Book of English Poetry. Helen Gardner, ed. New York: Oxford University Press, 1972.

Picard, Liza. *Chaucer's People: Everyday Lives in Medieval England*. New York: W. W. Norton & Company, Inc., 2017.

Pope, Alexander. *The Rape of the Lock*. London: Bernard Lintott, 1714. Reprinted by Oxford University Press, 1980.

Sandburg, Carl. *Chicago Poems*. New York: Holt, 1996.

Savoy Operas. London: George Bell & Sons, 1909. Reprinted by MacMillan & Co Ltd., 1957.

Robert Service. *The Spell of the Yukon*. New York: Barse and Hopkins, 1907.

Robinson, F. N., ed. *The Works of Geoffrey Chaucer*. London: Oxford University Press, 1957.

Shakespeare, William. *The Sonnets of William Shakespeare*. The Royal Shakespeare Theatre Edition. London: Shepheard-Walwyn, 1975.

Sisson, C. H. *The Divine Comedy*. Translated. Oxford University Press, 1993.

Skeet, Walter William, ed. *The Complete Works of Geoffrey Chaucer*. Oxford, UK: Oxford University Press, 1920.

Vergil, Publius Vergilius Maro. *The Aeneid*. Trans. by Robert Fagles. London: Penguin Classics 2008.

———. Trans. by Robert Fitzgerald. New York: Vintage Books, 1990.

———. Trans. by C. Day Lis. London: Hogarth Press, 1969.

Whitman, Walt. *Leaves of Grass*. Philadelphia: David McKay, 1882. Reprinted by Penguin, 1959.

Wright, David, ed. *The Canterbury Tales*. Oxford, UK: Oxford University Press, 1998.

About the Illustrator and Foreword Author

As an illustrator, **Cathy Morrison** is passionate about nature, science, and the environment. Combining her degrees in fine arts and education along with her background in animation and graphic design, she researches and illustrates a variety of books, including picture books, creative nonfiction, and chapter books. Cathy's studio is in the foothills northwest of Fort Collins, Colorado, with a panoramic view of the peaks of Rocky Mountain National Park. She enjoys travel, hiking, and gardening, especially with native, drought-tolerant plants that encourage pollinators.

Robert C. Baron is the founder of Fulcrum Publishing. He is the author of thirty books, including *Pioneers and Plodders: The American Entrepreneurial System* and *The Light Shines from the West: A Western Perspective on the Growth of America.*

About the Author

Josiah Oakes Hatch III was born in Savannah, Georgia, a fourth-generation Georgian. He attended Princeton University, where he graduated summa cum laude, majoring in Ancient Greek and Latin with a minor in music theory. A Marshall scholar at Pembroke College, Oxford, he studied Anglo-Saxon and Middle English. He spent a year in Italy studying Latin literature, history, and art.

After studying at Oxford, Josiah moved to Washington, D.C., serving as a museum administrator at the Smithsonian Institution, a speechwriter and political aide, and, after obtaining a law degree from Georgetown, a lawyer. In addition to his legal practice, he teaches courses in international business and economics at the Josef Korbel School for International Studies at the University of Denver. He is coauthor of a legal treatise on Director and Officer Liability, Indemnification, and Insurance.

Colophon

This book is set in the typeface Garamond Premier Pro with headings and emphasized type set in the display type Blackadder ITC. The font Blackadder ITC was designed by Bob Anderson and copyrighted by the International Typeface Corporation in 1997. It is an elegant yet menacing typeface perfect for dramatic flourishes.

Garamond Premier Pro had its genesis in 1988 when Adobe senior type designer Robert Slimbach visited the Plantin-Moretus Museum in Antwerp, Belgium, to study their collection of Claude Garamond's metal punches and type designs. Garamond, a French punchcutter, produced a refined array of book types in the mid-1500s that combined an unprecedented degree of balance and elegance, and stand as a pinnacle of beauty and practicality in typefounding. While fine-tuning Adobe Garamond (released in 1989) as a useful design suited to modern publishing, Slimbach started planning an entirely new interpretation of Garamond's designs based on the large range of unique sizes he had seen at the Plantin-Moretus, and on the comparable italics cut by Robert Granjon, Garamond's contemporary. By modeling Garamond Premier Pro on these hand-cut type sizes, Slimbach has retained the varied optical size characteristics and freshness of the original designs, while creating a practical twenty-first-century type family. Garamond Premier Pro contains an extensive glyph complement, including central European, Cyrillic, and Greek characters, and is offered in five weights ranging from light to bold.

The cover design is by the illustrator, Cathy Morrison. The interior design is by Patty Maher.